CHASING THE SLIPSTREAM

FULL THROTTLE

BOOK TWO

KANITHA P.

This book contains explicit sexual content, foul language, and mentions topics that could be triggering such as physical abuse, emotional manipulation from a parent, mentions of drug use, and anxiety.

Editing by Hannah G. Scheffer-Wentz, English Proper Editing Services.

Proofreading by Nyla Lillie.

Cover design by Ivy N. Isles.

To the ones who struggle with self-love; you are beautiful, unique, and worthy of every ounce of love the universe has to offer. You are enough - don't ever let anyone dim your light.

PLAYLIST

Kiss Me | Sixpence None the Richer
I Can See You (Taylor's Version) | Taylor Swift
Butterflies | Kacey Musgraves
You Should Probably Leave | Chris Stapleton
The Blue | Gracie Adams
A Sky Full Of Stars | Coldplay
Don't Let Me Go | Cigarettes After Sex
Wondering Why | The Red Clay Strays
You Are Enough | Sleeping At Last
Someone to Stay | Vancouver Sleep Clinic
After Hours | The Weeknd
Constellations | Jade LeMac
Dress | Taylor Swift
Fall Into Me | Forest Blakk
Wildest Dreams (Taylor's Version) | Taylor Swift
Stargazing | Myles Smith
Anchor | Novo Amor
The Prophecy | Taylor Swift
Boy With The Blues | Delacey
Falling Like The Stars | James Arthur

“SLIPSTREAM”

Aerodynamic technique occuring when a Formula 1 car is aligned behind another one to gain extra speed.

CHAPTER ONE

LONDON, ENGLAND

"I AM SO, so sorry."

Acting and sounding apologetic, when it was evident the expression of regret was anything but sincere, truly felt disheartening. Especially when the woman's lips were twisted in a pout, eyebrows knitted together, with a sigh nearly sounding dramatic escaping her nose.

Ava blinked, trying not to let her expression shift into suspicion as she kept her chin high. A lump had built inside her throat though, and even when she swallowed the dismay, she could still feel some sparks of anger starting to rush through her veins. Could feel her fingers tremble with rage. Could feel the sadness slowly spreading throughout her body.

"I'm not sure I'm fully understanding the situation." Ava let her hands fall on her lap. She had been busy rubbing the hem of her sleeve between her thumb and forefinger to keep herself grounded, but all she wanted right now was to go home and let all that pent-up anxiety out.

Sophie sighed. "It's not you."

She wasn't sure if she was being dumped or fired. Either way, this was starting to sound and feel like a breakup she hadn't anticipated.

Ava frowned. "Is it Thiago?"

"No, darling, no." The head of the marketing department pressed her lips into a thin line before allowing a smile to spread across them. "Thiago adores you, and I do think you were a great duo, but you know how everything works around here when we enter the new season."

Changes. But she hadn't foreseen this. At all.

Ava was downright confused. Through the thick cloud of turmoil fogging her mind, she managed to ask, "So why am I not his PR officer anymore?"

Absentmindedly, Ava started gnawing on her lower lip—an act of nervousness—and Sophie took notice of her demeanour. "Do you want some tea?" Ava shook her head in denial. "Alright. Well, even though you did an astounding job at keeping Thiago's reputation clean as much as you could despite his slip-throughs last season, I do think you would work better with Rowan. And as you may or may not already know, Ellie is pregnant. She has some complications and cannot work for the rest of the season. So, that's why you're replacing her."

In the span of ten minutes, Ava had been informed of two things that had caused her bewilderment to grow into poisonous vines:

1. She was being moved to another team and would stop representing Thiago Valencia, whom she had been working with for the past two years, and would now work with his teammate, Rowan Emerson.

2. Her colleague was pregnant, had complications, and hadn't told her anything.

"Okay." Ava scratched the side of her nose. "Who's replacing me?"

"Her name is Donna. She used to work for Imperium

Racing, but now works for us. You'll still see Thiago around at the factory and the paddock, if that's what you're worried about."

Oh, no, Ava wasn't worried about losing touch with Thiago.

She simply didn't want to work with Rowan Emerson, period.

She despised the man with a burning passion, and whilst he was an expert at hiding his true colours, she was convinced he wasn't fond of her either.

He was a skilled and talented Formula 1 driver—one of the public's favourites—but he was also the epitome of arrogance and masculine beauty. With a smug smirk constantly etched on his lips and unyielding mischief shimmering in his eyes, he thrived to be the best and do anything to win. He wasn't one to care about his entourage, walked the paddock like he owned it, constantly lived for the thrill of danger, and loved being the centre of attention.

In simple words, he was her polar opposite.

Ava didn't let her resentment show on her face and simply said, "That's fine with me."

She couldn't lose her job just because she wouldn't settle her differences with Rowan. She'd have to bite her tongue and accept everything he'd put her through—not that she wasn't already used to doing so on a daily basis, anyway.

Sophie smiled, threading her fingers together. "I knew you'd understand. You're never one to argue. You can move all your belongings into the office across the hall today."

"I'm even moving working spaces?" she asked, bemused.

"Into a bigger and isolated one." Until now, she'd been used to sharing an open space with her coworkers.

An office to herself? Say less. She felt like this was a win in itself despite the reluctance clouding her senses.

Begrudgingly, Ava responded with a tight-lipped smile and stood up. "On it." Uncertain if she was supposed to be grateful for this sudden change, she thought better of it and expressed her appreciation with misplaced bitterness. "Thank you for everything. For trusting me with the drivers."

"You're a hard-working, dedicated girl. One of my most trustworthy employees, so of course." Sophie didn't stand, instantly diverting her attention towards the screen of her computer. "You're coming to the launch party tonight, right? Might be a good opportunity to meet Rowan."

Ava blinked. *Meet Rowan?* As if she had never spoken to him. Had never glared his way, or snapped back at him, or scoffed at his pomposity. "I already know him."

Only the sound of nails hitting the keyboard resonated through the room. "I meant it as an official introduction of you as his new press officer."

Ava had turned on her heel, hand already grasping the doorknob as she halted in her tracks. She sucked in a breath, feeling her heart thunder. "He still doesn't know about the change?"

"No," was Sophie's nonchalant response. "I'm sure he'll appreciate you announcing the wonderful news."

Wonderful. Yeah, right.

At that moment, she couldn't help but wonder who, between herself and Rowan, would break first. It was no secret that behind his troublesome smirk and flirtatious regard was a hidden amount of equal disdain he shared towards her.

"Great," Ava chided, a lump in her throat. "I can't wait."

A MINI PLANT was the last item she deposited on her new bureau.

The sentiment of working in a new office with a new team was odd. She wasn't sure whether she was excited or terrified about this new journey. Perhaps both.

When she started working with the marketing team for Primavera Racing two years ago, Thiago welcomed her with open arms, always treating her like a sister. She had followed him all around the world, working day and night to help him maintain a good reputation despite his behaviour that had compromised his contract renewal last season.

In the end, he managed to sign again with Primavera, thanks to his tremendous efforts and great results on the track.

Obviously, Ava had spoken and worked with Rowan more than once. Whilst they had always managed to keep a professional relationship in front of cameras and prying eyes, the hatred was nothing but lethal and blazing behind closed doors.

She sunk into the chaise, propped her elbows atop the desk, and buried her face into her hands.

She inhaled serenity. Exhaled anxiety.

Ava wasn't sure why she was feeling so overwhelmed. Perhaps because she hadn't expected that news on her first day back at the office after a two-and-a-half-month break. Perhaps because of the February weather, where grey skies and concrete glinting with fresh drops of rain, weren't helping to uplift her spirits.

It was a knock on her door that startled her, bringing her back to this sudden and unexpected reality. Straightening herself, she peered at the silhouette casting a shadow in the doorway and instantly put her prettiest smile on.

"Ava," Nikki said coldly. As per usual, her expression was hard, her gaze full of haughtiness and derision. "Settling into your new office?"

Ava cleared her throat, pushing her glasses up the bridge of her nose. "Yes."

Nikki hummed and stepped into the room. Perched on her high heels, she scanned the nearly empty office, her lips pursed in disdain. Ava loathed this woman, but she couldn't show it because she was her boss. Whilst Sophie McKinnon directed the whole department, Nikki Bellinger was in charge of the PR and marketing team—the social media managers, analysts, content creators, and press officers.

Nikki was a rather beautiful person. Thriving in her thirties, her shiny, blonde hair always looked pristine, her lips were often coated with gloss, and she bore the physique of a mannequin. Only issue? She was an infuriating woman who thought she belonged on a pedestal that gave her the right to act like a queen.

Respectfully, Ava liked to call her a bitch.

You must have been thinking, *"Does Ava hate everyone she works with?"* Well, no. She merely had a wide sense of self-preservation that she loved to wear akin to a second skin, and selected her friends carefully.

She blinked up at her boss, unsure if she ought to be standing. Deciding to stay seated just so Nikki could feel superior, she chewed the interior of her cheek and waited for Nikki's anger to blow into her face.

"Just because Sophie has moved you into an office that you won't need to share with the rest of the team, doesn't mean you can spend your free time wallowing and staring at your nails all day."

Ava nodded. "I know."

"And don't think that because it's your first day back, now working for another driver, you can just sit here and do nothing. You can come back here this weekend to decorate your cute little office."

See? What a fucking bitch.

Nikki was a pro at acting like an angel in front of everyone else and being the devil in private.

"Got it," Ava answered quietly.

"Rowan is a handful," continued Nikki as she placed her hands on the edge of the desk, leaning forward. Her pale blue eyes were swamped with insolence, making Ava's skin prickle with irritation. "He isn't Thiago. He's exigent. Demanding. Likes everything to be perfect. He won't allow a single negative thing about him to be said in the media. You're young, naive, and quiet. You're used to working with Thiago, but Rowan isn't the sweet crown prince of the paddock. He's relentless and won't necessarily make your job easy. You're not here for a good laugh. Understood?"

Was she seriously trying to intimidate Ava? Unbelievable.

Ava tipped her chin higher. She wasn't afraid. She wouldn't falter. "I can handle him."

Rowan Emerson might have been shrouded in shadows, marred in tattoos, and imposing with lean muscles, but Ava was certain deep secrets were hidden behind his tough façade.

With a once-over, Nikki scoffed as though she didn't believe in Ava. She only lifted her eyebrows with that air of pomposity of hers and straightened herself. "If you say so."

She pivoted and marched towards the exit, her heels tapping loudly on the floor. Ava desperately needed to roll her eyes, and cry, and scream her frustration into a pillow.

Nikki didn't so much as turn around as she said, "Check your inbox. Sent you a few things to work on before tonight's car launch."

It wasn't until Nikki was out of sight that Ava stood up and mocked a reverence. "Yes, ma'am."

Shutting the door with a delicacy she didn't know she possessed whilst shaking with rage, she exhaled and leaned against a wall. Finally, she felt the tears burn her eyes, but she didn't allow herself to break down. Not here. Not now.

Ava wasn't ready to start this new episode. If only she had known what kind of storm was about to rattle her universe, maybe she would have considered not jumping blindfolded into the adventure. Still, she pressed play and dared not look back.

CHAPTER TWO

LONDON, ENGLAND

ROWAN'S FACE CONTORTED into a grimace the moment he felt a knot at the base of his shoulder blade, slight sparks of pain trailing down his ribs. Rubbing the aching spot, he stretched his neck out by rolling it, feeling a few strands of hair topple over his brows.

"You should take it easy."

A groan rose from the back of his throat at the sound of Tate's remark. Opening his eyes, he gaped at his physiotherapist busy closing his duffel bag, then let a scoff erupt.

From his seated position, Rowan leaned his elbows atop his thighs as the corner of his mouth curled into a smirk. "How is *taking it easy* going to make me win the championship?"

"The season hasn't even started," Tate noted dully as he stood up. "You injured yourself during the winter break and you know you need to stop being so hard on yourself."

Pushing his curls away from his forehead, Rowan lifted his shoulders in a lazy shrug. He didn't care about his doctor's opinion, nor Tate's, nor anyone else's. "It was a minor injury, I'll be fine. My goal is to beat Valencia."

The past two seasons were terrible for Primavera Racing. Both drivers had struggled with their cars and had been beaten by Imperium Racing consecutively. Even though Rowan had finished the season third in the drivers' rankings, he still craved to beat his teammate who, contrary to Rowan, had already been crowned World Champion once in 2020.

As Tate draped his duffel bag over his shoulder, he grabbed Rowan's and gave it to the athlete who had stood up and pulled a jumper over his training gear. "I'm sure you can beat Thiago. I mean, he's not Huxley—he's not the unbeatable Lion. But I'm not sure overworking your body and tiring yourself this early in the season is the way to do it. I know you want to stay in shape, but you know your mental health matters, too."

Rowan snickered and patted his trainer on the back before marching towards the exit. The gym at Primavera's headquarters was one of Rowan's favourite places. Set on the whole surface of the top floor of the building, it offered an incomparable view of the English countryside surrounding the factory, hence why he would spend most of his free time here.

Rowan hit the button to call the lifts, digging into his bag to retrieve a cap. Laying the hat backwards atop his hair, he looked at Tate. "Stop being so concerned about me, Ritchie. I can't take that much kindness."

Tate scowled. "I'm just doing my job, dickhead. Still can't believe how I put up with your annoying ass after all these years."

Rowan and Tate grew up as next-door neighbours in Brisbane. They had known each other since they were born, and when Rowan had decided to move to Europe to pursue his dream in motorsports, Tate had decided to follow.

They were like brothers.

Wherever Rowan Emerson was, Tate Richards was, too.

The doors to the lifts opened and they stepped inside in sync.

"What's the plan for tomorrow?"

Tate glanced at his friend, slight puzzlement etched on his features. "Nothing."

"No cardio? I love a good run on a Saturday morning."

Tate plucked his phone out of his pocket, snorting softly. "I'm not sure you'll be in the mood with the hangover that's waiting for you. Did you forget the car launch is tonight?"

Ah, fuck.

Rowan had forgotten.

And he'd forgotten he needed to retrieve his suit at the tailor's.

Every year, after putting on a pretty smile for the cameras, giving his opinion on the new livery and his predictions for the season, he'd grab a flute of champagne, one after the other, until he'd settle for an entire bottle to empty on the roof with Tate and his car mechanics.

"I forgot about that," he admitted, rubbing his flushed face and groaning in frustration.

"I'm going to start thinking I'm not only your physio, but also your assistant and your mother."

Rowan hummed, lifting his eyebrows. "My life would be such a mess without you."

Tate glowered at the sound of Rowan's sardonic tone. "Next time, show a bit more enthusiasm when you express your gratitude towards me."

Rowan was about to retort when the lifts stopped on the fifth floor, the doors slowly opening to reveal the bane of his entire existence. Cradling a box to her chest, she was smiling brightly to someone before she slipped her gaze towards the lifts when the bell chimed. The instant her dark, brown eyes collided with his, her grin faltered, allowing blatant annoyance to paint her face.

He clenched his jaw, sensing the muscle tick, and drifted his gaze away before glancing back her way, as though he'd been forced to watch her equally annoyed expression.

She pressed her lips into a thin line, exhaled, and took a step forward. "Gentlemen."

"Evening," Tate mumbled as he stepped to the side to allow her to stand in between him and Rowan. "How was your winter break?"

No amount of bitterness could ever overpower her genuine and natural grace. That sense of goodness was, for some odd reason, the cause of frustration rattling throughout his body until his bones hurt. Sweetly, she peered up at Tate, securing the box against a hip as she adjusted her ridiculously large scarf.

"It was nice," she responded softly, with that annoying feathery voice of hers. "Went skiing for a week, but I mostly got some rest."

"That's good."

"What about you?"

Tate shrugged lazily. "Same usual shit, you know. Went back home, caught some waves, stuffed my face with Tim Tam's."

Unconsciously, Rowan's jaw tightened when subtle notes of flowers and vanilla danced in the air, corrupting his senses for a flickering heartbeat. He leaned against the wall, buried his hands in the pockets of his shorts, and allowed a scoff to rise from the back of his throat as he witnessed their interaction like a phantom.

"Avery," he acknowledged, his coarse voice echoing through the small space. "My winter break was eventful, if you were wondering."

Though she had her back turned to him, he saw her shoulders tense at the sound of his words. She kept her chin high, continuing to stare ahead of herself. "It's Ava. And thank you, but no, I was not wondering."

He smirked because he knew she'd give him that exact response.

Popping a gum into his mouth, he observed her black hair

fall down her back. Had she cut it? "I'm pretty sure your name's Avery."

"I prefer going by Ava."

"Why?"

"Because," she bit out, her tone clipped.

"That's not even a response," he countered. "I'm going to keep calling you Avery."

"Don't."

It was impressive how rapidly his mood would shift in Avery Sharma-Maddox's presence. Instant irritation started to seep through his veins, causing his blood to boil and his pulse to drum against his temple. Whilst he'd been driving for Primavera Racing for seven years now, Avery arrived two years ago after graduating from university. She had instantly gained everyone's trust and affection with her pearly-white smile and contagious kindness. She was hired as Thiago's PR officer the moment she stepped foot inside the marketing and communications department.

Clicking his tongue against the roof of his mouth, he observed the box she was holding. "Are you quitting?"

He was sure she was rolling her eyes behind the big frames of her glasses. "Sorry to disappoint, but no."

"What's with the box then?"

Finally, brown eyes blazing with frustration found his gaze, causing his lips to tip into a roguish smirk. Over the years, he had found a particular pleasure in spiking her temper. "Aren't you a curious little thing?"

"Very curious," he confirmed with a nod, deciding to ignore the fact she'd called him *little* and *thing*.

She studied his demeanour with a slow once-over that made shivers roll down his spine, then spun on her heel to face the doors as they opened. "I'm going to disappoint you—again—but none of this is your business."

Rowan narrowed his gaze. All he wanted at that exact moment was for her to hold his defiant stare.

"Pleasure seeing you again," he called out.

She didn't so much as peer behind her shoulder. "Can't say the same for me."

He watched her walk out into the entrance hall, waving at the receptionist before pushing the large glass door to exit the building.

Tate was following Rowan closely, amusement edging his tone as he asked, "Remind me why you don't like her again? I think she's nice."

Rowan twisted his hat, pulled the hood of his jumper over his head, and dug into his pocket to grab his car key. "I don't know. But I can't fucking stand her."

He grinned broadly at the cameras sending blinding flashlights into his face, adjusting the collar of his shirt and winking before moving towards the entrance of Primavera's headquarters.

All workers—whether they were mechanics, engineers, marketers, or others—were filling the space in the entrance hall, flutes of champagne in hand whilst chattering joyfully. Primavera Racing would be launching their 2023 car in about twenty minutes. Whilst Rowan and Thiago would be interviewed by an F1 presenter, a live stream would be broadcast around the world for the fans to see the new livery. Primavera was also the last team out of the ten to present their new car.

Rowan was looking for blonde curls and signature red lips, but Ellie was nowhere in sight. Not that he'd be needing her help tonight, but receiving her reassurance would be comforting in a way.

He spotted Thiago grab two glasses of champagne and strolled towards his teammate.

"Have you seen Ellie?" He plucked one of the flutes.

Thiago paused, parted his lips, and frowned. "She isn't here. And give that back. It's for Kam, not you."

Now it was Rowan's turn to furrow his brows, absently handing the glass back. "What do you mean? She never misses anything."

Amusement glinted in Thiago's eyes. "Where have you been the past week?"

"What is that supposed to mean? Stop being so vague and weird, mate."

Pure bewilderment had drawn upon Thiago's face, and just as he was about to elaborate, his attention was brought towards the silhouette that came to brush Rowan's arm. Rowan thought how ridiculous his teammate looked as his features were suddenly illuminated as if a sun ray had started to shine upon him.

Rowan smirked at his teammate's girlfriend when she came to stand next to her partner.

He winked. "Evening, Kameron. Fancy seeing you here."

She scowled and accepted the flute Thiago handed her. Beautiful, devastating woman, but so cold and guarded. Ridiculous how tall she was, too. "It's Kamari."

"I know. I like taunting you."

"I don't return the sentiment." She grabbed Thiago's free hand, drawing Rowan's attention to their linked fingers. "I'm stealing Mister Sunshine for a sec."

Rowan dipped his hands in the pockets of his trousers, lifting his eyebrows. "I know what you mean when you say you need to steal him. You are not slick, Kam. Shagging right now isn't the best idea. We're launching in fifteen."

Kamari sent him a lethal glare which only made him laugh. "Goodbye."

He continued searching the crowd for Ellie, but was unsuccessful. Maybe she was hiding in the kitchen. Strolling towards the cafeteria that was less crowded—empty, even—he let confusion cloud his mind for a heartbeat as he still couldn't find his PR officer.

Taking his phone out of his pocket, he checked for a text message or even an email from Ellie, only to find himself thoroughly disappointed by the lack of updates. It was strange, unusual of her. He wasn't particularly used to being in touch with her every single day, but he was expecting her to be everywhere he was—especially during events like tonight's.

It was only when he turned around that the silhouette of a devastating angel hiding in the shadows caught his eye. She was a nightmare dressed like a daydream. An incandescent, divine being in simple disguise.

He rolled his tongue on the interior of his cheek, debating whether to turn on his heel or dive head-first into her spellbinding trap.

Intrigued by her solitude, he approached with wary steps, hands still in the pockets of his dress pants.

"Party's out front. Why are you hiding?"

Avery lifted her head at the sound of his voice, like he had managed to bring her back to reality. She was sitting at a table, chin in the palm of her hand as she stared at the moonlight's reflection on the lake.

"What do you want?" she snapped, straightening herself.

The light was dim, but he couldn't help himself from dropping his regard to her physique. She was unnervingly beautiful, effortlessly so, and it caused his temper to flare for some unknown reason.

"Rowan," she pressed, evidently impatient and annoyed by his unsolicited presence.

Doe eyes were staring up at him, waiting for a reaction. He had seen her without glasses before, but he had never noticed how thick and long her lashes were, making her dark gaze even more mystifying.

He lifted his eyebrows. "I asked the question first."

Avery rolled her eyes, her expression pinched. "To answer

your obnoxious question, I'm having a terrible night. So yes, I am hiding."

"The event has barely started," he stated impassively. "There's no way you're already having a bad night."

"Well, I am," she bit out, huffing an irritated exhale.

Feisty, she was.

His brows rose in bafflement at her clipped tone. "Are you going to tell me why?"

She blinked, like she was analysing his question. "If I tell you, will you stop invading my personal space and leave?"

"It's hardly your personal space," he retorted coyly. "We all eat here during our lunch breaks."

She didn't react to his remark. Didn't laugh, didn't scoff.

That was strange. She would usually always respond, quickly so. Most of the time, her wit would make him smirk in wry amusement.

After a few beats of them staring at each other, he threw his hands in the air in defeat and shrugged. "Yes, fine. I'll leave afterwards. I've got important shit to do, anyway. It's not like we're launching the new car soon or anything."

"No one's forcing you to talk to me."

"Thank God for that. So?"

Rowan observed the way her gaze trailed down towards his neck when he started fixing the collar of his shirt before smoothing out his vest. Raw, pure detestation was gleaming along the edges of her irises and he knew he was reflecting the same sentiment. It was a real mystery how they had managed to keep their hatred for one another a secret until now.

She then pointed to her left eye. "I lost my contact lens."

He snorted. "How does one do that?"

"When she's in a fucking rush and has no time to travel back to the city to change, so she has to do it at the office and then she's panicked as hell, so she just loses the contact down the drain."

"Woah," he whispered, eyes wide. "Please breathe. You're making me anxious."

Though she had exhaled, he could still see how taut her shoulders were beneath the thin straps of her black dress. Wasn't she cold? It was only February, after all.

"But you left at the same time as Tate and I earlier," he noted, taking a seat opposite her, which caused her to sigh.

"I only went to deposit that box in Nikki's car. I had more work to do, so I didn't have time to catch the train, then the tube, go to my flat, change into that dress, catch the tube again—"

He scratched his stubbled jaw and threw his head back. "Yeah, you could've summarised it and said you didn't have time. Why were you even working after hours?"

"One word: Nikki." Avery rolled her eyes. He wasn't that much surprised by the bitterness she shared towards that woman; not many people working for Primavera Racing were fond of Nikki Bellinger. "Anyway, the heel on my stiletto broke, too. So I will have to walk barefoot out there, or just wobble on my broken shoes and make a fool of myself."

Rowan winced—he knew Avery was the kind of person who couldn't stop talking whilst being a total nervous wreck.

"Just wear your Converse," he suggested. "The ones you wore today."

For a moment, she didn't let her expression break, then he saw a flash of surprise in her eyes.

It seemed like she was contemplating his recommendation at first. "I don't have time to go up there. All my clothes are in my office. It's whatever. Not that anyone will pay attention to me, anyway."

Rowan scoffed loudly. If one person could outshine the sun itself, it was Avery Sharma-Maddox. Despite being quiet and reserved, she had a vibrant energy that could put a smile on anyone's face. Had a soul so pure, so kind—sometimes too good. If anyone knew how to be the centre of attention, albeit unwillingly, it was her. She was full of life, full of grace, full of goodwill to her core.

He knew then that Avery was his opposite—a full, stark contrast. Because Rowan was guarding the true colour and value of his heart, hiding all the brokenness and dark corners of his soul so that no one could ever see the real him. He always knew that putting another version of himself out to the world was better, easier.

He folded his arms across his chest. "What kind of drug are you on? Something that causes you to spit bullshit and total nonsense?"

Avery only narrowed her eyes. "What are you doing here, Rowan?"

Understanding she wouldn't answer his previous question, he said, "I'm looking for Ellie."

He counted three heartbeats before she made her response audible. Her voice was quiet, nearly muted with the sound of the loud music coming from the other room, yet he managed to hear, "She's not here."

Rowan's eyebrows pinched together in a confused frown. "She's my press officer. Of course, she is."

She drifted her gaze away. "Not anymore."

"What do you mean '*not anymore*'?"

She let out an exasperated sigh. "It means what it means."

Ellie wasn't his press officer anymore? What the actual fuck?

He flickered his gaze down to her neck where she was toying with her pendant. He tried not to glance down to the rest of her physique, but he found himself struggling when the swell of her breasts lured his gaze downwards. He shook his head at the realisation, jaw tightening.

"Why am I being informed now?"

Her answer was a half-shrug.

"Who's replacing her?"

A beat passed. "You're looking at her."

Time stood still for a fraction of a second.

Next thing he knew, Rowan burst out in laughter, bringing his fist up to his mouth. If she was trying to be amusing, then she had succeeded.

"Funny," he chuckled dryly. "That's a good one."

But when he noticed she didn't so much as crack a smile or roll her eyes in pleasantry, he understood she wasn't lying.

His smile instantly vanished and he cleared his throat, poking his tongue on the inside of his cheek. It took him a few seconds to register the new piece of information. To process the news.

"Yeah, fuck no. That's not happening."

"Don't look so excited," she deadpanned before standing up, her small hands brushing her skirt. "You might set the whole place on fire by the look of utter delight on your face."

He rose to his full height, causing her stare to trail from his torso to his narrowed eyes. "I might set the place on fire for a whole different reason, Avery."

"Dramatic, much?" she muttered with a roll of her eyes.

Rounding the table, he came to stand before her. Flowers. Vanilla. Stupid, sweet scent—just as sweet as her. He truly detested her and the way she feigned innocence by blinking up at him.

"I don't want to work with you." She needed to understand this couldn't work. He just *knew* this wouldn't work, not even remotely close.

He wasn't certain why he didn't want to work with her. Perhaps they'd throw daggers at each other, continuously so. Perhaps he didn't want to spend time with her. Because his PR officer was supposed to be his partner in crime, his shoulder to cry on, his assistant, basically—and he did not want Avery to be that person.

She tipped her chin up so she could hold his fiery gaze. "And I share the same sentiment. I despise you and you despise me all the same. But I'm biting my tongue and doing my job because contrary to popular belief, I do not live off of my parents' money. I need this job to pay rent, and bills, and life. Quitting just to please your ungrateful ass is not an option, either. So yeah, Emerson, we're stuck together."

He ground his molars together, trying not to let his molten rage consume his thoughts. "I'm going to make your life such a fucking night—"

"Congrats because you've already done so."

"I can't stand you—"

"So glad the feeling is reciprocated."

"Hey, Rowan," someone said from the doorway, interrupting their argument. "We're launching in five."

Irritated, Rowan exhaled loudly and took a step back. He glanced towards the entrance of the cafeteria, only to see Nikki glare at Avery. When he looked at the latter, she was staring at the floor.

He nodded. "Be right there."

It was only when they were left alone with their respective wrath that he let out a loud scoff, obliging Avery to look back up at him. He could feel the tension envelop them in a blazing bubble—unwavering, powerful.

"This conversation isn't over," he bit out as he spun on his heel.

"It might as well be," she replied. "It's done. So act like the big boy you are and stop fighting me."

He'd always fight Avery. Always. And neither of them were ready for this battle.

CHAPTER THREE

LONDON, ENGLAND

"MY NAME'S ROWAN Emerson and I'm a car mechanic."

Ava couldn't help but chuckle behind the rim of her flute of champagne when Rowan introduced himself to the camera and the little crowd gathered around the new car. Soft laughter erupted from around, resulting in a wide grin drawing itself upon Rowan's face.

She kept her gaze on the fast car and its brand-new livery, admiring the shade of red the team had settled for—a mixture of maroon and carmine, something more savage and brutal than last year's burgundy.

She listened to the F1 presenter ask Rowan and Thiago their general opinion about the vehicle, and when Rowan's voice echoed first, she couldn't help but peer at him.

With one hand tucked in the front pocket of his trousers, he held the microphone to his mouth. She watched the spotlight cast a glow on his chest where tattoos were curling on the base of his throat and slipping underneath the unbuttoned dress shirt hugging his torso.

Whilst Rowan was all dishevelled, uncaring, and wild, Thiago was pristine, classy, and calm.

"I hope it goes fast," Rowan said, his stare focused on the car, taking in the halo, the sidepod, the rear wing. "As much as I loved staring at Valencia's behind last season, I need to give him a taste of his own medicine by offering him a lovely view of *my* behind."

Another echo of laughter.

Thiago slipped his free hand into the pocket of his trousers and shook his head in disbelief. "You'd have to be able to overtake first to be in front, darling."

Rowan narrowed his gaze. "I wouldn't be all pompous and proud already, mate. Game's on. But don't worry, if—and let me emphasise on the *if*—you're faster than me, I'll defend you like a king. The opposite is most likely to happen though, let's be real."

"I knew you loved staying close to me," Thiago joked, draping an arm around his teammate's large shoulders. "But let's not fight to become Minister of Defence. I'd rather wear the crown—the champion's."

Rowan's eyes rolled dramatically. "You're already the Crown Prince of the paddock. Give me something."

"You're the heartbreaker of the paddock," Thiago said, shrugging coyly. "Your title is just as sweet as your persona."

"That's so nice of you to say," Rowan droned, pushing his teammate's arm away. "*Your Highness.*"

Thiago grinned, slightly shifting to wink at the camera. "Your *Royal* Highness, please."

The banter between those two was always entertaining and amusing to watch. Ava bit the inside of her cheek to restrain her smile from growing and diverted her gaze back to the car as she listened to Rowan talk more seriously.

"How'd he react?" a voice whispered in her ear.

Ava startled at the sound of Kamari's voice, then turned towards her. With a subtle nod of her chin, she asked Ava to slip away from the crowd to stand further in the back.

Ava rose a brow in silent questioning, tilting her head to the side as she watched Kamari ogle her boyfriend like he was the most handsome man she had ever seen. Well, Thiago Valencia *was* a beautiful man. But to Ava, he was more like a brother.

Ava loved Kamari for Thiago and vice-versa. She was good to him—patient, loving, supportive; everything he had ever needed and wanted in a woman. After working for two entire seasons with Thiago, she had gotten to know the man deep to his core—minus all the secrets and burdens he kept to himself—and considered him as one of her closest friends.

The mere thought of knowing she'd have to spend countless hours and days with Rowan to follow him, check on him, and keep his image clean was already annoying her. Rowan was a handful—she knew that. She had always admired Ellie's capability at handling him, but she was not Ellie. Ava didn't know how to bring Rowan's barriers down without irritating him. Didn't know how to laugh at his jokes without rolling her eyes in annoyance. Didn't know how she was supposed to stand him.

"I know you're not Rowan's biggest fan," Kamari explained quietly. "And he isn't yours. Thiago filled me in on all the gossip."

"Oh." Ava chuckled, everything but amused. "Well, he isn't very pleased about the news, but whatever. I'm sure we'll both get over it and move on. I'm not going to let his dickhead energy ruin me. We can do it. We can work together and not kill each other."

At this point, Ava wasn't sure who she was trying to convince, herself or Kamari, but she teetered towards the former option, nonetheless.

"You'll get over that hatred," Kamari assured kindly. "You know, I didn't like Thiago at first."

She took a sip of the sparkling wine. "Why?"

"He was rude. And too pretty to be real. He made me feel things no one had made me feel before and I didn't like that."

But all Rowan could make Ava feel was thundering irritation, molten bitterness, and rare anger to the point of having her heartbeat batter erratically—and not in a good way. Those were everything but positive feelings.

A small tap on her shoulder obliged her to turn around and shock rippled through her body when she faced a tall, muscular man with brooding features.

Tate Richards was, undoubtedly, as handsome as his best friend, Rowan. With his light brown hair and piercing blue eyes, he knew how to attract a woman's—or man's—attention. The only issue was that he rarely smiled. Still, he was less infuriating than the driver whose voice echoed in the background.

"I've got something for you," Tate announced as he lifted a pair of shoes. Not any pair of shoes—her white Converse.

Begrudgingly, she grabbed them and gaped at Tate whose face didn't show a flicker of emotion. "Uh, thank you. But...why?"

She felt Kamari slip away, and she ached to turn around and beg for someone to rescue her. Because whatever Tate was doing was weird. Unexpected.

The physiotherapist's gaze dropped to her bare feet. "Boss made me do it."

In sync, they turned towards Rowan. His attention was focused on Thiago as the latter spoke, debriefing about his previous season.

"That's..." *Suspicious.* What was Ava supposed to say? That it was nice of him? Sure, it was, but Rowan was everything but nice. She offered a small smile to Tate. "Just thank him for me."

Tate nodded and turned around. "Will do."

The biggest cloud of turmoil was now fogging her mind. Rowan had gone from nearly shouting in her face that he refused to work with her, to asking his physiotherapist slash best friend slash brother to run upstairs to fetch her pair of shoes. That was madness. She didn't need to be saved.

Still, she appreciated the gesture.

Discreetly, she walked into the cafeteria and took a seat on the first chair she saw. Scrunching her nose when she realised she would put her dirty feet in her shoes, she sighed before slipping the sneakers on.

Better than nothing.

Leaning over to tie the shoelaces, a shadow came to loom overhead.

"I like this style. Converse with a fancy dress. Very Ava of you."

Ava chuckled and straightened herself, her gaze colliding with Eliott Dalton's blue eyes. His usually tied-back hair fell to the middle of his neck as he grinned down at her before gesturing towards the empty chair opposite her.

"Don't you have work to do?" she asked, though she nodded and permitted him to join.

"I'm sadly not in charge tonight. All I have to do is watch and sip fancy champagne like the lucky bloke I am."

Eliott was part of the creative team as a content creator. He would always roam around the paddock with a few cameras hanging around his neck, busy snapping amazing photos he would send to a teammate, who would post those on social media. He was probably the person she was the closest to on the team because they had started at the same time, and were around the same age. As she used to follow Thiago everywhere, Eliott would be following them alongside Alexander Myers, who was both Thiago's best friend and personal content creator.

"So, cat's out of the bag, huh?" He leaned back in his seat and smiled. "Excited?"

A small frown touched her brows. "About what?"

"Well, you're working for Rowan now."

Ah, that.

Trying not to show her annoyance, she nodded eagerly and forced a smile. "So freaking happy."

Eliott looked at her amusedly. She couldn't lie. Didn't know how to. "Are you sure?"

"Certain," she replied, tone clipped with a faux grin still plastered on her lips. "So, why did you follow me here?"

Eliott lifted his shoulders in a sheepish shrug. "Just wanted to make sure you were okay."

Her strained smile shifted into a genuine one. "That's sweet of you."

When Eliott drummed his slender fingers atop the table, he offered Ava a wicked glance. "Did you want to sneak out and drink champagne on the rooftop?"

She didn't so much as think as she stood up. "Can't say no to that."

When they returned to the busy entrance hall, everyone's attention was focused on the two drivers talking about their hopes for the new season. Eliott grabbed two glasses of champagne and, with a subtle nod of his head towards the exit, silently asked Ava to follow him.

They walked towards the lifts exchanging a small glance. What Ava wasn't aware of, was that someone had been watching her intently.

❧

"AND WHAT ABOUT YOUR BREAK?" Eliott asked, depositing the empty glass next to him. "I only talked about mine."

Ava shivered when the cold breeze caressed her bare skin. Wrapping her arms around herself, she glanced at the lake below, observing the silvery glow of the moonlight spilling on the calm water.

"It wasn't very interesting. Not as adventurous as yours."

Eliott hummed, placing his forearms atop the railing. "That's okay. Everyone's got their definition of taking a break. I travel and you take care of yourself. That's cool."

Ava snorted softly. "I'm not a cool person, Eliott."

She could feel his gaze on her, but she kept her stare on the lake, trying to seek a sliver of warmth by rubbing her cold flesh. "I think you are."

The compliment was akin to warm sunlight peeking through clouds. Tucking a strand of hair behind her ear, she smiled softly and nodded. Ava never knew how to respond to remarks like this.

"Listen," Eliott carried on, unaware of her slight discomfort. "I've been meaning to—"

The sound of his voice was concealed by loud laughter and the door opening. Ava pivoted to watch Tate Richards, Callahan Langdon—Thiago's physio—and a few other men stroll outside, followed by the one and only Rowan Emerson.

Though the men only waved or dipped their chins in acknowledgement when they noticed Ava and Eliott, they didn't comment on their presence as they walked to the other side of the rooftop. But when hazel eyes burning with unrelenting anger found her gaze, she held her breath, bracing herself for the tornado about to catapult into her face.

Rowan strode towards the pair in long, wrath-filled steps, fingers flexing by his sides. "Dalton," he said, barely looking at the photographer who had come to stand beside Ava. "May I have a minute with Avery?"

"Ava," she corrected grimly. The athlete only smirked smugly, like her frustration was amusing him.

"Sure. I was about to head back downstairs, anyway. It's kind of chilly out here. Ava, I'll see you on Monday?"

"Yes." She rapidly peered at her friend and smiled softly. "Get home safely."

Eliott returned her kind gesture. "You, too. Night, guys."

Rowan fluttered his fingers in farewell. "Bye-bye, sweetheart."

Ava counted three heartbeats before looking back at Rowan, and crossed her arms. He dropped his stare, tracing the route of her forearms until he reached her chest and the column of her throat.

"You're freezing," he noted coldly. "And that guy didn't even give you his jacket?"

Ava sighed through her nose. "I'm fine."

"You're obviously shivering." With a tight jaw and an expression full of blatant annoyance, he threw his head back and groaned skywards. Then, he took his jacket off and handed it to her. Ava blinked. Gaped at his tattooed and ring-clad hand extending the piece of clothing. "Just fucking take it, Avery."

She wasn't cold anymore; her blood had started boiling the minute he had stepped onto the rooftop, her pulse thumping against her temple in a nearly deafening rhythm. "I just said—"

"Don't force me to put it on you," he bit out. She still couldn't look at him. "I'd rather stay far away."

She scoffed. "At least we agree on something."

"Just put the jacket on." He released a grunt, like it physically pained him to muster the following word. "Please."

Ava gave in with a sigh and grabbed the blazer, although with slight reluctance. She rolled her eyes when he crossed his arms, waiting for her to shrug it on. His cologne enveloped her senses—masculine, intoxicating. She focused on the notes of citrus and pepper, ignoring how she was practically floating in Rowan's clothes.

"Thank you," she whispered, blinking up at him as she basked in the warmth of his jacket and scent. She fought the urge to linger her regard on the tattoos curling around the base of his throat and the lean muscle hidden beneath his unbuttoned shirt.

He was unnervingly handsome. And he knew it.

His throat worked as he swallowed. Jaw still clenched, he

nodded then jutted his chin at her feet. "Are you going to thank me for the shoes?"

She huffed. "I was getting there."

"Save your breath."

Rowan's eyes flashed as he stared down at her body, swallowed down by his oversized blazer. "See, Avery," he started, that coarse voice of his sending chills arising on her spine. "Your behaviour tonight is exactly the reason why I don't want you to be my press officer."

She wanted to bury her hands in the pockets of the coat, but to prevent herself from doing so, she simply curled her fingers until her hands were balled, her eyes narrowing into thinner slits. "Elaborate."

He took a step forward whilst she stood immobile. "I don't appreciate people leaving in the middle of an interview when I'm the centre of attention, even less when it's my publicist."

She had to crane her neck to look into his eyes. "I'm going to stop you right there. Before you lash out at me and fault me for all my wrongdoings, get it inside your head that I don't owe you anything. You didn't need my presence or services during the car launch. You were doing just fine being under the spotlight."

"You just fucking left," he seethed. "That was disrespectful."

"I get it. And I'm sorry for that. Don't you start believing that's how it's going to be once we start travelling and working together. You know I was good to Thiago, and as much as it flipping pains me to work for you, my work will be just as perfect and professional, if not even better."

The edges of his irises were illuminated with reckless anger. She now realised she had rarely seen him so angry, but she wasn't afraid. Wouldn't yield. For the most bizarre reason, she wanted to understand why he was so terrified to be let down. Surely, it wasn't because she had left the car launch party early.

"You're going to sabotage me," he accused, utterly convinced by his own words.

"That's where you're wrong." She stepped closer and folded

her arms beneath her breasts. Neither of them had noticed they were nearly standing chest to chest, their bated breaths entwining before curling into puffs of air. "I'm the best publicist you'll ever have. Your reputation will be perfect. I will make sure people worship you and never catch a glimpse of the vile man you are when you're not racing. People will love you more and more each day, and that's because I'll work hard on my end to defend you. Just because I snuck out during an event where I knew what you'd be saying anyway, doesn't mean I will fail at doing my job."

Rowan was starstruck. For a few heartbeats, he stared at her, his jaw going slack. He whistled then—*whistled.* "Damn. Small, but feisty."

Ava tipped her chin up, holding his burning gaze. "Do not underestimate me. If you're so convinced I'll make your life a misery, you're wrong. Get your head out of the gutter and stop acting like a baby. You're going to blow that cover one day, you know."

A frown touched his eyebrows, and she gaped at the deep crease forming between them. "What cover?"

She unfolded her arms, ready to push the jacket off her shoulders. "You know what I'm talking about. I need to leave—"

Rowan interrupted her. "There are no more trains at this time of the night."

She frowned as the jacket fell off her shoulders, the cold breeze causing shivers to skitter down her spine. His gaze dropped to her bare shoulders, her collarbones, taking in the way she couldn't hide the slight tremors corrupting her body. "I'm aware. I'll ask someone to drop me off."

She was confused. About his regard, about the whole turn this day had taken, her new job position, the encounters with Rowan, and the way he had been acting with her.

She presumed they were both on the edge of exploding, unable to know how to deal with this new situation.

At last, she looked away, fully taking the jacket off. "Enjoy the rest of your night."

His deep voice startled her, but not as much as the contact of their skin when he lightly touched her wrist to push it back towards her. "Just keep it. Wouldn't want my *amazing* PR officer to catch a cold. Don't be late on Monday. We've got stuff to work on. I'm so looking forward to being your worst living nightmare."

CHAPTER FOUR

LONDON, ENGLAND

THE PAIN AU chocolat was still slightly warm when she bit into it, a hum full of satisfaction vibrating inside her chest at the sound of the crunch and the buttery taste touching her palate.

There was always a small table full of pastries, fruits, coffee, tea, and juices set in the hallway for the employees to grab before going into their offices. Ava's guilty pleasure was a pain au chocolat, and she loved them even more when they were still fresh and crispy.

"Those are so bad for you."

Immediate irritation flared through her system at the sound of Rowan's low voice. Dabbing the side of her mouth, she peered at the door and watched him stroll inside her office without waiting for her permission to enter.

He took a seat opposite from her, leaning back in the leather chair as he let his lips curve into a smile. And just like that, he was the perfect portrait of indolence and arrogance.

"Good morning to you too, Rowan."

He grinned. The set of dimples adorning each one of his cheeks was just another weapon in his arsenal, but she wasn't fooled by his handsome smile. "Morning, love."

Ava wiped her fingers on a napkin after depositing the pastry on a plate. "Don't call me that."

"My bad," he said almost coyly. "Hi, Avery."

Letting out a heavy exhale, she shook her head in a barely noticeable motion. "It's nine in the morning and you're already here to annoy the shit out of me. What do you want?"

"You're a real delight," Rowan commented sardonically, yet coldly.

She offered him a faux smile. "Thanks."

A file she hadn't noticed he'd been holding landed on her desk. Warily, she grabbed it and made sure he saw the glare full of incredulity she gave him. All she received in response was a blank expression.

"What's this?"

Locking his fingers behind his head, he propped his feet atop the bureau and shrugged sheepishly. "Because I am a handsome, amazing, incredibly considerate man, I am saving you the burden of spending time with me. These are facts about me that you should know."

"I'm sorry... What?"

A smirk drew itself upon his lips. "Apology accepted. Just take a look at those. I promise you'll be thanking me."

Daggers were shot at him through her glare, but he merely lifted his shoulders in a lazy shrug again.

She despised how nonchalant he was.

"Are ten pages necessary for that?" Ava scoffed, taking the sheets of paper out. "You should've written an autobiography."

He smiled broadly at the sound of her derisive tone. "I did consider it. But my guess was that you'd DNF it, so I summarised everything. But I'll gladly tell you all about my life if you want."

"Please don't," she mumbled as she plucked her glasses from the top of her head to place atop the bridge of her nose.

"That's what I thought."

She took a sip of her coffee and allowed a frown to settle on her features as she gaped at the page before her eyes. "You can't be serious, Emerson."

"I am. Super serious."

"You're mad, that's what you are."

1. LIST OF VITAMINS AND MEDICINES I TAKE
2. MY ALLERGIES
3. BRANDS OF WATER I HATE (VERY IMPORTANT)
4. MY COFFEE ORDER (I ONLY DRINK OAT MILK)
5. WHAT NOT TO FORGET WHEN WE TRAVEL (E.G. FAVOURITE PILLOW)
6. AN INSIGHT INTO MY SUPER SPECIFIC DIET (I LIKE A PECAN PIE ON CHEAT DAYS)
7. SNACKS PRE AND POST-RACE
8. SONGS THAT HYPE ME UP + MY FAVE MOVIES (IN CASE I FEEL BLUE AND YOU NEED TO COMFORT ME)

Each bullet point was followed by a detailed explanation of the title. Rowan Emerson was not a simple man. He was eccentric. Arrogant to the point it was evident the whole world knew of his name. Complicated and mysterious in a way that strangely piqued Ava's interest.

When she looked back into his hazel eyes, she fluttered her lashes, dramatically so. "Do you want me to study those pages so I can know *everything* about you?"

A dimple made another appearance on his cheek when he grinned smugly. "That's the idea."

She rolled her lips, causing his stare to drop to her mouth. "Not happening."

"Well, you're going to have to," he argued. "I'm slowly

running out of vitamins, by the way. I need them before we leave for Bahrain."

The balls this man has!

Ava scoffed and put the papers aside. "No."

"No?" he echoed with raised brows. Something flashed in his eyes—as though he loved challenging her.

"Do you want me to say it in French?" she snapped. "*Non.* In Spanish? *No.*"

"Damn," he muttered. "Trilingual queen?"

She sighed, already exasperated by his presence. She still couldn't fathom why she was so bothered by his simple existence. "Can you please shut up?"

He laughed—*laughed*—and for some reason, his smile caused her irritation to spark, like angry fireworks exploding in her bubble. Perhaps because his smile was gorgeous. Perhaps because he was aware of his undeniable charm and his devastating looks—those intriguing tattoos, those piercings on his ear, that sharp jaw covered by a freshly shaven splatter of dark hair, and that intense scrutiny that could melt anyone's heart.

"I'm not your assistant," she clarified, tone clipped.

"Might as well be, love. We'll be spending *so much* time together." He winked. She huffed before pushing his feet off the table, eliciting a chuckle to rise from his throat. "Look at us already having fun. Becoming besties and all."

Ava leaned back in her seat, propped her elbows atop the armrests, and rubbed her temples. She inhaled. Exhaled.

"Can you just—" She wanted him to leave so she could finish her pastry and drink her coffee in peace. But she also needed to start working with him before leaving for the pre-season testings and have everything settled down. "Just sit there and don't say a word, please."

"Alright." Raking his fingers through his brown locks, he leaned back and spread his legs out, obliging her gaze to follow a route on his torso where a fleece jumper hugged his broad physique. "I will sit here and be pretty. I can do that."

Diverting her gaze towards her computer, she ignored his chuckle when she acted like she wasn't affected by his presence. "In silence would be great."

"Nah. I like a good chit-chat. Tell me more about yourself. It's crazy how we've been working together for, like, three seasons and know nothing about each other."

"Stop being weird." The fact that he was trying to talk to her settled an odd feeling inside her chest.

"How am I being weird?"

"I thought you didn't like me."

He huffed. "Well, I can't exactly deny it."

"So why are you trying to make conversation?"

The mischief shimmering in his eyes, the smirk pulling at his mouth, threatened to make her temper explode. "We're going to be stuck together for months, if not years. Might as well have fun with it. We should call a truce."

His remark was disregarded, but he didn't seem vexed by her lack of interest. On the contrary, he seemed amused as another soft chuckle erupted.

"Is this the moment you take out your sketchbook and draw me like one of your French girls?"

"Rowan," she hissed, trying to conceal the smile threatening to touch her lips. He was such a fool. One thing she had noticed was that he enjoyed making people smile and laugh, as though seeing his entourage grin was a personal reward. "We're working now, okay? No more *chit-chats* about trying to get to know each other. That's reserved for afternoon tea or something."

"Avery," he scoffed, feigning outrage. She saw him put a hand on his chest from the corner of her eye. "Are you asking *me* out? I would *love* to have a chat over a cup of tea. Does tomorrow work—"

She turned and scowled in his direction, which made him laugh again.

Lifting his hands in surrender, he shook his head. "Now's actually the perfect moment to resign. I'm always going to taunt and annoy you, just so you know. Sophie's office is right at the end of the corridor. Just a knock on the door, a heartfelt conversation with her, and you're out of this nightmare."

Ava narrowed her gaze on him, and he mirrored her action. "I'm not quitting. Sabotage me all you want, but I'm not letting you win."

Slowly, pure bewilderment drew itself upon his expression, and that glint in his eyes made her heartbeat drum faster. "Feisty. I like that."

Ava scoffed softly, diverting her gaze away. She couldn't stand that look in his eyes. Couldn't stand *him*, period. "Whatever."

She started typing on her keyboard, opening the notes she had prepared for this meeting. She could feel him staring at her, studying her allure, analysing each one of her calculated movements. Ava felt like burning up under the intensity of it all.

"Don't mind me," he said then, tone softer. A frown touched her brows at the sound of that sudden delicacy. "If you want to finish your breakfast before we begin, go ahead. Don't let my previous comment hold you back from enjoying yourself."

"Didn't you just say it was bad for my health?"

"Well, it is."

He was right, but she wouldn't let his words and judgment ruin her. "Food makes me happy," she retorted proudly.

He hummed. "Good for you."

She glanced at the pastry of which she had only taken a bite. "I'll just eat it later." He, too, was observing her plate, and she was slightly dazed by that strange look on his face. Ava did not like sharing her food, but for the most bizarre reason, she found herself asking, "Did you want some?"

"Nope. Strict diet."

"Of course." She focused her attention back on her computer, noting how his features had softened for a fraction of a second. "So. Media Day is next Thursday. They'll most likely ask about your summer break. Some nosy reporters might point out those pictures of you totally unhinged, partying in Dubai."

He snorted softly, gaze darting to the window behind her shoulder. "That was a fun party. Kind of blurry, but fun."

"I'm glad you enjoyed yourself." She wasn't one to care about any of the drivers on the grid, despite seeing all twenty of them more than she saw her own roommate, but she had seen a few pictures of Rowan partying during his break—dimpled smile, sparkling eyes, glasses of liquor in hands, women tucked under both arms. "I can't control everything on the internet, but do I need to clean your public image one way or another?"

He shrugged. "No, it's fine. I was on winter break, needed to get drunk and party. But I do expect you to have my back anytime I fuck up from now on."

She arched a brow, not appreciating how he kept underestimating her. "Don't worry about it. I'm good at what I do."

For a moment, he stared at her in silence. Ava couldn't read beyond his hardened expression and those eyes that reflected nothing but uncertainty. At last, the corner of his lips twitched upwards, and he shook his head in a slight motion, as if lost in his thoughts.

"So I've heard." He stood up then. "I have a seat fit right now, but you have my number. Whatever you need me for, just shoot me a text."

Ava leaned back in her seat, cupping her mug of coffee between her hands. "I'd rather not message you."

"Glad we feel the same way about each other."

She watched him wave in farewell and huffed behind the rim of her cup.

His tone was full of malice again as he sang, "Peace out. Don't miss me too much."

As if.

A sudden wave of realisation then hit her. "Wait."

Rowan abruptly stopped and peered over from his shoulder, raising a brow in silent questioning.

She pointed towards the small sofa where his blazer laid. "Your jacket. Thank you, by the way."

His gaze flickered towards the direction she was pointing at, and his shoulders sagged. Rowan took hold of his jacket, nodding stiffly. She could still smell the citrus enveloping her senses, could still feel the warmth of his large clothes on her.

"No problem."

Ava held her breath and looked away from the man, waiting for the moment he'd finally leave to sigh in relief. But, when his silhouette halted, she couldn't help but glance his way.

It was when he was at the door that their gazes collided again, a mischievous grin on his lips. "We're going to have so much fun together, love."

CHAPTER FIVE

SAKHIR, BAHRAIN

HIS PALM PRESSED against the steering wheel, the obnoxious sound of honking filling the silence and attracting annoyed glances his way. Rowan didn't care about all those people judging him for disturbing the calmness, because all he could see was red.

"Dude, you're the worst," Tate muttered from the passenger's seat as he put a Primavera Racing cap atop his hair.

"No, she is," Rowan countered, his gaze settled on the bane of his existence. "She's the reason why we're going to be late for the press conference. Best PR officer my ass. She's an absolute disgrace."

"That's rude," Tate said.

"It's the truth. Just look at her."

Avery was standing in front of the hotel's entrance with a few members of the marketing team, iPad clutched to her chest, bag hanging from her shoulder, and a radiant smile on her face.

The glow of the sunlight was illuminating her features, golden streaks creating the outline of a halo above her head—Rowan knew she was no angel, though. Dressed in her work attire, Rowan observed how the red polo and the black skirt hugged her pristine physique. She was annoyingly, effortlessly pretty.

Rowan shook his head when he realised where his thoughts had wandered off to, his palm now absently hovering over the steering wheel.

When he honked again, Avery took a deep intake of air and turned towards the car, lifting two fingers.

"Averyyyyy," he dragged through the open window. "Come on."

Hold on, she mouthed, causing Rowan to throw his head back against the seat as a grunt rose from his throat.

"You're an idiot," Tate fired at him.

Rowan didn't argue. Narrowing his eyes, he watched Avery beam brightly as Eliott Dalton lifted his camera to snap a picture. She then waved to her friends and strode towards the car, unhurried and taunting Rowan by taking her sweet time to cross the parking lot.

Shoulder pressed to the seat, he watched her climb into the back.

"That noise was very annoying." She met his angry gaze whilst pulling the seatbelt across her chest.

"Funny," he said, "that's my exact thought whenever you open your mouth."

"Hilarious," she bit out. "I'm still surprised you haven't gone and begged Romano to have another publicist."

Even though Simon Romano was Primavera Racing's team principal, he didn't have that power. He only had control over his team—drivers, car mechanics, rivals on and off the grid, etc. Therefore, he couldn't assign another press officer to Rowan.

Her gaze followed his hand when he placed his wrist on the top of the steering wheel. "If I ask for you to be replaced, that means I'm letting you win. And I don't lose, Avery."

Chocolate eyes meandered over his face. "There's a first for everything. Might actually be good for your ego to understand you don't rule the world."

He smirked. "Not the world, but the paddock, love."

"Whatever suits your fancy." She blinked, acting all innocent. "I thought we were going to be late, so maybe you should start driving?"

"I despise you," he grumbled, shifting in his seat to start the car.

"Feeling's mutual, honey."

"You're lucky you're forced to ride with me to the circuit, otherwise I would have left you to find a solution on your own."

She scoffed. "That's not very gentleman-like of you. Besides, I would have found a ride."

"Like who? Eliott Dalton?"

Rowan exited the parking lot and ignored Tate's stare full of incredulity.

"Yes," Avery answered, tone clipped. "Or anybody else on the team. Everyone's more delightful than you are."

Rowan glared at Avery through the rear-view mirror, and when she didn't yield and held his stare, he understood it would be a real challenge to work with her.

Tate cleared his throat. "When you two are done trying to rip out each other's throats, can we just hit the road?"

❧

VIBRATIONS JOLTED THROUGHOUT HIS BONES, causing frissons to appear on every single inch of his body. Rowan could feel beads of perspiration cascade down his temple, dampening his balaclava. His gloved hands were gripping the steering wheel, his vision entirely focused on the route ahead.

Racing in Bahrain was exhilarating regardless of the heat, because despite practising during the day, the actual race would take place during nightfall. The first race weekend of the season was always special—an entry to success, a way to prove himself to the team and the fans, a one-way ticket to pursue a dream of a lifetime.

"How does the car feel?" asked Jamie, his race engineer, through the radio. "Ten minutes left before FP2 ends."

Passing corner thirteen, Rowan accelerated and smirked when he saw his teammate fly past him. A mere push on the throttle and a rapid shift of gears resulted in him chasing Thiago. Free practice sessions weren't meant for racing, only for testing out the car, but it was a ritual for the two drivers of Primavera to race a little bit during those sessions.

He decelerated before turning in the next corner, feeling the engine's heat blend with the high temperature coming off the circuit. "Too much oversteer."

Just as he uttered those words, he felt the back of his car slip. Rapidly regaining control, he counter-steered to the right and drove through the next turn.

Because this session was dedicated to having several dry runs and experimenting with the new car's abilities, Rowan had faith his team would fix every issue in the blink of an eye. So far, the car felt different than last season's, but in a positive way.

He'd been able to drive on this circuit last week during pre-season testing, but there was still some work to do to improve the engine. The car had a great racing pace so far and the dragging felt minimal.

"Understood. Thank you." A moment later, Jamie's voice came through again. "Box, box."

"Now? Let me try and set the fastest lap again."

"It's not qualifying yet, Rowan."

"So?" He slipped through two cars driving at a slower pace and saw Thiago go into the pit lane. "I'm going to be the best this season. Watch me."

"You're ambitious."

He'd trained harder than any other driver during the winter break. Had spent hours racing on the simulator. Had sweated in the gym to strengthen his physique. He wouldn't let anything or anyone come in between his goals. Nothing would distract him.

❧

IT WAS QUALIFYING DAY, and Rowan had made it through Q1 and Q2 without an ounce of struggle, which felt strange compared to the beginning of last season where he'd either been out in Q2 or kept qualifying P9 or P10 until he would redeem himself during the race.

Waiting in the garage for Q3 to start, Rowan watched the screen above his engineer's head where the qualifying session was broadcast. The camera showed a clip of him sitting in the car, and when he saw that image of himself, he found the cameraman and winked.

"Okay," Jamie said, his voice echoing through Rowan's earbuds. "You've got enough fuel. What's your call?"

"I'm running my lap at the very end of Q3," Rowan said, confidence seeping through his veins. That feeling stirring inside his gut told him this was going to be a good weekend.

"Are you sure you want to take the risk?" Jamie gaped at him from his desk, brows raised as he adjusted his set of headphones. Rowan lifted two thumbs up. "You didn't have enough slip-stream during Q2."

"Yeah, but I have a nice balance between agility and top speed, so increasing speed shouldn't be too much of a struggle."

"Copy."

Four of his car mechanics were kneeling around his vehicle, holding heating blankets atop his tyres to keep them warm until he decided to go out. Rowan gaped at the television where a camera was following Thiago's car. His sectors one and two were purple, meaning he had set the fastest time in those two segments of the track. By the look of his current speed, it looked like he would have a purple sector three, too.

Rowan nodded—a sign of respect—when Thiago's name

flashed above the other nine drivers who had made it to Q3, setting his teammate as the provisional pole-sitter. Slight bitterness coursed through his veins at the realisation. No matter how much he respected and appreciated Thiago, he merely wanted to steal the spotlight for once and stand one step higher.

Rowan and Jamie exchanged a glance, and with a subtle nod of the head from the driver, Jamie gave a signal to the mechanics to take the blankets off.

Rowan then drove out of the garage and into the pit lane, a grunt rising from his throat when he saw all the traffic as he started running his outlap.

"This fucking traffic," he muttered.

Still driving at a slow pace like most of the nine other cars, he went around the circuit until he was nearly at the starting line.

Foot flat-out as he pressed on the throttle, he passed the chequered line, knowing he needed to set the fastest lap now.

He lifted his right foot and pressed the brake, his gloved fingers working on the left paddle to downshift his pace as he turned in the first corner.

He knew the route and trajectory of this circuit by heart, though he kept his focus on the invisible line, hitting the apex of corner five which delimited the first sector of the circuit.

Racing through the night was thrilling, exhilarating, incomparable.

Rowan breathed heavily as he braked, sweat dampening his suit and gloves.

"Full push," Jamie cheered on.

"Don't talk to me," Rowan snapped. "Especially in turns."

"Copy."

He flew through sector two as fast as he could, the smell of burnt rubber invading his senses.

He raced through the last long straight line, and when he finally passed the last corner, he pushed at full throttle to cross the finish line. The adrenaline rushing through his veins made his blood pump, made his heartbeat thump so loud that it was nearly as deafening as the roar of his engine.

"Tell me we have it," Rowan demanded, breathless.

Behind him, Thiago was giving his all to set the fastest lap again.

Jamie's response came through when Thiago passed the finish line.

"You're on pole, Rowan. You're on freaking pole, man!"

CHAPTER SIX

SAKHIR, BAHRAIN

"HEY, AVE. HEARD you were assigned to work with Emerson now."

Ava lifted her gaze from her phone before pulling her sunglasses up to rest them atop her head. An instant smile spread across her lips when her gaze collided with Miles Huxley's green eyes. He stood before her, arms folded across his chest hugged by a black fireproof shirt, his racing suit hanging at his hips.

The paddock was flooded with privileged fans, sports reporters and presenters, photographers, and cameramen. Ava had been enjoying the setting sun in front of Primavera Racing's motorhome, using that time to breathe and relax before spending the rest of the evening running after Rowan.

She lifted a hand over her eyes to shield her vision from the golden sunlight. "Oh, you mean Satan? Yep, that's my boss now."

Miles chuckled and tilted his head to the side. It was rare to see this side of the World Champion, but Ava assumed he had no struggle letting his walls down around her given they had known each other their entire lives. "I'm sure he's not *that* bad."

Ava's shoulders were lifted in a small shrug. "He's decent when he's not complaining about his coffee order or the brand of water he's drinking, or when he isn't checking himself in a mirror, or when he isn't making me run left and right for nothing."

He grinned down at her, mockingly. "Poor him, being described as decent. I just know his ego is taking a toll with you as his publicist."

She pocketed her phone, looking around the crowded paddock. "He's having a hard time processing the fact I'm not affected by his douchebag attitude. He can make me run kilometres to grab him a protein bar, and I'll still come back with a smile on my face."

Miles' smile didn't falter as he ruffled his chestnut hair. "There she is."

Ava and Miles had been friends long before his racing days. Prior to becoming an F1 driver and moving to Monaco, he lived in the same building as she did, all the while thriving in motorsports; karting, then F4, F3, up to F2 where he became champion, too. He was the one to convince her to pursue a career in motorsports when he'd realised she was as passionate as him.

She owed everything to Miles Huxley.

"Don't let him get to you," he continued. "I know how you are; pretending you don't care whilst you're the most sensible and sensitive person I know."

Ava's hands found the pockets of her skirt. "I'll be fine."

"I know you will," he quipped with a wink.

With a rapid hug, she told him cheerfully, "Good luck for the race."

"Careful," he teased as he rubbed her back gently. "You're fraternising with the enemy."

If only the world could see the authentic nature of the World Champion. Perhaps the people wouldn't call him cold, distant, and rude. Miles Huxley was everything but.

"Honestly? At this point, I'd rather work with Imperium than be glued to Rowan's side for another second. He's making my life a living nightmare. Not sure who's the enemy here."

❧

AVA WAS SITTING at the small table in Rowan's room in the motorhome, her attention zeroed in on the tablet in front of her, one earbud plugged in as she was busy transcribing the recordings from yesterday's interviews from the media pen.

Rowan's tone was delighted as he talked about the feeling of being on pole position for the first race of the 2023 season. She almost let a smile touch her lips when his laugh reverberated, and she remembered that blush coating his cheekbones, that dimpled smile that made the journalist grin timidly, those stars shimmering around his pupils. Happiness looked good on Rowan Emerson.

But when Ava realised where her train of thoughts had wandered off to, she shook her head and focused on the document open before her.

Laughter echoed again and she noticed it wasn't coming from the interview she had recorded. It was Rowan and Tate, laughing heartily as they watched a video on the physiotherapist's phone.

She glanced at the athlete, then back to her screen, and again to the man who had taken his cap off.

Ava had never truly paid attention to Rowan before. She was immune to his contagious dimpled smile, vibrant energy, and thorough love of attention for the sole reason that she always felt invisible whenever she was in the same room as him.

Because come on, why would a man like him pay attention to someone as simple as her?

But she couldn't fathom why she was being drawn towards him at that exact moment as he shrugged his t-shirt off to replace it with a fireproof shirt. The tattoos adorning his bronze skin suited him just as much as his red racing suit. She found herself wanting to trace every single one of those patterns with the tip of her forefinger whilst basking in the scrutiny of his honey eyes.

It was when he felt her stare on him that he turned around, catching her gaze settled on an intricate drawing on his ribcage. He grinned smugly and winked, and all she could do was look away and pretend she wasn't blushing.

Yep, she definitely hated him.

"Avery," he drawled, back turned to her.

His whole allure was enticing—his sun-kissed flesh, his toned, chiselled, muscular body, his confidence he wore akin to a second skin. He was devastatingly beautiful. And Ava despised that.

"What?" she snapped, focusing too hard on the wall opposite her where multiple Polaroid pictures were hung.

His gaze was already on her when she finally found the courage to look at him. "You've got a bit of drool there, love," he said, pointing at the corner of his mouth.

"It's probably vomit."

Rowan snickered. "Are you trying to convince yourself or me?"

"You know, I'd be offended if I were you."

"Right. My heart is broken into millions of pieces," he deadpanned.

She hummed. "I wasn't aware you had a heart to begin with."

"You're right, I don't." He ruffled his dark hair, rapidly drawing her attention to his arm. "I need my pre-race snack."

The audacity this man had—

She glared at him, hoping he'd see the invisible, yet lethal daggers thrown in his direction. He had the nerve to smirk sheepishly. "Get it yourself. You're a big boy, Rowan. Or ask Tate."

The physiotherapist raised his hands in surrender, his gaze still fixed on his phone. "Don't get me involved."

Rowan pulled his white fireproof shirt down as he turned to fully face her, and she fought the urge to glance at his contracted abdominals.

A grin touched his lips, taunting her. "Yeah, but it's no fun if I don't make you get it for me."

"While we're at it, do you want me to feed it to you, too?"

A small shrug of his shoulders was perceptible before he pulled the rest of his racing suit on. "I mean, since you're offering with so much enthusiasm and kindness, how could I ever refuse?"

Ava stood up, causing the chair to screech on the floor with the force of her movement. "You're terribly annoying, did you know that?"

"Yet you still haven't resigned. Admit that you like me deep down."

"I fear I won't be able to make your wish come true."

He could make her feel flushed and timid one moment, and the next, he would cause flaming annoyance to rush through her veins.

Cradling her tablet, two phones, and a pair of sunglasses to her chest, she narrowed her gaze on him. He had taken a step towards the desk, and she had put a distance between them by moving towards the door.

She was burning under the intensity of it all—his words, his gaze holding hers with equal defiance. "You want to make my life a misery? Go ahead. This is just as much of a nightmare for me as it is for you."

He only tilted his lips in a roguish smirk. Like he enjoyed seeing her so frustrated. Like he knew that, deep down, she loved the challenge as much as he did.

Turning on her heel, Ava exited the small room, but she

heard his footfalls follow her closely. "Oh, come on, Avery. I'm messing with you. You know I love annoying you."

"Why don't you find someone else to taunt?"

"You're my press officer. There's no one else I'd rather annoy."

"Wow," she droned impassively, spinning around. Her breath caught when she noticed he was standing mere centimetres away. "I feel so special."

Before Rowan could respond, the door to their right opened and Kamari appeared. Surprise drew itself upon her features when she saw the pair standing in the empty hallway.

Her brows rose as she flickered her gaze between Ava and Rowan. "Hi, guys."

Ava peered behind Kamari's shoulder to see Thiago busy zipping his racing suit.

"Oh, come on," Rowan grunted. "It smells like fucking sex in your room. You two are animals."

Kamari's cheeks flushed and Thiago only grinned before winking.

"I bet that sexy time will earn you a podium," Rowan commented.

Thiago's shoulders were lifted in a coy shrug. "That's the idea."

"Damn," Rowan mumbled. "Anyone volunteer as tribute to shag before every race? Avery? You could be my lucky charm."

Did he just admit he was somehow attracted to her?

No, of course not. She was just overthinking.

She smacked his chest nonetheless, eliciting a chuckle that rumbled deep inside his throat. She refused to look at him because she wasn't certain how she would manage to process that strange information.

"Tito," Ava pleaded. "Please take me back. I hate him."

She could feel the warmth emanating from Rowan's body as he leaned his palm against the wall, right above her head. His breath tickled the back of her neck when he chuckled, causing the hairs on her nape to rise, albeit against her will.

"Yeah," he agreed hoarsely. The depth, the gruffness of his baritone was something else. "Please take her back. She keeps giving me water I don't like."

Thiago snorted softly, shaking his head in disbelief. "You two are truly a duo."

Kamari exchanged a glance with her boyfriend, then pointed her thumb at him when she found Ava's gaze again. "If you and Rowan ever get married, Thiago needs to be his best man."

In sync, Ava and Rowan pretended to vomit just as she slipped away, purposefully bumping into his shoulder. "In his dreams."

"She wishes," Rowan said at the same time.

❧

HER HEART WAS RACING as she kept her stare on the television, holding the headphones against her ears just to feel, somewhat, grounded.

She was chewing nervously the inside of her bottom lip, a small crease between her brows as she stared at the screen. The palms of her hands were damp with perspiration, and she was certain her hair was a mess because of the heat.

It was no surprise that Miles Huxley had managed to lead the race after twenty laps. Thiago had overtaken Rowan after the latter had a front right puncture following a contact with another driver. Rowan was currently P3, and it was obvious that he was desperate to claim his front position back.

The thing with Rowan was that he was a reckless driver and he was taking too many risks. Obviously, he loved the thrill.

Fighting with his teammate was unsafe and dangerous. With five laps to go, Rowan was chasing Thiago, the front wing of his car nearly grazing his teammate's left rear tyre when he attempted an overtake on the inside of a corner.

"He's insane," she mumbled. At first, she thought no one would hear her comment, but the general hum of agreement floating around was proof her remark had been louder than intended.

Rowan braked late, drifting on the right to try and overtake Thiago, but when the latter's trajectory widened in the same direction, Rowan had to anticipate and let his teammate pass.

"God damn it, Emerson," Ava grumbled, holding her breath.

Eliott, who was sitting next to her, shifted the camera in her direction. She looked at the lens, sighed heavily, and shook her head. He chuckled and went back to filming everyone's reactions in the garage.

Ava kept glancing at the upper left side of the screen where the number of laps was counted. She truly felt like she couldn't breathe as she realised there were still four laps to go.

Rowan and Thiago were fighting each other, but at what cost?

She clasped her hands together, bringing the tips of her fingers to her lips as she maintained her gaze on the screen. Her heart was battering. Anxiety was emanating from everyone standing around her.

Only mechanics, Rowan's pit-crew, and a few guests were in the garage, yet the space felt cramped.

"Don't be an idiot."

Ava tended to speak to herself whilst she watched races, and it would always surprise her when others agreed with her comments.

Finally, after excruciating minutes of watching Rowan attempt to overtake Thiago, the chequered flag was brandished.

Rowan finished P3 in today's Grand Prix.

From the other side of the room, Ava caught Tate's gaze. He pressed his lips in a thin line, shaking his head slightly. Sending him a sympathetic smile, she went over to him, her heartbeat now steady as chaos didn't unravel. Only cheers of encouragement erupted because Rowan's finishing position didn't matter. Podium or not, his team would always celebrate him.

Ava didn't know much about Rowan, but she knew that he tended to unleash his wrath on his best friend, Tate. And right now, as he claimed the third position after tonight's race, she knew he was not happy about it.

❧

HER SHIRT SMELLED LIKE CHAMPAGNE. Whilst bubbles seared overhead when Huxley, Valencia and Emerson celebrated their podium, the latter had made sure to spray the team that was cheering below.

Despite Ava trying to hide behind Tate's large frame, it had been of no use to avoid the celebratory shower.

Busy tying her untamed curls in a bun, she leaned against a wall and tried not to stare at Rowan drying his hair with a towel.

He'd been silent since the podium.

He had asked for Ava to enter his room after he had showered, and Tate wasn't there.

"You're disappointed," she observed quietly. She wasn't even sure why she was trying to make conversation about something so evident.

Rowan scoffed. He threw his towel on the sofa and finally met her gaze. He had changed into loose jeans and his red Primavera polo. When he tucked his hands into the pockets of his trousers, he sighed deeply. Even that sound was filled with unrestrained distress.

She followed the route of a droplet of water falling down his temple because she didn't want to look into his eyes. But when she finally did, she found a crestfallen gleam in them that even his bright smile couldn't conceal.

"Rowan," she murmured.

"What?" He flopped down on the sofa, throwing the towel

on the chair of his desk. "Are you going to scold me like Romano did?"

She hadn't heard the conversation between Rowan and his team principal, but she had seen the anger in their boss' gaze.

"Of course not," she responded softly. Ava hated that she didn't know how to hide her good heart. No amount of misplaced acidity could ever overpower her kindness. She could resent that man as much as she wanted, but at the end of the day, he was her boss and she was a caretaker. "Why did you fight with Thiago? Even after being ordered not to take risks."

His head hung low between his shoulders. The floor seemed less intimidating than her stare. "Because I should have won, Avery."

She sighed, disliking that tone of his—laced with poison, low with sadness. "It's part of the game, you know that."

"I know."

"You could have caused so much unnecessary chaos. Could've injured yourself."

"I know."

"And you would have lost so much more than two places."

"I know." He leaned back into his seat and knocked his head back, staring at the blank ceiling. "You sound like you care."

"It's my job," she just said.

"Right."

The sound of her thundering heart was deafening. She inhaled. Braced herself, and demanded, "Can you look at me?"

And just like that, honey found chocolate. For a fraction of a second, his features softened, but she still could see that veil of vexation brimming his eyes.

She pushed herself off the wall. "Listen, I hate saying this, but you know you'll have to lie in the interviews we're going to go to now. They'll ask if a new rivalry was born between you and Thiago. The answer's no. They'll ask why you decided to battle him and you'll say that you wanted the end of the race to be exciting. That you had fun. Don't show them your disappointment."

His tone resonated bitterly. "Don't worry, Avery, I'm a pro at that."

She wanted to roll her eyes; tell him he didn't need to put that act on whenever he was in her company. But all she did was kindly say, "You'll come back stronger. Just stop being a dick. Think of the consequences of your actions."

CHAPTER SEVEN

JEDDAH, SAUDI ARABIA

Miles Huxley was unbeatable.

It was only the second Grand Prix of the season and Huxley's car was faster than any other one on the grid. With a gap of more than seven seconds between him and the second-fastest driver, he had been leading most of the race. Imperium Racing had dominated all weekend long—free practices, qualifying, and race; their two drivers were always at the top.

Good for them.

Undoubtedly, Rowan was very jealous. Utterly envious of their effortless success.

Still, he had finished the race third behind his teammate —again.

He knew he had to be grateful to be standing on the podium. Knew he'd driven brilliantly despite his overpowering thoughts that were intent on making him believe he hadn't been good enough.

After shaking his champagne bottle, he'd sprayed some of the bubbles down onto his team cheering on him and Thiago. Had poured some liquid into his racing boot and drank the contents from it.

He was now freshly showered and ready to head back to the hotel, but he still needed to attend a few interviews and the post-race debrief with the other F1 drivers. Slightly exhausted from the entire weekend and the heat, he stepped out of his room whilst rubbing his flushed and fatigue-stricken face.

Avery was waiting for him at the end of the hallway, but she was talking to Nikki Bellinger, the executive of the marketing and PR department.

Deciding he should wait for her in his room by turning on his heel, Nikki's high-pitched voice caused him to halt in his tracks.

"When are you going to fix it?"

"Tonight," Avery replied quietly. "I promise. As soon as I'm done with the interviews with Rowan."

"You better," Nikki bit out. "First you publish the article one hour late and then you dare not ask for someone to proofread. Result? There's a typo in the text."

Rowan couldn't help but look at the pair. Head hung low, Avery was fiddling with her rings as she nodded at every harsh, cruel word Nikki spat in her face. He studied the way she pushed her large glasses up the bridge of her nose and stared at the tips of her Converse.

He'd never seen her so quiet. Submissive. Small.

"It won't happen again."

"It better not. We're professionals here. The best team when it comes to content creation and media." After huffing, Nikki planted her hands on her hips and asked, "Why did you mess up?"

Though Avery's back was turned to him, Rowan could perceive how tense she was beneath her uniform. "I guess I was caught up in something else."

Nikki's gaze was all pomposity and haughtiness. Rowan had never really appreciated this woman, but he now decided he disliked her just as much as he hated Brussels sprouts. Disliked listening to the way she was talking to Avery. "Don't let it happen again."

Avery merely nodded. It was evident Nikki wanted to add something, but Rowan refused to watch his press officer be undermined again. Slamming the door to his room shut, the two women turned to see him stride lazily their way.

He found Avery's gaze—vacant but thoughtful all at once. "Ready to go?"

"I was just waiting for you." Her voice was so brittle, so cold —so unlike her.

He winked and patted his cheek. "This face needs extra care."

She rolled her eyes at his comment.

There she is.

"Of course it does," she chimed. "Let's go, then."

She walked past her boss without sparing her a glance, but Rowan dipped his chin when Nikki's stare lingered on his face then his chest.

There was no denying she was a pretty woman, but her personality was akin to a witch's. He'd seen her plaster an angel's face in front of everyone, but he wondered why she was so awful to Avery. There wasn't a shadow of a doubt that her superiors weren't aware of her double personality.

"Great race," Nikki said with a smile on her lips.

"I know," he answered dryly before catching up to Avery.

She was watching the starry sky outside the motorhome when he approached. Her shoulders tensed when she felt the heat of his body radiate on her arm. Then she looked up at him, exhaling.

Her expression was pinched, and for a beat, he thought how much prettier and electric she looked when she smiled. For a beat, he nearly cracked a joke just to watch her features relax.

He frowned lightly. "You okay?"

The question had slipped out naturally, easily, and Rowan wasn't sure why he cared at all.

She nodded subtly, yet he wasn't convinced. Pushing her hair away from her shoulder, she allowed a soft smile to touch her lips. Out of his control, he gaped at her plump mouth as she murmured, "I'm alright."

The corner of his lips tipped upwards. "Good."

But he couldn't help but wonder how many times she had uttered that blatant lie after being destroyed by people over and over again.

Perhaps Avery Sharma-Maddox wasn't that much of his opposite. Perhaps she, too, had secrets so hurtful and dark that she preferred hiding behind a smile. Perhaps she also bore an obliterated heart that had been shattered by different reasons than him, but still ached and craved for a delicate caress that would erase all the indentations.

CHAPTER EIGHT

LONDON, ENGLAND

ROWAN GRINNED DOWN at his phone, chuckling softly as he drew a small heart next to the picture of a baby Thiago before posting it on his Instagram story, captioning it with *"Hey, @thiagovalencia, you used to be so cute. What happened?"*

Just as he pocketed his phone, whistling delightfully, oxygen got knocked out of his lungs when someone collided with his chest.

"Fuck my life."

Rowan was about to open his mouth—to complain, or whine, or make a joke—but stopped himself. He could recognise that honeyed voice anywhere—metres away, in his dreams, in his nightmares.

He blinked and took a step back, only to find Avery crouched down in front of him as she picked up a to-go cup of tea that had spilled over the floor.

Rowan couldn't fathom why he always felt immobile in her

presence, like he'd lost his senses and become defenceless, and not necessarily in a bad way. It was just bizarre.

He pushed the thought aside and gaped down at the woman cursing under her breath.

Her lips formed into a small pout. "I was really looking forward to drinking that tea." She then rose to her full height and glared at Rowan. He ignored her regard full of disdain as he studied her outfit, a hint of a smirk drawing on his lips at the sight of her signature Converse paired with jeans and a blazer. "Thank you for that. Really."

The sarcasm dripping from the tip of her tongue was akin to poison ivy.

"Wouldn't have happened if you had been watching where you were going," he jested.

He found himself disappointed when she didn't fight him and only muttered, "Whatever."

Pivoting, she found a bin and threw the empty cup in it, aggressively. Frustratingly.

Their gazes collided.

He blinked. She blinked back.

How was she even blaming him? It was obvious she was the one who had bumped into him.

She then strode to the other side of the hallway and retrieved a bunch of napkins on the catering table before lowering herself to wipe the mess away.

Rowan could have walked away, but instead, he stayed and watched her with an incredulous expression. "You know there's people for that, right?"

She scoffed, but didn't look up. Her glasses slid down and she pushed them back up. "So? If you're just going to stand there and be a dick, just leave."

He folded his arms across his chest, his brows raising. "Having a bad morning?"

"It was decent until you knocked out my drink."

"It wasn't my goddamned fault," he grumbled.

Stepping away from the crime scene, he glanced again at Avery. A janitor had come to stand before her. When he asked if she needed help, Avery kindly replied that she had everything under control.

This woman was everything he had expected her to be: fierce, smart, and unpredictable.

Needing to clear his head by wasting his energy on the treadmill, he hit the button of the lifts just when another voice echoed.

It was Eliott passing by, holding two laptops, an iPad, bags hanging from both of his shoulders, and a camera strapped around his neck. That man-bun of his was fucking ridiculous.

"Hey, Ava," he said, grinning, just as she threw away the wet napkins. She found a hand sanitiser dispenser on the wall and washed her hands. "Are you doing anything tonight?"

Avery shook her head, dropping her gaze to look at Eliott's occupied arms. "Need a hand?"

"Oh, I'm fine."

"You're not," she chuckled. "Come on, give me your bags."

Why did she have to be so nice all the time?

Rowan narrowed his eyes when he saw Eliott's face flush. He handed Ava a bag, albeit slowly. "Thanks. So? Tonight?"

"Right. Uh, yeah, I'm not doing anything. Why?"

They pivoted, ready to walk in the opposite direction. Still, Rowan could hear their conversation loud and clear. "This new pub opened in Soho last week. Wanna join us and a few people from the team?"

Rowan caught a glimpse of the bright smile growing on her face. "I'd love that."

Shaking his head as the bell chimed, he stepped inside the lifts where Tate was already waiting, a bored expression on his features as he leaned against the wall, hands buried in the pockets of his joggers. Regardless of his nonchalance, he nudged his chin in greeting when he met Rowan's gaze.

"Don't you look happy to be here on this fine Friday morning," Rowan quipped, teasing his friend with a wink.

"Delighted." Gently, Tate slapped the side of Rowan's neck when the latter came to stand beside him. "We're strengthening your fat neck today."

"Moron." Rowan took his phone out and searched for the newest pub in Soho. "Down for a drink tonight? We should ask if the guys are free."

❧

"YEAH, RIGHT," Rowan scoffed, yet a wide grin had overtaken his features. "As if you'd agree to drink from my shoe."

"Not your stinky shoe, Emerson," Noa clarified, his nose slightly scrunched in repugnance. "But maybe from mine. Keeps me sane knowing where the shoe has been."

"That's just disgusting," Sasha complained from Rowan's side as she brought the rim of her glass to her lips. "The whole concept makes me want to vomit."

"Loser," Tate chimed in. "You said you'd do a shoey for Rowan's first win this season too."

Rowan snorted softly at Sasha's disgusted expression. She shuddered and huffed. "Is it too late to back out?"

"Nope," Noa said. "You pinky promised all of us."

"Damn the pinky," the blonde grumbled before taking three large gulps of her cocktail. "I'm really not looking forward to your first win, Ro."

With his arm draped over the back of the booth, Rowan pushed Sasha's head towards the table. She tried to resist him, and he ended up ruffling her hair. "Get lost."

Laughter echoed around the table, blending with the loud noise of happiness unravelling around the pub.

Rowan brought the bottle of beer to his lips, his gaze roaming around the crowded place.

Reuniting with Noa and Sasha felt nice—relieving in some way. When Rowan and Tate moved to London in their late teens, they first lived in a small house they had shared with other people: Noa and Sasha.

Noa Nguyen worked for a law firm in the centre of London. Rowan had clear memories of him crying over enormous law textbooks.

Sasha did a lot of things: she worked two times a week in a bookshop, helped her mother's art gallery grow, and took evening classes to open her own business. She had never known what to settle for, but she'd never been ashamed of that. Rowan liked her for that—for taking life slow, easy.

Sadly, with all four of them being busy with their careers and, well, life, it was only on rare occasions that they could reunite all together. Today was a lucky day for Rowan.

Rowan's attention was nearly brought to Sasha when she started rambling about her latest hookup, but not quite as his gaze was pulled towards the pub's entrance.

Through the mass of people standing before the bar, he saw Avery enter, and he smirked in triumph behind the mouth of his bottle.

He couldn't see her clearly, but she was wearing a long, black coat with a purse hooked under her armpit. She smiled politely when she pushed past a group of men, trying to get further into the cramped space.

When she spotted her friends, she waved and let her lips curve into a beautiful beam. Brushing past Rowan's table without so much as sparing a glance his way, she reached Eliott's table which was only a few booths down.

There were too many people around their table, yet a seat had been reserved for Avery. She squeezed in, took her coat off, and smiled at Eliott who was sitting to her right. Not even a second later, no one was paying attention to her anymore, but it seemed like she didn't care about the lack of attentiveness. Rowan observed her fold her arms across her stomach, before looking down at her outfit. Had it not been for the person who had come to stand between him and Avery, he would have lingered his gaze on her physique and wondered why she had frowned at herself.

Rowan decided he wouldn't be bothered by her presence or existence.

He focused back on his own friends, and when Tate's gaze found his, his friend scowled and mouthed, "*Are you fucking dumb?*"

Rowan frowned. He mouthed back, "*You're more dumb than me.*"

Tate's eyes flickered to Avery, then back to Rowan. His lips moved: "*Really, mate?*"

Rowan shrugged lazily.

Sasha's voice came through, "The fuck are you two mouthing about?"

❧

"EXCUSE ME? I'm so sorry to bother you. Could I just get a photo with you?"

Rowan's grin widened when he looked up at a woman with brown hair who had come to stand by his booth.

He took a sip of water and nodded before standing up.

The fan gave her phone to Tate who, with so much enthusiasm, got ready to take the picture.

Wrapping an arm around her shoulders, Rowan made sure not to apply too much pressure on her bare skin. She, however, looped her arm around his back as her other hand came to rest on his chest—just between his pectorals.

Rowan nearly rolled his eyes when her breasts were pushed into his side. Still, he grinned handsomely at the camera.

He'd been spotted taking pictures with several people tonight. Some fans more timid than others, and some girls more bolder—like this one in particular.

"Thanks," she beamed as she stepped away.

She had bright blue eyes, rendering her gaze seductive in a

way. She sure was an attractive woman.

"Cheers," Rowan said then when she didn't try to carry on the conversation—or simply try to make some as she kept checking him out in silence.

Her gaze travelled down his torso, leisurely. "Do you want to get out of here?"

Rowan heard Tate's low snicker. He was so used to this scenario. So used to accepting the flattery and whispering the rejection. "I'm not interested, love."

Offended—like they always were—she simply huffed and turned around. He didn't even look when she tried too hard to sway her hips or flip her hair.

He was still standing when Noa asked, bewildered, "Why the hell did you say no?"

Rowan shrugged and sat back down.

"What happened to the Rowan who used to dip his dick in every woman looking his way?"

He winced. "You're really tarnishing my reputation, mate. I don't know. Must be my age. I'm becoming wise and careful, y'know?"

His three friends snorted loudly.

"Sure, being twenty-eight is *so* old," Sasha said.

Rowan couldn't recall the last time he had hooked up with a random person at a party. Was it weeks ago? No, more like several months, if not over a year.

He wasn't interested in them anymore. Perhaps part of himself was yearning for something stable, more serious.

What a waste, right? He was a high-performance athlete, followed by millions of people who begged for his attention, but rejected beautiful women's offers to have fun just for one night.

Maybe something was wrong with him.

His gaze slipped to Avery, albeit unwillingly. Like he was naturally drawn to her. Like she was merely a sparkling ember, he gravitated towards her like a moth to a flame.

She was now sitting alone at the table as her group of friends had gone to play a round of eight-ball. Her attention was on them as they took turns exchanging the cue whilst she cradled her empty glass between her hands.

But when she stood up and walked to the bar, Rowan decided this was his signal to go and taunt her.

Because she couldn't escape him if she tried. Because there was no way he'd spend the night without annoying her. Without riling her up. He enjoyed seeing her so flustered and frustrated.

Forearms braced over the edge of the counter, she drummed her fingers to the rhythm of the music and waited for her turn to be served.

"Following me?" she asked when he approached, still looking ahead of herself.

He leaned his elbow atop the wood, fingers passing through his hair, a grin touching his lips. "Wow. Fancy seeing you here. Isn't it crazy how the world is such a small place?"

"Right. *So* crazy."

Dark eyes collided with his, and he couldn't help but wink. She rolled her eyes in blatant annoyance, causing his smirk to spread wider.

"How's your night going so far?"

Avery's gaze narrowed on him as she shifted to face him. He tried—he really, really did—not to glance at her outfit where a black top clung to her chest, its neckline so low that he could trace the shape of her full breasts.

It was no secret to Rowan that Avery was a beautiful woman.

Younger than him but still beautiful, very much so.

But she was more infuriating than anything, so he blinked.

"Funny you should ask," she started, "because it was decent before you appeared out of nowhere and decided to bug me."

A dry chuckle rose from the back of his throat. "Funny you should say that because mine was going so well before you decided to walk inside the pub where I was already in and enjoying my drink."

"Not everything belongs to you or is a fucking competition,

Rowan."

He smiled broadly because he knew that acting nonchalantly would irritate her. "I know."

When she pivoted, the bartender was in front of them. Apparently, smiling was optional for the man, but Avery still beamed at him and asked for a shot of tequila.

"Do you want something?" she asked coldly when she felt Rowan's stare roaming over her side profile.

"I'm good."

She rapidly peered at him. "What are you still doing here then?"

A lazy shrug of his shoulders was his next move. "Just wanted to say hi to my least favourite publicist."

He was enthralled by the faux smile plastering her lips. "How sweet of you. *Hi*. Bye, now."

Rowan couldn't help but snort softly at her sardonic tone. Couldn't help but let his gaze trail from her fingers gripping the small glass to her mouth when she downed the liquor in a swift motion. Couldn't help but raise his brows when she simply held his gaze and dabbed the corner of her mouth with the pad of her thumb.

"Please pretend I don't exist," she demanded as she turned on her heel.

Well, that was an order he couldn't execute, no matter how hard he tried.

❧

"AVERY. GET DOWN and sit your ass on the chair before I do it myself."

Pretending she hadn't heard him, Avery kept on dancing on the chair, screaming the lyrics of *Gimme! Gimme! Gimme!* at the top of her lungs.

He hadn't been able to look away from her—from her smile, her moves, her unwavering happiness.

Rowan felt as though he was a house of cards, ready to fall to his knees before this enchantress as she moved like she was a full-on rainstorm.

Rowan wasn't sure what he'd do if she fell and broke an arm or something. Someone would have to replace her for the next race. He didn't want that.

No one could fire back at him as well as Avery did.

No one knew how to handle his attitude the way she did.

It was only when the song ended that she finally decided to regain some senses, hopping down with a bright smile still on her face. Her chest was heaving as she cheered along with the rest of the patrons enjoying the night.

Tucking a strand of hair behind an ear, her gaze collided with Rowan's. "What are you looking at?"

He couldn't really hear her voice through the loud music or find the right words to say. She was still high on adrenaline, on euphoria. She was golden in this sea of people. Was, somehow, the only person he could see, and he couldn't fathom why.

"You," he said.

"Me?" she asked with a frown on her brows. Then she laughed and shook her head, like she didn't believe him.

Rowan's friends were busy drinking near the bar whilst he'd been watching over Avery. He wasn't sure why he couldn't simply live his life and not care about her. In the back of his mind he was well aware of the truth, but he'd rather lie to himself than face that odd reality.

"My friends left," she announced, a hint of sadness woven into her tone.

Rowan leaned back in his seat and crossed his arms over his chest. "They're not your friends, Avery. Where's your date?"

She tilted her head. Frowned. Leaned forward. "Sorry, what?"

Rowan had to focus on the back of someone's head so he wouldn't glance at her cleavage. Her sweet fragrance enveloped his senses, and he huffed. "Your date."

"I don't have a date."

"Dalton?"

Avery chuckled before straightening herself. "He left too. And he wasn't my date." Her shoulders were lifted into a shrug as she reached towards the table to grab another shot. "I don't care. I'm having fun. Getting shit-faced alone. No one's going to wait for you to be happy, so get up there and shine your light. Just do whatever makes you happy."

Rowan laughed heartily. She was drunk, delighted, talkative. She had spent an entire song telling him about the time she had danced to that music in front of her primary school, and he knew then that she was too drunk to know she was talking to him so openly. He didn't even know how she had ended up at his table in the first place.

"Is that your life advice?" he asked, grinning.

She lifted the glass. "That's my mantra. Cheers."

She downed the shot before taking a sip of her Coca-Cola. Then, her hand reached out to the last shot.

"You should slow down." Rowan had watched her drink with her friends before they left. He'd watched her more than he should have.

"But it's the last one," she countered with a pout forming on her lips.

"You've had too many already."

"You're not the boss of me," she bit out. "I want it."

"Your grammar is terrible."

"Says you." Her accusation was followed by a scoff.

He reared back, holding his laughter in. "My grammar is perfectly fine, thank you very much. I could write you a goddamn poem right now and make you fall in love with me."

Avery glowered. "Good luck with that."

"Is that a challenge?"

"I'm going to make you wish you were dead before you can even think of seducing me."

The laughter finally broke free before he took a small breath.

He tilted his head, arching an eyebrow. "And how are you supposed to get back home?"

"The tube? Walking? A cab? It's really not that far away."

He stood up abruptly. Her gaze trailed lazily from his torso, to his throat, and up to his eyes. "You're not walking home alone in this state."

She rolled her eyes. "Yes, I am. I'm a big girl."

"And you're stubborn. I'll drive you home." He was about to leave, anyway. "Come on."

She narrowed her eyes, planting her hands on her hips. "You had a drink, too."

"Just a beer," he admitted, slightly impressed by the fact she knew that. "Three hours ago, so I've sobered up. Let's go."

"But I want to take the shot."

"Avery," he grumbled.

"Rowan."

He sighed, throwing his head back. "You'll let me take you home afterwards?"

She nodded.

"Promise?" he prompted with raised brows.

"Promise." She batted her lashes. "Give me the shot."

"Say please."

"Nope," she said. "I might be hella drunk, but I'm not begging you for anything. Ever."

"We'll see about that." This woman would drive him to madness. "All right. I'll give it to you."

Grabbing the small glass, Rowan stepped towards Avery. All of a sudden, his entourage turned into vague, blurry shapes. He watched her pupils blow wide as he inched closer and closer, until his breath fanned across her skin. Until he could see how the artificial, yet dim light of the pub shone on the side of her face like she was meant to be under the spotlight.

He wasn't sure what had surged through him when he lifted his other hand to cup her chin, guiding her head to tip back. Too lost in another world, Avery didn't react. Didn't flinch. The pad of his thumb pushed on her chin to oblige her lips to part. When her mouth fell agape, he gently poured the contents of the glass onto her tongue, then guided her to close the gap.

Avery swallowed, keeping her wild gaze locked to his, and he suppressed a grunt at the sight of her gleaming, full lips.

He lingered his caress on her chin for a few beats too long before letting go, jolts of electricity dancing on his fingertips. "Good girl," he praised with a smug smirk, trying not to focus on the wild beat of his heart and the heat spreading across the back of his neck.

"What did you just call me?" Even her words were stuck in her throat as though she couldn't quite believe what had just happened either.

Rowan held Avery's bewildered gaze for a moment, but couldn't control the direction his perusal drifted to when the tip of her tongue came to wet her plump lips.

"Nothing." He poked her forehead, and she batted his hand away. "Let's get going."

"Wait," she said. "My coat and bag."

As she went over to the table where she had sat earlier, stumbling and giggling to retrieve her belongings, Rowan texted Tate to update him on the situation.

His friend stared at him from the bar. *You dumbass,* he mouthed.

ROWAN

I'll explain later. Do you need a ride?

I'm leaving now.

TATE

I'll crash at Sasha's. Closer than home.

Just get Ava somewhere safe.

Fucking idiot.

CHAPTER NINE

LONDON, ENGLAND

ROWAN'S FINGERS TIGHTENED around the steering wheel of his Porsche as he drove through her neighbourhood. With the faint melody of music filling the void of silence, he wasn't certain why he longed to hear her voice—the sarcasm dripping from her words, the delighted tone she'd take whenever she spoke of something that had made her laugh or smile, the way she'd spit out her phrase if he ever irritated her.

He couldn't help but glance at Avery who had been oddly silent since they left the pub. To be honest, Rowan wasn't sure why he had offered to drive her home in the first place.

Temple resting against the window, her eyes were closed as her brows were drawn together.

"You okay, sunflower?" he asked softly. Too softly. "Stay with me, yeah?"

He saw her nod from the corner of his eye. By the GPS' indications, they would be at her house in less than two minutes.

"Sunflower?" she echoed, straightening herself.

"Yeah," he said, focusing on the route ahead. "You remind me of one."

Rowan didn't care about the words slipping out. She wouldn't remember any of tonight's events, anyway.

"Why?"

He could now feel her regard on him. Curious. Intrigued.

Avery reminded him of a sunflower because she would always stand out amongst a field of flowers. Because she would always be attracted to sunlight, gravitating towards positivity, no matter how dark her entourage was. Because she was radiant in her own, unique way.

"Just because," was his vague reply.

"You're going to call me everything but Ava, aren't you?"

"Yes."

"Why?"

"Because it annoys you and I love annoying you." And he also knew that he was the only person to call her by her full name, which gave him a sense of ownership over her—like she was his in a way. But he kept that to himself.

"Charming."

"Don't be sick." He stopped in front of a two-story house when the GPS indicated they had arrived at their destination. "We're here."

"I wouldn't dare ruin your pretty car," she mumbled, straightening herself as she looked out the window.

"Thank you for caring about Percival's well-being."

"You named the car Percival?"

He put the blinker on. "Yes, and?"

"That's very Rowan of you." Her words were slow, slurred. Though she had been funny the entire night, he couldn't help but be slightly concerned about her state.

His response was a simple hum.

"Thanks, Rowan." Even now, her voice was feathery and sweet-sounding, like a soft caress against the shell of his ear.

"Hang on," he murmured. "I'll walk you inside. Is anyone home?"

"Gabe should be here."

"Gabe?" He felt his throat tighten as he put his left hand over the back of the passenger's headrest seat to parallel park. He used the heel of his palm to do so, smirking when he felt her staring at him.

"My roomie," she answered dully. "I call him Hercules because he's very muscular. Pretty sure his boyfriend calls him that, too."

Oh. Gay roommate.

"Makes sense. Come on, let's get you somewhere safe."

She laughed, and even though the sound was caused by her drunken state, it was a beautiful melody he wished she'd make more around him.

"Being home doesn't mean I won't jump and sing around," she supplied with a grin as she got out of the car.

Rowan shook his head and reached to the back seat to grab her purse and coat she had refused to put on. Stubborn woman.

She wasn't exactly walking straight to her front door, so he rapidly caught up to her just to make sure she wouldn't fall and hurt herself.

"Be quiet." Pressing her forefinger to her lips, she knocked on the door with her other hand.

Rowan couldn't help but chuckle.

"I said shut up," she hissed loudly, which caused him to snort.

He was about to retort when her back collided with his chest, his lungs suddenly giving up on him at the contact. He stilled. Ceased to breathe.

"Rowan..."

He swallowed. "Yes?"

"I think I'm going to be sick."

He winced and looped his arm around her waist. *Fuck*. She was tiny in his arms. Fitted perfectly. "No, you're not."

"You always have to fight me," she complained.

He grinned down at her, but her absent stare was on the door. "Yeah, I do."

When the door opened, Rowan didn't know why he couldn't let go of Avery.

A tall man with dark skin stood in the doorway, a set of headphones around his neck and a bowl of popcorn in hand. Plaid pyjama pants hung on his hips and a wool jumper clung to his muscular chest. That would be Gabe.

He blinked at Avery, looked at Rowan, stared at Avery, then burst out in laughter.

"Oh, this is fucking epic," he mocked before waving a finger in Avery's face. She tried to bite him and Rowan laughed. "This is even funnier than finding you in Green Park sleeping on a bench with a squirrel trying to get inside your bag."

Rowan made a mental note to ask about that later.

"Not a word," Avery whispered loudly.

Gabe didn't acknowledge her demand and slipped his gaze to Rowan.

The athlete nudged his chin. "I'm Rowan."

Gabe lifted his brows. "I know who you are. You're just the last person I expected her to come home with."

Rowan's jaw tightened. "I'm just dropping her off. She's smashed."

"I can see that." Gabe smiled softly at his friend. "That's nice of him. Right, Ave?"

Avery shrugged, yet she still leaned against him. "He's Satan."

"Wow," Rowan deadpanned. "Evermore the sweetest person I know."

Gabe gestured to Rowan. "I think you should thank Satan for driving you home, love."

Avery shifted to look up into his eyes.

Double fuck. Those dark, pretty eyes would ruin him. So

would her mouth. All of her, really. "Can you walk me to my room? Just to make sure I don't get sick."

Rowan threw his head back. Huffed. Watched the thick cloud of air fade away in the night sky. "I don't think it's a good idea, Avery."

"It's Ava," she countered. "Please?"

"God," he grumbled. "Just because I'm not an asshole."

"You are, though."

"Just not today."

"Not today," she agreed and stepped inside the house. He blinked before he could think of how he instantly started missing the warmth of her body.

Gabe stepped aside to allow them to enter, a grin on his lips.

"I'm Gabriel, but you can call me Gabe," he said as soon as Rowan passed the threshold. "I hope you know I'll never let Ava forget this."

"Oh, I'm fucking counting on it."

FROM WHERE HE STOOD, leaning against the doorframe, he watched Avery fall on her bed, a loud huff escaping her throat.

"Good night."

Her room was exactly the way he would imagine it to be. Not that he had ever thought about her, or her bedroom before.

Because she travelled a lot, she had a small room which, he supposed, wasn't occupied that often. There was a bookshelf next to the window where numerous books were organised by colour. Two shelves were dedicated to motorsports, though, a few car replicas adorning one of them. On the other were picture frames, paddock passes, and lanyards. He was in awe of her small cocoon; it resembled her personality a lot.

He pinched his brows together when he focused his attention on her. "You're not going to sleep in your clothes, are you?"

She glared at him as he crossed his arms across his chest. "Yes, I am. What are you going to do about it?"

"Take your shoes off."

"I don't take orders from you, Emerson."

"Actually, you do." He raised his eyebrows in defiance when she propped herself on her elbows and narrowed her eyes. "Come on. Don't make me come inside and do it for you."

She fell onto her back again. "But I'm so sleepy."

"I know, sunflower." With a resigned sigh, he pushed himself off the doorjamb. "Can I come inside or are you going to throw a pillow at me?"

"I'm too tired to throw something at you."

"Is that a yes?"

She nodded.

Rowan sucked in a breath and stepped inside, rubbing the back of his neck. He didn't even know why he was suddenly so nervous. He'd been inside women's bedrooms before.

"The room's spinning," Avery complained, using the pads of her pointer fingers to rub her temples.

He twisted his mouth in a grimace. "Ah, shit. Hang on, yeah? Gabe is getting you a glass of water and will give you painkillers for the morning."

She paused. "You're not staying?"

He clenched his jaw and kneeled on the floor next to her bed. "No."

"Oh," she whispered. "Okay."

Clearing his throat, he kept his gaze on her heeled boots. "I'm going to touch you now to take your shoes off, okay?"

He didn't hear a vocal response.

"Avery," he pressed. "I need your words."

He lifted his head to watch her prop herself on her elbows again. She blinked. He blinked back. "Yes, you can take them off. Thank you."

"You're welcome, sunflower."

Delicately, he took ahold of her calf and unzipped her boot

on the side. Just as gingerly, he took the shoe off her foot and repeated the action with the other one.

"Don't fall asleep," he demanded softly, suppressing the urge to caress her jean-clad shin.

"I won't." He rose to his full height and, as much as he wanted to look at her and linger his gaze on her generous curves and pristine physique, he slipped his gaze to the plant next to her nightstand. He wouldn't take advantage of her—not now, not ever. "You're nice."

The corner of his lips curved upwards. "Nice? Come on. I deserve a better compliment. Like, incredible, extremely good-looking, and hilarious."

Avery only huffed, shifting around in her bed, and tugged a pillow down to where she was lying to rest her head against it. "Good night. You know where the front door is."

"Fucking rude." Planting his hands on his hips, he sighed. "You need to take your contacts and makeup off."

Rowan himself was baffled by the fact that he had remembered she wore contact lenses.

"But I'm lazy."

"Just one last effort."

Honestly, Rowan didn't know why he was sticking around and helping. He could have left as soon as he had dropped her off—Gabriel would have taken great care of her.

"No."

"Don't make me drag your butt into your bathroom."

She gasped loudly. God, wasn't she dramatic. "You wouldn't dare."

His brows shot up as an amused smirk spread across his lips. "Don't challenge me."

"I'm not moving. My bed is very comfy."

"Well, then. You asked for it."

He grabbed her ankles and pulled her towards the end of the bed, gently. He could only feel a sliver of skin below the hem of her jeans, but the contact of her flesh beneath the palms of his hands made chills rush down his spine.

A surprised, soft squeal echoed in the room.

"You're manhandling me!" she exclaimed with outrage.

He chuckled and grabbed her wrist to pull her into a sitting position. "Yeah, because you're not listening to me."

Without letting his grunt of resentment be too audible, he slipped an arm beneath her knees with the other braced behind her back as he pulled her into his chest.

"You're not carrying me princess-style," she huffed yet looped her arms around his neck. "I'm heavy. Put me down, and I promise I'll walk like a big girl."

He glared down at her, a small crease making its appearance between his brows. A rapid surge of anger flared inside his chest as he said, "You're as light as a feather, Avery. I lift double your weight at the gym."

"Huh," she snickered. "I wonder who I should start calling Hercules now."

"Idiot." Yet he couldn't hide the way his lips were threatening to break into a full grin as he walked towards the en-suite bathroom. "Too late. I wanted to carry you like a potato sack, but you would have vomited on my jeans."

He flipped the light on with his elbow and set her on the countertop.

Putting as much distance as he could between them, and not appreciating the way he enjoyed having her in his arms, he leaned against the doorframe and jutted his chin in her direction. "Contact lenses out, love."

Avery rolled her eyes and hopped down. "So bossy."

"You're usually the bossy one, so I can, for once, give you some orders."

She threw a glare his way through the mirror's reflection. "Me? The bossy one? Have you met yourself?"

His smile was all smugness and pomposity. "The way I am makes me unique, sunflower."

"Whatever."

She washed her hands and took her contacts out as Rowan watched her, unaware of the admiration drawing itself upon his features. She was concentrated on her actions and, for some bizarre reason, he couldn't help but think she looked adorable with her rosy cheeks, her wild and big eyes, and her untamed curls because of the way she had moved at the pub.

"All done."

He blinked, regaining composure. "Makeup?"

Avery had the nerve to ignore his question. Brushing past him, she went back into her room and sat on the bed to take her socks off.

Rowan sighed, sliding his gaze to the bathroom counter where her beauty items were. Poking the interior of his cheek with his tongue, he shook his head and grabbed cotton pads along with the bottle of makeup remover.

When he stepped into the bedroom, his breath caught and disappeared somewhere inside his lungs at the sight of Avery passed out on the bed. She was lying on her back, one hand on her stomach as the other lay limp at her side. Steady puffs of breath escaped her parted lips, her chest rising and falling in sync with her serene breathing.

"You did not just fall asleep." He gently poked her knee, but when she didn't stir, he raked his fingers through his hair, sighing. "Damn it, Avery."

Sitting by her side, he poured some makeup remover on the pad before inching his hand towards her peaceful face.

"Sorry for touching you without your permission," he murmured, delicately pushing rogue strands of hair away from her forehead. He cupped her cheek and held her in place, finding every ounce of control he possessed not to caress her silken skin. Carefully, he removed her mascara, and she didn't so much as stir. "I have a sister, and I can't even tell you how many times I've had to help her take her makeup off before she went to bed totally smashed. She basically forced me to do it the first few times, but she told me it's very bad to sleep with all that shit on your face. So yeah, I guess this is me being nice to you, sunflower."

Refusing to linger his stare on her features, he went back into the bathroom to throw the used cotton pad away and turned the lights off. He couldn't leave until he was sure she was warm enough. So, he found the blanket she had left on a reading chair by the window and draped it over her body.

"If Ava had told me you had a soft heart beneath all those tattoos, I wouldn't have believed her."

Rowan's lips curled upwards at the sound of Gabe's remark. He found the man standing in the doorway, a bottle of water in hand.

Finally, Rowan stepped out of the room that smelled like soft vanilla and flowers. "Don't tell her what you've seen. She'll let it get to her head and never stop taunting me for my kindness."

Gabe laughed quietly. "You got it. Thanks, man. You really didn't have to do all that."

"I know." He patted Gabe's shoulder. "You take care of her, yeah?"

"Of course."

Rowan walked away and didn't turn around even though his head—or his heart, he didn't really know—screamed at him to go back and finish what he had started.

CHAPTER TEN

LONDON, ENGLAND

SHE HADN'T EVEN bitten into her pain au chocolat when the door to her office burst open.

"Ava, what the hell is this?"

Not only was it Monday, but Nikki had to have the pleasure of tarnishing the start of her day by pointing out Ava's faults.

Ava didn't even know what she had done wrong this time.

She set her breakfast down, frowning. "What do you mean?"

"You don't get to act like you don't know what I'm talking about."

Ava blinked. "I'm sorry, but I really don't understand."

Nikki's footfalls echoed as she marched towards the desk and shoved her phone into Ava's face. Ava thought she was about to collapse, yet she felt paralysed all at once.

Shit. Shit. Shit!

She blinked again. Inhaled calmness. Looked up at her boss only to see raw, pure rage etched upon her sharp features.

Before she could even try to explain herself, Nikki's shrill reverberated off the walls. "This is unacceptable, Ava. Going out for drinks with your colleagues is one thing, but seeing the drivers outside of work is inadmissible. This kind of behaviour is not tolerated."

Ava counted three heartbeats to process everything.

She hadn't been aware that pictures of her and Rowan interacting on Friday were flooding the internet.

How could she have missed it?

She would have done anything to take most of them down. Would have done anything to protect Rowan's image, because those pictures would certainly stain his reputation.

The blurry photo Nikki had shown captured the moment Rowan was busy pouring a shot down Ava's mouth, his tattooed hand cupping her chin, their gazes locked.

Ava had no recollection of this particular moment, but in the back of her mind, she wished she did. To wonder what his hand would have felt like on her skin. To remember their banter. To properly thank him for everything he'd done afterwards.

Gabe had told her she had arrived home safely, thanks to Rowan.

"It won't happen again," was all Ava could utter. Because, honestly, what could she say? She knew her energy would go to waste if she tried to defend herself. Knew that no matter what she'd say, Nikki would still bring her down.

Nikki shoved her phone in the back pocket of her jeans and placed her palms on the desk. Narrowing her eyes, she pursed her lips whilst roaming her gaze over Ava's frame, detestation brimming her pupils.

It was a true mystery why a woman in her mid-thirties loved tearing down her twenty-three-year-old employee.

Ava hadn't been gifted with self-love and self-confidence, but she never allowed negativity and sombre thoughts to overpower her true self. But the way Nikki Bellinger looked at her made her want to crawl under her blankets and never see the light of day again. Made her feel like she wasn't enough.

"Are you seeing Rowan?"

Ava reared back. Was that a hint of jealousy laced into Nikki's voice? "Like, dating?"

Nikki dipped her chin in a sharp nod.

The accusation was pure madness. "Of course not. We just happened to be in the same pub and—"

"Good. You're not allowed to date him."

"I don't—"

"Listen to me well." Nikki was enjoying her power way too much—pointing her finger at Ava, using that patronising and condescending tone. "I won't repeat myself. Interacting and fraternising with Rowan and Thiago outside of work is off-limits. This is a warning, understand? If you're seen one more time having a drink, or playing golf, or shopping within a ten-metre radius of the boys, you're out of here."

Ava nodded frantically. "Totally understood."

"It's your job versus a man who doesn't give a shit about you. Be smart for once."

Right. The non-fraternising clause. No one on this team had ever taken that clause seriously. If Nikki knew how many of her employees slept together... Was she that oblivious? Nevertheless, Ava wouldn't fight her.

Nikki didn't add a word and turned around, exiting the room with the loud taps of her high heels resonating.

Ava breathed in. Breathed out. She needed to get her nerves settled before going into the first meeting of the day.

"You're seriously going to let her talk to you like that?"

Cherry on top, Rowan Emerson had to bury his nose where it didn't belong.

She met with hazel eyes, doubtful yet burning with flames of wrath, from across the room. He was leaning against the doorway with his hands in the pockets of his jeans, his expression hardening by the second. Angry, he looked dangerous. Lethal, almost. She nearly shivered.

"Get lost, Rowan. It's none of your business."

"That's exactly where you're wrong." He stepped inside the office just as she leaned back in her seat, a lump building inside her throat.

"Elaborate."

"If someone messes with you, you'll be in a shitty mood, and then your performance at work won't be as good as usual."

Ava sighed. "I'm fine."

"You're fucking shaking, Avery," he pointed out angrily, gesturing to her hands. "This isn't okay. Why is she so mean to you?"

Ava had noticed that Nikki was this harsh only with her, and especially behind closed doors when her superiors weren't around.

"I can't answer that because I don't know."

"Tell you what," he started. "I think she hates that you have such a good position and reputation around here. She hates not having the attention on her."

She curled her fingers and dropped her hands to her lap—where he couldn't see how badly she was trembling. "How much did you hear, anyway?"

She watched his jaw tighten, a tick in the muscle perceptible. "Pretty much everything."

"I promise it's fine. I crossed a line, so I'm just dealing with the consequences of my actions."

Rowan took a seat on the chair opposite her, leaning back and spreading his legs. A lazy curl toppled over his forehead as he tilted his head and studied her, a furrow on his brows. "We *both* crossed a line."

"I'm sorry." She let out a long, heavy breath, freeing all the anxiety for a fraction of a second. She dropped her gaze to her untouched breakfast because she couldn't bear the intensity, the unsolicited concern in his scrutiny. "I haven't been on socials at all this weekend, but just know that I would have done my job to take those pictures down. I will get to it after my shift. I'll make sure your reputation is still shiny."

Too many heartbeats passed.

"Look at me." There was nothing she could do with his demanding tone, the gruffness in his timbre, but to follow his command. "I don't care about what they say about me, Avery. But the moment I see a fucking comment about you, I swear I'll break a neck. They'll have to go through me before even thinking of touching you."

She swallowed tightly. "You don't mean that."

"I do. I'm the only one who gets to mess with you, you understand? If you see one mean comment about you, you tell me."

She rolled her eyes despite the warm feeling flooding her chest. "I can defend myself."

Rowan rubbed his jaw with ring-clad fingers. "I know you can."

Ava cradled her cup of coffee—she needed to hold onto something. "That doesn't mean I won't do my job. You were seen partying with your PR officer,"—her voice caught inside her throat—"pouring some alcohol into her mouth. People might think you're not professional. Or they might think something—"

She stopped herself because she couldn't muster it out. Couldn't even think about it.

Rowan seemed to understand the idea behind her train of thought and only nodded, jaw still taut with some sort of unreleased anger.

He lifted his hands in surrender. "I was out partying with my friends, end of the story. I promise you, sunflower,"—*sunflower*—"that it's alright. It's not a big deal. Nikki just reminded you of the non-fraternising clause and that's fine. You're a professional, you'll respect those boundaries."

She breathed out again, nodding.

Her mind was spiralling. She couldn't fathom his sudden tenderness. Couldn't think straight after what had just happened in the span of a few minutes.

Regardless, she appreciated how, slowly, he was starting to trust her. This was what their relationship was supposed to be about: trust—an F1 driver and his press officer; partners in crime.

Her voice softened as she tucked a strand of hair behind her ear. "Thank you, by the way. For, you know, driving me back home."

His lips tipped upwards, that devastating dimple making its appearance. "Was it so hard to say? I've been waiting for your thanks all weekend long."

"You were waiting for me to text you?"

Rowan's gaze narrowed, but a glint of amusement was perceptible. "You should dream of more realistic things."

"That's basically what you admitted, though."

"Stop being delusional, love."

Silence fell, a slow smile spreading across her lips.

Damn him.

"You're much nicer when you smile," he stated with a wink, standing up and snatching the plate with her nearly-untouched pain au chocolat. "You should do that more often."

Her eyes widened, but she couldn't exactly ignore the tingles on her cheekbones. "Hey, that's mine."

His grin was smug, and he was back to being his usual self. "Not anymore."

"I thought you were on a strict diet."

Her remark elicited a wry chuckle. "Touché. See you at the photoshoot. And remember, I can snap a neck as quickly as I make the fastest lap around a racing track."

Her day was ruined.

But Rowan would ruin her more than anything.

CHAPTER ELEVEN

MELBOURNE, AUSTRALIA

The Australian Grand Prix was as important to Rowan as the British one for the sole reason that it was his home race.

He dreamed of brandishing the winner's trophy high in the air. Dreamed of being sprayed with champagne. Dreamed of finally proving everyone wrong.

But his dream was interrupted by the sound of his door opening.

Rowan turned around in his bed, the sheets rustling with his movements as he nestled in the warmth and comfort of the blanket.

"Get out, Tate," he mumbled into his pillow.

"Not Tate. Try again."

The echo of her honeyed voice was akin to a soft caress on the shell of his ear, yet his senses instantly heightened at the realisation that Avery was in his hotel room.

He released a small grunt and pulled the blanket up to his chin, keeping his eyes closed.

"Get out."

"It'd be my pleasure," she responded grimly. "But we have stuff to do today."

He braced his forearm over his eyes, suppressing a frustrated groan. "What kind of stuff?"

He listened to her footfalls as she walked further into the room, and to the sound of the curtains sliding open. He was expecting a bright ray of sunshine to filter inside the room, but all he could see was darkness.

"Don't fall back asleep," Avery demanded in that firm tone of hers that had the power to irritate him.

"What time is it?" He could hear the fatigue laced into his hoarse voice. Even his body was tired. All he needed was rest, not an infuriating woman trying to pull him out of bed.

Perhaps he should attempt to pull *her* in between his bed sheets and—

"Almost five thirty."

"Five? *In the morning?*"

She sighed softly. "Yes. I'm just as delighted as you, trust me."

After a few minutes during which he stretched himself and took the time to fully wake up, he opened his eyes only to see Avery's silhouette standing before the large window, her gaze fixated on the horizon where the sun was barely starting to rise.

He knew his vision was still hazy, but at that exact moment, the contour of her profile was ethereal. *She* was ethereal. Button nose. Pouty, full lips. Long, ebony hair flowing down her back. He wondered if her locks were soft, if her skin was—

Rowan had to blink several times to make sure she wasn't a trick of his imagination. To bring himself back to reality.

He propped himself on his elbows. "What kind of activity requires us to wake up this early on an off day? Are you aware you've just interrupted my beauty sleep?"

"Save the whining for later," she snapped. "We're filming content for this week's YouTube video."

"This should be illegal."

"Get up, *princess*. We need to get going."

"Where are you even taking me?"

"Somewhere."

He groaned, irritated. What a terrible way to start the day. "It better be worth it. Like, first date worthy."

"It's not a date."

He pouted, though she didn't bother sparing a glance his way. "I'm sad now."

"Are you going to move, or what?"

"Nope." He put his hands behind his head and grinned through the dark. She was still not looking at him, and he felt a desperate need to catch her attention. "If you're too lazy to leave, you can just join me and spend the day here. The bed's big enough for both of us. Can't promise I'll stay on my side of the bed, though. I like snuggles."

That was a lie. Rowan wasn't even sure he liked embraces—especially the kind that flickered inside his mind and instantly vanished. He'd never been used to being affectionate with the women he hooked up with. A rapid hug with his friends was fine in his opinion, but one that held more intimacy was just something he refused to experience.

She shook her head, evidently unfazed by his remark. "You're such a pain in the ass."

"I can turn the pain into pleasure, love. I promise I'll be gentle at first."

Finally, she turned. He wished he could see the shock, and distaste, and annoyance flaring around her pupils. Wished he could see the blush painting her cheekbones.

"I wonder if you're aware of how annoying you are," she grunted before coming to stand at the foot of the bed. Without warning, she pulled the cover off of Rowan's body, causing goosebumps to rise across his skin.

"Fucking hell," he exclaimed, falling on his back after a failed attempt at grabbing the blanket back. "What if I were naked? You'd have seen my dick in the air."

"Gosh, Rowan. Don't make this harder for me than it already is. Just get out of bed. The others are waiting."

Fuck her. Fuck Primavera. Fuck the entire marketing team for always wanting to film content at the most ungodly hours. Rowan really needed to rest because had spent the last three days in Brisbane with his family before flying to Melbourne to join the racing team.

"Fine." Begrudgingly, he sat up and rubbed his face. "I hate you so much."

"Feeling's mutual, honey."

She went to open the window to let fresh air inside, but all he could smell was her sweet fragrance.

He put his feet on the floor and sighed. "You, sunflower, are the absolute loveliest at dawn."

"Thanks," she deadpanned. Then, her voice softened, its delicacy feeding his soul. "Come on. We'll get coffee on the way."

"Oat latte?"

"Of course."

"HERE'S YOUR COFFEE, SIR."

Grabbing both cups from Avery's hands, he let a smug smirk touch his lips as she climbed back into the driver's seat. Somehow, her fragrance managed to overpower the scent of freshly brewed coffee, but only for a flickering heartbeat because he didn't allow himself to be distracted by this maddening woman.

When they left the hotel and walked towards the car that was assigned to them for the day, she had asked if he wanted to, perhaps, drive. He'd said no with a grunt, that he was too tired, and had begged her not to crash. All he had received in return was a scowl.

Placing the cups in the holders in the console between them, he asked, "What's your coffee order?"

He had realised, as she had gone inside the café, that he knew so little of Avery whereas she knew so much about him.

The wave of awareness had stirred an uncanny feeling inside his chest.

"Black," she responded, zipping her Primavera Racing jumper. With the morning haze still clearing from the sky, the breeze was crisp and chilly. "With one sugar."

"Like your heart?"

She glared at him. "Like *your* soul."

He grinned. "True."

As she ignited the car, Rowan scrolled through his playlists to find uplifting songs to scream at the top of his lungs, hoping he'd find a sliver of energy by hearing his favourite melodies.

"Where are the others?" He decided to play 2000s music, observing how a small smile spread across Avery's features when *Sex on Fire* started echoing.

The more he spent time with her and got to know her, the more he felt strangely drawn towards her. He'd finally met a woman with similar musical taste.

"Already en route."

He settled his gaze on the road when she finally exited the parking lot. "Why didn't we go with them?"

"That's a funny story." She reached to the console to grab her cup of coffee. "So, apparently, it's bothering everyone on the team that we keep trying to rip out each other's throats when we're not in the media pen, so Simon forced me to spend the day with you."

"Ah, shit," he mumbled. "So, it *is* a date."

"I'm going to start thinking you want to take me out."

He scoffed. "You wish."

"I don't."

Rowan cradled his cup and watched the sky painted in

orange create a beautiful canvas before his eyes. Adjusting the brim of his cap, he asked, curious, "Will you get in trouble?"

"For what?" A subtle frown touched her brows before she took a sip of coffee. "For firing back at you? I don't think so."

"For being here with me," he clarified, putting his elbow on the console. "Alone. You know, Nikki and her rules?"

"Oh."

She was silent for a moment.

He hated the way Nikki always talked to Avery.

Seeing Avery so powerless made his chest crack wide open, allowing misplaced anger to flow through his veins, seeping until his bones burned. He hated that too, because he couldn't fathom why he was letting himself be so affected by her situation.

He shouldn't care.

He *didn't* care.

"Nikki doesn't have a say when it comes to Sophie's or Simon's decisions," she said, tone clipped. "She only supervises my work, our team. So, if Simon tells me I must be stuck with you for an entire day, I guess that's my destiny, and she can't do anything about it. Besides, our little field trip is for work."

"And when are you going to stand up to her?"

Her fingers tightened around the steering wheel. "Why would I do that?"

"Maybe because she treats you like shit?"

"And why do you care?"

"I don't," he bit out. "But Avery... She's a bitch to you."

He glanced in her direction to watch her swallow thickly. "She's technically my boss when Sophie's not around. She just wants everything to be perfect. Being hard on me is her way of doing her job."

There was a difference between being hard on their employee to ensure a good result and being mean for no valid reason. Avery didn't see it—or at least stayed in the shadow of denial—and it was unnerving.

"You could talk to HR about her behaviour."

She sighed. "But I won't."

"Why? Sorry, but I'm just trying to understand why you're letting her boss you around like this. Sure, she might be your superior or whatever the fuck she's supposed to be, but it doesn't justify her words and actions."

"I don't want to cause any trouble. I just—I love working on this team, okay? The last thing I need is to get fired because it'll always be Nikki's words against mine. I get along with everyone, have a good position, and I'm doing what I love. I'm not going to let Nikki ruin this for me."

A scoff rose from the back of Rowan's throat when he tipped his head back. He tightened his jaw, unclenched it, and exhaled. "You're too good. Too nice."

A beat passed. "You're saying it like it's a bad thing. You're saying it like it's the exact reason why you can't stand me."

"Maybe it is," he snapped back, instantly regretting his words. He sighed, turning to look at her. "I just meant, that you're nice even to people who tear you apart. I don't understand why you keep doing that to yourself."

Avery shook her head. "I'm just like that, Rowan. I'm not like you, who tells stupid people to fuck off like you sometimes do with some journalists."

"That's a bummer because I know you can stand up for yourself. You have no trouble fighting me."

Silence.

"Besides," he continued after sipping his hot beverage, "I think you're decent. You keep up with my shit, work hard, and have good banter. It's fun."

"Wow," she droned. "Keep the flattery coming. I didn't expect you to throw so many compliments at me after being awoken so early."

He crooked a small smile. "I can insult you if you'd prefer."

"I'm good." They stopped at a red light and their gazes collided. He was suddenly hypnotised by the rising sun's light shining upon her face. "You're not too bad yourself."

He grinned, and her gaze flickered to his dimple. "I'm glad that we're always on the same wavelength, sunflower."

❧

HE EMERGED from the cold water, grinning like a devil with the feeling of sun rays beating down on him. Shaking his head before pushing his wet strands of hair away from his forehead, he turned to look at Thiago who was trying to keep balance on his surfboard.

Today's activity consisted of surfing. When Avery had parked the car near the beach where some members of the marketing team along with Thiago were already waiting, Rowan had *almost* embraced her. Happy to finally catch some waves. Delighted to be home.

Thiago fell once again in the ocean, emerging to the surface with a grunt rising from the back of his throat. "How do you do it?"

"It's in my blood, babe." Rowan grinned, adjusting the strap of the little camera attached to his torso. "Just accept the fact you can't be good at everything you do."

"Fuck you and your Australian genes," his teammate grumbled from afar.

Rowan laughed loudly. "Stop being petty."

As Thiago tried to surf another wave, determined to improve his skills, Rowan got out of the water, pulling the board with him.

Further in the water, Tate and Cal were surfing as well.

Whilst Eliott and the content creators for the team were discussing the next sequence they would shoot, Rowan slipped his gaze towards Avery. He wasn't sure why he was looking for her in a crowded place. Wasn't sure why he felt so drawn towards her today.

With her jeans rolled up to her shins, she let the water lap at her feet. Other people would memorise this scenery by taking a picture, but Avery was observing the ocean and the waves crawling gently to the shore, allowing the sun to shine softly upon her already bronze skin.

Rowan unzipped his wetsuit and looked away, but before he could even settle his gaze on something else, he looked back at her.

At Avery and her dark curls flowing down her back.

At Avery, laughing quietly when a rugby ball landed a few metres away from where she stood.

At Avery, who ran towards the ball, grabbed it, and threw it back to the group of teenage boys.

And when she turned around, their gazes clashed, her features softened for a rapid heartbeat before she blinked and walked towards the small blanket she had laid on the sand.

Rowan wanted to run up to her and annoy her. Perhaps by shaking his wet hair on her. Or by picking up the book she had been busy reading whilst he was shooting content for the YouTube channel.

There wasn't a single person in the world he loved annoying more than Avery.

"Don't even think about it." Tate's comment was followed by a harsh slap on the back of Rowan's head, causing him to grumble and pivot, catching his friend in a headlock.

"I wasn't thinking of anything."

"Exactly," Tate muttered, kicking Rowan's shin. "You cannot think straight whenever you're around her."

"I have no clue what you're talking about."

Rowan was a professional race car driver, but he was also a professional at hiding his true feelings.

"Do you want something?"

Avery jumped with a start, slightly startled by his presence and voice.

He snickered—she was so easily scared. He wondered if she ever watched horror movies. Probably not.

"I'm just looking." She still refused to meet his eyes, causing slight frustration to flare through his vessels.

Leaning in, Rowan aimed his finger at the corner of her mouth. "You're drooling."

"I'm not," she retorted, batting his hand away. "But these pastries look delicious."

As he was busy wrapping the day up, she had gone across the street to look at the shops lining the avenue. He had almost left with Thiago, Tate, and Cal, but remembered she had been asked to spend the entire day with him. He assumed that rule applied to him as well, so he forced himself to find her.

She wasn't hard to find, anyway. Standing in front of the vitrine of a bakery, ogling at the pastries the way he would look at watches or supercars. Standing there, under the amber glow of the sun, shoulders bare and curls untamed caused by the rustle of the wind.

"Do you like lemon meringue tarts?" he asked, surprising himself at the question escaping his thoughts.

She hummed, nodding. "Love them."

"Okay."

Without even shrugging his shirt on as he let the piece of clothing hang on his shoulder, he stepped inside the bakery, ignoring the perplexed gaze Avery threw his way.

"Howdy howdy," he chirped with a grin at the elderly lady. "Sorry for my attire, I'll be quick. Can I just get a slice of lemon tart, please? And a fork with it, if you have one."

The lady smiled softly. "Sure thing, honey. Take away then?"

He nodded and dug into his pocket to grab his wallet. "Please."

He paid the moment he had Avery's dessert, his smile not once faltering even when he bid farewell to the kind owner of the bakery.

Avery gaped at him, arms crossed over her chest, her gaze first landing on the box in his hand before travelling up his torso which was still slightly damp. Her perusal became slow, heady in a way that made his heartbeat pick its pace up. He clenched his jaw, forcing himself to stay focused on the way her expression shifted from hostility to pure surprise, instead of looking at her pushed-up breasts or the rest of her alluring physique.

He extended the box towards her. "Here."

She arched a brow. "Why?"

"Why not?"

"Did you hit your head or something?" She eyed the box warily.

"Oh, come on. I did not poison it. I would have already attempted to get rid of you weeks ago if I really wanted you gone."

"Evermore the sweetest person I know," she said sardonically, brows high.

Rowan chuckled, remembering he'd said those exact words to her when he had dropped her off after spending the evening in a pub. "Just accept it. I want to head back to the hotel as soon as we can, and you, staring at the pastries for ages, won't get us anywhere."

"How much was it?"

"You're not paying me back."

She chewed the inside of her cheek, peering up at him with those wide, doe eyes. "But..."

"I won't accept it."

A subtle line drew between her bunched brows. "What do you want from me? You can't make me quit by buying me food."

"I'm not trying to bribe you," he said. "You still think I want you gone after everything?"

"I don't know what you want, Rowan. One moment you're a total bellend and the next you're being... nice."

"I'm a nice man," he countered. "In fact, I'm a gentleman."

"I could argue with you on that."

Rowan scoffed, ignoring her remark. "Do me a favour and accept this. Take it as a token of peace."

Begrudgingly, she took hold of the box, her eyes shining as if a pool of starlight had started brimming the edges of her dark irises. "Thank you."

Rowan crooked a small smile. "You're welcome. Do you want to eat it now or save it for later?"

"Now," she said, excitedly.

God, had she always been this cute?

"Come on." He led her towards a bench with a direct view of the beach and the peaceful ocean. "So, is food the key to your heart?"

Avery sat down, placing a thigh atop the other as she opened the box. A great distance separated them, but he draped his arm over the back of the bench, keeping his focus on the waves.

"Why? Are you trying to find your way inside my heart?"

Rowan snorted, shaking his head. "I bet it's a labyrinth to get there."

He saw a shrug of her shoulders from the corner of his eye. "Maybe. I think it's easy access if you know the right path from the start."

He wondered if she guarded her heart as thoroughly as he did. Certainly not. It was easy to glimpse at her soul and its light. It was easy to see how good of a person she was. That didn't mean everything, though. Rowan was the first person to know that.

Rowan whistled softly to call a cat that had been wandering on the sidewalk. He wiggled his fingers to attract the animal, feeling sparks of joy when it approached.

"I didn't take you for a cat person," Avery noted amusedly.

He found her gaze, narrowing his eyes. "Why? Because I have tattoos? Cats love me."

"Congratulations. At least some creatures appreciate you."

"Brat," he muttered. "Do you like cats?"

A smile illuminated her features, and he felt his heart stop. "I do. But my dad is allergic to them, so I wasn't allowed to have one. And now, Gabe, my roomie—"

"I remember him."

Despite the warm tone of her skin, it was evident his comment had made her blush. "Right. Well, he travels as much as I do, so no cat. Maybe in another life."

A satisfied hum vibrated in her throat when she took the first bite from the pastry. He couldn't help but stare at her, like he was mystified. She had tipped her head back, eyes closed, a soft smile on her lips.

"So good."

Rowan could feel his heart batter erratically when his finger accidentally brushed her bare shoulder blade. Regardless of the featherlight touch, she didn't react, too enthralled by the tart in her hands, but he couldn't ignore the tingles dancing on his fingertips.

"I'm glad," he murmured.

She shifted to face him. "Do you want a bite?"

Rowan's mouth twisted in a grimace as he dropped his gaze to the dessert. "I'm not the biggest meringue fan."

Her scoff was rightfully outraged. "That's scandalous, Rowan. You haven't had good meringue before then."

He shrugged. "Probably."

"What's your favourite dessert?"

"Pecan pie. Mum's, specifically."

Her brows shot up, expression soft and eyes shining with happiness. That sight caused something uncanny to happen inside his chest: a sensation of flutters, like birds batting their wings, demanding to be set free from this tormenting cage that was his impenetrable heart. "I love pecan pie."

He smiled broadly. "Hers is the best."

"How, uh." She cleared her throat after taking a bite, rapidly glancing away. "How was your visit home?"

Unconsciously, his jaw tightened, and he looked back at the horizon. A lump started barricading his airway, and he swallowed it before it could affect his tone or voice. "It was fine."

She hadn't noticed the shift in his mood yet. Rowan hated how he was instantly shutting himself down, but he couldn't help it. It was as though a wall would immediately build itself to protect him at the mere mention of his family.

It was a sensitive subject, one he hated talking about. One he avoided at all costs.

Besides, he wasn't certain about Avery's motives behind her kindness. Her curiosity sounded genuine, though, and he didn't know how to proceed with the attention brought on him. The general act of goodness.

"Your family is coming to the race, right?"

"Yes," he answered coldly. Perhaps she would take a hint if he kept his responses dry and brief.

"Are you excited?"

Avery was so sweet.

And he was a man building a castle around him. A man shrouded in darkness hidden by that colourful veil he offered to the world.

He was a broken man who refused to let her in. If she saw all those shattered pieces within him, all those parts no one had deemed worthy of fixing, she would want to turn around, and it would destroy him even more.

"Fuck, why do you care?" he snapped harshly. "Why do you have to ask so many questions?"

He counted too many heartbeats before her reply came, quiet. "I won't ask anything anymore. I'm sorry."

Rowan inhaled deeply, raking his fingers through his hair before rubbing his face and turning towards her. "That's not what I meant."

She had closed the box with the almost untouched slice of tart inside, hurt etched on her expression. "It's exactly what you meant, and you're right. I shouldn't be caring or asking anything about your personal life."

"Damn it, Avery. That's—"

"Never mind." She stood up, her shoulders tense, her voice wavering. "It was dumb of me to think we could finally get along, but obviously, you prefer being a dick instead of trusting me. It's whatever. You were right earlier—I'm too good and too nice. This"—she gestured to him, evidently referring to his reaction—"is what I get for wanting to be a good person."

"Avery—"

"Let's get back to the hotel. You need to rest."

As she walked away, Rowan felt like drowning in an ocean of guilt. For the first time in years, he regretted his words and actions. Avery didn't deserve his anger. He was desperate to do anything to be able to go back in time. Give her a chance. Find a sliver of courage inside his gut to trust her, because she was a trustworthy person. He trusted her with her work, so would it hurt to let her further in?

As he watched her silhouette walk away, he decided he'd give it to her, no matter what it would take for her to understand he wanted to be forgiven.

CHAPTER TWELVE

MELBOURNE, AUSTRALIA

AVA KNEW THAT Rowan was an infuriating and unnerving man. A man with a mask he held onto so it wouldn't slip away or break, yet managed to offer a glimpse of the person behind that façade she had once despised.

She was so used to Rowan closing himself off. Was used to dealing with his mood changes.

But for the very first time, she was still lingering in the past and thinking of the way his features had dropped; how his jaw had tightened, and his eyes had shifted to ice because of the mention of his family. Most of all, she hated how she had made a fool of herself by simply wanting to be nice, and kind, and caring.

She didn't care about Rowan. Didn't want to let what happened a few days ago affect her. Wouldn't let him ruin her.

They had gone back to mainly ignoring each other if they were in the same room, occasionally firing a comment at the other and receiving equal banter in response.

But, whenever they were left alone—walking to the media pen, driving to the circuit (although with Tate in the back seat, always pretending not to be there), waiting in silence in his driver's room as he would warm up for free practice and she'd be occupied on her laptop—it was evident that Rowan wanted to talk to her.

She was waiting for his apology. For an explanation as to why he always needed to shut himself off. Ava was certain he was hiding something golden, beautiful, and rare beneath the tough surface he put on display.

Her train of thought was interrupted when an engine revving inside the garage roared to life.

She blinked, adjusted the set of headphones on her ears, and diverted her gaze to the TV screen that showed that Q3 had started. She watched as a member of Rowan's pit crew gestured for him to drive out, and his car bolted into the pit lane.

"Don't you dare fuck this up," she heard from behind.

Ava didn't turn around, but she knew exactly who had uttered those words.

Stephen Emerson wasn't exactly her favourite guest to attend the race weekend. Despite him being Rowan's father, she had always thought he was egoistic and downright rude. Walked the paddock like he owned it when he was a nobody in the racing world. Looked down at people from a pedestal where he didn't belong.

Ava knew very little about Rowan's family and his life when he still lived in Australia, but she knew his parents were divorced. Still, the whole family would reunite at the Australian Grand Prix to support Rowan.

Ava was sitting next to Rowan's mother, Julia, and his older sister, Riley. Stephen hadn't approached or talked to his ex-wife and daughter as though he was avoiding them, and kept standing at the back of the garage.

Ava inhaled deeply and focused on Rowan as he finished doing his outlap.

He had struggled during FP1 because of the bumpy and slippery circuit, but rapidly improved in FP2 and FP3 when the track finally rubbered in after each progressing session. Ava believed he could make it in the top three finishers for qualifying.

Albert Park Circuit was one of Ava's favourite tracks, not only for its beautiful and unique scenery as the track went around a large lake, but also because it was one of the fastest circuits on the calendar.

Keeping her focus on the TV screen, she watched the red car bolt through the racetrack. Rowan had set the fastest lap time on the first segment of the track, rendering his sector purple. Like every qualifying session, her heart was thundering erratically because of the anticipation.

Through the camera attached above the engine, she could see the way his fingers gripped the steering wheel tightly as he held clean control over his speed and the vehicle.

His sector two was purple, too.

There were less than forty seconds left before the end of Q3.

At the bottom of the screen, Thiago's time was also being monitored. Though all three of his sectors were green—indicating this lap time was his personal best—his lap time was the fastest of all ten drivers. He finished his lap before Rowan and secured provisional pole, eliciting a few claps of encouragement in the garage. Even if this was Rowan's garage, Primavera Racing was a family.

Rowan raced through the last turn, and just as he hit the apex of the corner, he lost control over the rear and slipped slightly, causing him to struggle to accelerate towards the finish line and lose time.

Passing the chequered flag, Rowan qualified second.

AVA WATCHED the way his fingers tightened around the railing as he listened to the journalist's question.

The tattoos.

The rings.

The veins.

Holding a recorder next to his mouth, she had a hand tucked in the pocket of her skirt whilst she did everything but look at his defined jaw and the tick in its muscle every time he clenched it. Obviously, he was disappointed with his qualifying results, and Ava knew he was too hard on himself at times. Knew he was a perfectionist, and that he'd secretly beat himself up for not attaining his expectations as well as the world's.

"I lost the rear after the last corner," he explained, "and that cost me the pole position."

"There's only five-hundredths of a second between your lap time and Thiago's," the journalist pointed out, impressed.

"Yeah." Rowan smiled faintly. "I'm happy for him. He's had a great weekend so far, but I'll do everything I can to win tomorrow."

"Can we expect a shoey from both Primavera drivers?"

His grin was all mischief when Ava looked up. "Oh, of course, baby."

The reporter thanked him for his time and Rowan turned on his heel. His shoulder brushed against Ava's, and despite having her gaze locked to the ground, she managed to catch the glance he threw her way before marching towards the motorhome.

Ava cleared her throat as she pocketed the recorder. "Want some water?"

Rowan slowed down and waited for her to catch up. A smirk touched his lips as he nodded, grabbing the water bottle she had tucked under her arm during the interview.

He uncapped the bottle. "You finally understood this was my favourite brand of water."

Ava rolled her eyes. "You've been taunting me for weeks

about giving you disgusting water, so how could I keep on continuing to treat *His Majesty* like this?"

With a snort, he bumped his shoulder into hers as they walked up the small stairs leading into the hospitality centre. "Admit it, you've been trying to poison me."

Lifting her shoulders nonchalantly, she peered up at him, only to find him already looking at her. "You caught me."

"I knew it," he huffed. "I knew you hated me."

"I know the feeling is mutual."

They walked towards his room, the echo of their footsteps blending in with the chatter reverberating around the place.

"I don't hate you," he said quietly. Lowly. Hoarsely. "Don't think I ever have."

Ava stilled, unable to look at him. But when he came to step before her, she was forced to find his honey gaze, like a magnet searching for its other half. "What?"

Rowan's gaze was promising utter destruction, yet there was a softness caressing the edges of his irises when he roamed his stare over her face. A soft scoff erupted. "How could anyone ever hate you, Avery?"

Rowan had rendered her speechless. Had caused her heartbeat to come to a halt before going back to thumping wildly. Had made her eyes widen in shock.

She hadn't expected this from him—ever.

"Listen," he started, "I wanted to apologise for what I said the other day at the beach—"

"Rowan," an angry voice interrupted from his room when the door opened. "Get your disappointing ass in here."

Chills skittered down Ava's spine at the sound of Stephen Emerson's voice. Taking a step back, she looked over to the room where the man stood, his gaze on his son, features hard with burning anger.

Rowan's sigh was audible. Clenching his jaw, he dipped his chin in a nod before turning to enter his room without sparing Ava a second glance.

Just as she started walking away, words resonating from the other side of the door forced her to stop.

"You imbecile kid. Not even capable of taking pole at his home Grand Prix. Did I raise you like this? Did I sacrifice everything for you to embarrass me? When are you going to realise you're a failure, Rowan? You've been in F1 for years and not once have you won a championship."

Ava's chest tightened with every syllable coming out of Stephen's mouth. Her heart cracked at every harsh word slapping Rowan's soul.

She knew she needed to walk away, but she couldn't bring herself to move.

When Rowan's voice didn't come through, she could only imagine his face, his reaction: the curl of his fingers, the tremble in his hands, the flex in his jaw, the raw sadness in his eyes.

Ava leaned against the wall, trying to calm the deafening drum of her heart.

"I don't have the energy to do this today, Stephen."

Stephen.

The fact Rowan called his father by his first name told Ava everything she needed to know about their relationship.

God, the way his voice was strained. Exhausted.

Stephen's punishing tone made her blood boil. "So when, hm? When are you going to stop being an embarrassment to the Emerson name?"

Rowan didn't respond.

But his voice came through after a moment, and it was woven with vexation. "If you're so fucking ashamed of being my father, why are you here?"

"Because after all this time, I thought I could come and support you and finally be proud of your achievements, but I was wrong. You're a total failure."

"A failure?" Rowan's voice rose slightly, causing Ava to frown. She'd never heard him angry outside of racing. Had never seen him so outraged. He was a loud man, mostly when happy, but he rarely showed negative emotions. "I qualified second. I'm working my ass off to improve every day. I don't care what you think because I'm happy with my results."

"You set the bar so low," Stephen bit out. "I didn't raise you like this."

"You didn't raise me at all," Rowan fired back.

"Watch your tone," his father seethed. "I paid for everything you had ever asked for. Everything."

"Oh right, because your damn money can make up for all your fucking mistakes? What are you going to do if I don't win the race? Walk out of my life again? Disinherit me? Go ahead. I've been making my own money for a decade—"

A sharp sound echoed, cutting Rowan mid-sentence.

Ava's heart ceased to beat at the same moment.

She swallowed thickly, feeling unwanted tears well in her eyes. Her mind was clouded, but not enough for her to stay put and do nothing.

Ava knew this was a battle she couldn't win, yet she still walked through the combat zone with her chin held high and a sudden urge to protect a man she supposedly loathed.

Knocking on the door, she blinked to make the burning feeling in her eyes go away. Sucking a deep breath in, she waited for the door to open. When it finally did a second later, Stephen stormed out of the room without glancing behind his shoulder.

"You're wasting your time with him, girl," Stephen muttered as he passed by her.

But Ava didn't acknowledge the remark. Didn't react. All she could do was look at Rowan, whose back was turned to her as he leaned against a wall, his forehead against it. His trembling hand was curled into a fist above his head, and his chest was rising and falling with every tremulous breath he took and released.

And then he hit the wall. Hard. Once. Twice. Three times.

Ava reared back, her heart somersaulting in tandem.

"Fuck," he whispered angrily, clenching and unclenching his fingers.

His upper body heaved again, and he passed his fingers through his hair with the unscathed hand.

Ava took a step forward.

"Avery," he called out, voice cracking. "Leave."

Ava looked down. Darted her gaze again towards his body still clad in his racing suit, its upper part hanging around his hips. His angry, ragged breathing resonated loudly.

"No."

"Don't make me repeat myself."

"My answer won't change."

"Avery."

"Rowan."

She watched him pivot, his handsome face now stricken with a form of vulnerability she'd never witnessed in him, his eyes so cold and sad, void of any sparks of joy. The reddish mark on his cheek caused tears to blind her vision for a rapid second.

"Leave," he repeated firmly.

"No," she said louder, reaching behind herself to close the door.

His nostrils flared before he let out a scoff. "You're so goddamned stubborn."

"Might as well get used to it, lover boy."

Rowan inhaled shakily, jaw clenched and shoulders taut with an obvious anger he needed to release. Carefully, Ava took another step forward, holding his gaze.

"I don't want or need your pity," he spat out bitterly.

A gentle frown touched her brows. "I'm not here for that."

Shaking his head, he tousled his locks and looked away. "What are you here for then?"

These past few years, Ava had witnessed multiple people walk away from Rowan during his lowest moments. She'd watched his team principal abandon him when he would fail at scoring points during a race. Had watched the media release negative reviews about his performances. Had seen the way his father treated him. Had seen how much he felt pressured into performing well just to be cast aside at the end of the day.

For a bizarre reason, she wanted to be the one who stayed even when he wanted to be enveloped by a solitude that would destroy him.

"Sit down," she ordered with a chilling softness.

"Why?"

"Stop asking questions."

A smirk started to play on the corner of his mouth, but she knew it was forced. "You love my questions."

"You know I don't."

"Keep telling yourself that."

He was still shaking, and it settled a heavy feeling inside her chest. She hated that. Hated seeing him like this.

She gestured to the sofa. "Sit down."

"So bossy," he mumbled. Still, he went and settled down. Throwing his head back, he rubbed his face, spread his legs out, and groaned in frustration.

Ava wanted to know about the thoughts fogging his mind. The demons obliterating his heart. The inner battles he'd been fighting alone.

The sunshine boy and the secrets he guarded so fiercely.

With a sigh, Ava walked to the chest of drawers placed on the other side of the room to retrieve a medical kit. She peered at Rowan; he was still lost in his world with his eyes closed and his head tipped back, hands curled into fists on his lap. His knee was bouncing. Up. Down. Repeat.

Gingerly, she walked towards the sofa and knelt on the ground, uncaring of her bare knees and the coldness of the floorboards.

Ever so carefully, she grabbed his right hand—the injured one.

Rowan startled at the contact of their skin, his eyes snapping open. His body stiffened, and Ava nearly regretted her actions.

She waited for him to retreat, to stand up, or ask her to leave again. But, after a few heartbeats, he simply relaxed and exhaled heavily.

"Is this okay?" she asked in a whisper.

Rowan's eyebrows were drawn together, but he responded, "Yes."

Ava brought his hand towards her, uncurling his trembling fingers. Staring at the bruised knuckles, raw from the punches he had thrown at the wall, she let out a soft sigh.

"Are you okay?"

"Marvellous," Rowan answered dryly.

Ava swallowed and whispered, "He hit you." Knowing this only constricted her chest, depriving her of oxygen. "He laid a hand on you."

"It's fine."

"No, *no*, it's not."

"Avery... Look at me." Through the buzzing in her ears, she hadn't managed to make out the gentle tone he had taken. When she finally peered up, Rowan tipped the corner of his mouth upwards. Subtle, but there. "I'm okay. This isn't the first time."

"Doesn't make it okay to—to—"

"Please," he whispered, closing his eyes. "Believe me when I say I'm grand."

Sniffling, she nodded, not wanting to push his buttons. Regardless, the weight on her shoulders didn't vanish. She cleared her throat, needing to hold clean control over her emotions. "You could've been a bit nicer to the wall."

A dry chuckle rose from the back of his throat. "The wall's fine."

"Your hand, not so much." When she let go of his hand and looked up, he was watching her with an unwavering tenderness that made warmth dance inside her chest. Before she could lose herself in the honey of his irises, she slipped her gaze to the medical pouch she had placed by her side. "You know you could get in trouble for behaving like this, right?"

Rowan hummed. "I know. But you're not going to say anything to anyone, are you? It can be our little secret."

She grabbed a cotton pad and poured some disinfectant onto it. "What are you going to say when someone sees your bruised hand?"

"I'll say it's nothing."

Holding his hand, she dabbed his splintered skin with the wet pad. She kept her focus on her motions, but still heard the way he hissed under his breath.

"Sorry. Does it hurt?"

"No," he responded smugly. "I'm a tough guy, sunflower."

Ava bit the interior of her cheek and continued to clean his knuckles. She threw the used pad into the bin and reached for the tube of healing cream.

"It's not *nothing*, you know," she said, her forefinger delicately tracing his rouge knuckles, gaping at the flower tattoo on his hand. She kept her touch featherlight, barely existent whilst applying the cream.

Time seemed to slow down as she felt the way his regard was burning on the bridge of her nose. He was studying, cataloguing, calculating each one of her motions.

"You sound like you care," he pointed out softly.

"I don't."

The corner of his lips tipped upwards when their gazes collided. "Liar."

Ava didn't respond. Didn't want to admit that, deep down, she wanted to care.

Just as she was about to retreat her hand, his fingers looped around her wrist. His eyes flickered between hers, his throat bobbing as he swallowed. At that moment, she wondered if he could feel the fast beat of her pulse. The sudden anticipation threatening to make her body quiver.

"Tell me a secret," she whispered.

Slight puzzlement flashed in his eyes. "Only if you give me one, too. A secret for a secret."

"Okay." She frowned when she felt his thumb brush the skin of her inner wrist—because chills started to arise on her skin, because the tension straining her shoulders vanished, and because she felt like she couldn't breathe. "Has he... Stephen... He's always been like this with you?"

It was apparent that Rowan didn't want to talk about it, but Ava knew he needed to release that pent-up anger and sadness. She thought they weren't that different from one another; always keeping their feelings bottled inside, always putting on a smile to conceal their chagrin.

Rowan blinked and dropped his head forward, allowing a few curls to topple over his brows. He breathed heavily, the silence becoming almost deafening.

Ava wasn't sure if she needed to put some distance between them, but the way he gripped her wrist was evidence that he wanted her to stay right here.

"You don't have to hide from me," she murmured, a sudden urge to coax him crashing through her veins. "You're safe here. You're safe with me."

Crestfallen eyes found her gaze, and her heart fractured at the sight of that sorrowful gloom misting over his irises. Finally, he admitted, "Yes."

She knew it—that he liked to joke to conceal the pain. That he smiled to hide what broke him. That he let playing pretence just so no one could see what truly hurt him.

Taking the risk, she placed her free hand above his. "I'm so sorry, Rowan."

The sad smile he threw her way was anything but genuine. "Don't be. It's not your fault."

"I know," she breathed out. "But no one deserves to be treated this way by their own father. I wouldn't wish this upon my worst enemy."

He blinked down at her, his features softening. "Thank you. I appreciate it."

When she smiled in response, she didn't know how to act as he dropped his glance to her mouth. "Of course."

She pushed herself up, forcing the warmth of his skin to disappear as he brought his hand to his lap. He clenched his fingers again before rubbing his face.

Ava turned on her heel, but before she could even take a step towards the exit, his hand caught her elbow. "Wait."

Gently, he made her spin around, and she almost collided with his chest when she faced him. Slowly, she trailed her gaze from his torso to his face, sucking in a breath when his eyes blatantly traced the contours of her mouth.

"You can't leave without telling me your secret," he said, his signature, cocky grin back on those lips of his.

She shrugged. "Ask away."

Without warning, Rowan lifted his hand until the tips of his fingers brushed her temple, delicately tucking a strand of hair behind her ear. Ava was immobile, totally consumed and enthralled by the look of awe, and admiration, and adoration etched on his features.

"Why'd you do this today?" Confusion laced his tone. "Why did you help me?"

Her heart started to thunder furiously, and as much as she wanted to leave and hide her foolishness, she held his gaze and didn't let her voice waver. "Because you deserve someone who stays and sees you when you're at your lowest. Especially during your worst moments. You deserve someone who stays when you beg them to leave you alone. So, until you find that person who is willing to do this for you for the rest of your life, I'm going to fill the void. You might be infuriating, cocky, and arrogant, but I still think you have a good heart behind that ruthless mask. And no matter what you think of yourself, or what people have told you, you are a good man. And you're enough. You are more than enough. I promise you this."

Ava lost sense of time, of her surroundings, when he started meandering his gaze over her face, like he was trying to understand whether she was real or merely a figment of his imagination. He only let out a small shaky breath.

"Do you have any idea of how unique you are, Avery?" he inquired in a low voice that made a shiver roll down her spine.

She dropped her stare to the base of his throat where tattoos were peeking from beneath his fireproof shirt. "This isn't about me."

Rowan lifted her chin with the help of his forefinger, obliging her to look into hazel eyes. He was devastatingly beautiful. With those long, dark lashes framing his flirty gaze, with that tanned skin and dimpled smile, those sharp features and sharp tongue.

He cradled her cheek, and she stilled. This was wrong—so wrong. But why couldn't she move? Why couldn't she push him away, find a snarky remark to spit into his face?

His gaze was focused on her lips. "What are you doing to me?"

She was uncertain of how to respond to that.

"Rowan," she whispered, his name caught in her throat. His thumb brushed her pulse and its thundering beat. She wondered if his, too, was hammering as violently to the point of coming to a complete stop.

"Push me away."

She frowned slightly at his demand. He didn't move. Didn't step back. His words were a whole paradox to his actions. "Let me go then," she countered.

"I don't think I'm capable of that."

Maybe Ava was getting drunk on the feel of him. Of his skin upon hers. Of his complete attention fixated on her.

Maybe she had lost her mind because she pushed herself on her tiptoes and placed her lips on his.

It was chaste, brief, and so quick before she realised what she had done. She stumbled backwards, hand over her mouth as she stared back at a wide-eyed Rowan.

"Oh my god," she whispered, her heart thundering. "I'm

sorry. I shouldn't have done that. I don't know what came over—"

Rowan cut her off by slanting his mouth on hers. She gasped, and he swallowed the sound like it belonged to him. He cupped her face in between his large, rough hands, seeking dominance over the kiss by brushing his tongue over the seam of her lips. Ava parted her mouth, allowing his tongue to find hers as she winded her arms around his broad neck.

Everything about him screamed power. Devastation.

The way he kissed her without allowing her to breathe. The way he angled her face by wrapping a hand around her throat as the other found her hip. The way he kissed her with such vehemence that she thought she would lose balance.

And the way he drank her in, tightened his grip, and touched her like he was starved and *needed* more. Like he'd been waiting for this moment.

"Fuck," he muttered against her lips. "We need to stop."

"We really, really do," she agreed, breathless. A soft gasp erupted when his lips skimmed over her jaw until they reached the pulse point on the side of her neck.

Rowan groaned before capturing her lips again.

Ava couldn't think. Couldn't worry about reality. Couldn't do anything but return his kiss with equal need.

"Rowan," she whispered when his hands found the back of her thighs. He hoisted her up easily, a grunt rumbling inside his chest when she pressed her front to his, her fingers tangling in his locks.

"Fuck," he repeated, pushing her against the wall. "Say my name like that again, and I'll make sure you scream it over and over until you show everyone in this place who's making you feel like this."

"We can't—" Yet she gasped softly when he pushed her skirt up to her hips, pressing his prominent, hard bulge into her centre. "Oh, God."

"It's Rowan." He smirked before nibbling her earlobe. "And

if you allow me, I'll worship your body because it's a temple to me."

"You're such a flirt," she fired, trying to hold her laughter in.

"You love it."

"I despise it."

"Whatever you say, love."

Rowan's mouth found hers again, tongues dancing and teeth clashing. Soft moans escaped his throat when she scraped her nails on his scalp just as he started rolling his hips on hers. Ava tipped her head back, allowing him to kiss his way from her throat down to her exposed collarbones.

Her mind had gone into a frenzy, her thoughts spiralling. All she could focus on was him. His hands. His mouth.

"You have no idea how many times I've wanted to shut that bratty mouth of yours by kissing you," he admitted, one of his large hands finding her breast over her shirt. "God, you're perfect, Avery. How are you even real?"

"How many times?" She met his hips by bucking hers forward.

"A lot. Too many to keep track."

He palmed her breast, causing her to arch into his touch as he kissed her jaw, her cheek, her lips. She wanted their clothes gone. Wanted to release that tension. She knew he needed that, too.

He continued to rock his hips into her, and she knew he'd destroy her. He was big. Hard. And there were still layers in between them.

"Last chance," he warned, "to push me away before I fuck you against that wall."

"Rowan," she gasped. "We can't."

He pecked her lips, his big hands cupping her bottom, guiding her to grind against his hard erection. She held a desperate moan in. "Are you saying you don't want to get it out of your system?"

"I—" She was slowly losing herself in a thick haze of pleasure.

"Got nothing to deny coming from that smart mouth of yours?"

She didn't say anything and stared into his eyes, observing his dilated pupils. His blood-rushed lips were gleaming, calling for her attention again.

"Is that what you want, Avery? Are you dripping wet for me right now?"

She shouldn't want him, but she couldn't help it.

Perhaps letting go of that tension would make her realise all this attraction was purely physical.

She trailed her fingers on his chest. God, he was crafted from marble. Everything about him was toned. Hard. Muscular. "Why don't you find out?"

Rowan smirked. "I knew you were a naughty—"

Three knocks on the door cut him mid-sentence.

They shared a panicked look.

He put her down on her feet, taking a step back just as she dragged her skirt down.

They couldn't look away from each other, their chests heaving in perfect sync, their ragged breaths echoing inside the room. She was ready to risk it all again.

And then, the realisation hit Ava like a tidal wave, nearly sweeping her off the ground. *She had kissed Rowan.* Had been willing to cross so many lines.

She couldn't believe it, and it looked like he couldn't, either.

The door opened, and Rowan turned around, adjusting his hard bulge and pushing his hair away from his forehead.

Ava grabbed the iPad she had left on the table just as Tate entered, her heart still racing at top speed.

"Damn," Tate said. "Is the wall okay?"

CHAPTER THIRTEEN

MELBOURNE, AUSTRALIA

"ROWAN," JAMIE SAID. "You are one point three seconds behind Thiago. Huxley is catching up and seeking slipstream."

"Hell no," Rowan muttered as he checked his rear-view mirror. The black car sporting the big number "1" was getting closer and closer. Because Miles was the World Champion, he had the opportunity to wear the number one as his own, and had grasped that opportunity with a broad grin. *Fucking bastard.* "I love having Huxley chase after me. He can keep kissing my bum."

"Okay," Jamie chuckled. "Nine laps to go."

Leading in front of an Imperium felt like a fever dream. A victory. A trophy Primavera Racing still had yet to claim.

"What's wrong with Huxley?"

"He doesn't have speed," Jamie explained. "His front end isn't as reactive, especially in corners."

"Understood."

Rowan's body vibrated in harmony with his car's energy as he raced through every corner, and turn, and chicane, finding the perfect trajectory to hit the apex at full throttle.

This was his home race. He couldn't mess it up. He couldn't win—courtesy of Primavera Racing's strategists who had decided that Rowan couldn't overtake Thiago—so he would stand on the podium right next to his teammate.

"Tito's slowing down," Rowan pointed out, frowning.

"He told his engineer it's on purpose."

Rowan narrowed his gaze and pushed on the throttle, a smirk slowly spreading across his lips at the realisation.

"He's trying to give me DRS," he announced delightfully. "That motherfucker. I knew he had some brains."

"Get him. And lose Huxley."

Rowan accelerated as they passed a slippery corner. When he was less than a second away from his teammate, DRS was available. The upper part of his rear wing opened, allowing him to gain more speed and causing the dragging of the car to be reduced.

He chased Thiago, a beam growing beneath his balaclava, just as the distance between him and Huxley grew bigger.

"In your face, Hux, baby."

"Get us that 1-2, Emerson."

His fingers hit the clutch. "I will."

❧

"Red flag in sector two," Jamie announced right as Rowan crossed the line to start the last lap of the Grand Prix.

"Shit." That meant the race wouldn't resume. Following Thiago to enter the pit lane, he asked, "Is everyone okay?"

"Just a McMillan losing fuel," Jamie said casually as if he wasn't surprised McMillan Motorsports was having trouble during a race, either.

"Ah."

Rowan was thoroughly disappointed; he wanted to have fun on the last lap to battle his teammate.

"Hang on." He drove slowly through the pit lane towards parc fermé. "Did we just make a Primavera 1-2?"

"Yes, you did!"

Rowan howled loudly, cheers and joyful screams heard on the other side of the radio. He waved his hand in the air as he passed in front of his garage, chuckling when he saw his pit crew jump up and down.

As he parked the car where the podium lay overhead, he killed the engine with so much enthusiasm that he could feel fireworks burst inside his chest. Rapidly, he unplugged the steering wheel and pulled himself out of the car.

He jumped down, fist pumped in the air, grinning like a devil when roars of excitement elicited from the crowd of mechanics lining up behind barriers.

Rowan engulfed Thiago in a hug, patting his teammate's helmet as he congratulated him on the win. Seeing stars shimmering in Thiago's eyes made warmth flood inside his chest. He knew Thiago was doing everything for his late father.

When Rowan approached his team, he was pulled into tight embraces, receiving encouraging pats on the back, the helmet, and his bum.

He moved towards Tate, exchanging their iconic handshake.

He fist-bumped his team principal who smiled proudly back at him.

He slipped towards his mother and Riley, pulling them both into his sweat-clad chest, smiling broadly when his mum said, "I'm so proud of you, honey."

His father was nowhere in sight, and Rowan felt like a douchebag for not caring.

Then, he saw Avery standing right next to his sister, a soft smile on her lips. Without thinking of the consequences of his actions, he wrapped an arm around her shoulders and pulled her in. Her small hand came to rest on his back, and he swore he felt a delicate caress touch his ribs when they pulled away.

She refused to meet his eyes, and Rowan refused to let this situation slip away.

❧

"DAMN, YOU'RE SET ON getting smashed tonight," Tate remarked, though amusement edged his tone as he watched Rowan chug down another shot.

Rowan grimaced as he slammed the empty glass on the table. "Feels good, baby. That 1-2 deserves the best celebration."

Cal, who was sitting next to Tate, lifted his bottle of beer. "Cheers to that."

Rowan couldn't pass on the opportunity of celebrating this weekend's results at the most famous club downtown. With all twenty drivers, members of all teams and guests, plus other people, Havana's was cramped, packed, and loud.

Rowan didn't want to get drunk until he would blackout, per se, but he did want to feel happy. But he also wanted to forget.

Wanted to forget his father's cruel words; the ones he'd received earlier after the race and the ones after yesterday's qualifying.

Wanted to forget about Avery—her lips, her body pressed against his. Because he hadn't been able to stop thinking about her since yesterday.

Avery and her tender caress on his back before he mounted the podium. The swirl of pride around her pupils. The devastating smile that shouldn't have affected his heartbeat's function.

Naturally, if his thoughts would derail to the bane of his existence, his eyes would search for her in a crowded place, too.

The light was so dim that it was impossible to make out a single face in this room. In addition to this, his vision was getting hazy and wasn't helping his spiralling thoughts.

"You looking for someone?" Tate asked as he came to sit on the stool next to him.

"Nah," Rowan replied absently.

The loud bass of the music vibrated throughout his body, causing him to bop his head to the rhythm of the song. He could feel other women's eyes on him, and as much as it was tempting to flirt with someone, he was intent on finding one particular woman who tended to run away from him.

And he found her.

Standing by a booth, a radiant smile on her lips. Maybe it was the alcohol playing tricks on him, maybe it was the dim light casting shadows on one side of her face, but Avery looked ethereal and heavenly. Gathering her hair over a shoulder, she laughed at something one of her colleagues said before leaning forward to reply into her ear.

Rowan's throat tightened when Eliott Dalton slipped behind her to head towards the bar, placing his hand against the small of her back to push her gently.

Avery didn't react though, too caught up in her conversation with Emily—or Emma, or Elise, whatever her name was. But Rowan swore he saw a flash of green blind his vision for a fragment of a second.

"Ritchie," Rowan started without so much as detaching his gaze from Avery. "I need you to do something for me."

"What?" Tate asked, sounding bored.

When Rowan looked at his best friend, the latter shrugged and brought the rim of his glass to his lips.

He motioned to the back of the room with a nudge of his head. "I need you to bring Avery to me."

"Emily?" Tate shouted through the loud music.

"Avery!"

"Emery?"

Rowan fisted his friend's shirt to pull him closer. "Avery Sharma-Maddox."

"Avery?" Tate echoed, slowly letting disbelief and curiosity etch upon his face.

"Yes."

"Your press officer?"

"Do you know any other Avery?"

Tate seemed to think for a second. "No." He narrowed his gaze. "Why don't you go to her like a big boy? You have no trouble running after her like the annoying bloke you are."

Rowan huffed and rubbed his jaw. "Because she can't be within a ten-metre radius of me outside of work."

Tate blinked and inched closer. "I'm sorry, what?"

Rowan shrugged. "Rules."

"For whom?"

"All the marketing team."

Tate took a sip of his beverage, face solemn. "Since when?"

"I don't know. Look, Nikki set that weird rule, and Avery can't be near me outside of the paddock or Headquarters, or else she'll get fired."

"That's stupid." Tate snickered, pointing a finger into the athlete's face. "Wait, is it because of that photo of you pouring alcohol into her mouth?"

Rowan scratched the back of his head, guilt pooling inside his stomach. "I think so..."

"You little troublemaker," Tate muttered with a shake of his head. "What is it that you need to say to her now, anyway?"

Rowan's jaw tightened. "I can't tell you."

Tate only nodded, unfazed by Rowan's secrets. "Whatever. Here, deal with the devil whilst I go fetch the other devil."

Just as Tate disappeared through the sea of dancing bodies, Nikki walked past Rowan's table, aiming for the bar.

"Nikki," he called as he stood up. "Hey."

"Rowan." Her gaze roamed over his chest before finding his gaze as a seductive smile spread across her lips. "Having fun?"

He grinned. "Having a blast. Listen, about my photoshoot

with GQ Australia on Tuesday, I was thinking of having Avery accompany me there instead of you."

Blatant offence appeared on her expression as she stared back at him. "Why is that?"

Rowan lifted his shoulders in a sheepish shrug. "She's my PR officer. She needs to attend the interview with me."

Nikki folded her arms across her chest. "I don't think her presence is necessary."

"It is to me. Besides, I tend to get a little nervy in front of cameras, and Avery is the best at soothing my nerves."

Nikki threw her head back and laughed. "You're Rowan Emerson. You live for the cameras; you aren't scared of them. And Ava? Quiet Ava knows how to calm your nerves?"

Quite the contrary. She was the reason his temper would spike. The cause of his skin prickling with irritation. But it appeared that, recently, her euphonious voice and doe eyes managed to make the tension rattling his body disappear.

A true mystery, all of it.

"You'd be surprised," Rowan said through gritted teeth. "She's not that quiet. You should get to know her before talking about her with so much open disdain."

Why the hell was he defending her?

Nikki's brows rose in both bewilderment and outrage. "Whatever. She can replace me just this once."

"Sweet." He winked and turned on his heel to sit back down. "Thanks. Enjoy the rest of your night."

He stilled when she came to whisper in his ear, "You can meet me at the backdoor in a few."

He tried not to purse his lips in distaste, backing away. "No, thank you. I'm not interested in you, and even less in hypocrites."

"Meaning?"

"Meaning you can try to seduce me or Tito, but the girls working in the PR team can't approach me? Your work ethic doesn't resonate well with me. See where the problem is? Oh, right, it's you."

"You can be such a dick."

He offered a faux smile to the blonde. "So I've been told."

"Just so you know, Ava has two choices: her job or you. Obviously, she's made her choice."

Rowan hummed. Still, despite his cool attitude, annoyance was thrumming through his veins. "Good for her. Still not attracted to you, Nicole."

Nikki left without a complaint, and Rowan exhaled loudly.

When he turned on his stool, Avery was walking towards the bar, ignoring her entourage.

Had Rowan always been attracted to her or was it because she had been bold enough to make the first move? Silly question. He'd always found her to be one of the most gorgeous women he'd ever seen, but there was something so enticing about her courage and boldness.

Rowan looked to where she had been standing and met Tate's wicked stare. His friend winked before sitting in the booth with Avery's coworkers.

She came to stand next to Rowan, elbows braced on the counter as she pushed herself on her tiptoes.

"Avery," he purred loud enough for her to hear. The people around them were too busy getting drunk, dancing, or chatting to even pay attention to them.

He had made sure Nikki was nowhere in sight before going to talk to Avery. As much as he was annoyed with Nikki, he wouldn't risk Avery's career for his own pleasure.

Avery glanced at him before turning back to the bartender. She kept her chin high, blatantly ignoring him.

"Seriously?" he scoffed.

He studied the way she nibbled on her lower lip whilst trying to get the bartender's attention. Well, she had it, because the man was busy ogling her chest whilst trying to make a cocktail.

Dickhead.

"Hi, Rowan."

"I just want to talk to you." Did he sound desperate?

She peered at him again, a rapid flicker of her eyes over his body perceptible. "Why?"

"Come here," he said gruffly, catching her elbow to pull her towards him.

Electricity rippled through his veins at the contact of their skin, and he couldn't fathom the reaction of his body. Couldn't understand what she was doing to him.

If it weren't for the loud music, Rowan would have been able to hear the gasp flying past her lips when she nearly stumbled in his lap.

He steadied her, a hand on her hip as he guided her to face him. She stood between his parted legs, eyes searching her surroundings.

Her skin was burning beneath his callouses, and he wondered if his body was reciprocating the same reaction.

"Relax," he told her. "She went out back."

Wide, brown eyes found his, and he instantly smiled. Keeping a hand on her hip and the other holding her elbow, he maintained her fiery gaze. "You're avoiding me."

"I'm not."

"You are."

"What makes you think that?"

"You can barely look me in the eyes." His fingers skimmed the soft skin above her elbow.

"Am I bruising your ego?"

"Deeply."

"Poor you," she deadpanned. "You must be devastated."

He smirked at her sardonic tone. "You have no idea."

Trailing his regard down her physique, he felt his breath catch and disappear. A black top hugged her torso, its neckline so low that he could see how her breasts were pushed together, whilst matching trousers hugged her waist and put her perky bottom in evidence.

He'd rarely seen her without her uniform on—or rather had never paid attention to her choice of attire before—but she was a real sight for sore eyes.

Black tendrils framed her face. It took everything in his willpower not to touch them and tuck those rebellious strands behind an ear.

"You look beautiful," he confessed softly, sincerely.

What the fuck was wrong with him? It was official; he was an idiot. A complete fool.

She scowled. "You're just trying to get into my pants."

"Maybe," he admitted coyly. "But you're still beautiful."

She tucked a strand of hair behind an ear, dipping her gaze to the floor. He wondered if she was blushing because he certainly could feel heat creeping upwards at the back of his neck. When a timid smile graced her lips, his chest tightened.

He couldn't stand not having her eyes on him, so he cupped her chin to let their gazes collide again. "Did you hear me?"

"Do you mean it?"

Rowan's brows pinched together. "Of course. I promise, you're drop-dead gorgeous."

Avery nodded slowly, as if trying to believe his sincerity. "Thank you. But I need to go. I can't get in trouble."

Her breath hitched when his fingers slipped beneath the hem of her top. "We have unfinished business, sunflower."

Her chest rose and fell as she held his stare. Her lips had parted, a small line of confusion appearing between her brows. "It was a mistake."

"A mistake? Really?"

She nodded as she took a step back. "It can't happen again. There's too much at stake."

Rowan tightened his grip around her hip—just enough to keep her close, just enough to make her understand he wasn't taking this as a joke, or a mistake, or a game. "See, I don't give a shit about many people in my life, but I pay attention to you. And I know you're lying right now."

"Rowan," she insisted. The music was so loud but, somehow, this rejection was louder and overpowering all his senses. "You were vulnerable, and I took advantage of you. I'm sorry for that. And I feel like you were entitled to kiss me back because you felt bad for me. Or because you're just used to making out with random people."

Was she being serious? Was this truly the way she saw him? As a playboy? Perhaps she'd been used to seeing the old Rowan —the one who would never leave a party alone. But all he needed, all he wanted, was for her to see who he was today. The man who only cared for *her* attention.

He let a frown touch his eyebrows, a spark of anger slowly making its way through his bones. "You don't know me, Avery. You have no clue what you're talking about."

"Exactly," she said. "Just let it go. Have fun. Celebrate your podium. Forget about me."

He scoffed and swallowed as she pried his hands off her body, albeit with a delicacy he didn't deserve. She walked away without sparing another glance his way.

Rowan was utterly frustrated, but he couldn't tear his eyes off her when she ordered drinks for her table before leaving. Multiple heads turned her way, but she didn't pay attention to anyone else. She sat down next to Tate and nodded in response when he asked her something.

His view was blocked when a woman came to stand in front of him. "Hi," she said. "I'm Jennie."

"Hi," he mumbled back.

He barely glanced at her before looking back to Avery.

He'd barely gotten his hands on her, and she was already slipping through his fingers.

He knew she didn't regret it—she couldn't.

Rowan couldn't stop thinking about the enchanting kiss.

Her words. Her touch.

It was as though his entire perspective about her had changed in the blink of an eye—or rather with the magic of a powerful kiss. One minute he was completely irritated by her presence and the next one he was desperate for her.

What was happening to him?

"My apartment is right down the street if you want," Jennie suggested sweetly, bringing his attention to reality.

It was now that Rowan noticed the other woman was pretty. Tall, but not as tall as Avery, with blonde hair and blue eyes.

A shadow of a smirk ghosted his lips. He wasn't interested, but perhaps he was allowed to have fun. "What's over at your place that the club doesn't have?"

She ran a finger over his chest. He couldn't help but compare her touch to Avery's. It was nowhere near as corrupting or enchanting. "Privacy. Me. Naked."

Rowan liked a woman with confidence.

His gaze clashed with chocolate eyes from across the room; Avery was fuming as she cradled her glass a little too tightly. But when her attention slipped to Eliott who came to sit beside her, an arm around her shoulders, she didn't move and smiled up at him.

Rowan clenched his jaw. His fingers tensed.

She found his gaze once more, and Rowan said to Jennie, "Yeah, sure. Let's go."

But before he managed to walk out of the club, he grabbed his phone and texted Tate.

ROWAN

Get Avery safely back to the hotel.

CHAPTER FOURTEEN

MELBOURNE, AUSTRALIA

ROWAN WAS A natural.

He was born to be under the spotlight. To be the centre of attention.

As music played softly in the background, Rowan was posing in front of the camera, a beautiful smile plastered to his equally handsome face. Occasionally, he would let a joke slip out, be his cocky self, or sing loudly, causing the people in the room to chuckle with him.

But Ava couldn't exactly ignore the few glances he would throw her way when he thought she wasn't watching.

She couldn't get rid of him. It was killing her that he invaded her thoughts night and day.

Those lips.

Those hands.

"You're drooling," a voice whispered in her ear.

Ava blinked and smacked Tate in the chest.

"I'm not," she said in a harsh whisper before crossing her arms.

Tate hummed. "Okay."

Come on, Rowan was standing under the bright lights of the studio, wearing nothing but Levi's jeans that weren't buttoned, hanging low on his hips. His inked chest was on display, the hard ridges of his abdomen contracted whilst two muscles formed a v-line, pointing towards an area she had thought of last night.

He ruffled his hair, his bicep flexing with the movement.

Rowan bore an ethereal physique, but it was his tattoos that had piqued her interest. Did they have a meaning? Or was he the impulsive type to get a tattoo whenever it pleased him?

Ava huffed under her breath and turned in another direction when the photographer asked Rowan to change position.

She walked towards the buffet where Tate was looking at the pastries with lazy eyes.

He then looked at her. Glanced back at the table. Lifted his gaze towards her again.

"What?" she snapped. "You're being weird."

"I'm not," Tate argued before snatching a brownie.

"You are," she retorted, grabbing a doughnut.

Ava narrowed her gaze on Tate, and he mirrored that look of incredulity before biting on his snack. He then turned around and sat on a chair before nudging his chin towards the purse she had set by his side. "What are you reading?"

"You read?"

"It's not because I'm all muscles and a pretty smile that I don't know how to read."

Ava raised her brows. "Arrogant like your best friend, that, you are. It's a romantasy. It's good so far."

He repeated the word, nodding. "Can I have a look?"

"Help yourself. I'm happy to lend you a few books if you're interested in any."

Tate's smile was a thing of beauty. "Thanks."

Her encounter with Tate at the club on Sunday night was as

clear as day in Ava's mind. She had been busy dancing with Eliott when he came up to her.

"Hey," he said, tapping on her shoulder to grab her attention. "I'm heading back to the hotel. You should come with me."

Ava snorted. "You're cute but not my type."

Tate wasn't fazed by the comment. "I'd just like to walk you back. As friends. Or whatever. No biggie."

When she peered behind her shoulder, she saw Eliott busy whispering in the ear of another girl from the marketing team, his hand splayed on her lower back.

"Where's Rowan?" she asked the tall man. "You're usually glued to his butt."

"He left."

Right. With that gorgeous blonde. Her chest was still aching at the thought.

Ava understood then. "I don't need a bodyguard."

Tate lifted his shoulders in a shrug. "Maybe you do."

"Is that what he told you?"

Tate grumbled and rubbed his face. "Look, I'm exhausted and I just want to sleep this long weekend off. But Rowan asked me to get you back to the hotel safely, so I'm not leaving without you."

"Do you do everything Rowan asks you to do?"

"Mostly."

"God, Tate."

"Dude, I don't know what's the deal between you two, but if Rowan asks me to look after you, it's for a reason. Besides, the way he's acting with you? All those annoying demands, the incessant taunting and bickering? He doesn't do that with other people. Ever."

She frowned, too drunk to process the information. "Dude," she emphasised. "This doesn't make sense."

"I know. I'm trying to understand, too."

"Let's take five." The photographer's voice boomed, snapping Ava out of her thoughts.

"Yes, please," Rowan agreed, stretching. "Should I change into the next outfit?"

"Sure."

When Rowan strolled towards the small changing room, he called out for her. "Avery, come in here for a sec. I need your opinion on something."

She blinked, inhaling sharply when she felt her heartbeat speed up. With a nod, unable to voice her agreement, she walked towards the small room.

"Close the door," Rowan asked, his back turned to her.

Leaning against the closed door, Ava needed to hold a semblance of control over herself, so she breathed out softly to calm her racing heart. She draped an arm across her stomach and bit into her doughnut.

"What do you think I should wear for the next round of pictures?" he asked. "I want to put one on my Instagram. Should I go shirtless again or go with that old-money look?"

As he pivoted to face her, he lifted a linen shirt and loose trousers.

"Depends," she started. "What audience are you trying to reach? Men who admire you for that classy side you sometimes show, or groupies who will zoom in on your abs and save the photo to their camera roll?"

"Talking about you?" He smirked, his gaze trailing down her body. Leisurely. Headily.

"You wish."

"Maybe I do."

"You need to sort out your priorities."

Rowan deposited his clothes on the sofa and sat on the edge of the table resting against the wall. His features hardened for a small moment, obliging her to look at the tick in his jaw and the bump in his cheek when he rolled his tongue over its interior.

When he slipped his hands into the pockets of his jeans, a few lazy strands of hair toppled over his brows before he pushed them away.

"Is there something you want from me?" she asked.

His voice dropped to a lower octave, causing a shiver to rush down her spine. "There are a lot of things I want from you, Avery."

Feigning innocence, she tilted her head before biting into her pastry, collecting a crumb from the corner of her mouth with her thumb. "Such as?"

A wicked gleam appeared in his eyes. "A secret for a secret?"

Ava managed to keep her smile from growing. "I'll go first. Why did you ask Nikki to have me here today instead of her?"

He pushed himself off the table and slowly, so slowly like a motion at idling speed, he made the distance between them disappear. "Two things: I'd rather be in your irritating company than hers—"

"Charming," she scoffed.

"—and there's nothing she can do to keep me away from you. She can say all she wants to keep you away, but I'll always find a way to break her rules."

Her breath caught inside her throat when he planted his hand above her head, his cologne invading her senses. "You're a fool."

A darker shade of honey shifted in his gaze. "Maybe."

The distance between them was barely existent. As her chest rose and fell, his bare torso nearly came in contact with hers. "You're taking risks."

And yet she was gravitating towards peril, not running away from this man who was set on ruining her.

"Baby, I race fast cars for a living. Taking risks and living for danger is my motivation. Trying to get your attention is nowhere near risky, and I think it's worth it."

She swallowed.

He watched her throat work up and down. Smirked, aware of the effect he was having on her. The destructive power he held over her.

"I'm distracting you," she whispered.

"You've finally come to the realisation."

"I don't want—"

"Me? Liar."

She glowered. "I don't want you to lose your focus."

When his fingertips came in contact with her cheek, she stilled and dropped the doughnut. She felt paralysed, spellbound under his burning caress as he tucked a strand of hair behind her ear.

"I'm touched by your worry." He lifted her chin, gaping at her mouth. "Do you want to know what I want from you?"

She nodded automatically, a smug smirk appearing on his bewitching lips. When his nose grazed hers, her lashes fluttered.

"I want you to finish what you started in my room on Saturday."

"Rowan," she whispered, somehow surprised by this confession.

From the way he had kissed her, had touched her, it was evident he had enjoyed it. But she was still confused as to why he had left the club with another woman. Actually, Ava had rejected him—he had every right to act like this.

"I don't chase after people," he said. "But I can't stand the fact that you're avoiding me."

"Do you not see where all of this is wrong?" she hissed. "We see each other every single day. We work together. Travel together. Things can get so complicated for both of us. You don't want whatever this is to be reported to HR. You could get in so much trouble."

He pecked her cheek, causing a certain weakness to rattle in her knees. "You are so cute when you're concerned."

"I'm not just concerned—" She stopped herself, inhaling deeply. "I'm trying to be rational. I could get fired, and your career could be jeopardised. God, what a shitshow it'd be if the press ever found out! Besides, it's obvious you regret everything because you left the club with that blonde—"

"Do I sense jealousy?" He had the nerve to smirk, to push her buttons.

Perhaps. "Just stating what I saw."

That cocky bastard was amused. "Thanks for the observation, love."

"Rowan," she breathed out, "I'm trying to make everything right."

"Pushing me away is not the solution," he murmured. "And for your info, I don't regret it."

"What?"

His lips started skimming her jaw, down her neck until they landed on her thudding pulse. Surprised, she gasped but tilted her head to give him access to her skin. She could feel his satisfied smile against her flesh. Could hear how his breathing was starting to stagger, too.

"I don't regret the kiss," he said hoarsely.

"You don't?"

He kissed the spot below her ear and pressed his hips to hers. His rock-hard arousal was nearly enough to make her succumb to the temptation. But she wouldn't let him win.

"And that other girl means nothing to me."

But then, he cradled her jaw, obliging her to look into his heady eyes and that salacious gleam alighting his irises.

"I don't regret kissing you back, sunflower. I would have taken you against that wall. I still want to rip your preppy clothes off and fuck you. I do. Not. Regret it."

"This is such a bad idea." She wanted to fight her thoughts, the misplaced desire she felt for him. Wanted to blink and wake up.

And as much as she was trying to convince herself this had been a mistake, he was intent on proving her it was everything but.

Everything could go wrong if they kissed again. But what if—

A knock resonated on the other side of the door. She startled slightly whilst Rowan dropped his head forward, grunting softly with unwavering frustration.

"Rowan?" It was the photographer. "You ready?"

CHAPTER FIFTEEN

MELBOURNE, AUSTRALIA

"THE HOTEL'S THE other way," Ava pointed out when Rowan didn't turn in the direction of the highway.

"I'm aware," he replied lazily, fingers drumming against the steering wheel to accompany the rhythm of the music.

"So why are we going this way?"

His gaze found hers through the rear-view mirror, eyes narrowing.

She was sitting in the backseat of the Ferrari Portofino whilst Tate was in the passenger seat. Courtesy of Ferrari, both Primavera drivers were lucky to drive a supercar whenever they travelled for a Grand Prix, and would benefit from the vehicle for several days after the race if they were still in town.

"I'm not kidnapping you," he huffed.

"You kind of are," she retorted, folding her arms across her chest. Weirdly, she could still feel the uneven beat of her heart, even though an hour had gone by since her encounter with him in the dressing room. "Where are we going?"

"Brunch. My mum and sister are still in town so we're grabbing a quick bite with them before they catch their flight to Brisbane."

"Me included?" Eyes widening, she peered at Tate who was busy selecting another playlist.

"Yes," Rowan said, clearly not wanting to elaborate on why he would want Ava to intrude on his family time.

"Already presenting me to your family?" she teased to ease the tension building inside her gut. "Take me out on a date first."

She saw the corner of his lips twitch upwards. "You already know them, sunflower. But we can still go on a date. Tonight? I'll pick you up at your hotel room."

"Ugh," she grumbled, slipping her gaze to the moving landscape. "I'd rather go out with Tate than with you."

"Don't get me involved," Tate interjected impassively.

"Yeah, right," Rowan scoffed at the same time, passing his fingers through his hair. Gripping the steering wheel with the other hand, Ava observed how his knuckles whitened for a rapid second. "I just want to point out that you were the one suggesting the date, so don't try to deny your unconditional love for me."

She huffed out an exhale of frustration. "I don't want to bruise your ego, but I was just joking."

"I'm starting to think I've rubbed off a bit on you now that you like to tease me and all that cute shit."

Cute?

"I hope not!" His amused chuckle resonated. "I'd rather fall off a cliff than become as annoying as you."

"Oh, come on," he protested with a sly grin. "You'd be so bored without me. You love me. I know you do."

"You wish."

He hummed, honey eyes meeting hers again. "Maybe I do."

Ava was about to snap back when Tate's voice rose. "Are you two done flirting?"

"Flirting?" Rowan's echo was full of disbelief. "I think she's trying to pick up a fight with me."

Ava decided to look out the window again, hoping he wouldn't notice the subtle blush blooming on the apples of her cheeks. "I'll bite harder."

"I know you will." She could hear the grin in his tone. "I like that. Turns me on."

"Jesus," Tate muttered. "Can you two stop?"

AVA WAVED when her gaze collided with Rowan's mother. She and Rowan had just shared a rapid hug, but when Julia saw Ava standing behind her son, her smile formed into a beam.

"You didn't tell me you were bringing your girlfriend," Julia teased her son, smacking his chest. Her Australian accent was rich and thick, contrasting slightly with Rowan and Tate's since they had been living in England for quite a few years now.

Rowan glared at Ava. "Girlf—nah, she's just Avery."

Why did her chest tighten?

"And do you bring your press officer everywhere you go?"

Rowan shrugged and took a seat across from his sister. Their table was set on the terrace of the café under the beaming sunlight. "Whenever I have public things to attend, yes. I had a photoshoot and interview with GQ Australia this morning."

"Poor you," Riley crooned when Ava approached the table. A toddler with blonde curls was perched on her lap, a piece of bread in her mouth. "You're going to have to deal with him and his humongous ego when he sees himself on the front cover of the magazine."

"Nothing I'm not used to," Ava said, dismissing the remark with a subtle wave. "I'll be fine."

He only sent her a dirty look. "Sit down, Avery."

Naturally, the only seat available was the one next to Rowan.

Reluctantly, she sat down and sent an apologetic smile to Julia. "I'm so, so sorry for intruding. Rowan dragged me here."

"Don't be silly," Julia replied. "I'm surprised Rowan is willing to introduce you to us."

"You guys already know her," he grunted, throwing his head back. Then, he stood up. "I'm going inside to order drinks. The usual for everyone?"

A general "yes" echoed.

Rowan looked down at Ava, his eyes looking like molten gold in the incandescence of the late morning sunlight. "For you?"

She blinked. "I'm good."

He studied her expression for a heartbeat before disappearing inside the café.

Ava smiled when the little girl on Riley's lap giggled. Tate had just tickled her side, causing soft laughter to reverberate.

"I believe you've never met Nora?" Riley asked. "She's Rowan's niece. My baby girl."

"She has your eyes," Ava remarked, waving to greet the toddler.

Nora giggled again.

"Rowan has a soft spot for her," Julia told Ava. "She was staying with some family while we were at the Grand Prix. I think Rowan would have loved having his little cheerleader there, though."

"She's precious."

Ava could sense Julia's gaze on her. "Something tells me he has a soft spot for you, too."

The heat creeping up her face set her skin ablaze, scarlet erupting on her cheekbones. A nervous chuckle fled past her lips as she waved her hand. "Oh, no, no."

Tate snickered as he pulled Nora on his lap. Maybe Ava had mistaken the look Riley gave Tate as longing. "They try to kill each other at least eighty percent of the time."

Nora peered up at Tate. "Kill?"

"No, I said kiss," Tate recovered, failing to hide his smirk when Ava glared at him.

Ava's face flushed. Thankfully, no one seemed to have paid attention to her sudden timidity.

"Kissy?" The little girl pouted her lips, obliging Tate to lean in so that she could kiss his jaw.

"Tate's, like, her other uncle," Riley clarified in a quiet voice.

"I see."

Ava flicked her gaze between Riley and Tate, unable to move past the secret glances and fleeting touches when they exchanged crayons for Nora to use.

Rowan's shadow loomed overhead like a brooding cloud when he came back, his fingers brushing her shoulder when he aimed for his chair. "Drinks will be out in a few."

A shiver rolled down her spine when he sat down, a whiff of his cologne swivelling in the autumn air. Not sure if the sudden appearance of chills on her skin was caused by his idle fingers or the cool breeze, she wrapped her cardigan around her torso.

"You cold?" Rowan asked in a murmur whilst the others were engaged in a conversation.

"I'm fine," Ava replied dryly as she reached for the menu.

"Liar." He took his jacket off and handed it to her. "Put this on."

She gaped at his vest and up into his eyes. She wondered how and why their entourage had blurred. "I can't. You'll catch a cold."

"Look at you being so concerned. I'll be just fine. Sun's beaming on my skin and I love it."

She took hold of the jacket because she was starting to get cold. "Thanks. Don't start making this a habit."

"Then stop giving me a reason to care for your well-being."

Ava was thankful for the waitress who arrived with a full tray. She placed cups of cappuccinos and a smoothie on the table, then gave Ava a cup of steaming black coffee. With a packet of sugar on the saucer.

"Ready to place orders?" the waitress asked.

As the others chose their dishes, Rowan leaned towards Ava.

"Black with one sugar. Just like your heart."

❧

"AVA, I HOPE THAT Rowan treats you well at work."

She swallowed the bite of avocado toast she had taken, and dabbed the side of her mouth with a napkin. Nodding frantically, she let a faux smile spread across her lips.

She felt Rowan nudge the side of her thigh with his knee, though he was focused on cutting his pancakes.

"He treats me really,"—she gritted her teeth and bumped his knee back—"really well. He's so nice."

Rowan elbowed her. "I'm an angel."

"The sweetest."

"Well," Julia quipped amusedly as she turned to Rowan. "I love that you're finally working with someone who keeps up with your shit."

Rowan huffed. "Thanks, Mother."

Brunch, so far, was going well. Between chuckling at Rowan and Tate's bickering and chatting with Julia, Ava felt at ease and delighted. Having this close insight into Rowan's private life was certainly a prize she'd never let go of. That man had been so intent on pushing her away and not opening up about his family, that she hadn't expected him to be so soft and gentle with his mother and sister.

Nora reached for Rowan. "Uncle Wawa—"

"Wawa?" Ava chuckled.

"She can't say my name," Rowan explained amusedly. "Cute, right?"

Adorable.

"Hold me," Nora begged.

Instantly forgetting about his food, he pulled his niece on his lap and kissed the crown of her head. "You want a bite?" he asked softly, planting his fork in a small piece of pancake.

"Yes!"

"Yes, what?"

"Yes, please."

Ava's heart burst into flames and instantly melted like molten lava. She was just speechless at the scenery deploying before her eyes.

"Rowan," Julia started, "I know you have three weeks of break until your next race. How about you spend an extra week here and come back to the ranch?"

His mood shifted in a heartbeat—his soft smile drooped, his features hardened, and his fingers curled atop his thigh. Ava saw everything, even when he tried his hardest not to appear affected by whatever storm was brewing inside his head.

"I don't know."

"But Tate is flying back. You should, too. Might be a great occasion to say hi to his parents and spend some time on the farm."

He exhaled. "I'll think about it."

Everyone seemed to sense the shift in his demeanour, the silence nearly becoming uncomfortable and the tension growing thick.

Riley cleared her throat. "Did you guys hear about the Smiths selling their estate?"

"Seriously?" Tate roared. "You're joking."

As gossip started spreading around the table, Ava nudged Rowan's thigh. He was absently cutting his pancakes in small bites for Nora as the latter was busy drawing.

"Hey," she whispered.

He didn't reply, only tightening his jaw.

Ava sighed. She truly disliked seeing him shut himself off from the world. She leaned towards Nora and pointed to a crayon. "Can I borrow this?"

Nora smiled brightly. She had a dimple on her chin—just like Tate. Subtle, but unique in their features. *Strange*. "Yes."

"Thank you, ma'am."

Nora laughed. "It's not ma'am! I'm just a baby."

"And how old are you?"

Nora lifted three fingers. "Two."

Ava tutted. "I think you're a big girl, Nora."

"Yes." She puffed out her chest and nodded vigorously. Her mother smiled from the other side of the table before returning her attention to Tate. "Big girl."

Grabbing a sheet of paper, Ava wrote down: *You okay? Want to talk about it?*

She slipped it to Rowan, and he chuckled. He grabbed another crayon and scribbled his response down, pressing his thigh against hers.

Nothing to worry about.

A secret for a secret?

I want to make a truce.
Make a deal with you after this three-week break.

What kind?

You'll see. Your secret?

I like your little family.

Their eyes collided. "They like you, too," he whispered.

But it was when her phone chimed that reality struck her face like a whirlwind, reminding her that all those secret glances and brief touches couldn't happen again.

"Shit," Ava mumbled. "I'm sorry, but I need to get going. I'll catch a bus to the hotel." She turned to the rest of the people surrounding the table, all watching her with perplexed expressions. "It was lovely chatting with you outside of the paddock. Thank you for brunch."

"You don't have to go," Julia said, frowning.

Ava tore Rowan's jacket off her shoulders, her lungs tight and her mind spiralling. "I do."

Tate's deep voice filtered through. "What happened?"

Ava sighed, gesturing towards Rowan. "We were spotted eating together, and I can't be seen with him outside of work."

"Nikki texted you?" Rowan asked, anger now woven into his tone.

She nodded. "She's not happy."

"I'll drive you," Rowan announced, standing up. "And I'll deal with that woman. She has no right to interrupt your free time outside of work. She wants to mess with you? She gets to deal with me."

CHAPTER SIXTEEN

LONDON, ENGLAND

"YOU SHOULD TOTALLY bang your boss."

Ava choked on her coffee and coughed until she breathed normally again and the faint haze of confusion inside her mind dissipated. Eyes wide, she tried to process and comprehend the sudden suggestion.

Sitting on the other end of the sofa, she delicately kicked Gabe's shin before making herself comfortable. She wrapped the blanket around herself and brought her cup to her lips.

"What are you on about?"

Gabe didn't peer up from his phone, one hand draped behind his head. "Your boss."

Ava blinked. "Sophie McKinnon? Simon Romano?"

"Rowan," Gabe clarified, smirking.

"Why would you say that?"

She had done everything in her power to stay busy, to keep her mind occupied and away from the bane of her existence. But it occurred that, sometimes—mostly at night—she would think of Rowan and the way his lips had felt on hers. Of the deal he wanted to make with her.

"Because he's so tall," Gabe answered dreamily. He turned his phone towards Ava, displaying the most recent picture Rowan had posted online: a shot from his interview with GQ Australia. "And handsome as hell."

Ava hummed. "Maybe *you* should bang him."

He locked his phone and tossed it aside. "I wish. But I think he's more into you than into me."

Her breath caught. "Me?"

"The way he looked at you when he dropped you off the other night? I'm pretty sure he was devastated you were drunk. Otherwise, he would have ripped your clothes off."

"He hated me back then."

"Hate is a strong word."

"Gabe," she grumbled, feeling heat spread upwards to her cheekbones. "We swore to never talk about that night again."

"You forced me to forget about it," he protested.

"Don't mention it."

Her roommate eyed her amusedly. "Are you blushing?"

"I'm not."

"You are."

"Am not!"

"Babe, come on. You read romance novels to pass your time. You must have read books where the main characters are coworkers and bang in the boss' office."

"Yes, and?"

"Reenact a scene with him, please? To spice up your life?"

Ava released a small scoff of disbelief. "My life has plenty of spice."

He raised his brows. "Really?"

"Gabe," she groaned, regardless of the splatter of blush that made her cheeks burn with some sort of timidity. "Rowan is my boss—"

"Exactly."

"—and he would never get with me. Nothing would ever happen between us."

"You're really in denial."

She placed her cup of coffee atop the table and dragged the blanket up to her chin. "And you're being delusional."

The fantasy of having a wild night with Rowan was nearly driving her to insanity, and she wondered if it would ever happen. If Rowan was still intent on finishing what they had started in Melbourne.

Gabe's lips turned upwards into a mischievous smirk. "Admit that he's hot, though."

She let out a long exhale, sinking further into the sofa. "He is. He really, really is."

❧

AVA HADN'T SEEN Rowan in almost two weeks. Whilst she had gone back to London, he had decided to stay in Australia and spend some quality time with his family.

She had seen a few pictures he had shared on his socials, but hadn't heard directly from him once.

Not that she had been expecting a message or a call, anyway.

Stepping out of the lifts, she smiled brightly to greet her colleagues standing in the corridor. She received equal sympathy in return as she unfastened her coat, walking towards her office.

Her body reacted weirdly when the sound of a specific laugh echoed. Perspiration started clamming her hands, and her gaze instantly went to search for the creator of that melody.

He stepped out of Sophie's office, cradling the new Primavera Racing merch in hand.

A flickering heartbeat later, Rowan's gaze found hers, and he tipped his lips into a polite smile. Ava scoffed. That man was everything but polite.

She saw him walk towards the table at the end of the corridor, where food was always scattered on top of it, mumbling something to the girl standing before the basket of croissants. The girl gaped at him and nodded before turning on her heel. Ava swore she could see her face stricken with fear.

As Ava looked away, intent on finding shelter in her office, she inhaled sharply when Rowan's familiar scent danced in the air. He brushed past her in the hallway without so much as meeting her gaze, but when his fingers caressed her hand, she swore a zip of electricity coursed through her veins.

He slipped a note through her fingers and disappeared into the lifts.

I NEED TO TALK TO YOU. IN PRIVATE. HOPE YOU DIDN'T FORGET ABOUT MY PROMISE.

SHE COULDN'T STOP THINKING about the little note Rowan had scribbled.

When she pushed the door to the meeting room open, he was sitting on a chair, head tipped back and gazing at the ceiling, absentmindedly twirling a pencil between his fingers.

His attention snapped towards her, an instant smirk appearing on his lips. It took the greatest effort for Ava not to blush under that magnetising gaze of his. Walking in, all indifference and insouciance, she sat opposite him in the large, empty room.

The walls were made of glass, so each one of their moves were being observed and studied. Ava couldn't make a fool of herself.

"Miss me much, sunflower?" The deep baritone of his timbre sent a chill rolling down her spine.

"Not really, no."

"Liar," he droned. As she slid a foam cup of coffee towards

him, he grabbed it, brushing his fingers against hers on purpose. "Oat latte?"

"Of course."

The corners of his lips tipped upwards, yet she didn't miss the faint glint of suspicion in his eyes. "You know me so well."

She raised her brows, opening her laptop. "How could I not when I was practically forced to learn every single thing about you?"

"Oh, tone it down with that miserable voice. I am undoubtedly the most fun and interesting person you know. I bet you read all those papers I gave you before going to sleep so that you'll dream of me."

"More like having nightmares."

"There she is." When she looked up, he was grinning behind the rim of his cup and eyeing her amusedly. "How did you enjoy your breakfast?"

"Did you ask Mandy to leave the last pain au chocolat for me?"

He waved an idle hand. "Whatever her name was seemed very compliant. All those pastries should be for you."

What was he playing at? "That's nice of you."

If he had noticed her perplexity, he didn't show it. "Nikki give you trouble yet?"

She tucked a strand of hair behind an ear, drawing his regard towards her red-painted nails. "I haven't seen her today. Thank you again for last time."

"I told you," he murmured. "I've got your back."

The day she had been spotted having brunch with Rowan and his family in Australia, Nikki had messaged her and told her to leave the café on the spot or else she'd lose her position as a press officer.

Rowan had driven them back to the hotel, and he had defended Ava without an ounce of hesitation.

"Nikki," Rowan purred as he approached the blonde perched

on a stool at the bar of the hotel. Ava was in tow, somehow hiding behind his broad frame.

"Rowan," she greeted softly. Ava didn't miss the seductive smile she threw at him, but Rowan didn't seem to be affected.

"Listen. What Avery does outside of work is none of your business. Not that I should explain myself, but I invited her to brunch and I'll keep taking her out for food if I want to."

"But—"

"Let it go, Nikki. Be nice to her. Start respecting her."

Nikki's gaze found Ava's, anger dancing around her pupils. "Be smart."

Her job or Rowan.

"I have a question for you," he continued coldly, bringing Nikki's attention back to him. "Why is it that you're still working for us? Everyone knows you're awful to the employees, especially to Avery, yet you manage to get away with it every single time. What has she done to you?"

Nikki stared baffled at him.

"That's what I thought," he said. "She didn't do anything except be a phenomenal, fierce woman. I'm not going to be the person who rats you out to HR, but I hope that one day you come clean about your attitude."

"Anyway." She turned the laptop towards him as she finished setting everything up for the video call with Indigo Bailey and her sports podcast. "How was Australia?"

Rowan ran his fingers through his hair and, even if it was barely noticeable, she watched how his features hardened. "Fine."

"Just fine?"

"Yes."

Here he was again with the one-word answers any time she'd mention his family or life back home.

"Rowan," she murmured after releasing a sigh.

His gaze found hers, and a rare tenderness came to veil his honey eyes. "What?"

"I'm not your enemy." Despite the coldness in his tone, she kept her voice soft and soothing, hoping he'd eventually warm up to her delicacy. "You know that, right? I'm not here to judge you. I'm not here to tear you down."

"Why are you being nice to me?"

Why was he resisting her goodness?

She smiled softly. "Do I need a specific reason?"

Deep down, Ava was tired of the misplaced hostility. She and Rowan had been spending so much time together and would be in each other's company even more these upcoming months. She needed to put that bitterness aside to find a way to his heart and discover the secrets that had obliterated his organ. She'd crawl if she needed to.

It felt like an eternity before he spoke. "Thank you. I appreciate that. I appreciate you."

It was a knock on her door that interrupted her wild thoughts.

When she peered up from her computer, she saw a devastating angel leaning against the doorframe—a man with a broad grin and crestfallen eyes that reflected an affliction caused by his past. A pain he couldn't hide from her no matter how hard he kept that anguish a secret. That boy with the blues, that boy who was secretly broken, was shrouded in tempestuous darkness and was the embodiment of danger, yet she was ready to run into his open arms. Despite that tenebrosity, she saw a golden light in him.

Ava knew it was now that she needed to run away, lest she got heartbroken because of something that had been born from lust and impulsiveness.

But, as Rowan stood there with a smug smirk playing on the corner of his lips, her mind forgot to remind her that he was a terrible idea.

"Why are you still here?" he asked.

"What do you want, Satan?" she demanded at the same time.

A cold laugh broke free as he threw his head back. He lifted his hands in semi-surrender, that mischievous grin only widening. "I come in peace; I promise."

Sitting back in her seat, she flicked her gaze to the window and noticed how dark it was outside.

Shit.

Before she could say anything, he took a step forward and entered her office. He closed the door, though she was too stunned by his presence to ask why he would give them privacy. She knew all her colleagues had already clocked out. She was probably the last person left on this floor.

"Are you still working?"

"Yes. I just have a ton of paperwork to turn in tomorrow."

"Are you aware your shift ended, like, three hours ago?"

"And how do you know that?"

"I know more about you than you think."

"That's not creepy at all," she noted, arching an eyebrow as she watched him stride towards the sofa placed against a wall.

"I didn't mean it in a stalker-like kind of way," he grumbled, making himself comfortable. "It just means that I pay more attention to you than you think."

"Oh." She felt her cheeks tingle with a sudden timidity, and shifted her gaze to her desk.

"When are you going to be done?" He seemed oblivious to the corrupting effect he was having on her.

"Why?" She looked back to where he was, lying on the sofa with his hands behind his head and his eyes on her—observing, admiring. "What are *you* even doing here at this time of the evening?"

"Late sim test," he replied with a nonchalant shrug. "Have you had dinner yet?"

"No. Why?" she asked slowly, pivoting her chair so she would face him.

His gaze dropped to her bare thighs. He wasn't even trying to hide the blatant attraction, the risqué and sensual gleam in his eyes. She gulped. Felt her heart rate starting to increase its rhythm.

"I was thinking we could grab a bite together. Borough Market? Primrose Hill? I'm hungry," he said, still staring at her legs. "I'm meeting a few friends at a pub and thought I could drop you off at home afterwards."

"I can go home on my own just fine," she answered, passing on the fact he'd told her he wanted to eat out in her company.

Was he insane? Did he not understand what was at stake for them if they continued to be spotted hanging out outside of work?

"Baby," he started gruffly, finally meeting her eyes, "you missed your bus to the train station. The next one is in an hour."

Checking the time on her phone, Ava released a soft grunt filled with frustration. He was right.

"You're taking risks." And apparently, he was doing it on purpose.

He raised his brows—like he was accepting the challenge. "I love taking them."

When she didn't react, he sighed.

"Take it this way, sunflower: just one handsome, extra talented, and super cool F1 driver helping his amazing PR officer get back home safely just because he's a nice dude and can't stand the thought of her being out in the dark, all alone."

Her mind went into instant overdrive as she blinked.

"Rowan."

"Avery," he deadpanned.

"What do you want?"

One moment, he was spread out on the sofa, somehow lazy and acting like he owned the place, and the next moment, he was sitting up, gaping at Ava with flames dancing around his pupils.

"I already told you; there are a lot of things I want from you."

The sound of her rapid pulse became deafening. "Tell me more."

He ran tattooed fingers through his dark hair, jaw ticking as he seemed to be thinking carefully about his words. Legs spread out, elbows resting atop his thighs, he was watching her with a vehemence that made the hairs on the back of her neck rise. His stare dropped to her heaving chest, and a smirk appeared on the corner of his sinful lips.

His tone was gruff, gravel-like, dangerous. "I want you to finish what you started weeks ago in my room after qualifying."

Feigning innocence, she tilted her head. "I don't know what you're talking about."

Rowan scoffed. "Like hell, you don't. I thought you were smart."

If Rowan was an ember yearning to burn lethally, she was the match that would set him ablaze. "Why don't you be more specific, lover boy?"

His smirk widened at the sound of the name she had given him. He rubbed his jaw, a flash of defiance darkening his eyes.

He shifted to sit on the edge of the sofa, holding her gaze. She wondered if his pulse was hammering as wildly as hers. "Remember that time you kissed me, and I kissed you back until I left you breathless? That time I pinned you to the wall, your thighs wrapped around my hips, your chest pressed to mine? Remember my hands all over you, ready to slip under your uniform?"

She couldn't form a single sentence, let alone have a coherent thought run through her mind. All she could do was nod, lips parting ever so slightly.

"See?" he asked hoarsely. "I knew your pretty mind wouldn't just forget about it. Do you think about our kiss as often as I do?"

She suddenly grew hot—in that small room with only

Rowan, under that intense scrutiny that made her feel as though she was standing completely bare before him. "Careful," she droned teasingly, her voice a sultry whisper she'd never used before, "or I might think you're a tad obsessed."

His voice didn't waver as he said, "What if I am? What if I can't get you out of my mind?"

It was after a few heartbeats too long that Ava's shoulders fell as she released a long, heavy exhale. "We can't."

Rowan saw right through her. When their gazes collided, she found his features sharp with irritation. He watched her like he didn't believe her. Like he didn't want to believe that she refused to give in to the temptation.

"Why not?"

Ava closed her agenda aggressively and put her pen back into its holder before standing up, tugging her skirt down her thighs. "Do you not think about the consequences?" she gritted out, gesturing towards the door where reality lay beyond.

"Come on," he groaned, standing as well. "When are you going to start doing things for yourself? This is about your pleasure, about what you want. Fuck these people. Fuck them all."

"And it's also about our careers, how it could impact your future, Rowan. Why are you wasting your time on *me*? There are millions of women who would die to be in your bed, who are ten thousand times prettier than me, and who aren't your publicist, for fuck's sake. I'm nothing compared to them, and you know it. You just like that I'm not afraid of talking back to you, that I'm indifferent to your smug smiles and flirty gazes."

The faintest furrow of his brows was noticeable, then his tone was a firm affirmation. A fierce assurance. "I don't care about those women."

"Well, you should! You're going to go back to hating me in no time when you realise this,"—she gestured between the both of them—"isn't going to work out. You're going to get what you want and then what? Do you need to get it out of your system and move on? Is that it?"

"Move on," Rowan parroted, followed by a scoff. He took one step forward, his demeanour burning with some kind of untameable wildfire. "Do you think I'm going to be able to pretend nothing happened? Do you expect me to *move on,* just like that? I've been trying to get your attention for years, Avery. And I promise that you won't so much as try to move on once I fuck you nice and hard."

Ava's chest rose and fell. "You're wasting your time."

"Don't tell me what I'm doing. I'm not leaving this room until I get what I want. And don't say you don't want it either."

"What *do* you want?"

Rowan didn't answer the question. Like he was thinking of a reply that wouldn't scare her off.

"Sex?" she whispered. "Just—sex."

Something flashed in his eyes, but all he did was nod subtly. "Only sex. That's why you kissed me, right? It wasn't for nothing."

She frowned. Swallowed. "I took advantage of a moment of vulnerability. I shouldn't have done that."

"Good God, you're so fucking stubborn." He observed her, studied her expression, catalogued her movements. Chest heaving, jaw tight with its muscle flexing, he was the perfect picture of annoyance. "What would you do if I went to touch you now?"

She wanted to convince herself that Rowan did not affect her. Wanted to tell herself that she did not want him, but… he had been right—she needed to do what she wanted for herself. For her own pleasure. She hadn't realised she'd been craving his touch until she felt her fingers tremble from holding back from him.

"Why don't you find out?"

Nothing else seemed to exist or matter at that exact moment.

Rowan paused, as though analysing her words and studying her body language.

"Fuck it."

He closed the distance between them with long, furious strides and grabbed her face, angling it so she could stare up into his dark eyes. "For someone who's so fucking intelligent, you can be so stupid sometimes."

And then he stole her breath away by pressing his lips to hers.

Nothing was gentle or tender or delicate about the way he was kissing her. Nothing was kind or nice about Rowan Emerson.

Though Ava felt her knees weaken, she immediately responded by returning the fiery kiss, arms winding around his broad neck. He moaned in the back of his throat, and she instantly lost sense of everything.

Ava couldn't believe Rowan Emerson wanted this with her—whatever this was. Couldn't believe he was kissing her. Couldn't believe his hands were on her.

"That's what I fucking thought," he bit out before attacking the side of her neck with open-mouthed kisses that left her panting. "Be quiet, though. I checked all the rooms, and they were all empty, but we don't want any janitor to hear you screaming my name tonight."

"I hate you." Ava arched into him, eyes nearly rolling when his tongue flicked over the sweet spot below her ear.

He hummed against her skin. "I'm glad the feeling's mutual."

A low growl rumbled in his throat when his hands slipped to her bottom, fingers digging into her flesh. She tugged at his hair, her mind racing when his lips found hers again.

"Fuck," he mumbled against her mouth. "You're insanely hot. Can't believe I'm pulling you."

Ava couldn't help but bark out a laugh, slightly backing away to look into his lust-filled eyes. "Are you drunk?"

"No," he answered amusedly. "Why?"

"Do you hear yourself? Have you met yourself? I'm so basic and boring for you."

"Stop saying that." For a fraction of a second, that glint of destruction swirling along the edges of his irises became a tender glow. "You're beautiful. Inside and out. You're quite literally the most interesting woman I've ever spoken to."

Rowan Emerson was the first man to ever call her beautiful.

A line appeared between her brows as she pushed him to sit on the sofa. Straddling his hips, she shivered when his calloused palms ran over her thighs until they settled on her waist. "You're so confusing."

His gaze was fixated on her blood-rushed lips when he dragged her cardigan off her shoulders. "How?"

"You left with another woman in Melbourne, but now you come running back to me?"

He had the nerve to smirk. "Are you jealous?"

"You wish."

Unbuttoning her silk shirt, his lips came in contact with the swell of her breasts, teeth nipping at her flesh. He pulled her into his chest until the hard bulge in his trousers was pressed against her centre. "I think you are," he countered smugly. "But I didn't fuck her. Didn't even kiss her. Just walked her to her place."

"Why?"

"Because."

"That's not an answer."

"Well," he breathed out, hand cupping the back of her head, fingers tangled in her hair. "The real answer's that I wasn't interested in her because the only one I have eyes on right now is the stubborn, infuriating, and snarky woman who's sitting on my lap."

"Promise?"

"I promise I'm being sincere. Not even a kiss on the cheek," he whispered, holding her gaze. "Nothing. Went straight to the hotel after dropping her off."

"Did you stop your random hookups? I've seen you leave pubs with women before."

"I'm not the same man I was two years ago. I don't just sleep around anymore. One-night stands are over for me."

She ran her hands over his muscular pectorals. "So what is this?"

"Just a sexy F1 driver hooking up with his equally sexy publicist?"

She threw her cardigan on the floor and pushed Rowan to lie down. Dimples appeared on his handsome face, a quiet laugh vibrating in his broad chest. "I'm not sure if I want to slap that shit-eating grin off your face or kiss it away."

"Second option's the safest, baby."

Safe? Ava wasn't sure of that. To keep on kissing Rowan would ruin her. But Ava had always had a tiny love for the thrill of danger.

She felt Rowan's heartbeat under her palm as she rested her hands on his chest, and for a second, an eternity, she looked into his eyes and watched how lust morphed into something more vulnerable—intimate, almost.

And she didn't want that. Couldn't possibly want that.

Everything was so confusing.

So, to clear her mind, she locked her lips with his.

It seemed like Rowan had read her overbearing thoughts as he let his tongue stroke against hers, punishing her with a kiss that left her moaning softly whilst rocking her hips against his.

She felt him grow even harder. The sheer size of him pressing against the inside of her thigh caused arousal to pool inside her underwear.

She felt his fingers trail on the back of her thighs, creating a sequence of shivers in their wake. He pushed her skirt up to her hips, keeping his hands there to guide her against his erection. Bucking his pelvis upwards, he rutted into her, causing her to gasp, and moan, and writhe.

"Fuck," he groaned. His hands were touching her everywhere, like her body was his favourite sculpture. She liked having his touch on her, as if his fingers could erase all her worries. "Keep those pretty sounds coming."

"Don't tell me what to do."

He chuckled before letting his hand slip towards her front, his fingers pressing against her clit. "Only you would get into an argument with me whilst I try to finger-fuck you."

Her hips jerked when he started circling her clit. She straightened herself, allowing him to look where they were connected, and he groaned at the sight of her lace underwear, damp with arousal.

"You can't stand the thought of having someone being able to handle your attitude, can you?" she asked, breathless.

Rowan's smirk was all destruction. "Me? *I* have an attitude? You should see yours."

"Oh, please," she scoffed, "Don't let me stop you from being the biggest drama queen to ever walk the paddock."

"Good God, woman," Rowan muttered, pushing her panties to the side. He cursed when he saw her bare, gleaming, ready for him. The pad of his middle finger touched her clit, and she sighed in pleasure. She threw her head back, a quiet moan stuck in her throat when he coated his fingertip with her arousal and spread it over her core. "I'm trying to fuck you. Just shut up."

Ava couldn't respond when he started circling her clit, putting the perfect amount of pressure that left her heaving bated breaths. Her fingers fisted his shirt as she pressed her lips in a thin line, holding her pleasure in silence.

"I'm starving," he stated huskily, his dark gaze travelling from her face, to her chest, to where he was touching her. "Sit on my face."

Ava ceased—to move and breathe and think. "W-what?"

"I'm going to eat that pretty cunt of yours." He grabbed the back of her thighs, nudging her towards his face.

"I—"

Rowan paused, frowning. "Has no one ever gone down on you before?" Pure concern was now etched on his face.

"Twice. It wasn't necessarily good, but—"

Fingers dug into the flesh of her bottom. "The very instant my tongue lands on your clit, baby, you'll forget about those idiots who haven't been able to make this an enjoyable experience for you. In fact, I intend to erase the memory of every man you've had before me."

Ava scoffed. "You're overly confident."

"Have you met me? I always am. And I keep my promises. Come here."

Ava swallowed, and Rowan's face softened.

"Wait. Shit." Gently, he pulled her in to level her face to his. He pecked her lips once. Twice. A few times to ease her. "Are you okay with all of this?"

Ava could only nod, going in for another soothing kiss.

"Words, sunflower."

She pulled back just enough to look into dark eyes shining with so many emotions—ruination, admiration, lust, and desire.

"Yes."

"Good. Now come. On my face, preferably."

Once her thighs were bracketed on either side of his face, he didn't waste a second to latch his mouth to her clit.

Ava cried out, a wave of pleasure taking control of her body.

He groaned. "You taste so sweet. Like heaven."

Throwing her head back, she closed her eyes as she let herself enjoy this foreign sensation of pleasure. Her fingers tangled through his curls, pulling softly at the roots.

She could feel him smirk whilst he tried to push her against his mouth, the gruffness of his beard tickling her flesh.

"I'm going to suffocate you," she protested, nails scraping his scalp. He moaned at the sensation, the vibration sending a jolt of intense pleasure through her core.

"Good." She was now riding his face, his tongue flat against her core, its languid strokes making the moment last. "I'd die a happy man with my head buried between your thighs."

Ava had always been self-conscious about her thighs—her

whole physique, actually—but the way Rowan worshipped her silently by running his hands everywhere, as though he wanted to ingrain the route of her curves into the back of his mind, made her forget about all her worries.

She bit on her lower lip when his mouth wrapped around her clit to suck on it before he went back to devouring her with abandon, tongue lapping fiercely against her wet folds.

"Rowan," she gasped just as he gripped her bottom, fingers digging into her skin. He was holding her exactly where she wanted him to be.

"Ride my face, baby." Her hips rolled in tandem with the rapid motions of his tongue, eyes shut closed as she enjoyed every second of this moment. "Good girl. So hot."

His words, the way he praised with both his voice and hands, caused her stomach to clench.

One of Rowan's hands trailed up her stomach until it reached her chest, fingers palming her breast through the flimsy fabric of her bra. When he pinched her taut nipple between his thumb and forefinger, he groaned shamelessly.

Ava leaned back, bracing herself by placing her palms on his firm thighs, causing Rowan to grunt again, as if encouraging her to continue rolling her hips against his flat tongue.

"I'm close," she announced breathlessly.

She felt him smirk, then he went back to stroking her clit, humming like he was satisfied. Ava was a writhing and moaning mess, rocking her hips against his mouth, seeking the pinnacle of pleasure.

He tugged the cup of her bra down to properly play with her hard nipple, switching between rolling the bud between his fingers and palming her breast, testing its weight and fisting the full flesh.

The weight of his other hand left her backside, and she opened her eyes just to see him adjust himself in his pants.

And before she could do anything about it, she felt her legs shake, her core clenching as she reached her high.

"Fuck," she cried out, falling forward to grab his head again. Her body spasmed as white stars blinded her vision. Rowan's tongue kept lapping over her clit, and he moaned with her when she tugged at his hair, her cries of pleasure filling the small room. "Rowan."

He didn't remove his mouth as she rode through her orgasm, not stopping until she stilled, trembling.

Ava blinked at the ceiling as she listened to her heavy breaths. Pushing herself up on her knees, fingers passing gently through his hair, she looked down at Rowan, only to see him looking up, grinning like the devil. His lips and chin were coated in her arousal, and he had never looked so good.

"You're fucking unbelievable," was all he said as he observed her catching her breath.

Ava fell forward as he adjusted her underwear before cupping her face. He pulled her in to kiss her softly—too softly—and she moaned at the taste of herself on his lips.

Rowan's fingertips dug into her skin as he tilted her head, obliging her to look into his dark eyes. That gleam around his pupils promised destruction. Power. And under that magnetising touch, she was simply defenceless.

"Say that again," he seethed, the pad of his thumb brushing over her lower lip. She knew he was referring to the comment she had made earlier.

But she couldn't even voice her thoughts. Couldn't move out of his punishing grip. She was still trying to catch her breath, her mind spiralling with memories of him—his demanding lips, his rough hands, his dirty words.

Pulling her in, he let his hand slide until it bared her throat, thumb pressing into the side of her neck. He smirked when he felt her pulse quicken. "Next time you see me interact with another woman, sunflower, you're going to remember it was *my* head that was buried between *your* thighs tonight. Say once more that you're nothing compared to these girls, and I promise I'll fuck and ruin you until you put into that head of yours that it's you that I want."

"Okay," she whispered after a moment of staring at him, utterly speechless by his confession. "Thank you."

Rowan Emerson wanted *her*.

He chuckled. "Thank *you*." When she reached down between them to cup his throbbing erection, he whimpered, but caught her wrist before she could rub her hand against it. "Not today."

"But I want to."

"I know. But I don't expect anything in return. All I wanted was to make you come. Besides, it's been so long, and I know I'll last a total of thirty seconds, and my ego can't handle that. I'll jerk off in the shower later tonight, though. You better believe me when I say I'll come with your name on my tongue and think of how pretty you looked riding my face."

Ava felt her cheeks burn up, so she hid her face in the crook of his neck, inhaling his addictive scent. His laugh echoed as he caressed her back, coaxing and tender. "The mouth you have, Emerson."

He kissed her cheek, her jaw, her neck, then slapped her bum. "You haven't heard anything yet."

Being in his arms after experiencing such a high—possibly the best one she'd had yet—was more comforting than she cared to admit. Calm. Natural. Easy. She found herself basking and lingering in the moment, wishing it wouldn't end. Wishing things weren't so complicated and confusing.

His lips came in contact with her ear, and she shivered again. "Will you let me drive you home now?"

CHAPTER SEVENTEEN

BAKU, AZERBAIJAN

AVA'S HEART BATTERED furiously as she watched the twenty drivers warm up their tyres during the formation lap.

It was warm yet windy in Baku, and she knew the race would be tricky and physical, especially on this circuit which was known to have a mixture of wide and open, tight and twisty turns.

Primavera Racing had struggled during free practices on Friday as both drivers had to find a perfect balance between downforce in the twisty corners and less dragging in the straight lines. Ava had watched both Rowan and Thiago be frustrated with their performance, their car, and their team. Both teams of mechanics had spent Friday night working on the cars, and qualifying had gone better than expected. Rowan had qualified third and Thiago fourth.

Ava adjusted her headphones as she watched the five red

lights come to life one by one. Four seconds later, the lights went out, and the cars started in sync.

Rowan had a good start, slotting in between Huxley and Beaumont, claiming P2 with a mere push on the throttle. While chaos unravelled at the end of the grid where there was contact between two cars, Ava was unimpressed by this typical first lap incident, caused by too many cars driving side by side into the corner.

The yellow flag was brandished then because debris was scattered on the track.

Ava watched the board on the left side of the screen where the drivers' names were, hiding her smile at the sight of Rowan behind the race leader.

"Come on, mate," Tate said. "Show 'em what you've got and how good those three weeks of break were to you."

❧

ON THE EIGHTH LAP, DRS was open for Rowan, but no matter how hard he tried to chase Miles, the Imperium car was fast. Miles slipped away, but it was evident Rowan wanted to fight.

He was ruthless in his driving style. Skilled in a way that left Ava speechless, breathless as he took tight corners, handling his car with such precision that the front wing never came in contact with the walls.

Rowan now had Thiago on his tail. Maybe Primavera Racing would make a double podium at the end of the fifty-one-lap race.

❧

ON LAP FIFTEEN, Ava frowned as she noticed the gap between Rowan and Miles increase.

The exchange between Rowan and his race engineer, Jamie, resonated through her headphones.

"The engine braking is not good," Rowan complained.

"Understood," Jamie said. "Keep pushing."

"That's what I'm trying to do."

"How's tyre management?"

"They're fine. I've got grip."

"Good. Full push now."

ROWAN HAD JUST PITTED and changed his set of medium tyres to hard ones. With fresh rubbers on that shouldn't degrade rapidly, he was hoping to finish the race with those compounds.

He was currently chasing Charlie Beaumont, Huxley's teammate, who had managed to steal his position whilst he had boxed.

Ava was gnawing on her bottom lip when she observed Rowan chase after Charlie. Despite the hard tyres' resistance, they were less performant, rendering the race to be more challenging for Rowan. Braking late after the straight line, he didn't seem to be complaining any longer about the engine brake and slipped on the inside of the corner. Wheel to wheel, their front wings were centimetres away from touching. Charlie couldn't do anything but yield and give his position to Rowan.

"Yes!" Tate hollered, pumping a fist in the air.

Cheers erupted around the garage, and Ava clapped.

He was back to being P2.

THERE WERE ONLY ten laps left when Rowan started slowing down.

"Is he losing power?" Tate whispered to Ava.

"Shh," she said, smacking his chest.

"Engine brake is shitty again," Rowan grumbled through the radio.

"Understood. Keep pushing to finish the race."

"I've got it." Ava could hear the frustration in his tone.

"Let Thiago through. Team order."

Ava shook her head, sighing. The atmosphere in the garage shifted drastically when everyone realised what was happening.

"Fuck," Rowan said. "Sorry."

One second later, Thiago was in front, Rowan on his teammate's tail and trying to keep his pace.

Charlie wasn't far away now.

And when Rowan turned too widely in corner fourteen, Charlie slipped through, gaining one position.

Rowan was P4.

❧

AVA ONLY HAD the chance to hand Rowan his water bottle, without receiving so much as a glance in response, before he turned on his heel and walked through the paddock. Anger and deception emanated from his demeanour like a tempest ready to strike anyone who dared to cross his path. Ava knew it was best not to say anything right now.

He got away from her, went into his room, and slammed the door, causing the walls to rattle.

Ava sighed, hand on the doorknob, hesitant. Tate, who had been following, rubbed her back gently.

"I've got him. I don't want him to say the wrong thing to you because he's angry right now."

She blinked up at Tate, heart pounding as she glanced around, surveying the empty corridor. "Is it wrong that I want to comfort him? Instead of telling him what to say to the reporters?"

"It's okay. It shows how big your heart is. Caring for him is okay."

"Is it, though?" she whispered.

"You're a good person," Tate said with a smile. "You're good for sticking around even during his worst moments. He and Ellie got along quite well, but she used to leave him with his burden and let him deal with it alone."

Ava wasn't sure what to reply, so she stayed silent, only gaping at the tall man before her. Did he know about what they —she—had done the time Rowan punched the wall?

Tate rubbed the back of his neck, exhaling. "You know how he is. He's going to beat himself up for his mistake. Just give him a few minutes to cool down before going in and starting the PR debrief."

She only nodded, taking a step back to allow Tate to enter the driver's room.

All she could do as she waited was to wish she had been brave enough to follow Rowan inside the walls that tended to cage his pain, and to hold him through that turbulent storm of anger.

CHAPTER EIGHTEEN

BAKU, AZERBAIJAN

ROWAN NEVER TALKED about it to anyone, but today, he felt like his panic was suffocating him. Like the world, and the people, and the media were trying to choke him. Drowning him under all that guilt that was destroying him.

It was so hard, so painful, when he felt like everything was his fault—well, it was his fault. That result was because of him. That missed podium was because of his own mistakes.

And even when his entourage kept cheering him on, kept telling him he had done great, he couldn't help but feel like he wasn't enough.

It was only when he was alone in his hotel room that he decided it was okay to let his smile fall and unwelcome tears escape. It was then that his lungs felt tight, and his head started spinning. It was then that he punched his pillow, furious at being so stupid.

And it was when he read his father's messages that he cried in frustration, wondering when the hell he would be enough and good in the eyes of his parent. Perhaps never. And Rowan had to live with that.

When his breaths became even and the fog inside his mind cleared, he regained composure and changed into his swimming shorts. He knew the pool had closed hours ago, and it made everything better for him to know he'd be alone.

The still warm air caressed his bare skin when he stepped on the rooftop. His heart ceased to beat when he saw a silhouette sitting on the edge of the pool. He instantly knew who it was by the reaction of his body.

Hearing the door close behind him, Avery turned around. "Oh, it's you."

Rowan scoffed softly. "Hide your joy."

She didn't say anything as she watched him put his towel next to hers on the lounge chair. He walked towards the pool, ruffling his hair before diving in.

The lukewarm water soothed the ache in his body, especially his shoulder after the minor injury he had a few months ago.

When he resurfaced, he sighed contently.

"Do you want me to go?" Avery asked quietly.

He found her gaze, breath catching inside his throat. Basking in the soft glow of the moonlight, she looked like an angel sent from above. Her dark hair framed her face, the luminescence of the silver orbit drawing stars on her tender expression.

Rowan realised she had been fated to crash into his orbit like a comet, a shooting star that would change his life. But he still wanted to live in denial. Wanted to keep his walls intact and unwavering.

He couldn't help but roam his gaze over her physique—one he couldn't forget about—and found himself swallowing when he watched the lavender swimsuit hug her body perfectly. Her breasts were nearly spilling out of the fabric, pressed together in a way that made him wish he could bury his cock in between and fuck her generous tits.

Rowan cleared his throat, finding her gaze again. She had

tilted her head, a line drawn between her brows as she studied his features. He already knew that she could sense something was wrong with him.

And Rowan felt like a dick for ignoring her the entire evening. He had barely spoken to her when he went to do the interviews in the media pen. Hadn't spoken to her when he left the circuit with Tate. Hadn't asked if she wanted to ride with him. Hadn't answered her message when she had asked if he was okay.

"Stay," he finally answered. "I'd like you to stay."

Nodding, she tucked a strand of hair behind her ear. "Okay."

"I'm surprised to see you here. Thought you didn't like to break rules."

She shrugged sheepishly. "I broke quite a few last week, so what's one more rule to ignore?"

A smirk ghosted his lips. "I love the way you think."

"Why aren't you partying and celebrating?"

Rowan fell on his back and started floating. He stared at the starry sky, silent for a few beats. "Didn't feel like it. Don't feel like I deserve to celebrate."

Her response was muffled by the water lapping around his head, so he straightened himself again. "Sorry?"

"I asked why you would think that. If there's one driver who's deserving of celebrating today's Grand Prix, it's you."

Rowan curled his lips into a taunting smirk. "Look, I appreciate the flattery, but I don't really look like Miles Huxley. I'm ten times more attractive."

Rolling her eyes, Avery shook her head, but a small smile was trying to creep on her face. "You know you had a great race, right?"

He only responded with a shrug of his shoulders.

"Are you okay?" she asked, her features stricken with concern.

Another shrug.

Even if he responded vaguely, he knew she'd try and rattle his barriers. That fierce, unyielding layer of her personality made her even more attractive from his point of view.

Slipping into the water, she faced Rowan. Doe eyes scrutinised his face, not a single flicker of judgement sparkling in those chocolate irises. "A secret for a secret?"

Rowan wanted to close the small distance between them, to catch her lips, to touch her skin, but he knew she'd push him away. Because that demand to share a secret in exchange for another one was a moment of vulnerability. There was no place for foolishness, for distractions.

Inhaling deeply, he decided he needed a moment to collect his thoughts and to decide which secret to spill. There were so many secrets he was willing to share with Avery. So many things that he kept hidden in his heart that he wanted to lay open. There was just something about her that procured him a solace he shouldn't long for, yet he craved for it—that comfort, that serenity, that feeling of understanding.

He started doing a few laps around the pool, and when he came back to stand before Avery, she was leaning against the wall, patiently waiting for him.

"You don't have to rush," she told him with a delicacy that cracked his heart open. He didn't deserve her kindness. "Take your time. I'm not going anywhere."

Rowan nodded as he rubbed the back of his neck. He swam towards Avery to rest next to her, draping his arms over the ledge and leaning his chin atop his forearm, staring absently ahead.

"I'm bad at this," he whispered.

"At what?"

"Communicating. In general."

"You're doing a good job right now," she praised. "Keep going."

The walls he'd built around him were intact. Had never once so much as wavered. But it seemed like Avery knew the secret to see past them, intent on tearing them down.

Though he allowed a tiny smile to settle on the corner of his lips, he didn't want to look at her, terrified of how his heart and body would react once he found chocolate eyes. "I grew up in a broken home," he confessed. No one except Tate knew about this. "My parents sacrificed a lot for me, and sometimes I still think I'm the reason why they split up in the first place. I was ten when they divorced. I can still hear my parents yelling at each other, getting into argument after argument over my racing and the money they were spending on me. I can still hear my mum crying in the middle of the night because my dickhead of a father would blame her for everything that went downhill in their relationship."

The water lapped around him when she turned, inching closer until she braced her arms on the ledge, too. Her bare shoulder brushed against his, a zip of electricity trailing through his veins at the contact.

"You're doing great," she encouraged in a murmur.

"Because of my broken home, there was never space for me to learn how to communicate properly, to talk about my needs, or fears, or joys. My mum would try to talk to me when I would close myself off, but I could never manage to speak up, resulting in me pushing her away." He inhaled deeply, already feeling a heavy weight lifting off his chest. "I was such a goddamn angry kid, always keeping all my feelings bottled in. I would never be here without my folks; let's be real. I know they gave up a lot for me, and I'm super grateful for them. But, whilst Mum and Riley have always cheered me on and loved me despite my mistakes, my father is just...I don't even know. He's messing with my head. He's fucking with me over and over. He wants me to be the best, but doesn't support me—never has. We were never close. I can barely call him Dad, but you know, sometimes it hurts to be in this position."

"How's your relationship with Riley?"

He shrugged, keeping his stare on nothing in particular. "Okay. We weren't very close as kids. She's the oldest, right? She's the golden girl with a bright future, a great corporate job, and a beautiful life ahead of herself. She isn't close to Stephen, either, but I've always kind of lived in her shadow. We only started to bond when she had Nora."

"Who's..."

"Nora's father?" He saw the nod of her head from the corner of his eye. "We don't know. She won't tell us. All I know is that Nora's the gift of a one-night stand."

"That's tough."

"Yeah. It sucks to grow up with an abusive father, but imagine growing up without one."

"I can't imagine how much it hurts," she said softly. "I'm sorry that I can't understand what you're going through."

He smiled faintly. "Don't be sorry."

"Can you tell me more about what happened with your father?" Rowan understood she was doing this to help him heal. Avery wasn't the type of woman who would try to change him like his past girlfriends. Wasn't the type to judge him for his past, for his story.

Rowan's jaw tightened as he let unwanted memories flood his mind. "I don't want to be a burden."

"You're not," she assured. "You'll never be a burden, but it's okay if you don't want to talk about it. I'll understand."

"He was just"—he paused to take a deep breath—"a total asshat. I once had a karting competition when I was eight. Finished third. He wasn't happy and left the circuit without me, leaving me to find a way back home. When I was safely home, he just yelled at me for being a failure. He hit me. I'm quite literally his biggest disappointment—always have been. I'm fine now. I try to not let him affect my mental health the way he used to. The only thing he still makes me believe is that I'm not good enough to be in F1. I just feel so, *so pressured* every time I get in the car. It's a weight I can't seem to shake off."

"I'm sorry you had to go through that, and I'm so sorry you feel this way. Does your mum still talk to him?"

"I appreciate your apology, but it's not your fault at all." He swallowed his grunt then. "Unfortunately, Mum talks to him more than she should. They tried to maintain a good relationship to co-parent as best as they could, but deep down she's hopeful. She's hoping he's going to change and come back. It's been twenty years, and she still thinks he can be a good man, but she knows he's not. She deserves so much more than him."

"Do you think she still loves him?"

"No. I know the divorce hurt her a lot, but she just loves what they used to have before having kids. She clings too much to the past."

"I don't think you were the reason your parents separated."

"Sure. Maybe you're right. But when you see the two people who raised you grow apart, you can't help but think love is only ephemeral."

"You don't believe in love, then?"

He shook his head. "Not one bit. I don't think it's meant for me. At least not in this lifetime."

He'd been told, repeatedly, that he didn't deserve good things in life. Love included.

"Is this why you're so scared of opening up?"

"Maybe." Of course, she'd been able to sense his resistance, his will to keep her away. But how could anyone resist her charms?

She placed a comforting hand on his shoulder, but retreated quickly. Rowan found himself instantly missing her touch. "Thank you for sharing this part of you with me. It means a lot."

The sincerity in her gaze made his breath hitch. Caused a lump to build inside his throat.

She leaned her cheek in the palm of her hand, a soft regard meandering over his face. "It's hard to believe you're hiding such a deep background under your tough and arrogant façade."

He lifted his shoulders. "Yeah, well, I'm an expert at showing that cocky side of me and hiding my true self. The world loves me for who I am."

"You know, no one goes through life unscathed and

unharmed. Shit happens to everyone, and I believe each of our stories makes us who we are today. Your past doesn't define you, and what the world expects of you shouldn't define you, either. You're more than enough. You know how worthy of that F1 seat you are. You know how hard you've worked to get here. You deserve to be amongst those other nineteen Formula 1 drivers. You don't come from a family of racers, but Primavera Racing has welcomed you into their family with open arms, and you're here to stay. Those scars, whether they're hidden or not, make you beautiful, Rowan."

He wondered how, even in his worst times, Avery saw the best in him.

How, even in his worst lies, she saw the truth in him.

How, whilst he was in the aftermath of an earthquake, she was a tranquil ocean, stable, and calm, and peaceful even when she'd been through reckless waves.

"I'm sorry you had a difficult childhood," she continued when he was unable to voice his thoughts. "And I'm sorry your father can't see you for the real talent you are. I promise there are millions of people out there who admire you."

Swallowing, he nodded. "Thank you, sunflower. You've got no idea how much your words mean to me."

A beautiful, devastating smile spread across her full lips. "Of course."

He pushed himself off the edge and dipped into the water just to soak all the emotions in. Only now did he realise how good it had felt to speak up, to confess to someone other than Tate. Emerging to the surface, he caught Avery's hip to make her turn around, pressing her back to the wall. He braced both hands on either side of her body, caging her in.

"I'm supposed to stay away from you," he whispered lowly. "But how am I supposed to do so when you're being like this with me?"

She narrowed her gaze. "Do you want me to go back to being a bitch to you?"

"To be honest, your attitude turns me on."

She pushed his chest, but he didn't so much as move. He loved the feeling of her soft skin on his, even if it was brief. "You're an idiot."

Her gaze fell to his dimples when he grinned broadly. "I know."

Her fingers twitched in the water, like she wanted to touch him, but she kept her hands by her sides. "Don't beat yourself up because of today's result. You did amazing; it was just a little mistake. Don't listen to the media. Be the Rowan everyone adores: the guy who smiles and has no regrets. The guy who turns bad moments into simple memories."

He nodded, determined. "I will." He made the first move, brushing her messy fringe away from her forehead. "What's your secret?"

"What do you want to know?"

He liked how open she was with him. She used to be so reluctant towards him, so cold and uncaring. But now, she was allowing him to catch a glimpse of what had been laying beneath that open disdain.

"Why aren't you partying with the rest of the team and your friends?"

"Because I don't have any friends."

"Lies," he scoffed. "You're a social butterfly."

She shook her head, eyes dropping to his tattooed chest. "Not really. My only friends are Gabe and his boyfriend, Elijah."

He knitted his brows together. "You're always surrounded by so many people. You always talk to everyone."

"I see you've been keeping a close watch on me."

He chuckled. "Just like you do with me, love."

Truth was, no matter where they were, no matter how many people stood between and around them, he would always find her in a crowded place. Like a magnet craving to find its other half.

Avery slipped her gaze to the waning crescent moon, a soft

sigh flying past her lips. "Being around a lot of people doesn't mean I'm close, let alone friends with them. I enjoy the team's company; we have fun together, we laugh a lot, and we get along. But there's a part of me that doesn't want to get too close."

"Why is that?"

As she looked away from the constellations brightening the night sky, she settled her gaze on the chain around his neck. "I've had bad friendships in the past. I think I'd rather be alone than in bad company. To have a few close friends rather than be surrounded by hypocrites."

"What happened?" He cupped her chin, obliging her to bask in the raw concern shimmering around his pupils.

It took a few beats for her to open up. As she searched for the right words to express her quiet anguish, she started biting her lower lip. It was an effort for Rowan not to brush her mouth with the pad of his thumb.

"People take my kindness for granted, and that's sad. They use me, make fun of me and what makes me happy, and I try not to care. But when I try to befriend someone, they don't return my excitement. I'm very often belittled and I don't know why. It's tiring. I wish I could become friends with someone who listens without judging, who won't make everything about them. I don't ask for a lot, but it always feels like I'm begging for the moon."

Rowan's hands started shaking with unrestrained anger. Why and how could someone hurt someone as good as Avery? And how was she still so stunningly mystifying after being obliterated by people in her past?

"Do you—feel lonely?"

Sorrow misted over her eyes, and his throat tightened. "Sometimes. All the time, actually. Do you know how hard it is to feel lonely when you're in a crowded room? But I'm used to it. Honestly, I don't mind the solitude. I embrace it and make the most of it."

"Avery," he started, voice hoarse. "I had no idea you felt this way. I'm sorry."

"I'm fine," she assured. "I don't need to get drunk and party to have fun. Besides, after this exhausting week, relaxing by the pool at midnight is exactly what I needed."

Looping his arms around her waist, Rowan pulled her into his chest. He heard her breath catch inside her throat, and he wondered if she could feel the rapid pulse of his heartbeat against her own. She winded her arms around his neck, wide eyes flickering between his.

He found himself wanting to hold her, curl into her warmth. It was a strange feeling; he couldn't recall the last time he'd been held. The last time he'd sought a hug, comfort. But desire took over his tenderness.

"I'll be your friend," he murmured, nose grazing her jaw until his lips hovered above the side of her neck.

"Really?"

"Yeah." He kissed her neck, smirking as he felt a shiver rack through her body.

She passed her fingers through the wet hair on his nape. He loved it when she did that. "What kind of friend?"

He continued to trail kisses down her throat, her sweet fragrance enveloping all his senses. He could see her as a new addiction. Dangerous. Compelling. "I can be the friend who listens to you when you need to talk to someone. Who comes to you when I need to lift things off my chest. I can be the friend who tells you a secret in exchange for one of your own. I can also be the friend who makes you scream at night, who shows you how perfect you are and how your body deserves to be worshipped. I can be whatever friend you need."

"What about the *just sex* deal?"

"We can alter it."

"Friends with benefits?"

"*Lots* of benefits. Tons of them. Sounds good?"

"Why not," she breathed out.

"Why not?" he parroted, bemused, his hands running down her ribs. "Will you ever stop being a brat?"

"But are you sure you want this with *me?*"

He stilled, a deep crease forming between his furrowed brows. He found her gaze, gaping at her incredulously. "Yes."

"But..."

"But what? Tell me."

She sighed heavily, shoulders sagging. "I don't know, Rowan. You seem like a stable guy. Steady. Well-balanced and anchored to your commitments. I don't want to hold you back from hooking up with other women. I just—sorry. I'm rambling. Whatever I'm trying to say doesn't make sense. I'm nervous."

"I make you nervous?" He smirked. "One point for Rowan Emerson."

"I'm trying to be serious here."

"And I'm trying to tell you that,"—he grabbed her hand to place it above his prominent bulge, causing her eyes to widen slightly—"I don't want anyone else. No one can be a better friend with a cunt as sweet as yours, Avery."

She couldn't help but laugh at the foul words leaving his mouth, yet a crimson blush had appeared on her cheekbones. When he placed a tender kiss on her nose, then her cheek, and on her jaw, he heard her sigh softly.

Rowan was baffled by his actions. His affection.

With her head tilted to the side, she had granted him more access to her skin just as he grabbed the back of her thighs to wrap her legs around his waist.

"Okay, but wait."

"Anything you want, sunflower."

"We need to set a few rules."

He groaned. "Seriously?"

"Yes." She cradled his face, prying him away from her soft skin to force him to look at her. Unconsciously, he leaned into her touch. The look on her face shifted from aggravated concern and seriousness to a certain tenderness. "I don't want this—us—

to impact your performance and especially your career. If we get caught—"

"We'll be careful. I'd never put you in danger. Would never take the risk of getting caught because I don't want you to be fired."

A tantalising smile illuminated her features. "Are you finally admitting I'm the best PR officer you've ever had and that you don't know what you'd do without me?"

He rolled his eyes. "Let's not go too far."

"It's always going to be work before anything else, okay? I'm not going to distract you. You'll come to me only when you need to get it out of your system, and I'll do the same, but we have to stay professional."

God, that overbearing, controlling side of hers. He was so turned on. Could fuck her right then and there. "Rules. Okay. Yeah. Anything you want."

"No hooking up when we're travelling."

"Are you shitting me?" he bellowed with disbelief. "We travel ninety percent of the season, dude. When can we bang, then? Winter break? Yeah, no, fuck that."

She was amused. He wasn't. "Fine, *dude.* No hooking up during race weekend—that means Friday through Sunday night. You need to focus."

"Okay, but what if I need to release some tension before a race or something?"

Avery shook her head. "Not happening."

"Fine. I respect that. You want us to be professional. Fine."

She giggled. *Giggled.* Hooking a finger under his chain, she said, "You sound petty. Stop. I just don't want it to be weird between us."

"It's not. It won't be."

Doe eyes blinked up at him. "Promise?"

"I promise, sunflower."

"We have to be *extra* careful of everything we do. Where we meet. When we meet."

He nodded. "You got it."

"We can't tell anyone."

"Obviously. My lips are sealed. You're my secret."

Something flashed in her eyes, but he couldn't put a word on that strange emotion.

"And when you meet someone else, someone new, you tell me so we can end things. Same goes for me."

Rowan nodded, but he didn't want to meet anyone new. Didn't want her to meet another man.

None of this sounded like two friends seeking a relationship where only lust could take over, where feelings were unwelcome. But, somehow, he didn't care.

"Deal," he said despite the tightness in his chest.

"Deal." She extended her small hand, and he shook it with a firm grip. She tried to grip him harder, causing him to chuckle.

"Good. Now, come here."

Cupping her chin, he brought her lips to his, and the contact set his entire universe on fire. Explosions of overwhelming sentiments. Fireworks of incomprehensible yet unyielding desire. Kissing Avery had never felt so good.

Her lips parted, allowing his tongue to explore her mouth whilst their breaths entwined. Slipping his hand to her neck and aiming for her chest, he pushed his hips into hers, eliciting a gasp to echo.

When her hands fell onto his pecs, he smirked, but she pushed him away.

He blinked.

She had the audacity to shrug sheepishly.

He let her go, confused, and she pushed herself out of the pool.

And then, she bent over to grab his jaw, pecked his lips, and whispered, "Goodnight, Rowan."

He watched her walk to the lounge chair to retrieve her towel, hips swaying and perfect round, generous ass in his field of vision.

"Are you fucking serious? Leaving me here alone with a raging hard-on?"

She didn't look at him when she waved in farewell. "Sorry, lover boy, but you'll have to take care of it on your own tonight. Sweet dreams."

CHAPTER NINETEEN

MIAMI, UNITED STATES OF AMERICA

Sprawled on the sofa, Rowan waited for her answer. Regardless of his patience, he could feel his fingers tremble with anticipation as he stared absently at their message thread.

Today wasn't necessarily his favourite day, but he had forced himself to smile and pretend he was having a great time. He'd had cake, had received numerous wishes, but he didn't care that much for his birthday.

After celebrating with the team and participating in PR activities for Media Day, Rowan had managed to get a hold of a Polaroid. He'd snapped a photo of Avery busy eating a piece of cake and scribbled a note on the back of it before slipping it into the back pocket of her jeans when no one was watching.

All he needed now was to let go of that pent-up stress, get laid, and see Avery. Obviously, he had spent some time with her these past few days, that mutual hostility now long forgotten. He hadn't managed to get some alone time with her though, and it was slowly yet surely driving him mad.

ROWAN

Did you get my note?

Meet me tonight, the note said.

SUNFLOWER

Yes.

ROWAN

Meet me in my room

SUNFLOWER

What are we going to do?

ROWAN

Each other

SUNFLOWER

You have no filter whatsoever.

Rowan, the hotel is flooded with team members

ROWAN

So? We're young and reckless baby. Nothing has stopped you before.

Room 555

SUNFLOWER

I'll kill you if we get caught

ROWAN

As long as I get to bury my head between your thighs, I'm fine with the consequences

❧

Rowan was electric with need. He was yearning for Avery's touch. He craved her like he was addicted, but he refused to find a cure to lure him out of this bewitching spell.

The instant a soft, almost inaudible knock resonated, he opened the door and pulled Avery in by her wrist. He pushed her against the closed door, instantly slanting his mouth on hers. The gasp she emitted was swallowed by him as he let his tongue stroke hers in a languid motion. Avery moaned softly, winding her arms around his neck as his hands found the back of her thighs.

He hoisted her up effortlessly, refusing to break their fervent kiss.

She was wearing cotton shorts, and imagining her walking around with those on made his cock swell. He pushed himself into her centre, a moan catching inside her throat. She made him feel like a teenager; he could come inside his joggers just by rolling his hips against hers, listening to her soft whimpers.

"Wait," she breathed out.

A frustrated groan rumbled inside his chest. "I've been wanting to kiss that bratty mouth of yours all day long and now you're stopping me? It better be for a good reason."

Gently, she pushed him away just enough so that he could stare into her eyes. Doe eyes glinting with tenderness. Mesmerising, doe eyes he couldn't get out of his mind, no matter how hard he tried.

"Happy birthday," Avery murmured, extending a small box his way.

"What is it?" His eyebrows had drawn together in slight confusion.

Damn it—why was she constantly, continuously good to him? What had he done to deserve her?

"The birthday present you've been dying to receive."

A smile danced on the corner of his mouth as he reminisced

of the moment he'd taunted her for not gifting him anything. Her reply had been: "*You're already gifted by my presence.*"

He let her down on her feet, forgetting about his painful erection. He grabbed the box and opened it. He blinked. Raised his brows in shock. Looked at her.

"Is it poisoned?"

She scoffed. "You're hilarious."

He expelled a breath.

"Sunflower," he whispered in awe. "That's very..."

She folded her arms across her stomach, as if self-conscious. "That's too much, isn't it? I knew I shouldn't have done that."

"I was going to say that it's very thoughtful of you."

She stared up at him, uncertainty etched on her beautiful face. "Really?"

"Yes."

There was a small pecan pie in the box, its smell heightening his senses and making his stomach grumble.

"I know it's not your mum's recipe," she started, "but this is mine. Well, with a slight twist because Kam gave me her recipe for the cream, but yeah."

"That's adorable," he acknowledged with a smile. "Thank you."

He placed the box on the desk before grabbing her face. His lips skimmed hers, a shiver rolling down his spine when her fingers looped around his wrists.

"You're too good for me," he whispered.

"Don't say that," she whispered back.

"It's true."

She shook her head before kissing him softly. But Rowan didn't want delicate touches and lovers' caresses tonight—he wanted to release the tension corrupting his body.

Angling her head to kiss her deeply, he groaned when her hands fisted the front of his shirt. He walked them to the bed and pushed her onto the mattress, pinning her wrists above her head.

He didn't allow her to break the kiss until he heard her panting. Locking her legs around his hips, she pulled him into her, and the contact of his bulge on her centre made her writhe.

"Patience, baby," he rasped, smirking.

Slowly, he ground into her, his breaths as heavy and staggered as hers. His lips found the curve of her jaw, trailing kisses down the side of her neck. He nipped at her skin, his hands skimming her thighs.

"No hickeys," she ordered.

"Bummer," he said. "I really want to mark you as mine."

"I'm not yours," she argued, followed by a scoff of disbelief.

"Really? Is this why you're under me, ready to beg for my tongue or cock to fill you up?"

He pulled away to watch her reaction. As expected, her tanned skin flushed, allowing patches of red to colour her cheekbones. He loved the power he held over her.

"I hate you."

He grinned. "I know."

He watched her chest heave as they held gazes. Slowly, he trailed his perusal down her physique, his breath catching for a heartbeat. She wasn't wearing anything beneath her cotton top, showing peaked and hard nipples straining against the fabric. Dark hair spilled over the pillow. Avery looked good in his bed.

"God, Avery," he breathed out. "Your beauty is otherworldly. You're stunning."

He smirked when she blushed again, but a smile spread across her swollen lips.

"Do you say that to all your no-strings-attached hookups?"

"No. Just you. There's only you."

He kissed her again. Claimed her by roaming his hands all over her body. Stole each one of her breaths away.

Avery arched her back when he palmed her breasts over her clothes, fingers threading through his hair. He groaned because she felt heavenly in his hands. Perfect. Made for him.

He trailed his hands down and pushed her shirt up, but she grabbed his wrists, stopping him mid-movement.

"Can you leave my shirt on?" Her question was almost inaudible.

"Anything you want. Can I ask why?"

He left coaxing caresses on her hip, encouraging her to use her voice.

She lowered her stare elsewhere. "I'm a bit self-conscious about my body. I just—I'm not ready to show it to you yet."

Rowan's heart shattered. Avery was one of the most exquisite women he'd ever seen, to the point he'd always thought she was out of his league.

He kissed her softly. "I hope that one day you trust me enough to lay completely naked. But just so you know, I think you're perfect the way you are. I respect you, your body, your demands, but you don't have to hide from me. This is a safe space for both of us."

Avery pulled him in. "Thank you, Rowan. You have no idea how much this means to me."

After easing her again with kisses, he plunged his fingers inside her shorts. They skimmed over her lace panties, and she bucked her hips upwards.

"Are you already wet for me?"

She mumbled incoherent phrases against his mouth, causing him to chuckle. Pressing his fingers on her clit, she released a heavy sigh as she held onto the back of his neck. Rowan circled her clit whilst peppering kisses down her throat, her collarbones, and the swell of her cleavage. He found her taut nipple over her shirt, wrapping his mouth around it. Sucking on it, he looked up at Avery to find her already staring at him, lips agape and eyes dark with desire.

But just as he was about to slip his fingers inside her panties, her phone rang.

She sighed, digging into the pocket of her shorts to take the device out. She threw it on the bed, letting it ring as she got lost in a haze of pleasure when Rowan's fingers quickened their pace.

"Answer it," he demanded.

"Later."

"Answer it," he repeated. "Be a good girl and act like you're not busy with me."

She threw him a glare and grabbed her phone, then hit the green button. "Hey."

"Speaker," Rowan mouthed, tugging her shorts down her legs. "Now."

Avery rolled her eyes, and he slapped her covered clit. She yelped, throwing him a dangerous glare.

"No, no, I'm fine," she answered, breathless. "Just bumped my hip on the corner of the desk."

"Speaker," he whispered as he spread her legs open. He bit the interior of his cheek at the sight of the red lace contrasting with her dark skin.

When she finally hit the speaker button, Eliott's voice filled the stillness in the room. Rowan was drowning in jealousy and possessiveness, but he reminded himself it was him who was between her legs at that exact moment. He caressed her shins, her knees, and her thighs, holding her gaze as he pressed his thumb on her clit.

"Are you still joining me?" Eliott asked.

Rowan stilled and narrowed his eyes. Avery raised a defiant brow.

"Oh, uh..." She bucked her hips, eyes nearly rolling when he applied more pressure. "Rain check? I'm not feeling very well."

"Really? Do you want me to bring something to your room?"

"N-no." Rowan started kissing the inside of her thighs, inching dangerously close to her core. "I think I just need to go to bed. It's been a long day."

"That's fine." Disappointment was laced to his tone regardless, and Rowan couldn't help but snicker in triumph. "We can do that another time."

"For sure," she quipped.

"Are you sure you're okay?"

Rowan latched his mouth around her nipple, dampening her top. He was now drawing circles on her clit with two fingers, fast and hard, ready to make her come.

"Totally fine. I need to go. Bye, Eliott."

"Good night, Av—"

His sentence wasn't even finished when she ended the call and threw her phone somewhere on the bed. Rowan rose to face her lips, jaw tightened.

He dipped his fingers lower, pushing into her entrance, her panties still creating a barrier between them. "What was all that about?"

Avery gripped his forearms, nails digging into his skin. "Oh, fuck."

"Answer me," he said, slowing his pace down. "Why the fuck does Eliott call you late at night?"

She huffed. "He wanted to have a drink with me."

"Like a date?"

"No. Like two colleagues catching up."

"Sounds like a date to me."

"Are you jealous?"

Rowan scoffed. "No, because you're here with me."

"Exactly."

He retrieved his hand, causing her to whine. "You know what? Since you're such a brat, I'm not making you come."

"Why?"

He stood up, taking his shirt off. Her eyes sauntered over his chest, and there was something about her gaze that made him feel seen and beautiful. Other women looking at him boosted his ego, confirmed he was an attractive man, but everything was different when it came to Avery.

"Because you left me with a raging hard-on at the pool on

Sunday, and now you make plans with other men when I ask you to meet me. Come here and get down on your knees."

She obliged in a heartbeat.

"Good girl." He bunched her dark hair around his fist, smirking when she watched the sheer size of him throb inside his joggers. "You're going to suck my cock now."

She nodded, lustful eyes holding his stare as she hooked her fingers in the waistband of his trousers, tugging the fabric down. He wasn't wearing briefs underneath, causing her eyes to widen when his shaft sprang free.

"Jesus, Rowan," she exhaled. "Not only is your ego enormous but you have a massive dick, too."

Throwing his head back, he laughed. "You're the one who doesn't have a filter whatsoever."

A vicious smile played on the corner of her lips as she caressed his tattooed thighs. She swallowed, wrapping a hand around the base of his erection. Rowan emitted a groan when he realised she wasn't able to fully hook her fingers around it.

Slowly, she stroked from base to head, causing Rowan to whimper.

"Rowan," she called, dragging his attention back to her. She looked so pure. So innocent. God, he would destroy her. "I've never done this."

He stilled, frowning. "Wait. Are you a virgin?"

Avery shook her head. "No, I just don't have much experience. All my past hookups were bad. Like, really bad. Can you—will you teach me?"

He brushed her bangs away from her eyes. "That's okay, baby. I'm going to guide you. But if it ever gets too much, you stop, okay? You're in complete control with me. You always will be."

She nodded, her grip tightening just enough to make his abdomen clench.

"Understood?" he asked, demanding for her to use her words.

"Understood."

"Good." He gathered her hair in both hands, looking down at her. Just the sight of her on her knees, breasts nearly spilling out of her top, wide eyes teasing him could make him come. He'd already come so many times whilst replaying their secret moment in her office in London. "When you're ready, wrap your lips around the head. Be careful with your teeth."

The moment her full lips came in contact with the leaking tip, he whimpered loudly. She gathered a drop of precum on her tongue before wrapping her mouth around the head of his cock, slowly taking in as much as she could.

Rowan breathed heavily, head tipping backwards when she started bobbing her head, her tongue sliding across the underside of his shaft.

"Use your hands to touch me where you can't reach. Breathe through your nose and relax your jaw."

He felt her hand wrap around the base, pumping in tandem with the languid strokes of her tongue.

He looked down, colliding with her gaze that had been watching his expression carefully. Her tongue flickered over the slit, making his legs tremble. He moaned, his fingers tightening around the makeshift ponytail he was holding onto.

"Fuck, just like that. Look at you, you're doing so good."

She used her free hand to massage his balls, and Rowan blinked away the stars threatening to blind his vision. She was breathless, a string of saliva mixed with his precum descending her chin as she took him deeper. The tip hit the back of her throat, and she pulled away to take a breath.

"You're perfect," he praised as she pumped his length with both hands before going back to sucking on the head. "Can I fuck your mouth, baby?"

She nodded in approval, and he bucked his hips into her mouth. She applied hard pressure with her hands around the base whilst sucking on what she could take, her tongue sliding over the slit, the crown, the length.

Rowan had always been a vocal man, but something about this woman made him unleash a side of himself he hadn't seen until now. He was panting, whimpering, moaning, cursing, and sweating, all the while guiding her head as he fucked her mouth with abandon. She gagged when he hit the back of her throat, but he watched how she pressed her thighs together, searching for friction.

"Does sucking my cock make you wet, Avery?"

She looked up at him with teary eyes and nodded.

Rowan had to think about the F1 World Champions of the past decade to keep himself from coming. About the expensive watch he had recently purchased and its complex mechanism.

"Touch yourself," he commanded in a low voice.

Surprise alighted her eyes for a heartbeat, but then she continued to pump his shaft with a hand, the other snaking in between her legs.

"Pull your panties to the side. Put a finger in your sweet cunt and show me just how soaked you are when I'm fucking your bratty mouth."

He slowed his pace to watch her tug her underwear to the side. She spread her legs just enough to pleasure herself, her middle finger thrusting inside her core. She moaned, the vibration around his erection causing chills to spread across his entire body. He watched as she circled her clit, rolling her hips on her hand before lifting her fingers to show Rowan the mess she'd made.

He grabbed her hand, hunched over, and wrapped his mouth around her fingers to suck her arousal.

"So sweet," he hummed. "I've been dreaming of eating you out every single day."

As Avery continued to suck him off as best as she could, he guided her head and continued to fuck her mouth recklessly as she started circling her clit.

Rowan was close to unravelling, but he refused to come before she did.

"Do you touch yourself often, baby?" His gaze was strained on her hard nipples.

He couldn't wait to see her entirely bare. Naked just for him. He simply knew she was a goddess waiting to be worshipped by the right man. And he would be that man who would praise and applaud every single inch of her.

She nodded, humming.

He smirked, but the imagery made his stomach clench. "That's so hot."

Her nails grazed the underside of his erection, and he felt himself twitch inside her mouth.

"Fuck," he breathed. "You're taking my cock so well. I can't even imagine how well you'll be taking it when I fuck you properly."

Her fingers' rhythm fastened over her clit. She was writhing, moaning every time the tip of his cock hit the back of her throat. Every time she was getting closer and closer to attaining the pinnacle of pleasure.

"You close?" Rowan asked, panting.

Avery nodded, and he pulled out when he noticed she was picking up her pace. He took over, fisting his cock, pumping rapidly to match her rhythm.

"Can I come over your tits?"

"Yes," she answered, breathless.

"I'm going to fuck those one day. And you. I'm going to fuck you until you understand that no one will treat you as well as I do."

Those words seemed to make her fall apart. A loud moan escaped her mouth as she unravelled, shaking as her fingers stilled. She rolled her hips, head tipped back as her brows drew together.

The sight of Avery finding pleasure and coming before him made his cock twitch. The next second, he was spilling all over her chest, a moan rising from the back of his throat.

"Fuck," he whispered, continuously stroking until every drop of his release stained her skin and shirt.

Avery was always unexpected and surprising. Taking his cock in her mouth, she sucked on the sensitive tip, swallowing the last few drops of cum. Rowan swore he had never seen stars so bright and blinding before.

"Holy fuck, woman. Are you sure it was your first time giving head?" he asked incredulously, tugging his joggers up.

She nodded, cheeks flushed and lips swollen, wiping the trail of saliva and release off her chin. Rowan grabbed a washcloth from the bathroom and kneeled in front of her to wipe her chest. He leaned in to peck her mouth, but he melted into the softness of her lips and the tenderness of her kiss, lingering in the moment and not pulling away.

"I read a lot," she stated when they parted ways.

He raised his brows. "What kind of books do you read?"

She shrugged sheepishly, and he chuckled. "Instructive novels."

"Instructive," he repeated, followed by a hum. "Any chance I could read them soon?"

"Why?"

"I could learn a thing or two." He winked, then brushed the apple of her cheek where a blush had bloomed. "Well, thank you. Best head I've ever gotten."

She frowned slightly. "You don't have to lie to me."

"I'm not lying," he said, cupping her jaw. "It was really good. So good I nearly collapsed."

"Oh." A small smile tugged at her lips. "Good."

He pecked her lips again. "I'm going to have so much fun teaching you stuff."

She simply nodded, suddenly timid.

Rowan reached for the shirt he had thrown on the floor and handed it to her. "Go clean up. We'll eat your pecan pie afterwards."

"I should—I should probably leave, though."

"Do you *want* to go?"

She blinked, chocolate eyes flicking between his. "I don't want to be a burden. I know we said just sex and no-strings attached, so I don't expect anything afterwards."

His chest tightened, the sensation almost painful. He tucked a strand of hair behind her ear, not allowing her to see the dismay her comment had caused. "What's the harm in wanting to hang out with you? As far as I know, there's no written rule about the way I should handle my situationship."

She wasn't just someone he fucked and left behind. She was no ordinary friend with benefits.

Her brows pinched together. "You want to hang out with me?"

"I told you I'd be your friend, didn't I? Besides, we barely talk outside of work, and—" He stopped himself as he felt his cheeks heat up. "I really want to spend more time with you."

"Okay," she whispered. "Good."

As she stood up to go to the bathroom, he slapped her bare bottom, causing a giggle to fly past her lips. The sound of her laughter made his chest swell, made something uncanny bloom in the pit of his stomach.

Rowan felt as though he was already too well-tangled in this situation, but he wasn't sure he wanted to disentangle himself from her.

As he watched his reflection in the mirror, observing his glinting eyes and rosy cheeks, he wondered how in the hell he would be able to keep this situation casual when he was already tethered to Avery as though she was his anchor.

CHAPTER TWENTY

MIAMI, UNITED STATES OF AMERICA

"ANOTHER DOUBLE PODIUM for Primavera Racing this season," Franklin Harlow, the Head Presenter of F1, exclaimed enthusiastically. "How are you guys feeling about this weekend?"

"Well, it was a tricky race," Thiago started as he sat to Rowan's left, whilst Miles—as per usual, the winner of the Grand Prix—was to his right. They were in a room filled with sports journalists and all three drivers had been answering questions about the race. "It's not easy to seek slipstream here and overtaking can be tricky. But we had a good strategy, and everything went smoothly."

"What was the cause of this great result?"

Rowan draped an arm over the back of the sofa they were sitting on, pointing a finger at himself. "You're looking at him."

Soft chuckles resonated around.

"You're so cocky," Miles noted amusedly.

"Hey, bud, if no one can love you, you've got to love yourself," Rowan joked, though he wanted to look at a particular person standing in the back of the room. He lowered his gaze, forcing himself not to meet chocolate eyes. He didn't even know why his thoughts had drifted towards her, as though he couldn't control that heavy gravity between him and Avery.

For the entirety of the interview, he made sure not to be obvious and kept his gaze either on his shoes or on Franklin, but he felt like he would combust.

He had finished the race P3; and to him, that was an amazing result.

So far, the season was great—reactive car, powerful engine, overall great strategies.

But his phone had been vibrating in the pocket of his jeans for the past hour. Rowan knew who was busy blowing up his notifications. He wasn't sure he wanted to face his father's wrath. All he wanted was to bask in chocolate moons that procured him an unsolicited solace and get lost in her whispered sighs and her dreamy body.

He simply couldn't handle any more pressure today.

"True," Miles agreed, his voice keeping Rowan away from his daydream.

"The next Grand Prix is Monaco's," Franklin said then. "Are you looking forward to it?"

❧

ROWAN WAS PACING back and forth in his driver's room, trying to calm his uneven breaths and regain composure over his racing thoughts. He passed his fingers through his hair, inhaling. Exhaling. Repeating. But nothing seemed to be working. Nothing he tried could erase the harsh words his father had told him over the phone.

It wasn't the first time he had been belittled and torn apart by Stephen, but Rowan wasn't exactly sure why he still let those words affect him so much.

He heard the door to his room open, but he didn't turn around.

"Rowan?"

He wasn't certain if his name had been called out, or if he had imagined it.

An ache inside his chest had bloomed, and he rubbed at the painful spot to make it go away.

"Hey, what's wrong?"

Her voice was distant, but he could recognise that honeyed tone anywhere. He just couldn't pull himself to the surface to breathe properly.

Gentle hands touched his upper arms, startling him. He blinked, and there she was. Standing in front of him, wide eyes brimmed with concern stared up at him, studying his features that were stricken with panic.

"Breathe," Avery demanded. "With me. Inhale. Exhale."

He followed her instructions, steady breaths soon replacing the ragged ones that had once reverberated off the walls of this very room. The buzzing in his ears disappeared slowly, his vision clearing up in tandem.

"Good job," she praised in a whisper. "Again."

He felt her hands on his trembling arms, smelled her sweet fragrance enveloping his senses, listened to her voice guiding him.

"I'm sorry," he croaked out, rubbing his face. His pulse was still thrumming erratically, his head spinning like it refused to rest.

"Don't apologise. What happened?"

She stepped back, and Rowan instantly craved her touch. Its soothing power. Its delicacy. But he simply watched her turn around, bending over to grab his phone from the floor.

"What did this poor phone do to you?" She studied the shattered screen, grimacing before handing him the device.

Rowan threw the phone on the sofa and took a seat. "More like what did the person calling say to me?"

"Daddy issues?"

"Yeah," he scoffed. "Nothing new."

Taking a seat next to him, she bumped her shoulder into his. He smiled softly, returning her teasing gesture. "Do you want to talk about it?"

Rowan shook his head. "Nothing for you to worry about. Just same old Stephen messing with my head and telling me to go to hell."

He had always struggled with being satisfied with his performance, but he had learned to see the positive side in every situation. He craved to be able to cope with the pressure, though. To be able to overcome the fear of disappointing a man who had walked out of his life decades ago.

"Rowan," she murmured sorrowfully. He obliged to look into her eyes, and something bizarre happened inside his chest: his heart fissured at the same time as it mended itself back. "You're a good man. You know you're enough. You know you're an amazing driver. Don't let him ruin your mood and energy."

"Thank you, sunflower." He wanted to embrace her. Wanted to feel her. But all he did was throw a sad smile her way. "I thought you left the circuit. What are you doing here?"

"I left my recorder here. I can't forget to send a report to Nikki."

He frowned. "Are you going to work tonight?"

"Probably. I'd rather be done with it sooner than later."

He shifted to face her, tucking a strand of hair behind an ear. Her lashes fluttered, as though she was getting lost in his electric touch, too. "Come to the club with me. We can sneak and fool around."

"You know I can't," she replied softly.

"Come on," he huffed. "We're in Miami. You need to come. We can bang in the bathroom or something."

She rolled her eyes. "You just want to get some."

"Always with you." He winked as she gave him a dirty look.

"Celebrate your podium and this amazing weekend the way

it deserves to be celebrated. Be the Rowan everyone adores. But you can be yourself when you're with me. I hope you know that."

"Yeah, I do." He cupped her jaw, skimming her lower lip with the pad of his thumb. "Be there. Please."

He didn't give a shit if he sounded desperate.

Rowan didn't know why he wanted to spend every minute of every day with her. To talk about everything. To laugh. To bicker. He simply couldn't fathom this urge to be around Avery all the time.

A line drew itself between her brows. Still, she didn't make a move to get away from him. "You're not being careful."

Damn her and her rational logic. "Does it look like I care?"

Silence fell, honey staring deeply into chocolate. It felt as though she was sharing a secret with him, and he was giving one of his own.

She frowned, leaning into his touch. "What are we doing?"

Rowan's mind was still hazy, but all he knew was that she had managed to coax him through that storm of wild emotions. His body didn't hurt anymore. On the contrary, it was now thrumming with anticipation, as if her existence had brought him back to life. He'd never felt like this before.

"I don't know."

Not a single soul could know about them, or else Avery and Rowan would lose everything. But part of himself wanted someone to know about his hands in her hair, her clothes in his room.

Rowan was downright confused about the way he felt.

"Can we meet tonight?"

A soft smile tugged her lips upwards. "You really do want to see me today, don't you?"

His response was a mere nod.

"Rowan," she started, delicately brushing a rebellious lock away from his forehead. "I—"

She got interrupted by the door opening. Scrambling away,

he sat on the other side of the sofa whilst she stood up, glancing at the walls filled with Polaroid pictures.

"Okay, I need to ask you something, bro." Tate's voice resonated, followed by eager claps in his hands. "Ah, Ave, we need to talk books! You coming to the club? I'm happy to share my thoughts about—"

"She's not coming," Rowan interrupted gruffly. "What did you want to ask?"

Tate looked at him and smirked. "Who are you shagging?"

Rowan's breath caught as he blinked slowly. "Sorry?"

"I heard you the other night. Our rooms are right next door."

Ah, shit. Shit. Shiiit.

Rowan rubbed the back of his neck. "Just this girl."

Avery slipped away, winking at him.

Tate gaped at the woman set on running away. "Ava, do you know about this?"

She shook her head vigorously. "His sex life doesn't concern me. Who would even want to sleep with him?"

"I bet you dream of it every night," Rowan bit out. What a brat.

"Do I dream of wiping that shit-eating grin off your face? Yes." She blew him a kiss, followed by a faux smile which caused Tate to snicker. "Have a lovely evening."

He scoffed. "Not returning the kindness."

"How surprising," she mused.

Perhaps their incessant bickering could cover them just enough.

"Your girl sounded hot," Tate muttered, and Rowan saw a flame of rage blind his vision.

"She was," he said, tone clipped.

"Nice," his friend cheered. Avery had walked out of the room, but Rowan hadn't missed her reddened cheeks and timid smile. "Hold on... Did you break your phone again?"

CHAPTER TWENTY-ONE

MIAMI, UNITED STATES OF AMERICA

"IS OAT MILK okay for you?"

"Pardon?" Ava chuckled as she came out of Rowan's bathroom.

She had changed into his shirt after cleaning up and tying her hair into a messy bun. His musky cologne was slowly becoming her favourite scent, and she couldn't deny she had taken a whiff of the piece of clothing after shrugging it on.

Earlier tonight, she hadn't managed to fall asleep, so she watched One Tree Hill on her iPad whilst Rowan was clubbing. But when he came back at one a.m., he had texted her to see if she wanted to hang out.

He had kissed her until she was weak in the knees the instant she entered his room. Had ended up kneeling before her, head between her thighs and tongue on her clit, one of her legs hooked on his shoulder as she leaned against the wall for support. She had barely taken her shorts off, only leaving her in a tank top.

Though she was comfortable with everything they were doing, Ava wasn't ready to show her whole body to Rowan. She was still terribly insecure, lacking self-confidence even if she felt beautiful under his scrutiny.

She was grateful for him because he'd never pressured her into undressing—in comparison to boys she had slept with before. He'd never rushed her for anything. Actually, it seemed like he wanted to take his time to explore her likes and dislikes.

After he had made her come for the first time, he had asked if she wanted to try something new. Ava had then sat on his face whilst sucking on his thick shaft, and she had swallowed every drop of his release.

"Oat milk," Rowan said when she marched further into his room. "With your cereal."

He lifted two bowls, grinning coyly. His dark hair was ruffled, the tops of his cheekbones slightly rosy. Basketball shorts were hanging on his hips, all his tattoos on display just for her.

"That's fine." She smiled and sat on the floor across from him. "Is this going to be a ritual for us? Eating after hooking up?"

He handed her a bowl and a spoon. "It can be."

She chuckled at the sight of Cocoa Puffs filling her bowl, shaking her head in bafflement. She took a spoonful, humming in delight when the sweetness collided with her palate. When she looked up, she found Rowan staring at her, a soft smile tugging his lips upwards.

"What?" she asked, hand shielding her mouth.

He shook his head, lowering his gaze. "Nothing."

"You're not looking at me like it's nothing."

"No, really," he said. "It's silly."

"Come on," she said, nudging his knee with hers. "A secret for a secret."

Delicately, he collected a drop of milk on the corner of her mouth, smiling tenderly when her face flushed with thorough embarrassment. He winked to put her at ease, and she rolled her eyes, feigning annoyance.

"You look so cute in my clothes," he murmured.

"Wow," she droned mockingly. "Look at you complimenting me."

"This is usually the moment you thank me."

"I was getting there." She pushed her glasses up her nose. "Thank you."

Was hanging out with him and wearing his clothes after hooking up too intimate? Certainly, but some parts of her didn't mind that domesticity.

"What's your secret?" he asked after swallowing.

Ava looked down at her cereal, shaking her head at the first thought that invaded her mind.

"You have to tell me," he pressed gently.

"You're going to think I'm stupid and immature."

He shrugged. "Your words, not mine." She glared at him, and he laughed. "Sorry. Sorry. I promise I won't laugh at you."

She breathed heavily, looking out the window. "I'm a bit terrified, Rowan."

"Of what?"

"Of this." She found his gaze, her chest tightening at the sight of stars shimmering along his pupils. "Of us. I'm scared you're going to hurt me."

She was growing some kind of affection for him. As his press officer, she was protective and wanted what was best for him. But as his...friend, she was starting to get attached. And her first mistake had been letting her walls down too easily and quickly.

He frowned and settled his bowl down to the side. He did the same with hers before pulling her onto his lap. "You know, I'm terrified, too."

"You are?"

"Yeah." He breathed out, looping his arms around her waist and burying his face in the crook of her neck. She relaxed in his embrace, returning the hug, aligning the drum of their heartbeats so they could thump in harmony. "You make me feel some type of way, and it's scary. But I'm never going to hurt you. Ever. I'm not going to be the guy who treats you like you're not the sunbeam that you are. I'm not the guy who's going to make you believe you're a burden in any kind of way. I'm going to be the one who gives you the entire world if you ask for it. And I'm not going to let you push me away just because I'm getting close to you."

"Why?"

"Because I think you're worth fighting for. As a friend. As my publicist who goes through thick and thin to keep my reputation clean. And as the woman who, for some weird reason, sees me for someone else other than the cocky driver."

To her, Rowan had always been more than an arrogant and smug driver. He'd always been secretive in a way, urging her to know everything about him. And now that he was allowing her to see more of his true nature, she wasn't certain she wanted to imagine a life where Rowan wasn't part of hers.

"Your cockiness is sometimes a bit overbearing," she taunted.

"You love me the way I am."

"You wish." She held her breath then, tightening her hold over him. "Doesn't seem super casual to me."

Rowan didn't say anything for a few heartbeats as he sighed. Then, came his honesty: "I don't care. Is it bothering you?"

"No," she said earnestly. "I just don't want either of us to be confused."

"I'm not. I think we're on the same wavelength."

"So do I."

"This is nice," he mumbled. She noticed how his embrace had tightened as well.

She smiled, loving this soft side of his. With her, Rowan Emerson wasn't the handsome, fearless, tattooed driver. He was just a human being, seeking affection, and not realising he was fully adored. "It is."

"Come." He stood to his feet, dragging her with him before walking them over to the large window.

Music was playing softly in the background. He lifted their hands above her head to make her spin around, catching her and making her dip.

She laughed. "You dance?"

"Only with you," he answered with a broad smile.

The moonlight was spilling on them, and she was enthralled by his effortless beauty. The silvery glow cast an almost invisible halo above his head—a simple proof from the universe that Rowan was an angel despite the fact he was convinced he wasn't a good man.

He made her spin again. "You love romance and cliché gestures."

"How do you know?"

"I've seen the books you read. Is your dream coming true by dancing to *Kiss Me* by Sixpence None The Richer?"

She retained her smile from growing as she made him pivot, a heartfelt laugh erupting from his throat. "It would be even better under the pouring rain."

Rowan scoffed. "Of course. Do you also dream of an angry love confession under the rain?"

"Every girl does," she said promptly.

"I see."

"You're not that much of a romantic, are you?"

"How can I be when romance wasn't something that existed in the house I grew up in?" Rowan lifted his shoulders in a small shrug. "I don't know a single thing about love."

Ava wanted to tell him that even if he didn't believe in love, he was doing a great job at opening up. At slowly accepting that he was deserving of love, too. She was secretly hoping to mend the shattered fragments of his heart so that he could feel how appreciated he was.

They danced under the moonlight filtering through the

window, sharing secrets and quiet laughter, engulfed in their own cosmos.

There was something so innately beautiful about this man—this man who'd deemed himself unworthy of every good thing life had to offer.

Basking in the silvery splatter of the moonlight's glow, Ava forgot about the song playing in the background as she allowed his fingers to tighten around hers. She scanned his sharp profile and its enticing features, listening to the vibration in his throat as he hummed to the music. Rowan made her spin around again, caught her, and placed a delicate caress on her hipbone which nearly made her tremble.

The corner of his lips twitched upwards. Like he knew exactly what she was thinking and why she'd become immobile all of a sudden.

"I know I'm pretty to look at." The baritone of Rowan's voice sent a chill rolling down her spine. "Should I pose for you? I bet I look handsome under the moonlight. You could use the photo as your new lockscreen."

She scoffed. Such a conceited prick. "No, thanks."

After five songs, Rowan winced slightly.

"Are you okay?" Ava asked, concerned.

He let go of her hands to rub his shoulder. "Just a bit sore from today's race."

Ava should have told him to get some rest. Should have wished him a good night of sleep then. Instead, she found herself saying, "Come lie down. I'll give you a massage."

"Aren't you a sweetheart?" he mocked, yet he went to the bed, lying on his stomach with his arms folded under his cheek.

Straddling his backside, she started to rub his tense shoulders, causing him to sigh in relief. His skin was smooth, but the muscles beneath were firm, taut—a body honed by years and years of intense physical exercise.

He moaned, his features morphing into pleasure. "Oh, *fuuuuck*, yeah."

Ava chuckled. "Didn't you stretch with Tate after the race?"

"I did, but that dude has aggressive hands. Yours are gentle and soft and delicate." He peered at her, wiggling his brows. "Do you want to become my physiotherapist? We'll have so much fun, and you'll get to touch some parts Tate can't come close to."

Ava pinched his bum, causing him to squirm and laugh. "You're insufferable. I'm very happy being your PR officer."

"Ha! So you're *finally* admitting you're having the time of your life working with me."

"That's not what I said." She rubbed a particular knot that made him sigh in relief again. "Feels good?"

"Yeah," he breathed. "Don't stop."

He was humming to Chris Stapleton's *Tennessee Whiskey*, eyes closed, a soft smile plastered on his lips. Ava was starting to get lost in him, observing that serene expression etched on his face, her hands running over his bronze skin like she couldn't get enough of him.

She rubbed a tense spot between his shoulder blades where a small dragon tattoo was inked. She traced its contours, watching with awe the details and complexity of the drawing.

"A dragon?"

"Yeah," Rowan answered. "I loved *Eragon* as a kid. And Mum always referred to me as a dragon."

"Why?"

"She's always said I'm very protective of what I love and what's mine. She also says that I can easily burn my surroundings when I'm angry."

She hummed. "I think it's the creature that represents you best."

"You do?"

She smiled, running her finger down his spine, feeling chills rise beneath her touch. "Because you're confident, charismatic. But you're also naturally gifted with that talent for racing. And you do everything with the intention of doing your best."

She felt Rowan's torso rise and fall beneath her hands. The steady thump of his heartbeat.

She changed subject to forget about the tingles burning her cheeks. "Tate came by to borrow another book before you left for the club."

Rowan's lips twitched. "I love that you're bonding over books."

"Did you tell him about us?"

"No, but he's most definitely heard us tonight. Again."

Ava's face flushed further. "I'm embarrassed."

A chuckle rumbled inside his throat. "Don't be. I trust him with my life, but I won't tell him anything unless you're okay with it."

"He's your best friend. What is he going to say if he ever finds out?"

Rowan frowned slightly before opening his eyes. Then, he rolled over, keeping Ava sat on his lap. He braced a hand behind his head, causing her to look at his bulging bicep.

"He's going to call me stupid, but he's going to be happy for me. I haven't been seeing anyone for the past year and a half or so, so I think he's going to be happy to know I've finally broken my rules."

"How come you haven't been hooking up or seeing anyone?"

He shrugged, his free hand coming to rest on her thigh, caressing her warm skin. "I don't know. One-night stands and girls wanting me just for fame and money became boring. Sure, getting off is fun, but I think I've reached a point in my life where I think that, maybe, I deserve something more."

"You *do* deserve more," she whispered, running her hands over his hard abdomen until they rested on his chest. She heard Rowan inhale sharply, the rhythm of his heartbeat unsteady and wild beneath her palms. "I hope you find your special someone soon."

Their gazes locked, and time stood still. "I hope so, too."

With the tip of her forefinger, Ava started tracing the butterfly tattoo on his bicep—a featherlight caress as though she was drawing over those intriguing designs. She observed goosebumps appear in the wake of her touch, Rowan's breath catching when she continued to draw over the rest of the ink adorning his body.

He was magnificent. She wondered if he was aware of it. Wondered if he knew she'd worship him—body and soul—the way he'd been doing with her.

"Thank you," he whispered.

"For what?"

"For not trying to fix me like I'm some lost cause, but for seeing me. For being patient, supportive, and caring. I truly don't deserve you."

Ava had to blink multiple times. She wasn't sure if it was fatigue or his earnest confession that made her eyes burn.

She didn't trust her voice at that exact moment.

She couldn't feel something more than lust for Rowan.

She just couldn't cross that line.

"You don't have to thank me."

He applied pressure on her thigh—another silent act of gratitude. "Can I ask you something? You don't have to answer if you're not comfortable."

Ava had found herself enjoying opening up to Rowan. It was so easy to talk to him. "Anything."

"How come you struggle with self-confidence?" He frowned, as if doubtful about the way his question had been voiced. Ava supposed he was referring to more intimate moments, when they were in the bedroom alone. Because he'd seen her wear more revealing clothes than others—at the pub a few weeks ago, at the pool a few nights ago.

She ignored the burning feeling in the back of her throat. "I care too much about what people think. I try not to let it get to my head, I try to wear clothes that make me feel sexy and pretty, but when I'm with you… I fear you won't like me for who I am. I'm terrified that you'll compare me to—"

"Avery," he breathed out. His thumb grazed her skin lightly. "When I'm with you, all I think about is *you.* I think you're insanely sexy, and I'm sorry that I made you feel this way. What can I do to make you understand you're the only woman I have eyes for?"

"It's not because of you. I think… I think it's a fear I need to overcome on my own. I compare myself to others too often. I undermine myself too easily. But I'm learning to become a better version of myself. I'm getting there."

Colour bloomed on Rowan's cheeks. "Your way of thinking is just as sexy as your body. You're smart. Fierce. You're beautiful, Avery. Don't let anyone make you feel less than that."

As she blushed furiously, she debated hiding behind her hands, but all she did was nod, giving her gratitude with a timid smile. "What do these numbers represent?" she asked then, pointing to a date in the crook of his elbow.

He slipped his fingers under the hem of her shirt. There was nothing sexual about that act, but something bizarrely and innately intimate as he touched her hip.

"The year Mum was born." It was evident that, despite everything he went through as a child, his mother was his entire world and beyond.

"And this one?" She traced a flower on his rib—one that had caught her attention months ago.

"It's a Chrysanthemum. Nora's birth flower."

Rowan loved his family so strongly. It was odd how a man who adored his loved ones so deeply had concluded he could never be loved in return.

Ava smiled down at him. His features softened even more, sleepy eyes staring back at her. "Is she a November baby?"

"Yes. You too?"

She nodded in response.

She'd point to a few patterns, and he explained each of their meanings. He showed her a smiley on his thigh—one Tate had tattooed on him when they were eighteen—and she laughed. Not once did he retreat his hand from her hip, as if he needed that physical contact to feel alive.

And when she finally grazed the spot on his pectoral, he stilled.

"There's a blank space here," she noted. "Right above your heart."

She watched Rowan's throat work as he swallowed. "I'm saving this spot for the most special thing to have entered my life."

"Whatever it is, it'll be a privilege to be placed over Rowan Emerson's black heart."

"You're a brat."

"And you're an absolute prick," she fired back.

He looped his arms around her waist and flipped her on the mattress before pulling the covers over both of them.

Ava's body went rigid the moment he wrapped his arms around her body, pulling her as close as he could. "What are you doing?"

"I'm exhausted. Going to sleep."

"Okay," she breathed out, somehow affected by his nonchalance. She tried to pull away, but he didn't let her. Wouldn't loosen his hold. "I'll go."

His breath fanned across her temple. Being here with him felt incredibly good—wrapped in a cosmos of unfathomable serenity where reality couldn't break them apart. "I want you to stay."

"Rowan," she warned in a whisper.

"I'm so used to people leaving me," he mumbled, causing her heart to crack and leave all the shattered fragments to turn into dust inside her chest. "Don't be someone who lets me go, too."

"Why do you have to make things so complicated?" She sighed, burying her face in the crook of his neck. It was difficult to understand how fitting they were. How safe she felt in his arms.

"Please. It's late. I don't want you to walk back to your room alone."

"Is this your way of saying you care about me?"

His voice was quiet, tired. His hold tightened even more. "You know I do. I care about you so fucking much, Avery. I shouldn't, but I can't help it."

Before she could say anything, his breaths became heavier, steadier, and she understood he had fallen asleep.

She sighed, tempted to linger in the moment. She wanted to bask in his warmth, wanted to fall into a deep slumber whilst hanging onto him.

But she couldn't. It was too risky. His room was on the same floor as most of his mechanics, Thiago, and his team principal.

She waited a few minutes, ensuring he was sound asleep. And when he started snoring softly, she carefully got out of his embrace.

He didn't wake up, only shifting to make himself more comfortable.

"I'm not abandoning you; I promise. I'm just trying to protect you because I would never forgive myself if they took away the only thing you love." Ava kissed the crown of his head. "Good night, lover boy."

CHAPTER TWENTY-TWO

MONTE CARLO, MONACO

"I'M GOING TO kill her."

"Will you stop?" Tate groaned, his gaze fixated on his phone.

"We're going to be late."

"So? You've never made a fuss about arriving two minutes late to an event before."

Rowan wasn't certain what had caused his nerves to spark. Perhaps it was the fact that he was going to attend an important event with Richard Mille—Primavera Racing's biggest sponsor. But Rowan wasn't one to be afraid of too many cameras aimed towards him. So maybe he was nervous because he hadn't seen Avery in over a week.

They had promised each other to keep things casual, but why was Rowan craving her like oxygen? Like an addiction he couldn't live without?

As his PR officer, she was obligated to attend the event—not as his date, though he wished he could've asked her to accompany him.

He was waiting for her inside the lobby of his building. He had recently bought a flat here, and his plans for the upcoming years were to spend more time in Monaco instead of his house in London. From here, he, his date, Indigo Bailey (whom he had no interest in apart from helping her find a place in the motorsports world), Tate, and Avery would go to the venue together.

"I bet you're going to leave the party early," Tate said to Indy who was busy fixing her blonde hair in the mirror.

"Me?" she asked, outraged. "Please."

"You never stay during these kinds of events," Rowan accused. "And you don't try to be discreet when you leave."

"True." Indy shrugged sheepishly.

"How's your new job coming along?" Tate inquired curiously.

Rowan glared at his two friends. "Are we seriously making small talk?" He wasn't usually like this. He was just too nervous to think of joyful things.

"Grumpy," Indy muttered. "No one's forcing you to participate. But to answer your question, Tate, I'm miserable. I'm dying to host and present more on TV, but that'll happen when my internship is done."

Indy was a journalism intern at Thunderbolt Sports, a global motorsports channel. Everyone knew her dream was to become an F1 presenter. Already hosting a motorsports podcast, she was a force to be reckoned with—she was intent on proving women belonged in this universe, too. Rowan knew she had worked hard to attain her goals, and her persistence would get her on top of the world. He wouldn't tell her, though. If he was the epitome of arrogance, Indigo was his female equal.

"Look at you go," he said. "I can't wait to be interviewed by you in the paddock."

Indy eyed him amusedly, catching on to his sarcasm. "I know

you're thrilled. Anyway, Tito's throwing a party on his yacht tonight. You guys coming?"

Tate answered, but Rowan didn't hear the response because Avery entered the lobby.

"Sorry, I'm late." Breathless as though she had run to arrive, her gaze was on her shoulder as she tried to adjust the strap of her satin dress. Dark locks framed her angelic face, a smattering of rose colouring her cheekbones.

Rowan felt his breath catch somewhere in his lungs and disappear. His lips parted, but no sound escaped as though she had managed to render him speechless.

Their gazes clashed, and the world came to a full stop. Rowan's entire entourage crashed down to dust, her mere presence nearly sending him into an endless precipice of ruination.

She blinked, admiration slowly drawing upon her face. As she tucked a strand of hair behind an ear, she let her stare fall to his tailor-made suit, a beautiful smile touching her red lips.

Rowan grunted in annoyance when Tate hit the back of his head.

"Ow," Rowan whined. "Fuck off."

"You, fuck off," Tate argued in a whisper. "You're drooling by the way."

Rowan punched his friend's arm as he turned around to fix his suit and touch the corner of his lips. Obviously, he hadn't drooled.

Tate Richards was so fucking stupid. But maybe Rowan was a bigger fool.

"Rowan was about to have a stroke," Indy announced, chuckling as Avery approached. The sound of her footfalls matched the rhythm of his heartbeat—rapid, hurried. "He kept checking the time every ten seconds."

"Drama queen," he heard Avery mutter.

He rubbed the back of his neck and finally faced the woman who had been invading his thoughts.

"You look beautiful," Indy praised her friend.

She did.

"Thank you," Avery chimed in sweetly. "This dress looks fabulous on you. Bet you're going to change into something more comfortable and fitting for a party later, though."

"Wow." Indy reared back and furrowed her brows. "Is my reputation that bad?"

"Yes," all three responded.

Avery and Rowan collided gazes again.

"You look..." There was no adequate word in the English language that could describe Avery's immaculate beauty. Her elegance. Her grace. He trailed his gaze from her face down to her physique, his jaw nearly going slack at the sight of the dress clinging to her body akin to a second skin, its fabric cinched at her waist before flowing down her legs seamlessly. A long slit followed the route of her right leg, allowing him to catch a glimpse of smooth, tanned skin. "Decent."

"Jesus fucking Christ," Tate mumbled quietly. "Get a grip, mate."

It was evident that Avery wanted to laugh. She saw right through him—she always could. Lips tipped up into a mocking smirk, she lifted her brows in defiance, tracing her perusal over his frame with equal admiration.

"Thanks. You look okay, I guess."

As he narrowed his gaze on her, she winked playfully. Rowan only pressed his lips in a firm line, anchoring himself to the floor so he wouldn't go up to her and kiss her attitude away.

"Now that we're done checking each other out," Tate started, amused, "shall we go?"

Indy grinned, clapping her hands. This woman was a walking ball of sunshine. "We shall. I'm so excited. I bet they have good champagne."

Rowan didn't pay attention to Indy and Tate walking away, as he couldn't stop staring at the devastating angel standing before him.

"We'll be waiting for you in the car," Indy called out, arm

hooked under Tate's.

"Got it," Rowan mumbled. "Bye."

Avery blinked up at him, timidity evident on her face. "Why are you looking at me like that?"

He exhaled, a ball of nervousness obstructing his airway.

"Let's skip the event." He wanted to drive her out of the city. Wanted to take her someplace where they could be in a world alone.

"Why?"

"Why?" He lowered his voice, leaning towards her. "Avery, I haven't seen you in a fucking week. How do you expect me to react when you left after I told you to stay, when I woke up alone? I don't let anyone stay in my room; you know that. If you expect me to act like I don't want to be near you, then you're wrong."

She blinked, as though processing each one of his words.

Stepping forward, she reached towards him until her pinky finger wrapped around his—a rapid, secret touch.

"I promise we'll find time to talk later."

Then she brushed past him, her fragrance nearly bringing him to his knees. He'd bow before her. Would do anything for her.

"Come on, lover boy. The cameras aren't going to wait for you."

He scoffed, following her out. "Sure, they are. I'm the only star of the show."

"There he is."

❧

"GODDAMN IT, Indigo. Stop looking at me like that."

Indy giggled behind the rim of her flute of champagne before taking a small sip. She shook her head, gaping up at him with a smile on her lips.

"Seriously. What?" Rowan groaned again, frowning. "I don't

like that sneaky little smile."

She batted her lashes dramatically. "You don't like my smile?"

"You're annoying. You're not my type, so stop whatever you're doing."

"What's your type? Dark-haired women with snark and wit who aren't afraid of putting you in place?"

Perfect description of Avery.

"Maybe."

"I knew it," Indy mused, looking proud to have discovered one of his secrets. "You should put your arm around my shoulders. I'm not opposed to that."

Baffled by her sudden suggestion, he frowned down at her. "Why are we doing this?"

"I know you're trying to get someone's attention." Had he been that obvious? "I'm sure she'll stop acting like she doesn't care if you start flirting with me."

Rowan sighed and gulped down the rest of his champagne. "You're as infuriating as your best friend."

"Kam?" she asked, confused. "She's the classiest person here."

They both turned to look where Kamari and Thiago stood, chatting with another couple. Something uncanny stirred inside Rowan's chest when he observed the way Kamari was smiling at her boyfriend. Rowan wanted to be loved the way Thiago was loved—for the person he was; not for the driver he was known to be.

Rowan lifted his shoulders in an indifferent shrug. He looked away, one hand tucked in the front pocket of his trousers and his empty flute in the other.

"She never smiles."

"That's because she doesn't like you," Indy countered.

"Everyone likes me, Indigo."

"That's debatable."

Rowan narrowed his gaze on the blonde standing by his side.

"Did you side with Avery? Cause you're being rude to me."

Indy snorted softly before covering her nose with her hand. "Was bringing Ava up necessary?"

"Wasn't intentional," he grumbled, looking at the dancing crowd because he didn't want Indy to witness his cheeks turning red.

"Whatever you say."

Just like that, as though there was an invisible thread tying Rowan to Avery, he found her in a room full of people. She was dancing with Tate to a slow song, a smile on her lips as she listened to him rambling.

There was something about seeing her with another man that angered him and made his blood boil. His grip tightened around his flute, his jaw ticking when it clenched. Tate was harmless, though; his hands were resting on the middle of her back, a respectable distance stood between their chests, and there were no fleeting glances and secret smiles.

Unlike with Rowan and Avery.

She found his gaze from across the room, her smile dropping ever so slightly. Her perusal scrutinised the entirety of his physique, making time slow down. Rowan felt like combusting into a hellfire just with the intensity of it all—like she was holding the matches, and he was a moth to the flame.

Their secret moments in a crowded room caused frissons to roll down his spine, setting him ablaze with intense anticipation. He'd give everything to be in her arms. To make her smile and laugh.

And he'd give up forever just to touch her. Just to feel the sensation of her soft skin on his. Just to be with her.

"You can fool everyone, but not me, darling," came Indy's voice.

Rowan blinked. Just like that, all sounds became loud and clear, taking him back to reality just as Avery brought her attention back to Tate.

He looked down at his date, shaking his head. "I have no clue what you're talking about."

Indy's small, knowing smile never once faltered. She finished her drink, head tipped back before tapping his back amicably.

"Your secret's safe." She winked, her expression morphing into mischief. *Fuck.* Rowan knew that look on her face—she was planning something. "Go to the balcony on the fifth floor, the one that faces the ocean in five minutes. Wait for my signal to leave, though."

"What signal?"

"You'll see."

❧

INDIGO BAILEY WAS both a mastermind and a mad woman.

She had gone on the dance floor, kindly asking for Tate to have the next dance with her, then murmured something in Avery's ear as the latter was leaving.

Then, Rowan had watched Indy say a few words to Tate, causing him to grunt in annoyance before accepting whatever this woman had planned.

In Indigo Bailey style, she had convinced the DJ to play some early 2000s hit songs, causing all the guests to join the dance floor a minute later.

She had created a distraction just so that he could meet with Avery. And of course, she'd used her charms to do it.

When Rowan stepped onto the balcony, he felt like losing sense of everything—time, himself, his once-coherent thoughts.

He wondered how many times he had fallen speechless and felt his breath catch in the span of a few hours.

She was standing near the ledge, observing the burning sky where, on the horizon, the sun was bidding farewell to the universe. He could only see her profile, but the softest light gleamed in her eyes, indicating she was adoring this exact moment. And Rowan adored watching her love the smallest, simplest things in life.

He closed the door, bringing Avery's attention to him.

"Woah," he breathed out gruffly, ruffling his hair as he revelled in the view; the work of art she was. "How do you expect me to stay away from you when all I'll remember from tonight is you, standing in this dress and staring at the sunset?"

She stared at him amusedly, watching how he closed the distance between them with slow steps. "Did you hit your head recently?"

"Why?"

"You keep on complimenting me. Is there something you need?"

"Very witty," he drawled sardonically. "I'm a nice man."

She tilted her head, taunting him with those red lips and rosy cheeks. "I already told you: we could argue about this statement for hours."

"Brat," he bit out playfully. Now standing in front of her, he couldn't look away. Even the sky painted in vibrant colours wasn't as breathtaking as the woman before him.

"Why are you here?" she asked softly. "You had all these people's attention on you tonight."

"I don't care. The only woman's attention I want is yours."

He wasn't certain what he needed to do to assure Avery that *she* was the sole person to rock his world.

She stared at the inked pattern on his neck, his mind flashing with the memory of her delicate fingers drawing over most of his tattoos—like she had healed his wounds.

"You have it. All of it."

Rowan expelled a breath, losing himself in the moment. "You're a goddamn distraction, Avery Sharma-Maddox."

He said it like he blamed her for winding herself into his life. Like he hated her for having this corrupting effect on him. Like he didn't want to fall.

"I'm sorry."

But she wasn't the reason for his downfall anymore; she was slowly becoming his guidance towards light—salvation with the silhouette of an angel. "Have you been avoiding me?" he demanded then, taking another step closer.

"Have you?"

"You don't get to use reverse psychology on me, sunflower."

Avery's breath hitched when he finally stood before her, hands finding the railing behind her and caging her in between his arms. Holding her captive in his world, secretly hoping she would never escape.

"I don't know what you want, Rowan," she murmured.

His forehead fell forward, strands of hair toppling over his brows. Delicately, she cradled his face, her touch bringing him back to life. She pushed his hair off his forehead, watching him with awe, which caused his heart to burst into flames. Despite that inconsistent and wild beat, he could feel broken pieces mend themselves back, one by one.

He exhaled tremulously, leaning into her hand. "I can't stop thinking about you."

"Is it a bad thing?" she whispered.

"You tell me." He grabbed her hand, planting a soft kiss on the inside of her wrist. "Hey, sunflower."

She smiled, ruining him just like that. "Hey, lover boy."

"You look..." Once again, he had to take a deep breath before voicing the words that had been deafening and ricocheting inside his mind. "Beautiful."

"Finally found the right word?"

"I mean, you kind of rendered me speechless, so it took me a while to find the exact words to describe you."

"What a flirt."

He pulled her away from the edge of the balcony, lifting her hand to make her twirl. She was electric. Exquisite. Rowan had never felt so starstruck by anyone before, but it was evident Avery was intent on tilting his entire world onto its axis by simply existing.

He pulled her into his chest. "You owe me a dance."

She winded her arms around his neck. "Do I?"

"Yeah. I watched you dance with Ritchie all evening long."

"Do I sense jealousy?" she taunted, running a finger across his chest, where his shirt wasn't fastened.

"So what?"

"Not even denying it? You must have lost your mind."

He tucked a strand of ebony hair behind her ear, purposely lingering his touch so that he could observe goosebumps arise on her skin. "My offer still stands; let's get out of here."

"Rowan," she murmured, her tone edged with an unfathomable pain. "You know we can't. As your publicist, I need you to think about the consequences."

"And as my... Avery?" *His sunflower.*

She held his gaze, indecipherable emotions shimmering along the edges of her irises. "Maybe we can have it all in the next life."

He sighed heavily, dropping his forehead against hers. "What if none of these rules existed?"

This situation was slowly, yet surely, tearing him apart.

He wasn't exactly sure when he had allowed himself to be consumed by those foreign feelings—ones he'd never thought possible to experience in this lifetime.

"Then things would be different."

"What things?"

She brought his gaze back to hers. "Everything."

When Avery looked behind his shoulder, blatant deception drew upon her features. She sighed softly when sounds of laughter came from inside, and she took a step backwards, the heat and comfort of her hands only leaving tingles in their wake.

Rowan had always hated how his fate was written in the stars, but he loathed destiny even more now.

She brushed past him, and he caught her pinky finger with his. "When can I see you?" he asked. "*Really* see you?"

"We'll find a moment. Now go back downstairs and shine your light."

CHAPTER TWENTY-THREE

MONTE CARLO, MONACO

PULLING THE VISOR of his helmet down, Rowan took a deep breath in as he watched four of his mechanics scurry to the side of the track.

With his gloved hands, he gripped the steering wheel tightly, blocking out his surroundings and only letting the sound of his loud heartbeat take over his senses.

He inhaled. Exhaled. Repeated.

The signal was given, and that was his cue to push on the throttle to begin the formation lap.

Zig-zagging, accelerating, braking, and pushing the gas pedal again, he dragged the tyres on the asphalt to warm up the compounds. The sensation of the engine vibrating was his favourite; he was able to feel the car's power, its loud roar as it zipped through the streets of Monaco.

Monaco's Grand Prix was one of Rowan's favourite races on the calendar because it was a challenging one. The circuit had always been iconic, but the twists and turns were narrow, causing overtaking to be nearly impossible.

He was starting on pole today.

He wasn't going to let the universe ruin anything for him. This win was his, and no one else's.

He had worked night and day with his engineers to fix all the issues the car had faced during free practices.

Back on the grid, he watched from the rear-view mirror as his rivals lined up in their respective positions.

He focused back on the route ahead, waiting for the five lights to shift to red.

The green flag was waved in the air.

Inhale. Exhale.

The first light lit up, followed by the four others.

Rowan's mind flashed with everything he needed to do during the race—all the corners he needed to put his skills to use; all the turns where he'd need to show millimetric accuracy whilst driving at top speed. The iconic hairpin where he'd need to control the vehicle before roaring off into the next few turns and flying through the well-known corner of the Casino.

The lights froze for six seconds, then went away.

Rowan pushed on the throttle, flying down the long, straight line.

Compared to Thiago who was starting P2, he had made a bad start, causing his teammate to slot to the front, but he kept his pace and stayed close.

Just as they were about to take turn one wheel to wheel, Charlie Beaumont, who had started P4, managed to overtake Huxley. Charlie found a gap on Rowan's left, resulting in Rowan being sandwiched.

"The fuck is Charlie doing?" Rowan bellowed. The track was tight enough as it was.

All three took the turn, but Rowan couldn't go anywhere. His front wing came in contact with Charlie's side pod and pushed his rival into the protective barrier.

"Fuck!" Rowan regained control of his car, chasing Thiago down the track. "Sorry. Tight corner."

"You okay?" Jamie asked.

"I think I got damage on my front wing."

"Copy. Stay out. We're checking."

❧

HE RUBBED HIS FACE, wet and sticky with droplets of champagne and slid down the wall. Taking his hat off, he sighed and watched Thiago accept a hug from their team principal, Simon.

Rowan wondered if one day he would be as loved and appreciated as his teammate. He'd always considered Primavera Racing as family, so it was simply natural to crave equal affection like air.

Rowan wondered if one day he would be as good as Thiago. If one day the world wouldn't fault him for something he hadn't been able to control. If one day he'll stop living in his teammate's shadow.

A silhouette loomed overhead, obliging him to look away from the cause of his affliction. He met with kind doe eyes that made him breathe in slight relief.

"Here," Avery said, handing him a bottle of water.

"Nice," Rowan quipped. "You're not trying to poison me with some water I don't like."

She chuckled, sitting next to him. He wanted to tuck her into his side, let the warmth of her body and comfort cocoon him. But he couldn't. Their shoulders didn't touch, and he forced himself not to linger his stare on her face.

"I made that mistake once," she coyly said.

"More like four times," he corrected, uncapping the bottle.

"My bad."

He took a few sips of water, only wanting to hide from the world and release his anger. He didn't want to speak to anyone, but he knew pushing Avery away would only destroy him further. She was his press officer above all, and she needed to know what he was feeling at this very moment.

He tightened his jaw. "You don't have to pity me because all those people booed me earlier."

She stared ahead, but her voice echoed softly. "I'm not here for that, Rowan. You don't have to block me out because you think I'm going to judge you, or be rude, or leave you, or whatever you're thinking."

"Why are you here?"

"Which answer do you want?" she asked softly. "The answer as your PR officer or as your friend?"

Friend.

They had agreed on not letting feelings interfere with the situation, but why did hearing this particular word feel like a wound opening itself?

"Both."

"Well, as your friend, I think you're too hard on yourself. You finished P3 with damage to the car. You're extremely skilled and talented when it comes to tricky races like today's. You managed to overtake, which doesn't happen quite often in Monaco. As your PR officer, I need you to get your shit together, go up to Thiago, and hug him so that people don't think there's bad blood between you—"

"Why would they think that?"

"Because you didn't congratulate each other before the podium. You're going to smile in the media pen and tell every reporter that it wasn't your fault. There's nothing you could have done to avoid the contact."

Swallowing the lump in his throat, he looked at her, head tipped back against the wall behind him.

"You're really pretty," he whispered, causing her cheeks to flush.

"Don't deflect," she bit out.

"You're supposed to thank me when I compliment you."

She rolled her eyes, pulling her phone out of her pocket. “Look.”

She pressed play on a video she had received from Julia. He frowned, making a mental note to ask Avery why she had texted his mother. But the confusion brimming his senses tapered off when Nora’s face appeared on the screen. The happy toddler was wearing Primavera merch—Rowan’s jersey—as she waved at the camera whilst smiling brightly.

His heart swelled. He wouldn’t refuse a hug from his precious niece. Sadly, she was still in Australia.

“Hi, Uncle Wawa,” Nora said. “Congrats to my favourite driver. I miss you.”

After a moment, Avery stood up and grabbed the bottle from his grip, brushing her fingers to his on purpose. “You’re a lot of people’s favourite driver. Don’t beat yourself up, lover boy.”

❧

“WHAT THE FUCK ARE YOU WEARING?”

Tate applied more pressure on Rowan’s bare back just as the words fled past his lips. Rowan observed Avery stroll inside his room, closing the door behind her.

“Clothes?” She walked to the small bureau and took a seat, ready to start her routine after each race: write down a report of the interviews he had gone to and send it to Nikki.

“Thank you for pointing out the obvious,” Rowan spat. “Why are you wearing *my* shirt?”

She glanced down. “It’s merch, lover boy. With your name and number, so what? I spilled tea on my shirt, so I had to change into something. Do you want me to wear Tito’s number instead?”

“Fuck no, sunflower.” The simple thought made his blood boil.

Seeing Avery wear his name and number made him believe she was *his*.

Tate's snort was audible as he tapped the back of the athlete's neck. "Lover boy and sunflower. You two are unbelievable. Still don't know how you haven't killed each other yet."

She hummed, her gaze settled on her iPad. "I think about it every day."

Rowan scoffed. "I think about it every minute of every day."

"Damn, okay." Tate walked away from the massaging table, and that was Rowan's cue to sit up. "I'm going to grab something to eat and hang out with the crew before we have to leave. You guys coming?"

Avery shook her head. "I want to send the report tonight, so I don't have to do it tomorrow whilst hungover."

"That's fair," Tate said. "Rowan?"

"I'll be a minute."

Tate glanced from Rowan to Avery, lifting an eyebrow up. "Don't kill each other, please."

"We'll try," they answered grimly in unison.

When Tate was gone, Rowan went to lock the door and slouched on the sofa, exhaling loudly before tipping his head back. Even if he was busy staring at the ceiling, he could feel Avery studying his defeated demeanour.

He heard her close her iPad before she came to sit next to him.

"What's wrong?"

"Do you think Primavera Racing is keeping me because they pity me? I'll never be as good as Tito."

"Rowan," she said softly. From the corner of his eye, he saw her move until she was in front of him. Gingerly, she grabbed his hands, pulling his attention towards her. "Is this okay?"

She was kneeling between his legs, staring up at him with those big brown eyes whilst coaxing him through that tempest of emotions by caressing the back of his hands.

"Yes," he whispered, a small smile tugging his lips upwards when she started tracing the tattoo next to his thumb.

"You know, I think you're the most underrated driver on the grid."

"Oh?"

She held his gaze, the tenderness and unwavering delicacy glinting along the edges of her pupils causing his heart to swell. "You don't come from a family of racers. You don't come from a wealthy background. You had to work hard and sacrifice a lot to get where you are today. You're here because you're talented and because you deserve that F1 seat. A lot of people see your brilliance, you know. The raw talent, the precision in your driving style, the ruthless and fierce driver who represents number thirty-three. So no, Rowan. Primavera isn't keeping you out of pity. I know comparing yourself to your teammate is inevitable, but whatever your father has been telling you all these years isn't true. Do you know how many rookies arrive in F1 and sign an eight-year deal with a top team? Not many. You're one of the rare ones. And that says a lot about the man that you are. A number of World Championships will never define you as a driver."

Through his blurry vision, he could see his whitened knuckles as he had curled his hands into fists. Still, Avery hadn't loosened her grip around his hands—as though she didn't want to leave even when he was trying to shield himself. As though she wasn't afraid of breaking those walls down.

He swallowed the lump that had built inside his throat, unable to voice his thoughts. Unable to do anything.

She lifted herself up, brushing his under-eye with the pad of her thumb.

"You're a good man, Rowan Emerson. There's always going to be people who will try to tear you down and sabotage you. But look around; you're appreciated and admired. Just because you've been left multiple times by people you loved, doesn't mean you should stop yourself from wanting to be loved and to love. Not everyone is going to leave—I promise you this."

He blinked several times, taking his time to breathe in and out just to hold a semblance of control over his emotions. "How do you always find the right words to say?"

She sighed softly. "I don't know. I just don't really like seeing you like this."

"You're the only one besides Tate and my mother who's seen this side of me. "

"It's an honour. Thank you. I know how hard it is to show your vulnerability to someone else."

"Thank *you*," he whispered hoarsely.

"Can I—can I give you a hug?"

He nodded. "Please. I really need it, baby."

Pulling Avery onto his lap, she looped her arms around his shoulders as he wrapped his around her waist. He embraced her tightly, afraid to break down, but he knew she'd still hold him.

"You're okay," she whispered, stroking the hair on his nape gently. "Nothing bad happened to you."

"No, but Stephen's words always mess with my head. And today's booing, the way I'm being neglected by my team... I'm just tired. I want to perform well."

"I don't care what it's going to take for you to understand that you're more than enough. I don't care how long it's going to take for you to believe me. The fact that you feel pressured into performing well is a good sign. It means that you care and that you have a good soul. My words might not be meaningful or important to you, but you deserve to hear them."

She was wrong. So, so wrong.

All his life, he'd been yearning for someone as good as her. All his life, he'd been craving for someone to see him the way she did.

Avery Sharma-Maddox was slowly, yet surely becoming *everything* to him.

Burying his face in the crook of her neck, he inhaled her scent, embracing her just a little tighter and a little longer.

"Thank you," he murmured.

"I've got you... *dude.*"

Rowan huffed out a laugh, pinching her side. "Way to ruin the moment, *dude.* You're such an idiot."

"At least I managed to make you smile."

He planted a kiss on her jaw. She shivered, and he smirked, knowing all too well he had a devastating power over her, just like she did with him. "You always know how to break down my walls. How to make me smile."

He placed a kiss over her pulse point where he could feel the steady beat, trailing a route towards the sweet spot below her ear. He nipped at the skin, feeling her fingers dig into his shoulders as she held her breath.

"Rowan," she sighed.

The way his name sounded on the tip of her tongue was akin to spun sugar—warm, addictive. He wanted her to chant his name, just so that he could replay it like his favourite melody.

He pecked her jawline, causing her to tilt her head to the side to grant him more access to her neck. Then, he kissed her cheek until his lips grazed her parted mouth.

He cupped her jaw, his fingers resting on the back of her neck and tangling into her hair. His forehead fell on hers, his brows knitting slightly as he felt his heart go into overdrive. His brain still couldn't fathom how strong and unyielding that invisible thread tying them together was. How it felt as though she was controlling every drum, every beat.

"Rowan," she whispered, her breath fanning across his lips, only urging him to close the distance between them. "Don't do this."

"Do what?" He kissed her nose, her cheek, the other one, and her forehead.

"Don't use me after a moment of anguish. Don't let me take

advantage of you when you were being vulnerable just two minutes ago."

"This is a new moment. This isn't related to what just happened. I'm trying to heal, and what would help me feel better is kissing you."

"You speak such nonsense."

"Seriously." He groaned, slightly frustrated. "Can I kiss you?"

"Since when do you have to ask?"

"Since you think I want to do this to forget about my demons. I just want to kiss you because seeing you wear my name and number is doing things to me."

"Oh, really?" she asked, feigning innocence.

"Yeah."

She held his defiant gaze, equal mischief glinting in her eyes. "Do something about it, then."

So, Rowan kissed her. But he didn't want to rush it, didn't want her to believe he simply wanted this to relieve the tension. No, he kissed her slowly, allowing a certain vehemence to join the dance of their tangled tongues. He kissed her softly, but his desperate heart was crying and aching to feel something else other than pain. He kissed her like he had all the time in the world, like nothing else mattered.

When her tongue stroked his and her lips wrapped around his bottom one, he melted into her touch.

He poured unspoken words, silent promises into the kiss, and it felt like she was returning the same sentiments.

He cradled her face, angling her head to kiss her at a different pace, causing her to moan softly as she pulled herself into him.

And just like that, the atmosphere in the room shifted.

Entwined breaths were heavy, tongues were battling for dominance, and hands started to discover each other's bodies.

"You're going to ruin me," he mumbled against her mouth.

"Good."

"Good?" He pulled away and pushed her off his lap.

She stood in front of him, slightly dazed and confused. Her chest was rising and falling, her cheeks flushed and her lips blood-rushed.

"Take off your clothes," he demanded. "But leave my shirt on. I'm about to ruin you and make you understand who you belong to."

CHAPTER TWENTY-FOUR

MONTE CARLO, MONACO

"DON'T START ACTING all innocent now, Avery. Take your clothes off."

"B-but," she stammered, panic burning through her veins. "The entire team is still in the motorhome."

"So?" He leaned back, draping his arms over the back of the sofa whilst spreading his legs out. This man was the portrait of arrogance, indolence, and masculine beauty. "I'd love to make you scream and let everyone know you're mine. But since we're breaking hundreds of rules right now, I'm going to keep all your pretty moans to myself, because they belong to me."

"I'm not yours," she breathed out.

"Yeah?" He smirked, jutting his chin towards her. "Is that why you're wearing my name and number?"

Her chest heaved. "I hate you."

"I know."

Trailing her gaze over his alluring physique, she sucked in a breath at the sight of his hard muscles and the obvious arousal straining against his basketball shorts.

"Don't look at me like that, sunflower. And don't make me ask you again. Clothes. Off. Now."

Chills arose on every inch of her skin at the sound of his low, hoarse voice. Kicking her shoes off, she watched the way his eyes darkened as he took her in with a slow once-over. She unbuckled her belt and pulled her trousers down, trying not to melt under the intensity of his scrutiny.

"Good girl," he praised huskily. "Now, come here."

Straddling his lap, Ava shivered when his calloused palms came in contact with the outsides of her thighs. "I'm obsessed with your thighs," he murmured. "Just fucking obsessed with all of you."

Ava couldn't help but blush at his words. She buried her face in the crook of his neck, hating how she would always become timid whenever he worshipped her. She still couldn't understand how and why Rowan had chosen her in a world full of other women.

"You're gorgeous, Avery," he whispered when she didn't say anything. His hands curved around her bottom, palming and remembering. "Everything about you is."

She kissed his jaw in response.

Rowan then cupped her face, obliging her to find honey eyes darkened by intense desire. "What do you say, baby?"

"Thank you," she said softly.

"That's right."

And then, his lips found hers.

The kiss was different from the one they had shared earlier. This one was messy, eager, filled with lust.

Rowan pulled her closer by the waist, letting his hands slip under her shirt. She could feel his prominent bulge pressing against her centre, so she rolled her hips, causing him to groan in the back of his throat.

"Can I touch you here?" he asked, fingers dancing across her ribs just as he peppered open-mouthed kisses on the curve of her jawline.

"Yes," she answered in a breath.

"Here?" His hand caressed her stomach.

That was the part of her body she was most self-conscious about. Because it wasn't flat or toned.

But his touch made her feel like she was a work of art; one in a million.

Instead of rearing back and hiding, she accepted his silent adoration, leaning further into his touch like he was drawing stars over her insecurities.

Butterflies took flight inside her stomach when time stood still as his gaze found hers, a foreign gleam alighting his starlit eyes.

So she found herself saying, "Yes."

"Thank you." They shared another kiss before he broke the contact, his hand finding her cleavage. "What about your tits?"

They were heavy, aching. She couldn't help but moan softly when he grazed his thumb over her peaked nipple through her bra.

Ava nodded. "You can touch me everywhere."

He placed a kiss above her heart, where his number was. "Am I the first one who gets to touch you like this?"

"Yes."

"What a privilege," he said, smirking. His hand slipped lower until his fingers skimmed over her clothed core, teasing her with a featherlight touch. He pressed on her clit with his middle finger. "Am I the only one who can make you come this hard?"

Her fingers tangled through his hair as she tried to keep her breathing even and her whispered sighs quiet. "Yes."

"And am I going to be the only one who gets to fuck this tight little cunt?"

Ava nodded, already lost in a haze of pleasure. "Yes."

"Good."

She cradled his face, lifting herself on her knees to take

control when she kissed him. She felt his smirk against her mouth just as he drew circles on her clit, causing a moan to get stuck in her throat.

"As much as I love the pretty sounds you make, you've got to stay quiet, baby. Thiago isn't next door right now, but he can come into his room anytime. He can't hear you, okay? The walls are thin."

"How do you know?" She tugged at his roots, tilting his head back as she peppered kisses down the column of his throat.

"Can't even tell you how many times I heard him and Kam shag."

"Oh."

"So, you're going to have to be extra quiet. Okay, sunflower?"

She trailed her hands down his pecs. "Same goes for you. You're a vocal man, so let's see if you can make it when I suck you off."

His brows were lifted in slight puzzlement. "Who gave you that much confidence?"

"My books."

"Your books," he scoffed. "Yeah, right."

He tugged the waistband of her underwear down until she was out of it. Bunching the lace, he pulled her lower lip down until her mouth was agape.

"You have such a bratty mouth." He put the ball of lace on her tongue, closing her lips. "That'll shut you up for now."

She glared at him, but the annoyance didn't last long before his fingers found her core, collecting her arousal.

"For someone who's been claiming to hate me, you sure are soaking wet for me."

She rolled her eyes annoyedly. Her nails dug into the skin of his shoulder when he circled her clit fast. She watched his gaze follow his fingers' motions, totally enthralled.

"The only time you're going to roll your eyes at me is when I make you come." He then thrust a finger in, his thumb applying pressure on her clit.

A gasp tried to break free when she threw her head back, rocking her hips in tandem with his finger's rhythm. His other hand trailed upwards until it cupped a breast, tugging her bra down.

She loved the feeling of his hands on her because even with rough callouses and scarred palms, his touch was delicate and careful.

Rowan inserted a second finger in, a grunt rising from the back of his throat. "You're so fucking tight. I'm going to wreck you."

He'd already wrecked her. And the more she kept being pulled towards him, the more she felt like plummeting from the edge of a precipice, unable to pull herself up to the surface. Ava knew that if she played too dangerously close to the border, she would simply crash. Hard. Unexpectedly. She wasn't sure if she wanted this.

He pulled his fingers out and pushed them back in, played with her clit, causing her stomach to clench. When his digits curled and brushed her sweet spot, she bit back a moan. Rowan's lips were parted as he watched his arousal-coated fingers thrust in and out.

"More," she tried to say.

"What's that?" he asked huskily, dropping his other hand from her breast to her hip.

"More."

The panties bunched in her mouth were bothering her, so she took them out under the glare Rowan threw at her.

"Did I say you could take it out?"

She ignored his question, dropping her forehead onto his. "Rowan," she gasped as quietly as she could. The sound of her arousal made her legs tremble just as he picked up his pace. "I need more."

"You needy brat," he spat out before putting a third finger in.

Ava bit her lower lip to stifle her moan. As she pulled Rowan's hair, he groaned softly.

"You like that?" he asked. "When I finger-fuck you like this?"

Ava nodded.

"Words, baby."

"Y-yes," she breathed out, grinding against the heel of his palm. "I need more."

"Jesus, Avery, you—"

"Fuck me. Properly. I want you."

He stilled, the loss of pressure on her clit causing her to whine and buck her hips in search of friction.

"Sunflower—"

"Please," she whispered.

She didn't know it was possible, but his eyes darkened even more. "Are you sure, baby?"

She nodded. "Please," she repeated. "The rule doesn't apply anymore since you've already raced."

"You're so pretty when you beg."

He pulled out, and she could feel her entire body thrum with intense desire, aching for release. He brought his soaked digits to her lips. "Open." She wrapped her lips around his fingers, sucking them clean and moaning softly at the taste of herself. "Good girl."

"Rowan," she murmured, caressing his chest and holding his gaze. "I want you to fuck me. But if you don't want to today, it's fine. We can just—"

"I want to," he interrupted gruffly. "So bad."

"Are you sure?"

He grabbed her hand to put it over his erection, bucking his hips upwards. "Feel that? That's how bad I want you. You get me so hard all the damn time. And I've wanted you for so long, Avery. It's just that the moment I fuck you, everything is going to feel different."

She brushed her lips to his. "And what happens if this gets real?"

She heard Rowan swallow thickly. "You tell me."

For a moment, for an eternity, she watched all those fears of being abandoned mist over his eyes. She knew Rowan had been used to hookups with no strings attached, to fuck women and leave them because they didn't mean anything to him.

But this was different. Ava knew it, and so did Rowan.

Neither of them knew exactly what it was. So, for the time being, they let lust take over until something more powerful could replace that ephemeral feeling.

Ava kissed him softly—a promise to never leave, even if he pushed her away. Rowan deserved to have someone who would fight for him.

He returned the kiss with equal fervour, cupping her face. When their tongues brushed with more intensity and their breaths became heavy with need, she dragged the heel of her palm against his shaft, making him groan.

"Can I keep going?" she asked.

"Please."

She smiled against his lips. "*You're* so handsome when you beg."

Tugging his shorts and boxer briefs down, she wrapped her hand around his thick shaft, pumping it a few times. All the while kissing him, she collected his arousal on the pad of her thumb, spreading the wetness around the head before shifting so she could sit on his erection. She slid along his length, causing them both to whimper quietly.

He threw his head back, hands on her hips. "Fuck."

He guided her, occasionally meeting her halfway by bucking his hips upwards. Her clit brushed against his throbbing cock, and she could already feel herself on the cusp of falling apart.

But Rowan had other plans.

Pushing her away, he kissed her cheek before reaching into his duffel bag at the foot of the sofa.

He pulled a condom out, smirking smugly.

"Do you carry these with you everywhere?"

"Yes," he said, opening the foil packet. "Bought these when we started seeing each other."

"Really?" She took the condom to roll it down his length, and he sucked in a breath at the sensation. "You don't have old ones in your bag?"

"No. I bought a new pack for us. I told you; I haven't had sex in over a year. You're not a simple fuck to me, Avery. Understand?"

She lifted herself on her knees, bringing the tip to her entrance. "Yes."

Rowan leaned in to peck her lips. "Are you sure about this?"

"Certain," she whispered. "Are you?"

"Yes. Go ahead, use me."

She lubricated the condom by rubbing his erection along her folds, holding her breath when she pushed the tip in.

"God," she mumbled.

He was holding her waist, coaxing her with a soft caress. "What the fuck are you complaining about?"

"You're so fucking big."

He smirked, guiding her down on him. "We'll make it fit, love."

She tried to relax, sinking down inch by inch. She'd never had anyone as big as Rowan. Never had anyone better than Rowan.

She winced, feeling him stretch her out.

Rowan kissed her softly, rubbing soft circles on her hip. "Relax, baby. Take deep breaths for me. I'm not even halfway in."

"You and your massive dick," she said to ease the uncomfortable sensation skittering across her body.

As she found support on his shoulders, he grabbed her hand to kiss her inner wrist. "Loving all these compliments."

"And your fucking ego."

He chuckled, making that slight flicker of pain vanish.

Once she had sunken down and he was buried to the hilt, a groan rumbled in his chest as he leaned his head on the back of the sofa. He pinched his eyes shut for a second, breathing in before finding her gaze with lustful eyes.

"Holy fuck," he mumbled. "You good?"

Ava nodded, that feeling of discomfort now gone as he started rubbing her clit with his middle finger. "I'm okay."

"Move when you're ready."

She pushed herself up on her knees, glancing to where they were connected. Lowering herself down, she let out a pleasured sigh.

Switching between rolling her hips and bouncing up and down, Ava rapidly found a rhythm that made the both of them pant heavily.

He was holding her hips, nails digging into her skin as he guided her.

"Perfect." His cheeks were rosy, his eyes black with unrelenting desire. "That's it. Atta girl, ride my cock like it's all yours."

"Rowan." She felt herself clench around him as he thrust his hips upwards to meet her halfway. The sound of their arousal and their skin slapping echoed inside the small room, and she prayed no one would hear them.

"I know, baby." He pressed his thumb to her clit, drawing rapid circles. "I'm close, too."

She looked at his heaving chest, watching a bead of sweat roll down the valley of his pectorals. "Does this feel good?"

He cupped the back of her head to pull her forehead towards his. He continued to circle her clit all the while thrusting hard and fast. She knew he was driving himself to insanity for not letting a sound out, just like she was trying to be as quiet as possible.

He kissed her messily. "Feels fucking incredible. You feel like a dream, Avery. So tight. So wet. So perfect."

Watching how his brows were knitted together, complete pleasure etched on his face as he tried to fuck her with as much passion as she was giving him, Ava couldn't help but tip her head back.

Her eyes rolled in pleasure, and when Rowan accidentally let out a moan, she felt her walls tighten. The pressure on her clit made her unravel. Shaking hard, she fell forward and bit his shoulder to keep her screams silent.

Rowan continued to fuck her deeply, the tip of his cock continuously brushing her sweet spot as he helped her ride out her high by pressing on her clit.

Then, his thrusts became sloppy, unsteady, and he fell apart. His legs trembled as he spilled into the condom, hugging Ava close to his chest as his body spasmed. He whimpered in the back of his throat, heavy breaths fanning across her neck.

"Holy shit," he whispered before kissing her neck.

She could feel his hands caress her thighs as she was still trying to recuperate her breath, that haze of intense pleasure slowly vanishing away.

"You okay, sunflower?"

Ava pulled away just enough to look into his eyes. "Yes. You?"

The smile illuminating his features was akin to a ray of sunlight beating down on her skin.

"I'm perfect. I mean, I just got laid by the prettiest girl walking the paddock."

She pushed his shoulder. "You're an idiot."

He kissed the tip of her nose. "I promise I'll fuck you very soon in a place where you can scream all you want."

"Great." Her cheeks flushed, and he chuckled. That adoration, that tenderness drawn on his face made warmth invade her chest. "Can't wait."

"Someone's greedy," he teased playfully, though that blazing devotion burning in his eyes never once wavered.

After helping her stand up and laughing at her because she

felt weak in the knees, Rowan discarded the condom in the bin. He helped her clean up and fix her hair, complimenting the locks and her body.

"How do I look?" she asked once she was fully dressed.

He grinned. "Like you've been freshly fucked by yours truly."

Ava rolled her eyes and walked towards the door. "Fuck you, Emerson."

She didn't have to look at him to know he was still smiling. "You just did."

She opened the door, acting all nonchalant and indifferent despite her hammering heart and the anxiety coiling in her gut. "I hate you!"

"Feeling's mutual, sunflower," he called after her.

The corridor was empty. Loud chatter and laughter were coming from the hospitality room, and Ava sighed in relief.

Just as she started walking towards the main room, Thiago rounded the corner with a bowl of pasta in hand and a bottle of water in the other.

He smiled, jutting his chin towards her. "Sup, girl."

She waved. "Hey, Tito. Great race."

"Thanks."

She brushed past him, and he pivoted, gaze narrowed on her face.

"Come in my room for a sec."

She followed him, albeit reluctantly. His room was empty, which made her sigh in relief. As much as Ava loved Kamari, she didn't want anyone to hear what Thiago was about to say. Because Ava had a feeling he was going to mention Rowan.

Thiago placed his bottle of water and bowl on the small table and leaned against it, tucking his hands in the pockets of his jeans.

"Are you being careful, Ave?"

Ava blinked. "Careful?"

"With Rowan." He rubbed the back of his neck, emitting a

nervous chuckle. "I mean not sexually. I mean, I hope you're being careful, but I mean—shit, sorry. Are you sure you know what you're doing? I'd hate for you two to get in trouble."

Ava tucked a strand of hair behind her ear, chewing the inside of her cheek. "How do you know?"

"Come on, Ave," he said, a soft smile on his lips. "I'm not daft. That bickering? Those secret glances? That incessant '*He hates me, but I hate him even more*'? You can't fool me. I know you enough to know how you act around other men on this team, and the way you're with Rowan is not how you act with the other guys."

It took a few seconds before she said, "Don't tell anyone." What was the point of hiding it from Thiago?

"You know I won't."

She released a long sigh. "Do you think other people know?"

Thiago shook his head. "I don't think so, no. I just pay attention to things most people ignore. Your secret's safe with me."

"Thank you, Tito. It just... happened."

He shrugged. "Good for you."

"We're not together."

He smiled mischievously. "Yet."

"I'm not sure what we are."

There was a small beat of silence as Thiago observed Ava's features. She wondered if she looked happy, serene. She surely felt like it. After a moment of contemplation, his voice echoed softly. "You're good for him. Probably the best thing he's ever had. And he's good for you."

She couldn't help but smile. "Yeah, he's whatever."

Thiago laughed. "Just be careful, alright?"

"I will. Thank you."

He winked. "I've got your back. You should come to my boat party. It's just the inner circle and Rowan's circle. Would be a good opportunity to be with starboy away from prying eyes and the team, you know?"

The idea was tempting, but she shook her head. “I can’t be seen with you outside of work.”

“Come on,” Thiago pleaded. “You’ll be fine if I tell them I was the one who invited you.”

Ava sighed. She’d been wanting to spend time with Rowan outside of work, anyway. Still, she was reluctant. She just hoped no one would get in trouble. “I’ll kill you if we get caught. You and Rowan both.”

CHAPTER TWENTY-FIVE

MONTE CARLO, MONACO

"SPILL THE BEANS, girl."

Taking a seat next to Kamari at the table, Ava accepted the glass of wine Indy slid her way.

Indy and Kamari had dragged Ava into the cabin to chat the very instant the yacht left the harbour.

Regardless of the hesitancy flowing through her bones, Ava had been convinced by Kamari to leave the circuit and attend the private party. Still, she wasn't totally comfortable with being seen in the company of the two drivers outside of work.

"What beans?" Ava demanded, feigning innocence before taking a small sip of wine.

Indy cupped her hands around her mouth and whispered, "About you and your secret lover."

Ava blinked, but the blush coating her cheekbones betrayed her. "Who?"

"Oh, come on!" Indy exclaimed. "I spent an entire evening

watching you and Rowan eye-fuck each other from across the room."

Ava glanced at Kamari who was observing her with an indecipherable expression.

"Thiago told me," Kamari said casually. "But don't worry, your secret's safe."

Placing her elbow on the table and leaning her chin in the palm of her hand, she let her stare drift towards the deck where Rowan was. He was leaning against the railing with a bottle of beer in hand as he was chatting with Tate and Cal.

The breeze brushed his hair away from his forehead, a soft smile touching his lips as he spoke. He then winked at Cal, causing Tate to bark out a laugh. Rowan grinned, proud of whatever he had said. He was devastatingly handsome, and he didn't even know it.

Ava looked back to where Indy and Kamari were. "You guys promise not to say anything to anyone?"

"My lips are sealed," Indy said earnestly. "And Kam always keeps everything to herself."

"True," Kamari confirmed before taking a sip of her beverage.

Ava let out a small breath. "We're just hooking up."

"Just?" Indy asked, a brow raised. "Honey, that man doesn't look at you like he's *just* banging you."

Ava's heart started to pound ferociously, as though it needed to escape the confined space of her chest to explode into fireworks. "How does he look at me?"

"He looks at you like you're the only person in the room. Like you're that ray of sunshine peeking through clouds on a stormy day. He looks at you, and he simply refuses to look away." Indy glanced towards Rowan, a chuckle flying past her lips. "You can grab his attention the moment you walk into a room. I was there to see it with my own eyes. And I know that he's into you beyond physical attraction."

Ava wasn't sure what to say. What to do. She took a sip of

wine, trying to haze her mind, but all she could do was look at Rowan.

He found her gaze, winking before looking away.

Ava no longer had control over the butterflies resting inside her stomach. They found their freedom, circulating through her system, setting her vessels ablaze.

"Do you like him?" Kamari asked softly.

"I can't," Ava whispered.

"But you do."

Ava reared back at the realisation. "I'm trying not to."

There was a gleam of comprehension in Kamari's green eyes, as though she could understand Ava's feelings more than anyone.

"I'm sure you two can figure it out," Indy comforted. "It's kind of thrilling to be sneaking around, right?"

Ava chuckled. "Very. I don't know, he brings out a side of me that I always keep hidden. And I feel so safe with him."

"Cute," Indy mused, her blue eyes gleaming. "But on a scale from one to ten, how good is the sex? No offence, but I've observed that man, and I think he is *packed.*"

"Indigo," Kamari sighed. "You need to stop asking and thinking about the F1 drivers' dicks. It's weird."

Indy's lips formed into a pout. "It's the most action I'm getting. All I'm asking is for a man to look at me like I'm their whole world."

Ava tilted her head. "I thought something was going on between you and Miles Huxley?"

Indy downed the contents of her glass in a gulp. "I wish. The only times he looks at me, we end up banging and he leaves without saying a word."

"That's tough."

Regardless of Indy's small, nonchalant shrug, Ava could still see the hurt in her eyes.

"He's a good guy, you know," Ava said. "He's probably

pushing you away because he doesn't want to hurt you or something."

"Or maybe because he's best friends with my brother? Men are so complicated. Anyway, don't deflect. How good is Rowan in bed?"

Ava bit her lower lip, allowing earlier events to flash inside her mind. "So good. A twelve out of ten."

Indy used a hand to fan herself. "God, I'm going to faint."

Kamari hummed. "No wonder why he's so conceited. He knows what he's doing."

❧

AVA FOUND ROWAN sitting on a bench alone, an empty bottle of beer cradled between his hands as he observed the starry sky and the splatters of constellations illuminating the heavens.

For a moment, she stood still and watched the light draw minuscule stars on his skin. The way he was revelling in the view, marvelling at the sight as though he was grounding himself to the stars—constant elements in his turbulent universe.

"Looking for some company?"

An instant smile took over his features at the sound of her voice. "I suppose your presence is okay."

She took a seat next to him, handing him a new beer. She made sure to keep a certain distance between them, even though she was craving his familiar touch. "I'm glad I find your company tolerable too."

"Thanks," he said, lifting the bottle to his lips. He motioned his chin towards the small plate she was holding. "What do you have here?"

"There's a cheeseboard inside," she explained excitedly, plucking a piece of baguette out of the plate. "Do you want to share with me?"

When he didn't respond right away, she looked up only to

find him staring at her amusedly, that set of killer dimples adorning his face.

The heat crawling up to her cheekbones set her skin on fire, like his gaze was made of sparks. "What? Why are you looking at me like that?"

There was something about this moment that made her want to forget about the rules they had. About the distance that had been forced to stand between them. There was something about this moment that made her entire surroundings a mere element that couldn't be as attention-grasping as Rowan.

"I love how you always get excited about the smallest things in life," he murmured. "Especially food. But are you sure you're okay?"

A small frown touched her brows. "Yes. Why?"

He jerked his chin towards her occupied hands. "Because you're willing to share."

His comment elicited a scoff. "I'm not always a brat."

"Depends," he retorted with a smirk before plucking a grape from the plate after she set it down in between them. "So, making new friends?"

"Sorry?"

"Indigo and Kamari," he clarified. "I saw you three giggle and gossip."

"Watching me?"

"When am I not?"

She tried to glare at him, only to fail miserably when he threw a grape in the air, catching it swiftly in his mouth before sending a roguish wink her way.

"They're fun," Ava admitted as she took a small sip of wine.

He leaned forward, elbows on his thighs as he gripped the bottle of beer, settling his stare on the horizon. "Don't push them away. I know you have a hard time trusting people and making new friends, but I think they're great. Indy is wild as hell, but she's an angel beneath that surface. Kam is more closed-off, but I think she's a bit like you in a way. She's really nice, though."

She dropped her stare to her shoes. "I'll try. It's just hard to let people further in when the friendship starts to develop because, you know, I can't help but build those walls up naturally. I'm just so tired of getting hurt. Of giving my all to end up drained and questioning myself for what I did wrong."

She watched the tip of his shoe nudge the side of hers, drawing her attention back to him.

"Yeah," he said. "I get it."

If there was a person who could understand her better than anyone else, it was Rowan.

"But I'll try," Ava promised. "I have a good feeling. I hope I'm not wrong about it this time."

The corner of his lips twitched. "I'll be your friend."

"You already are." She trusted him. Fully. Whilst it had always been a challenge to befriend someone, letting Rowan in had come naturally.

He was so much more than a simple friend. Rowan was everything. He was a vast ocean of tranquillity, a galaxy glowing with unwavering solace.

She shifted to face him. "Why are you alone?"

His jaw tightened for a flickering heartbeat, causing his features to harden into coldness. "Just needed to clear my head."

"Want to talk about it?"

"My father happened, and I made the mistake of checking my messages."

That glint of pure sorrow in his eyes made her chest ache. She truly couldn't comprehend the pain Rowan was going through by always wanting to please someone who took his efforts for granted. Who constantly underestimated his talent. Who had never loved or appreciated him.

That realisation hit her like a tidal wave and cemented her into voicing her thoughts.

"I'm sorry." She didn't even think about the people around.

Didn't think of the consequences of her actions. Gently caressing his back, she felt his body stiffen before relaxing under her coaxing touch. Then, she tangled her fingers through the hair at his nape, making him close his eyes and sigh heavily. When honey irises looked at her again, a gloom had misted over. "I wish you could see yourself the way I see you. You're beautiful beyond measure, Rowan. Your soul holds a light so innately bright and your heart is big and made of gold. Please don't beat yourself up because your father can't see you. The true you. I promise there are millions of people all around the world who love and admire you. Me included, but I just tolerate you."

The last sentence was the reason a broad smile broke free on his face, but Ava couldn't miss the way unshed tears had veiled his gaze.

Deep down, he was just a broken boy looking for love. Not even the toughest façade or the coldest mask could conceal his vulnerability.

He grabbed her wrist and planted a soft, lingering kiss on her palm. He closed his eyes, a little divot appearing between his brows when he frowned slightly.

"Want to know something?" she whispered. He nodded. "I grew up watching F1, and before coming to Primavera Racing I was terrified to meet you. You were one of my favourite drivers. I love your driving style and how ruthless you are when you're behind the wheel. You take so many risks when racing and not many drivers are as daring as you. And then I met you..."

"And I was an asshole to you."

"The biggest bellend I had ever talked to. You suddenly became my least favourite driver."

Rowan's laughter boomed through the noises surrounding them. "I guess I deserved that. Is that why you started disliking me so much? Because I was rude and annoying?"

"I guess so. I didn't understand what I'd done wrong for you to dislike me so much. Why *did* you hate me?"

"I told myself that the only way I could push you away was

by being a disgrace to you. Because I couldn't get you out of my head. Couldn't think straight whenever you were around. I haven't been able to stop thinking about you from the moment I met you."

Was Rowan aware that the grip he had around her heart was becoming more firm, more powerful?

"I hope I didn't hurt your feelings," he said. "I'm sorry if I ever did. And I'm sorry if my actions made you think you were a bad person, because I swear that you're the best, most selfless, incredible woman I know."

There had been a time when second-guessing herself was inevitable because all she'd wanted, her whole life, was to be a good person, a good friend. She now understood that Rowan had used his rudeness as self-preservation.

"I forgive you," she whispered.

"I don't deserve you." She tried to swallow through the lump inside her throat, exhaling tremulously when he brushed another kiss on her knuckles.

"Please don't say that." She brushed a curl away from his forehead, allowing a soft smile to spread across her lips. His stare instantly fell to her mouth as she cradled his jaw, her thumb brushing his cheek where a dimple would appear if he grinned. "My sad boy."

Rowan leaned into her touch, closing his eyes to linger in the moment.

Ava still couldn't understand how a man like him was allowing himself to be vulnerable with her—only with her. How he blatantly showed her this side of him without being scared.

He pulled away, and as he was about to say something, loud music started blasting from a stereo.

Ava reared back, startled by reality before laughing heartily.

Rowan then stood up, extending his hand. "Dance with me?"

"Always with you."

He made her spin around.

He made her laugh.

He spent the entire night with her, both ignoring the incredulous glances their friends were throwing at them.

And for an eternity, Ava forgot about the real world as she drowned in honey eyes, wondering what would happen if she let herself completely fall.

CHAPTER TWENTY-SIX

LONDON, ENGLAND

Her fingers tightened around the steering wheel as she pressed on the brake, taking the tight corner as she followed Rowan closely.

She focused on the route, now knowing the shape of the karting circuit as she had driven through it multiple times for the past hour. The raw, unbridled speed made excitement rush through her bloodstream as she felt her bones vibrate.

She was milliseconds away from overtaking Rowan, who had been leading the race. This was the last lap, and they would cross the finish line soon.

When Ava accelerated in the long straight, she slipped through the gap and passed in front of Rowan before driving at full speed towards the chequered flag.

After parking the kart, she jumped out and bounced excitedly on her heels, watching the others line up after her.

Her heart was beating erratically, a grin growing on her lips as she laughed heartily. At that exact moment, the sensation of thrill was incomparable.

"I did not just lose to my PR officer!" Rowan exclaimed furiously as he unbuckled his helmet after getting out of his kart.

She folded her arms across her chest, feeling her heart momentarily stop at the sight of his angry eyes staring into hers. "You did and now you're going to have to live with that for the rest of your life."

Rowan strode towards her, tearing the helmet and balaclava off. She had seen him do this hundreds and hundreds of times, but she couldn't help but find the movement thoroughly sexy. Especially when he ruffled his hair afterwards.

"You cheated," he accused as he stood before her.

She took her helmet and balaclava off before taking her hair out of her ponytail. "Sorry to hurt your ego, Rowan Emerson, but I think I'm a better racer than you are."

The corner of his lips tipped into an amused smirk. "I'd like to see you in an F1 car."

She lifted an eyebrow. "Is this a challenge?"

"God," he whispered, dropping his gaze to her mouth. "I could kiss you right now."

She tried not to blush, failing miserably. "Careful, lover boy."

Ava knew he would have done it without a flicker of hesitation if they had been alone.

"Awesome!" Nikki's high-pitched voice burst their bubble open. Ava saw Rowan huff before shifting to stand behind her. His fingers brushed her hip, and she fought the urge to lean into his chest. "The fans will love this week's content."

"It was Ava's idea," Thiago chimed in with a broad smile before grabbing a bottle of water.

Nikki trailed her gaze over Ava's physique, obvious disdain perceptible in her eyes. The silent judgment coming from the woman didn't help Ava overcome her self-consciousness.

Ava felt Rowan stiffen behind her, and she simply lowered her gaze.

Perhaps in another life she'd be tall, and skinny, and confident, but in this life, she was learning to embrace who she was. So, to start trusting the acceptance, she lifted her chin and held Nikki's gaze, standing her ground and not yielding.

"Whatever," Nikki said. "Doesn't take a genius to think of something as dull as go-karting for F1 drivers to have fun. Ava's ideas are okay once in a while, but I'm glad you boys enjoyed yourselves."

"Watch your fucking tone when you talk about Avery," Rowan warned through gritted teeth.

Nikki merely blinked, the silence in the large room nearly becoming deafening as all eyes flicked back and forth between Ava and Nikki.

Ava didn't want to say anything. Didn't want to create unnecessary drama. She knew Nikki hated her guts, so it wouldn't be in her favour to open her mouth.

"You're not even going to apologise?" Rowan bellowed. Wrath started to emanate from his demeanour, almost allowing Ava to feel how he was trembling with rage.

No reply came from Nikki as she only folded her arms across her chest.

"Unbelievable," Rowan muttered. "You're an evil woman, Nikki. No one likes working with you."

Then, Ava felt Rowan's shaky hand in the middle of her back, pushing her towards the exit as he grabbed the helmet from her hand.

"Where are you going?" Nikki asked.

"I'm driving Avery back home."

"You can't!"

"Just watch me," he said, without so much as turning around as he urged Ava out. "Fucking bitch."

"If you leave this place with him, Ava," Nikki said menacingly, "you're fired."

Ava felt paralysed, unable to fight. Unable to defend herself.

Her job or Rowan.

"Pardon?" Thiago interjected. "I don't think you can do that, Nicole."

"It's Nikki."

Thiago swallowed his sip of water. "Really? I always thought it was Nicole."

"You have no right to act this way," Rowan seethed, facing the other woman. "I'd suggest you start respecting Avery unless *you* want to be fired."

"Are you threatening me?"

"I'm making you a promise. Don't mess with her, and I won't mess with you."

"Rowan," Ava whispered, listening to the sound of her voice cracking. "I can go home on my own. Just let it go."

Ava didn't miss the evil smile pulling on Nikki's mouth.

Bitch.

Frowning, he searched her gaze. "Not happening. You're not letting her win."

Rowan brushed past Ava to open the door, letting her exit the building first. He didn't say a word. She watched how his hands gripped the helmets tightly, his knuckles white with tension.

"Rowan," Ava said softly, following him towards his car. Her mind was still spiralling, struggling to process what had just happened. "It's fine. Go back inside."

He ignored her statement, spinning on his heels to face her. He inhaled deeply, obvious anger tensing his shoulders. "You okay?"

She simply nodded.

"Are you sure, baby?" He clenched his jaw then released a small sigh. "I hate that woman. I hate how she treats you like shit. I hate the way she speaks to you. Damn it, I want to run her over."

The only thing Ava needed right now was to bask in his

warmth, settle in the firmness on his chest, and feel his arms engulf her in a tight embrace.

Her chest tightened at the realisation; Rowan had defended her in front of everyone. It was evident that he didn't care about getting in trouble.

She felt a sudden urge to touch him, but she only let her fingers twitch. Glancing towards the building, she saw everyone looking at them. "Let's get out of here before you commit a crime."

"How are you so fucking calm?" He threw a hand in the air before taking a deep breath, tucking a helmet under his arm to ruffle his hair frustratingly. "Okay. Sorry. Do you have your purse?"

She shook her head. "It's inside."

"Shit. So are my car keys. I'll be right back."

"DID NIKKI SAY something when you went back inside?" Ava ended up asking once they hit the road.

"She can say whatever bullshit she wants to me. I don't care about the rules or that stupid non-fraternising clause."

Her chest tightened. "Do you not care if I get fired?"

"You know I wouldn't be able to breathe without you," he said firmly, his knuckles whitening as his fingers gripped the steering wheel. "But I will not let her speak to you that way. I will not let her belittle you again. She cannot get you fired, anyway."

"She can report this to HR or Sophie."

"Avery, it's going to take more than her words to get you fired. There would be no good comms team without you. You hold the entire PR team together, and I know you don't see how good your work is, but I promise you're a wonderful publicist. Nikki is just jealous of your position. So she can wave her witch's finger in your face, but I'm not afraid of telling her to shut her fat mouth."

"Rowan..."

"What, sunflower?" He rapidly glanced her way before focusing back on the road. "She doesn't have any power over me."

"Did you threaten her again?"

"Yes. I'm tired of standing there and watching her be like this with you. I just told her to get her shit together or else I'd expose her to HR."

"Expose what?"

He shrugged. "I don't know. But I enjoyed the way she blanched and started stuttering."

"You're a bellend. But thank you. Thank you for standing up for me."

"I don't think you realise it, but you're a force to be reckoned with, Avery." His hand found her thigh and she allowed his warm caress to coax her. "I'll defend you with my life. I hope you know that."

"I do."

The ride from the karting circuit to her house was rather short. When Rowan parked in her street, he pivoted to face her after unbuckling himself. Part of Ava didn't want to leave, because being with him procured her an intense sense of serenity.

Even if they sat in silence, she loved his company. His voice. The way he spoke. The way he looked at her.

"You let me win, didn't you?" she asked, referring to the karting race.

He chuckled, and the sound of his delight brought a smile to her lips. "Obviously."

"Why?"

"To see this." He leaned his head on the seat, watching her with an unwavering tenderness. He catalogued her features, like he was photographing this moment and ingraining the image inside his mind. "Your smile. That little dimple on your cheekbone. That little squeal of joy you emit when you're happy."

She drew her brows together. "You've noticed all of this?"

"I notice everything about you, sunflower." He tucked a strand of hair behind her ear, causing her to shiver. *What was he doing to her?* "Spend the evening with me."

The suggestion made her heart clench. The thought of Rowan needing her as much as she needed him fed her soul. Her sentiments weren't unrequited, and it made relief seep through her system.

Ava was teetering towards the temptation, but sighed. "I can't. I promised my parents to have dinner at their place. I haven't seen them in a while."

Disappointment gleamed in his gaze. "Oh. That's fine."

She bit the inside of her cheek, locking her pinky finger with his. "You could come if you'd like."

"Yeah?"

"My father will faint the moment he sees you, but my parents will definitely enjoy your company."

He arched a brow. "Aren't we supposed to stay away from each other outside of work?"

Nikki's voice echoed inside her head, reminding her what was at stake if she crossed the line.

"What's one more rule to break?"

Rowan's lips broke into a broad grin. "Well, I guess it's time to meet the in-laws."

CHAPTER TWENTY-SEVEN

LONDON, ENGLAND

Rowan paced back and forth, raking a clammy hand through his hair. Taking a deep breath in, he slowly gained control over his emotions before ringing the doorbell.

Not even a second later, Gabe opened the door, a smirk dancing on the corner of his lips.

"I was wondering when you'd finally grow the balls to knock," Avery's roommate commented as he stepped aside to let Rowan enter.

After he had dropped Avery off earlier, they had agreed on meeting up in the evening to have some time to get ready and freshen up. He had insisted on picking her up again and driving to her parents' house.

Rowan scoffed. "Were you watching me?"

"Yes," Gabe admitted bluntly. "Pretty funny to see the ruthless F1 driver lose his mind over my beautiful roommate. But y'know, I get it. I'd also be down bad for Ave if I weren't gay. Oh, and that's my boyfriend, Elijah."

Gabe had pointed to the man spread out on the sofa, but Rowan only kept his gaze narrowed on the dark-skinned man.

"I'm not down bad for Avery," Rowan hissed quietly. Gabe gave him a disinterested look, and Rowan wasn't entirely convinced by his own words, either.

"Sure." Gabe gestured to Rowan's hands. "The bouquet you're holding says otherwise, honey."

Rowan was about to argue until footsteps echoed from the staircase. He glanced in the direction of the distraction, finding Avery walk towards him whilst securing an earring.

"Sorry for the wait." She stumbled in front of him, invading his bubble with her addictive fragrance and radiant smile. "You ready to go?"

Rowan nodded.

He was speechless.

Why was he downright starstruck like this?

He dipped his chin in a polite nod, holding her gaze. "You look nice."

Wry amusement started to shine around her pupils. "Thanks. Are these for me?"

"What?"

She glanced at the flowers he'd been holding and forgotten about. "The bouquet? Unless you have a thing for Gabe."

"I'm not opposed to that," Gabe chimed in from where he was leaning against the doorframe that lead towards the living room.

Rowan swallowed, unable to control the blush heating the back of his neck. "Yes." He cleared his throat and extended the bouquet towards her. "Here. I hope you like them."

She grazed a petal between her fingers, smiling softly. Knowing he was the cause of her delight made him feel alive. "I love them. You didn't have to get me anything."

"I, uh," he stuttered, rubbing the back of his neck. He was a total nervous wreck. "I went to get your parents something and I thought I'd give you flowers, just because you deserve them, too."

Her smile only widened, her cheeks tinted with a rosy tinge. "That's very sweet of you."

He shrugged sheepishly. "It happens once in a while."

Nothing else seemed to exist every time he stood in the same room as Avery. The more he spent time with her, the more he found himself lingering too close to the track limits, where the unknown lay beyond. But he also found himself wanting to shower her with goods and everything she deserved.

"So cute," Gabe supplied with a dreamy sigh that was more taunting than anything. "Now off you go, or else Mama Sharma will be mad."

Avery blinked, like she was also snapping back to reality.

"Right," she whispered, handing her roommate the bouquet. "Let's go."

Rowan held the door open, allowing her to head outside first. Her arm brushed his chest and there it was again; his heart going into overdrive just by the contact of their bodies.

"Have her home by midnight," Gabe chastised, waving dramatically.

Rowan snorted amusedly. "We'll see about that."

"Use protection!" Elijah, who had come to stand next to his boyfriend, shouted.

"I hate you two!" Avery shouted back before making a beeline towards Rowan's Porsche.

Rowan had other plans, though. With the slight drizzle glistening the concrete, he didn't want her to walk in puddles of rain. He caught her wrist, listened to her gasp of surprise, then lifted her up to carry her bridal-style.

"What the hell?" She winded an arm behind his neck, laughing softly.

"Don't want you to dirty your shoes."

He opened the passenger door, and she smiled brightly in

return when he lowered her to the ground. "Look at you being a gentleman."

He winked. "Always for you."

In the car, he allowed her to put some music on as he typed her parents' address into the GPS. He couldn't keep his smile from widening when Zach Bryan's voice echoed through the speakers.

"You into country, sugar?"

Avery's laugh was akin to an addictive melody—a harmony of soft delight, slowly imprinting itself inside his mind like his all-time favourite song. "Don't call me that again. But yes, you're always humming to country. Indy sent me a playlist with her favourite country hits."

"I'll make you a playlist, too." He started driving off, rubbing the back of his neck with his free hand. "Indy has relatives living in Montana, doesn't she?"

"Yes. Actually, Simon Romano's daughter grew up with Indy's cousins."

Rowan peered at her, baffled by this new piece of information. "Really? Simon's from Montana?"

"You didn't know? And Charlie Beaumont, too. Well, his mum is. His father's Monegasque."

"Really?" he repeated.

She chuckled. "Yes."

"I had no clue. Imagine if Beaumont and Romano's daughter were hooking up. War would be declared."

"I mean, Romano would definitely hate Imperium Racing and both drivers even more. Aïda's off-limits. Especially from Imperium guys."

"They should bang," Rowan encouraged. "There would be so much drama in the paddock."

Avery fell silent for a few heartbeats too long. "What if we're being spotted together? We would create some drama, too."

His fingers tightened around the steering wheel. "So? I told you, people will have to get through me before they can even think of saying a bad thing about you."

"And if I get fired because of my reckless choices?"

"Then you better teach me how to use PowerPoint, because I'm ready to walk into Sophie's office and do a whole presentation as to why you're a great publicist who deserves to keep her job."

"Wow," she breathed out. "That is the best compliment you've ever given me."

"You're a brat."

"But still a good publicist?"

He smirked. "Depends."

He caught a glimpse of her small smile before focusing back on the route.

Despite the serene ambiance in the car, Rowan couldn't ignore the overpowering sensation of nervousness stirring inside his stomach. Taking a deep breath in, he tried to control his rapid heart rate, rubbing the palm of his hand on his thigh.

"Are you... I can't believe this. Are you nervous?"

Her tone was edged with mockery, causing him to narrow his gaze on her when they stopped at a red light. "Yeah, so?"

He released a long sigh when he felt her gaze on his profile. She grabbed his hand, weaving their fingers together and causing his shoulders to drop with relief.

"Talk to me," she asked softly.

"I've never done this," he confessed, pressing on the throttle when the light turned green. He let go of her hand to change gears, then twined his fingers to hers again. "Never met my... *friend's* parents."

"This is a first for me, too." She pecked the back of his hand. "This is the first time I'm introducing them to a boy."

It was his turn to kiss her hand, repeatedly so, causing her to laugh softly. "Baby, I'm a gentleman in this world full of boys."

"Right. A gentleman who fucks me real good."

Nearly choking on air, he tried not to let shock lace his tone.

"Behave, sunflower. Don't make me act like a bad boy the night I meet your folks."

❧

"I GREW UP HERE," Avery explained as she pointed to a building on their right. "Huxley was my neighbour. He lived across the hallway."

"You're kidding me."

Rowan slowed down, a crease forming between his brows at the sight of the building. Small, private—a stark contrast to the World Champion he knew today.

"He lived there with his dad and big sister," Avery said. "But he was the one to take care of his family."

"What about his mother?"

"It's not really my story to tell, but she's not in the picture anymore. Hasn't really been, anyway. I don't think I've ever met that woman. All I know is that she started doing drugs with the money Miles won with karting competitions and all."

"Shit. That's tough. I had no idea."

"Yeah," she murmured. "Like a guy I know, he's a pro at hiding his secrets."

The rivalry between Rowan and Miles was burning, mostly on the track, but that didn't mean he wished for Huxley's downfall outside of racing. Rowan hoped the rude, cold, heartless World Champion would find his own sunflower one day—the person who would be able to see past the thick walls of self-preservation.

Avery pointed to a small house at the end of the street. "That's me. We moved here before I got into uni."

"This is lovely," he acknowledged as he parked in the driveway.

Everything about Avery was his opposite, yet that was why he felt so complete and whole in her company. Like she was the other half his soul had yearned for his entire life. Like she was the missing piece magnetised to his heart, providing that sense of pure rightness he thought he'd never experience.

That's when he realised he could accept being loved. That he *wanted* to be loved.

"Okay," she started when the engine of the car was turned off. "Fair warning, my parents are still teenagers in their minds, so don't be freaked out if they're more outgoing than what you're used to. They had me at a young age, so that can explain their chaotic energy."

"Yeah? How young were they?"

"Nineteen."

He blew a breath. "Wow."

"Yep. But they're my best friends. I think you'll love them."

Rowan smiled. "I'm excited to meet them."

She flickered her gaze between his, her features softening. "Really?"

"Really," he whispered. "I can't wait to meet the people who helped you become the incredible woman you are today."

She swallowed, an emotion he couldn't name misting over her eyes. "Rowan…"

"Listen." He pivoted to face her, reaching for her hand. Until her, Rowan wasn't the biggest fan of being so touchy with another person. Wasn't one to seek the comfort of someone else's skin. But there was something so grounding about her, which was why he felt so desperate to touch her. Absentmindedly, he started tracing intricate shapes on the back of her hand. "You know I'm not really good with big words, but I think you're the most exciting woman I've ever met."

She teased him by arching a brow. "Are you professing your unconditional love to me?"

He couldn't help but chuckle. "Stop being so unserious."

Avery's lips parted to argue, but the front door to her house opened. She rolled her eyes in faux annoyance and turned to wave to a woman who was standing in the doorway, smiling brightly.

No doubt this was Avery's mother.

"Ready?" Avery asked.

"Ready."

Rowan stepped out of the car, rounded it, and opened the door for Avery. The base of his neck was burning, his cheekbones tinted with blush. That ball of anxiety stirring inside his gut hadn't diminished yet, but he took another deep breath in to remain calm.

Rowan was so used to messing everything up, but he wouldn't dare ruin it with Avery.

He couldn't lose the only person who had faith in him.

As Avery went to hug her mother, Rowan opened the trunk to retrieve a bottle of wine and a bouquet of flowers.

He stepped towards the threshold, smiling timidly to the woman who was eyeing him curiously with a beam on her lips.

Avery looked exactly like her. Rowan had to blink a few times to understand they weren't twins.

"Good evening, Mrs. Sharma," he said, extending the flowers. "It's so nice to meet you. I'm Rowan."

"I know who you are. Please, call me Zoya." She chuckled, accepting the flowers. "These are gorgeous. Thank you."

He cleared his throat, meeting Avery's gaze. She smiled, and he smiled in return. "You're welcome."

"Come on in," Zoya urged eagerly. "I was so happy when Ava told me she was coming over with someone special."

Rowan grazed his fingertips to Avery's arm as he took a step inside the foyer, closing the door behind him. "Oh, I'm flattered."

Avery narrowed her gaze when he grinned broadly. "You're not *that* special, Rowan. Get your head out of the gutter."

Zoya chuckled at her daughter's remark before disappearing into another room.

Her home was small, but cosy. Welcoming. Warm. No wonder Avery was such a good person deep in her core.

Footfalls echoed from the staircase, and Rowan watched a

man descend the steps whilst shrugging a jumper over his shirt. As he halted in the foyer, he instantly found Rowan's gaze, his mouth gaping as he blinked once. Twice.

"Zoya?" he called out slowly, not looking away from Rowan. The latter dipped his chin in a polite nod, unsure of what to do.

"Yes?"

"Have I gone to heaven?"

"I'm pretty sure there's a place for you in hell," Zoya snapped.

"But, love, Rowan Emerson is in our house!" he exclaimed excitedly, causing Avery to grunt. "Holy freaking hell."

"Dad," Avery sighed.

"Oh, hey, kiddo." Avery's father glanced from Rowan, to Avery, back to Rowan, and to Zoya who had returned. "You're dating Rowan Emerson? No one has prepared me for this day."

"Not dating," Avery clarified as she walked further into the house.

Rowan wasn't sure why those words had felt like receiving a punch straight into the gut, the pain spreading ever so slowly towards his heart to wrap around the organ like lethal vines.

"Shagging then?"

"I'm not answering this question."

Smiling, her father stepped towards Rowan and offered his right hand to shake. "Come in, man. I'm Andrew. I'm honoured to meet you! I'm such a big fan."

Rowan emitted a quiet laugh and shook Andrew's hand. "Thank you. Pleasure's all mine, sir."

Andrew turned to his daughter, wide eyes glittering with surprise and admiration. "You've hit the jackpot, girl."

"Stop being weird," Avery mumbled, unable to hide the blush coating the apples of her cheeks. "He brought you some wine."

Rowan then handed Andrew the bottle he'd been holding, a sheepish grin spreading across his lips.

Andrew whistled as he read the label. "Ava, I hope you say yes when this guy asks you to marry him."

"Dad!"

But all Rowan could do was look at Avery and imagine what eternity resembled like with her by his side.

And it looked golden.

❧

"SMELLS DIVINE IN HERE, ZOYA," Rowan commented as he walked into the kitchen.

He had spent the last twenty minutes conversing with Andrew, sometimes about Formula 1, sometimes about his career as a divorce lawyer, all the while snacking on appetisers.

Zoya turned around, smiling. "Thank you. Do you eat Indian food often?"

"As surprising as it might sound, it'll be my first time."

"There's a first for everything, right? I think you'll love it."

"I don't doubt it. Do you need help with anything?"

Zoya took her apron off, shaking her head. "I'm all good. You can take the naans out into the dining room, if you'd like."

After Rowan had deposited the plate on the table, he couldn't help but glance at Avery and her father sitting on the sofa, laughing together.

"So, what are your intentions with my daughter?" was the question Zoya asked when he emerged back into the kitchen.

"Isn't that supposed to be Andrew's question?" Rowan teased as he took a seat on one of the stools surrounding the central island.

Zoya's lips tipped upwards. "Touché. But he doesn't see you as a threat."

Slight panic flared through him. "You do? I'm sorry, Mrs. Sharma. It was never my intention."

"I'm messing with you." She leaned the small of her back against the counter behind, holding her glass of wine. "I'm just curious. Ava hasn't introduced us to her friends in years. To be honest, her only friends I remember meeting are Gabe and our ex-neighbour, Miles, who you race with. When Ava lets us meet her friends, it means that she trusts them with her life."

"I trust her with everything," he said softly. "Your daughter is an incredible woman. She's intelligent, works with an intense professionalism, and knows how to handle every situation with beautiful delicacy. She's caring, passionate, sensible. Sometimes, I feel like she understands what I'm feeling more than I do. She's funny, sarcastic, and she's brave. I'd protect her with all I have."

Zoya's brown eyes shone with a veil of unshed tears. She took a step forward, setting her wine glass down with a trembling hand. "Is this how you're asking for my blessing to ask for my daughter's hand in marriage?"

Rowan barked out a laugh. "I see where she's got her snark and wit from."

A soft chuckle erupted from Zoya's mouth, her features softening. "You know it only comes once in a lifetime, right?"

"What does?" Rowan asked, unable to ignore the lump clogging his throat.

"What you and Ava have. Don't ever, ever let it slip away from your grasp. Once it's gone, it's terribly difficult to find something close to that spark again."

"I don't plan to," he whispered truthfully.

"And don't hurt her. Because if you do, Andrew will kill you. Favourite F1 driver or not, no one harms his baby girl."

Rowan swallowed. "I won't hurt her. I promise."

❧

"God that's a nice car." Andrew whistled as he leaned against the doorway, hands tucked in the front pockets of his trousers as he looked at the Porsche.

A gust of wind blew Rowan's hair away from his forehead whilst thunder rumbled in the dark sky.

"Hit me up when you're free," Rowan told the man. "I have an old 911F sitting in my garage. You could take her for a ride."

"Seriously?" Andrew's eyes were wide with excitement. "I'd love that."

"Dad," Avery chimed in as she exited the house, planting a kiss on her father's cheek. "Did you just become best friends with your favourite F1 driver?"

"Yep," Andrew said proudly. "Biggest life goal has been accomplished."

Rowan chuckled and extended his hand for a handshake. "Thank you for having me for dinner. The butter chicken was excellent."

"That's all Zoya's culinary talent."

"Are you flirting with me, Andrew?" Zoya mocked, tucking herself into her husband's side.

"For the past twenty-five years or so, but whatever," he shot back.

Zoya grinned at Rowan. "Come by anytime you want. It was so great having you around."

He nodded. "For sure. I'll see you two at Silverstone?"

"Count on us," Andrew responded with a wink.

Avery brushed his hand after embracing both her parents. "Let's go."

Once buckled in the car, they waved at Andrew and Zoya, then hit the road.

Rowan felt content, humming to the faint melody resonating in the background. He was happy to know Avery had people she could count and rely on; people who loved her unconditionally and supported all her choices.

"Your parents are great," he told her earnestly. He understood why Avery was so loving, gentle, affectionate. She had grown up in a healthy environment, where there was space for open communication—where vulnerability wasn't an asset to failure.

"They're the best."

He slipped his hand to her thigh, applying a soft pressure. When she held his hand, he felt a surge of heat spreading from his digits towards the rest of his body.

"Am I dropping you off now?" he asked.

"Unless you have a suggestion?"

Anything. Anything just to spend more time with her.

"Come back to my place."

He could feel her gaze on him, analysing and studying, uncertainty filling the space of the car. Brushing his knuckles with the pad of her thumb, she murmured, "Are you sure?"

"If there's one thing I'm positive about, it's you, Avery. So yes, I want you to come home with me."

CHAPTER TWENTY-EIGHT

LONDON, ENGLAND

AVA HUMMED TO the notes blasting from the speaker, smiling to herself when she perfectly flipped the golden crepe in the pan.

"Not only did you inherit your mother's snark, but her culinary talent, too?"

She jumped slightly at the coarse baritone of Rowan's voice still laced with sleep.

Turning around, she lifted her shoulders in a sheepish shrug. "I can't promise these are good, though."

"Trying to sabotage me?"

"When am I not?"

Rowan's lips curved upwards into a devastating smile, and she felt her knees weaken at the sight of his dimples. He was leaning against the doorframe, hands in the pockets of his joggers. Tattooed chest on display, she couldn't help but glance at the drawings she had traced late at night.

"Good morning, sunflower."

"Morning," she said softly. She turned back to the stove to put the crepe on a plate. "How did you sleep?"

She listened to his footfalls, focusing on the new crepe she had poured on the pan. When his arms looped around her waist, she felt her heart skip a beat. Then, he placed his chin atop her shoulder a moment after nibbling the shell of her ear.

"Like a baby," he admitted hoarsely. "Never slept that well."

She hadn't planned on staying the night at Rowan's, but after multiple rounds of intense, breathtaking sex, she hadn't been able to combat the fatigue. Hadn't been able to tell him no when he'd pleaded for her to stay.

She had woken up to the soft morning light filtering through the curtains, and when she saw how peaceful he looked sleeping, she had decided to let him rest.

"How'd you sleep?" he asked, tightening his hold before letting go to make himself some coffee.

"Pretty well."

Truth be told, sleeping next to Rowan had procured her an unfathomable amount of serotonin.

He had made her climax time and time again last night. In different positions. Different rooms. Too addicted to each other's bodies, they hadn't had sex fully unclothed once, but Rowan had touched her everywhere. Had praised her with the touch of his hands. The scrape of his nails. The bite of his teeth.

In between rounds of intense sex, they had lain in his bed, talking about everything their minds came across before letting lust take over again.

She had understood then that he, too, was starting to find it impossible to disentangle himself from this situation. That he also wanted to stay hidden in this cosmos of pure solace. That he wished reality wouldn't be so complicated.

"I fucked you real good, didn't I?"

Ava scoffed and turned the stove off. "You need to take it down a notch, dude. You're not that good."

"Hmm." She watched him take a sip of his coffee, studying

her bare legs. "Pretty sure you were saying the opposite when you were screaming my name."

She glared at him. "I hate you."

He grinned handsomely. "You know your resentment towards me turns me on."

There was a tender gleam swirling along the edges of his irises. Something new, yet addictive. Something that made her pulse drum hastily.

"Come here," he urged gruffly, setting his cup down.

Ava couldn't help but succumb to his demand. As she stood before him, he cupped her jaw, brushing her lower lip with the pad of his thumb.

"Beautiful," he murmured, and she watched how his features morphed from lazy tenderness to unrestrained admiration. "Thank you for last night."

"For being a good fuck buddy?" she teased with a wry smile.

"For being my everything."

Her heart exploded, flames setting every vessel, every nerve on fire.

"For listening to me," he continued, oblivious to the corrupting power he had over her. "For spending time with me. For being my favourite person."

Ava held her breath, forcing herself not to be consumed by emotions.

She'd never been anyone's favourite.

"Tate would be so jealous."

"He would be," he confirmed, grinning, a malicious glint alighting his eyes. "Don't tell him I said that."

Ava only chuckled and lifted herself on her tiptoes to kiss Rowan softly. Slowly. As if she had all the time in the universe to pour all those foreign, terrifying yet euphoric feelings through the tangle of their breaths.

The world had stopped spinning the moment he had entered the room, but now she was finally accepting that he had tilted her entire universe onto its axis. She was flying in his orbit like a constellation, and there was no way out.

He pulled away, a soft smile on his lips. And when her own grin widened, he blushed and dropped his forehead against hers.

"What?"

He shook his head. "Nothing."

Rowan pecked her lips again. And again. A growl erupted from the back of his throat when he deepened the kiss, letting his tongue dance with hers for a few beats. Catching her waist, he hoisted her up effortlessly and set her down on the counter, parting her legs to stand in between them.

Ava's fingers twined with his hair, pulling him closer. Shivering when his calloused hands caressed her thighs, she sighed softly into the kiss, forcing herself to pull away.

"I have to go soon," she whispered against his lips.

"Nope. I refuse," he argued, squeezing her thighs. "You're staying with me."

"Rowan," she breathed out.

"I'll never get over how sexy you are when you say my name like that."

"I need to go." Still, she accepted his kiss when he pressed his lips to hers again. "Need to get home and pack. Did you forget we're leaving for Spain today?"

"Didn't forget."

"Stop distracting me, then."

"*I'm* distracting *you*? Jesus, look at yourself, Avery."

She couldn't control the heat creeping up her face. "How about I eat breakfast with you, then I go home and pack?"

When a smirk started dancing on the corner of his lips, she knew exactly what was going through his mind. His hand slipped to the front of her panties, middle finger pressed to her clit. "I know what I'm having for breakfast, and it's your soaked cunt."

She tapped his wrist, feigning shock by gasping. "You have such a foul mouth."

"I won't be able to touch you for days," he said. "It's going to drive me to absolute insanity."

But before she could give in to the temptation, she heard the front door open then slam. Rowan stepped away, groaning and adjusting his obvious erection inside his joggers.

Ava looked at him, panicked.

"It's just Tate," Rowan announced with a baffling nonchalance. "He's got a key."

She jumped off the counter, listening to the deafening thrum of her pulse.

"Where do I hide?" She pulled the oversized t-shirt down her legs, which was doing absolutely nothing to cover the love bites branded all over her flesh.

"Nowhere." Rowan grabbed his cup of coffee, kissing her cheek. "I'm tired of hiding."

"But—"

"Emerson!" Tate bellowed from the foyer. "Why does it smell like crepes in here? You're on a diet, asshole. Are your bags packed? We're leaving soon."

"Told you," Ava muttered, fixing her hair.

"Told you," he mimicked with a roll of his eyes. He then started muttering behind the rim of his cup, causing Ava to narrow her gaze on him.

"What are you doing?"

"Naming F1 World Champions to get my dick down. I'm painfully hard. Thanks for that, by the way."

The door burst open, and Tate reared back when his gaze collided with Ava's. The keys he'd been holding fell to the ground, the loud clatter blending with his confused, "What the fuck?"

"Sup, bro," Rowan greeted, grabbing the plate full of crepes to set it down on the table.

Ava wasn't sure how to react. All she did was wave when Tate studied her physique. He allowed his mouth to part in shock, looked at Rowan, back at Ava, and again at Rowan whilst blinking.

"I'm not sure if I'm supposed to say 'about damn time' or 'you two have some explaining to do'. Either way... What the fuck, guys?"

CHAPTER TWENTY-NINE

BARCELONA, SPAIN

"Ready to kick some ass, mate?"

Rowan pulled the visor of his helmet down and smirked. "Bring it on."

Jamie's chuckle rang through his earbuds. Adjusting his grip around the steering wheel, Rowan waited for his team of mechanics to pull the warming blankets off his tyres. Once done after the signal was given, they scurried off the track, leaving the starting grid to be flooded with the twenty racing cars.

Rowan took a deep breath in.

Starting from pole, he led the queue of cars for the formation lap.

He accelerated, decelerated. Hit the brake.

Pushed the throttle, turning his wheel to zig-zag.

Dragged his tyres on the asphalt to warm them up.

Stimulated the engine, feeling the car's vibrations send jolts of thrilling electricity throughout his bones.

His blood was boiling with anticipation. His heart was thundering wildly as he focused on the route ahead.

When he stopped again on the starting grid, he watched the other nineteen drivers line up behind him.

Rowan's fingers tensed, ready to hit the forward gear clutch.

The first red light flashed. Followed by the second one, until all five of them were bright.

They stood still. Then went away.

Rowan hit the gas pedal, flying down the long, straight line. His pulse was drumming in his ears, his entire entourage a vague semblance as he roared off down the track.

As he took the third turn, he felt a strong resistance in his steering wheel. At first, as he tried to control the car by thinking he had understeered, he couldn't manage to get back on track. Smoke came from his front tyres when he understood he had locked up. He slipped off the limits, just a millisecond before Thiago's car drove past him, and spun.

Rowan's foot pressed on the brake as he tried to work the steering wheel to stop spinning.

Before he could hit the barrier, his car came to a full stop on the gravel, a cloud of dust rising and enveloping him.

"You okay, Rowan?" Jamie asked.

Rowan tipped his head back, slamming his hand on the steering wheel. He pressed his eyes closed and shook his head. "I think I lost the hydraulics."

"Ah, shit. Get out ASAP."

"What happened, though?" Rowan was utterly confused. He'd had a great weekend until now. The car hadn't shown a single sign of weakness.

"I don't know," was Jamie's panicked answer. "Get out of the car, Rowan. Turn the engine off before it blows up."

Rowan's ears were buzzing as he kept the heels of his palms pressed against his closed eyes. He felt like drowning, his lungs begging for some oxygen and his breaths staggering as he felt like the entire world was speeding up.

He heard the door open, cracking his bubble just enough for Tate's voice to filter through.

"I hate you two," Tate muttered. "Be quick before you get in trouble."

Rowan sensed another person walk towards him as the door to his room shut. A second later, soft hands grabbed his wrists with a delicacy that made the fog of anxiety diminish.

"Is this okay?" came Avery's question as she rubbed the back of his hands with her thumbs.

Rowan only nodded, unable to voice a response, fearing to hear the anguish in his tone. But he knew that it was okay to be vulnerable. Especially with Avery. Because she understood his feelings. Because she didn't judge. Because she only pushed him towards daylight instead of pulling him to bask with his demons.

"I don't have much time," she whispered. "Eliott's been acting weird. He's always following me. He won't leave me alone for a minute. I told him I was doing a quick debrief with you, but I need to get back to the garage and watch the end of the race."

He nodded again.

Prying his hands away from his face, Avery looped her arms around his shoulders and pulled him into her chest.

The moment Rowan's ear collided with her steady heartbeat, he breathed out in relief as though he had finally resurfaced from shallow waters. Wrapping his arms around her waist, he held her tightly, trying to regain control over his shaking body.

"You're okay," Avery whispered softly. Gingerly, she pulled him away just enough to force him to look up into her eyes. A small line had appeared between her knitted eyebrows, a soft exhale escaping her mouth when she studied his hardened features. "I've got you."

"Don't go." He hadn't realised her shirt was bunched between his fist—as if he needed to hold on to the sliver of promises she was giving him.

"I wish I could stay." She started caressing his cheekbone—a lover's touch. "But I have to go. I'll meet you for the interviews after the race."

She leaned over and planted a brief kiss on the crown of his head, causing his lungs to tighten.

"Can I see you tonight?" Rowan asked, uncaring of how desperate he sounded.

"Yes."

He hadn't been able to catch a single moment alone with her since they had landed in Spain. It was destroying him to be standing next to her, forbidden to touch her just because they were surrounded by other people.

"You're okay," Avery repeated. "It was not your fault. Jamie said it could've ended badly if you had raced. So, you will bounce back next weekend. You will prove to them you never left. But I also want you to understand that you're a phenomenal racer. I know what's happening inside your head right now and I don't want you to drown in guilt. Okay?"

He swallowed, nodding. His voice cracked when he answered, "Got it."

She kissed his forehead. "I'll see you later."

Rowan watched her leave, feeling all the fissures in his heart widen until all those splinters of pain obliterated his entire chest.

He wanted to cling to her. Wanted to hold her and never let go. Wanted to tether himself to that invisible thread of hope, needing to know he was worthy of something—worthy of her.

It felt as though she was the only person in this universe who was willing to run a finger over the indentations bruising his heart, not even caring if she got injured in the process.

Her feathery voice echoed inside his head like an unforgettable memory. *You're enough. You're enough. You're enough. I promise you this.* She had said those words months ago, but he hadn't been able to put them aside.

But he couldn't have Avery and, secretly, it was destroying him piece by piece.

As he watched her exit the room, he promised himself to start being good for her. Because maybe, just maybe, Avery would be his just like he was already hers.

CHAPTER THIRTY

LONDON, ENGLAND

"WHO'S MAKING YOU smile like that?"

Ava locked her phone and looked up at Indy, lifting her shoulders in a coy shrug to conceal how affected she truly was by Rowan's flirtatious messages.

Because there was a two-week break before the next Grand Prix, Indy had asked Ava if she wanted to grab a coffee at Dawn's Café, the popular coffee shop owned by the one and only Kamari Monroe.

As she walked in, Ava had wondered why she didn't spend more time here. There were shelves upon shelves filled with books, including a romance section. Delicious pastries were on the menu, as well as a long list of homemade beverages. Perhaps this place would become another home to her.

Ava took a sip of her coffee, contemplating whether to tell Indy the truth or try to change subjects.

"It's just Rowan being Rowan," was her response.

Indy nodded. "He *is* a funny guy. Is he a prankster? I feel like he is."

"Not really. But he does like to make the people around him laugh."

"Remember that interview I did with him at the beginning of the season? I have tons of bloopers of me laughing at his stupid jokes."

Ava couldn't control her growing smile, letting her mind wander to all the moments he had made her laugh to the point of curling over whilst holding her stomach as tears welled in her eyes.

Perfectly manicured hands came to deposit pastries on the table, attracting Ava's regard towards Kamari's face.

"What are we talking about?" Kamari inquired curiously.

"Her boyfriend," Indy whispered, winking.

"He's not my anything," Ava retorted.

"Yeah, sure."

"How are things going between you two?" Kamari took a seat next to Ava, deciding to take a small break and let her brother manage the shop.

Cradling her cup between her hands, Ava sighed softly. "We're still just hooking up. I stayed over at his house before we had to leave for Spain, though."

Kamari raised her brows. "Is it some sort of casual dating?"

"I'm not sure... There's always been more than just sexual tension, but I'm very confused about my feelings."

Indy squealed excitedly before covering her mouth, though she wasn't able to hide that spark of enthusiasm from shining in her eyes. "You mentioned feelings! *And* stayed over at his place. So, are you, like, exclusive?"

"Exclusive friends with benefits," Ava clarified. She didn't enjoy that pang in her chest. That burning sensation in the back of her throat. "Just friends."

The café's owner clicked her tongue on the roof of her mouth. "That's bullshit."

"Who knows about you two? Except from us and Tito," Indy inquired.

"Tate. He caught us in Rowan's kitchen."

"Were you fucking?" Indy asked in a whisper before earning a gentle smack on the arm from Kamari.

Ava's cheeks were flaming. "We were teasing each other. But you guys know how Tate is—he was just unfazed. Besides, he's been suspecting Rowan of seeing someone. He even heard us hooking up multiple times. Now he knows it was me all along."

"Rowan is head over heels for you," Kamari added softly. "I watched him dance with you on Tito's boat. Watched him drag you into that world where only the two of you existed. Watched how he did everything in his power to make you smile when it was obvious he was busy combating the demons inside his head. I've observed Rowan a lot, and I'm aware that we're not particularly best friends, but I just know that you're this man's world."

Ava's heart felt like combusting. She exhaled tremulously, finding Kamari's tender gaze.

"Ava, Rowan would do anything for you. He'd yell from a rooftop that he likes you. He'd do something stupid and cheesy, like write *Ava + Rowan 4 life* on his helmet just to prove that he isn't afraid of showing the world who he wants to be with. The only thing that's blocking you both is because you're working together. He's just respecting your boundaries."

Perhaps Kamari was right. The only thing that was standing between Ava and Rowan was work, their career. And that clause forbidding her from dating or befriending Rowan or Thiago.

"He knows I'll have to choose between my job or him," Ava said, a lump inside her throat.

"Who would you choose?"

She didn't even hesitate. "Rowan." Months ago, she'd have chosen her career before a boy, so was she a fool for letting her focus slip away? "But he'd pick racing over me."

Ava's phone vibrated, and her surroundings blurred again.

ROWAN

What are your plans for today?

AVA

Missing me?

ROWAN

Yup. Loads.

AVA

I'm at Dawn's Café with Indy and Kam

But I'm free later tonight.

Why? Want to go on a date?

ROWAN

Dude, I'm supposed to ask you out.

AVA

Ask me out then

ROWAN

Will you go out with me, sunflower?

AVA

I'll think about it.

ROWAN

You're such a pest.

My place 7pm?

I don't want to risk being spotted out in the wild. But you do know I'd take you to the stars if I could, right?

AVA

I know. See you tonight.

❧

Ava pecked Rowan's cheek when he stepped aside to let her enter his house.

It was already too late when she realised what she had done, so she only glanced his way to see him rub the back of his neck as a wave of blush made an appearance on his cheeks.

He crooked a timid smile, as if her fleeting kiss had rendered him speechless and powerless.

"Smells nice in here," she observed as she kicked her shoes off.

"That would be me."

She chuckled, allowing him to take her jacket off her shoulders to hang it amongst his coats. He grinned and grabbed her purse before lacing his fingers with hers. He then pulled her towards his living room. "I made you dinner."

"You did?"

"Don't sound so shocked," he drawled. "Just because I'm an F1 driver doesn't mean I can't cook."

Ava felt her breath catch and disappear somewhere inside her lungs as she halted in the middle of his living room. She felt his fingers release her hand before they came to tuck a rogue strand of hair behind her ear. She suppressed the urge to close her eyes and lean into his touch, keeping her amazed gaze on the small candles lit up around the dining table.

"Cigarettes After Sex?" She drifted her stare towards the record player where music was playing softly.

"I love that band," Rowan said gruffly before coming to stand before her.

"So do I." She obliged and looked up into his eyes. "You did all of this for me?"

When he gently grabbed her chin, she felt a certain weakness in her knees that only he could provoke. "I'd do anything for you."

She felt an invisible thread tighten around her heart whilst she accepted his boundless adoration that felt akin to an eternal embrace.

Ava didn't know how to voice her affection to him. She only let out a breath. Perhaps he had understood everything she wasn't capable of saying by simply observing her reaction.

"I did a crazy thing," he admitted then, passing his fingers through his hair.

She blinked, unfazed. "You always do insane stuff."

A nervous chuckle rose from his throat. "Hang on."

Ava let him scurry off into another room as she looked at his helmets and trophies lying on several shelves amongst small picture frames. There were photos of Rowan standing with Tate as they held a tyre after Rowan had claimed his very first pole position; photos of Rowan hugging his mother; another of him holding Nora when she was a newborn with his sister sitting by his side.

And when a particular Polaroid picture caught her eye, she paused and took a closer look at it. It wasn't framed, and it looked recent. But most of all, it was a photograph of *her*, smiling at something he had said. Alex Myers must have taken the shot before giving it to Rowan.

She wasn't allowed to form a coherent thought because Rowan came back into the room.

"Turn around," he said softly.

She obliged and felt her breath hitch at the sight before her.

"Rowan," she mumbled, eyes rounding. "Why are you holding a kitten?"

A tiny cat with white, smooth-looking fur was cradled between his tattooed arms, purring loudly as he stroked its head.

A devilish grin touched Rowan's lips. "It's yours. I mean, it's kind of mine. But it's ours."

"That was very clear," she deadpanned as she inched closer towards him. "Can I pet it?"

"Yes."

Carefully, she allowed the animal to smell her hand before delicately caressing the top of its head.

Ava felt like melting on the spot. "When did you get it?"

"She's a female," he said. "I got her earlier this week. For you."

She looked up into his eyes, brows lifting in stupefaction. "Me?"

He nodded, that soft smile never faltering. "You once told me you've always wanted a cat, so here it is. I don't know, I went to the shelter just to take a look, and this little one caught my eye. She was in a room with a dozen other kittens, but she was minding her business in a corner alone. She reminded me of you in a way."

"How so?"

"You're constantly surrounded by people, but you know how to thrive and find joy in the smallest things whilst being on your own. I admire you for that so much because I don't know how to do that. I constantly need validation from other people, I always need to be surrounded because I'm scared of being alone."

She frowned slightly, lifting her hand to cradle his cheek. He leaned into her touch, closing his eyes to linger in the moment. "You're not alone. I'm not going anywhere."

"Promise?"

"Promise."

He raised a taunting brow, smirking. "What happened to wanting to get rid of me?"

"I think it was the other way around," she countered. "You tried to poison me."

Rowan barked out a laugh. "You're so full of shit."

The kitten emitted a small meow, causing Ava to look down.

"What's her name?"

"Praline," he revealed. "You can change it if you want."

"Praline is perfect."

❧

After playing with Praline and exhausting her until she started napping in the middle of the carpet, Ava's stomach grumbled from the smell of Italian aromas wafting in the air. Rowan chuckled before leading her into the dining room.

Like the gentleman he was, he took the chair out for Ava to sit down. He rounded the table to sit opposite her, a grin dancing on his lips.

As she returned a smile, his gaze settled on the dimple on her cheekbone. "Your mama raised you well."

"Do you think so?"

"I know so. You're a good man. Thank you for welcoming me in your life."

"I wouldn't want anyone else but you," he said, sincere and honest. "Mum was struggling so much with the divorce, with finding happiness again. She was constantly worried about not being able to raise good kids."

"She raised wonderful people. She has got nothing to worry about."

Rowan's chest rose then fell as he exhaled. He offered her a longing look filled with gratitude before finally changing subjects. "Red wine, miss?"

"That would be lovely, sir."

The nervousness racking his entire body was apparent as he poured the burgundy beverage into her glass then into his. He rubbed the back of his neck, peering up into her eyes when he set the bottle down.

She frowned slightly. "Are you nervous?"

Rowan's throat worked up and down as he swallowed. "Very."

"Don't be," she murmured, reaching across the table to grab his hand. He didn't hesitate to accept her touch. "It's just me."

"Exactly. It's you. I don't want to mess it up."

"You're doing an amazing job," she praised.

She observed his throat work up and down as he swallowed tightly. Frowning, she tilted her head, encouraging him through her silence to express his thoughts.

"Sometimes—all the time, actually—I think I'm not worthy of you," he admitted quietly. "That I won't be able to give you the moon."

A splinter was being twisted in Ava's heart—shattering, breaking the organ. "Don't say that. What I love most about you is that you take your time to make things right. Besides, fetching the moon doesn't happen in the span of a few days. It takes time, and I'm here to match your pace."

His hazel eyes flickered between hers, all that unyielding adoration he only kept for her shining around his pupils. He placed a soft kiss on her inner wrist, and stood up.

"Almost forgot about dinner. I could stare at you for a lifetime."

She huffed out a mocking laugh. "You need to get over your obsession with me."

Was his heart battering as wildly as hers? She had slept with him multiple times, for fuck's sake. Why was eating with him so nerve-racking, then?

"Impossible," he replied from the kitchen.

He appeared a moment later with two plates in hand.

"Pasta with homemade pesto," he announced, setting a plate in front of her.

"Homemade pasta, too?"

He scoffed softly. "Don't ask too much of me, please."

She chuckled. "This looks great. Thank you for inviting me over."

"You're welcome, sunflower. Tell me, where would I take you on our first date if things weren't so complicated?"

She felt her heart stop. Would Rowan truly break all the rules to be with her? He'd always been one to take on mad challenges, but this could impact his entire career.

"The Planetarium & Astronomy Shows at the Royal Observatory," she answered dreamily.

"Yeah?" He nodded, smiling. "I'll take you to the stars. I promise."

She clinked her wine glass with his. "It's a plan."

Winking, he took a sip from his drink, humming when the taste hit his palate. "Bon appetit."

Under his patient scrutiny, Ava took a bite of her meal, then a soft snort escaped her nose. With a napkin, she dabbed the side of her mouth, laughing at Rowan.

"Dude," she chuckled.

"What?" He was confused, a frown on his face as he started twirling his pasta around his fork. "Stop mocking me."

"I hate to break it to you, but the pasta isn't cooked."

With his gaze narrowed on her, he brought the fork to his mouth then barked out a laugh. "See? You wanted al dente, but I gave you *croquante.* Maybe I should hire a personal chef."

❧

THEY WERE LYING on the carpeted floor of his room, staring at the ceiling where he had projected a sky full of constellations.

"This one is my favourite," Ava noted softly as she pointed heavenwards. "Orion."

She pressed on the small remote he had given her, changing the scenery to another starry sky. It was the closest to the Planetarium he could give her, but this—everything about him, his intentions, his growing affection for her—was bigger than the whole sky.

"This one is yours," she whispered.

"Which one is it?"

"Draco; the Dragon. The eighth biggest constellation."

When he didn't respond, she turned her head to look at him. Silver splatters of stardust were reflecting on his face, his absent gaze was roaming around the stellar ceiling. He was divine. The stars were shining for him, and he didn't even know it.

"Something is going through your mind," she observed quietly.

A subtle tick in his jaw was perceptible, causing her entire attention to drift towards the silent man.

"A secret for a secret?" she demanded then, causing the barest smile to touch the corner of his mouth.

He exhaled loudly before shifting to prop himself on an elbow. "I'm starting to get tired of hiding you. Us."

She felt her heartbeat skip a thorough thump. She held his gaze, noticing that pure sincerity. "You are? But—"

"Avery, I can't find the right words to express how much I adore you. How much I crave touching you in a crowded room. How much I want to hold you after qualifying or a race when you give me the support I've always yearned to have."

When he started grazing her arm with the tips of his fingers, she understood how much he felt anchored whenever he was touching her.

His whisper caressed the shell of her ear, its meaning sending her heart into racing mode. "You feel like home to me."

Her chest rose and fell. "I feel the same way about you."

"Good." His dimpled smile was her weakness. Rowan himself was her weakness.

"What is this? What are we?"

"We're whatever you want us to be," he said softly. "But I want you to know that there isn't anyone else for me. I don't want anybody else. But I'll do anything you want, I'll be anything you need."

"You're such a softie."

He winked, causing her to emit a soft chuckle. "Look what you did to me."

Ava sighed, eyes fluttering when the tip of his forefinger came to trace the contour of her nose. "I don't want to mess up our situation at work. I want this to work out, but I don't want you to hate me if something breaks us apart."

"I could never hate you," he assured fiercely. "And we'll make it work. I would tear myself apart if I ever let you slip away. You're everything to me, Avery."

"We'll figure it out," she guaranteed, though she didn't know who she was making this promise to; herself or Rowan.

"Together."

"Always."

As he brushed a wild curl away from her face, he couldn't retain his smile from growing until dimples adorned his cheeks. "God," he breathed out, his wild eyes meandering over her face as though he didn't quite know where to settle his gaze.

"What?"

"I always thought you were the most beautiful girl I've ever laid eyes on."

She could feel her face burning as she bit the inside of her cheek. She lowered her gaze to his tattooed neck, unable to hold his stare.

"Me?"

"Yeah, you. No one compares to you." He lifted her chin with the help of his forefinger. "You know the first time I saw you, I think I was downright speechless. You were shining brighter than anyone else, you were smiling beautifully. I remember watching you and Tito talk, and the admiration etched on your face as you introduced yourself as his new PR officer... I wondered if you would ever look at me that way."

"But you hated me."

"I hated the fact I couldn't stop thinking about you. You'd be in the same room as me, and I would be distracted. I always needed to catch your attention and annoy you because you're the only one who isn't afraid of being a brat with me. To be fair, I also disliked your attitude and the way you had no trouble standing your ground. I wasn't used to being put back in place until you came along. I always found myself wanting to talk to you, and I hated that."

Her cheekbones tingled. "I had no clue." Now she knew why he'd never leave her alone, why he always needed to irritate her.

"Tell me your secret."

She counted three heartbeats before saying out loud the words that had been, secretly, obliterating her soul. She wasn't afraid of opening up to Rowan because he made her feel seen. Made her feel important. Made her feel understood.

"I don't know how to love myself," she admitted almost inaudibly.

A crease between his eyebrows appeared when he frowned. "Why is that?"

Lifting her shoulders in a small shrug, she slipped her gaze towards the ceiling. Again, Ava immediately found his constellation, as though he was the only bright star in her universe. "You know, I have nothing to complain about the environment I grew up in. My parents had me at a young age, but they taught me everything. How to communicate and work through an issue, how to be kind and resilient. And despite it all, it's always been so difficult for me to look in a mirror and tell myself 'You're good. You're enough. You're beautiful.' When I look at myself, I just wonder why people undermine me so easily."

"Jesus, Avery," he breathed. "You've got no idea, do you? Of how you steal the spotlight when you walk into a room. How your unconditional kindness brings me an unbreakable sense of peacefulness. All I can breathe is your life, your energy, you."

Ava blinked, feeling her eyes burn. She exhaled shakily when he pressed a delicate kiss in the centre of her palm. "I have a hard time believing you want me when there are tons of women chasing after you."

"I don't care about anyone or anything but you." When he kissed her softly, she felt herself relax, accepting the promises he was pouring into the entwine of their breaths. "If I show you what I love about you, will your perspective change?"

"I don't know," she responded through the heavy lump stuck in her throat.

"Come here."

Rowan helped her sit up. He sat against the bed and pulled

her in between his legs, wrapping his arms around her shoulders whilst her back came in contact with his chest.

She watched their reflection in the mirror, smiling when she realised how fitted they were—like two puzzle pieces that had been made for one another.

He winked. She smiled.

"I love your spirit," he murmured against her temple. "The way you think and your perspective on things and life are my favourite things. I love how fierce and passionate you are about your job and motorsports. How driven you are, and how it's so painfully obvious that you want everyone around you to feel appreciated. You're brave, courageous, and whilst I know there are people out there who like to give you shit for your hard work, you will never let their words get to you to tear you down. Not a lot of people are like you, Avery. In fact, I don't think I've ever met anyone like you before."

Tears were prickling her eyes because no one had ever said those words to her before. Because he always made her feel like one in a million.

Rowan brushed her hair away from her shoulder and kissed the spot behind her ear. "I love your skin. How soft it is. How tiny goosebumps appear on your arms whenever I touch you. I love your face so much. The shape of your nose, the fullness of your lips... Beautiful."

She leaned into him, allowing him to pry her legs open. A shiver racked through her entire body when his palms ran along the outsides of her legs, pulling her skirt up to her hips.

"Is this okay?" he asked, meeting her gaze in the mirror.

"Yes."

"Perfect." He pecked her jaw. "I love your body. It's sexy and feminine and beautiful. I love the sounds you make when I kiss you. Those whispered sighs when I touch you. Those moans when I fuck you."

"Rowan," she whispered in desperation. She watched his

fingers trace circles on her thighs, always inching towards the place craving for his touch, yet never coming close enough.

"I know, baby." He braced her throat with a tattooed hand before tipping her head backwards, obliging her to look into his eyes. "I love everything about you, Avery. I wish you could see yourself the way I see you."

His lips hovered above hers for a fraction of a second before stealing her breath by kissing her slowly. Ava gave in to the power of devastation by returning the kiss with equal vehemence, listening to the moans erupting in the back of his throat.

But the way he kissed her made her head spin. Made those butterflies inside her chest bat their wings so wildly that she thought they might combust. Made her skin burn as it craved for Rowan to caress every surface of her physique.

She felt his other hand trail down her chest, slip down her stomach until it dipped between her thighs. She bucked her hips upwards, searching for friction, causing Rowan to smirk smugly against her lips.

"I want you to watch us in the mirror," he ordered, his chest heaving. "You're going to watch how I fuck you, how I worship your body."

All she could do was nod and follow his command as she shifted to face the mirror.

"This is very sexy," he rasped, tracing the hem of her underwear with his forefinger. "Did you wear this for me?"

"You wish."

He started planting open-mouthed kisses on the side of her neck as he started rubbing her clit over the lace. "You should try and sound more convincing when you lie to me."

Ava only glared at him, grabbing his wrist to encourage him to fasten his pace.

"I bet you're already soaking for me," he muttered, palming her breasts through her top.

"Why don't you find out?" She directed his hand inside her underwear, causing a low growl to rumble deep inside his chest.

"Fucking hell." He collected her arousal on the tips of his fingers before circling her clit. "You're so desperate for me, aren't you?"

Ava only nodded. He watched how enthralled she was by his hand hidden under her flimsy piece of clothing, but procuring her the best, teasing sensation.

He retrieved his hand to hook his fingers under the hem of the panties. "Let's take this off."

Though Ava felt exposed with her legs spread out and his eyes on her, she didn't feel like hiding.

"Touch yourself," he asked. "Show me what you do when you think of me."

Although a faint coat of blush touched the apples of her cheeks, she still followed his instructions as though she was utterly powerless under his command.

She sighed softly when her fingers came in contact with her clit. She drew fast circles, desperate for release since she hadn't had any these past few days.

"So sexy," he praised, his dark eyes following her movements. She could feel his hard erection press against the small of her back as he gripped the hem of her blouse. "Do you trust me?"

"Yes."

"I'm going to take this off, okay?"

Ava sucked in a breath. "Okay."

She had to retreat her hand to allow him to undress her. When her back collided with his chest again, she watched his reaction as he observed her nearly bare body.

"You're breathtaking," he whispered, fingertips touching her stomach.

She found her slick core again, teasing herself by rubbing slow circles. "Thank you."

"I fucking love your tits." He took hold of her breasts, kneading and palming before pinching her nipples through the lace bra. "Your whole body's a temple."

Halting her motions by grabbing her hand, Rowan brought her fingers to his mouth. He sucked her arousal, grunting.

"I'm starving. Come here."

Rowan told Ava to lie down on the mattress. Standing at the foot of the bed, he let his perusal travel over her body. Imprinting the image in his head. Memorising this very instant, like he was studying his favourite sculpture. Stars shone in his eyes, and Ava didn't feel like shielding herself.

"Wow." He repeated the word over and over, shaking his head in disbelief. "You are the most beautiful woman I've ever seen. Please don't ever hide from me."

"I won't," she whispered with equal softness.

His gaze kept roaming over her body, those sparks ignited around his pupils feeling like poetry, like a serenade meant to make her fall.

Pulling her towards the edge, he fell to his knees and draped her legs over his shoulders, instantly latching his lips to her clit.

His big hands found her breasts, pulling the lace down to touch the bare skin. Ava moaned loudly when the languid stroke of his tongue went from her entrance to her clit, working in tandem with his fingers pinching her taut nipples.

He broke apart for a heartbeat to spit on her core before going back to devouring her like a man starved. She met his lust-filled stare, whimpering when he reached down to adjust himself in his jeans.

She tangled her fingers through his hair, pulling at the roots when his tongue lapped fiercely against her folds. She felt her legs shake when he groaned against her skin, the vibrations sending jolts of electricity throughout the rest of her body. She ground against his sinful mouth, holding him exactly where she wanted him.

Soon enough, Ava came hard, crying out his name.

Rowan stood up with a smirk on his lips, wiping her arousal from his chin. She propped herself on her elbows and watched him undress himself. He, too, was a work of art.

"Keep looking at me like that and I'm going to fuck you until you beg me to stop."

Ava tilted her head, arching an eyebrow in defiance. "Maybe that's my intention."

"Be careful with what you wish for," he drawled, crawling on the bed.

She thought he would kiss her or perhaps tease her some more, but he grabbed her waist and flipped her over on all fours. He bunched her hair into a makeshift ponytail, tilting her head backwards and obliging her to stare at their reflection.

"Look at you," he said huskily, grazing his fingers to her sensitive core. "So ready for my cock to fill you up."

Ava felt her arousal pool down the inside of her thigh. Arching her back and spreading her legs further apart, she offered a heavenly view of her backside to Rowan. He muttered something inaudible under his breath, before his palm came in contact with the skin of her ass. Hard. Fast. Ava whimpered.

"Hang on," he said quietly before releasing her hair. "Condom."

"Wait." She watched Rowan still before he came to hover above her, planting a kiss on her shoulder blade.

"What is it?"

She found it fascinating how his features would soften into tenderness when only a second ago, he was more than ready to ruin her.

"If it's okay with you, I'd like to do it without a condom."

Rowan's lips parted as his fingers found the back of her neck. "Are you sure?"

"Positive. I'm on birth control."

"Baby," he murmured, holding her gaze through the mirror as he straightened himself. She watched his hand wrap itself around the thick base of his shaft, stroking slowly, torturously. "I've never fucked anyone bare before. You do realise what is at stake now? I can't let you walk away after this. I can't pretend this is only physical between us."

"It's always been more than that," she whispered. "I don't want anyone else other than you like this."

An emotion she couldn't decipher flashed in his eyes. As he held her hip, he continued to pump his erection before lining himself with her entrance.

"Good." Then, he slid in with a swift motion, causing Ava to fall forward onto her forearms. He whimpered loudly, this sensation being a new one for him as well. "Fuck. *You're mine.*"

Her fingers tensed around the bed sheets when he pulled out slowly then slammed in roughly, the tip brushing the most sensitive spot that made her scream out his name.

"Eyes on me," he demanded, pulling her hair again to oblige her to look at herself. "Look how well you're taking my cock."

As much as she tried to hold his gaze, she couldn't keep her eyes from rolling in pleasure when he started thrusting rapidly. The sounds of skin slapping mixed with their moans. She could already feel a bead of sweat cascade down the valley of her breasts.

"You like being fucked like this, don't you?" His breathing was staggered, heavy, bated with whimpers and guttural moans.

"Oh, God." She met him halfway by moving her hips in tandem with his animalistic thrusts.

"It's Rowan." He slapped her bottom again. "I asked you a question, baby."

"The answer is yes."

"Good girl." Slowing his pace down, he breathed heavily, letting go of her body for a few beats just to unclasp her bra. She moved her hips forward, backwards, fucking his hard cock in a slow motion. He leaned forward to kiss her back, a hand coming to grab her breast. "Shit, you feel so good."

A throaty moan escaped. "Enjoy it while you can."

He emitted a hoarse chuckle, digging his fingertips into her waist. "Brat. That's my intention, don't you fucking worry."

He started pounding into her again, keeping his eyes on her through the reflection. A sheen of sweat had started to glisten on his bronze, tattooed skin. He looked like a Greek God on the cusp of ruining her, and she was at his complete mercy.

Her entire body gave up on her as she lied down on her stomach, dragging Rowan along with her.

And then, something shifted.

He fucked her slow and deep, pressing coaxing kisses on her shoulder blade whilst slipping his hand to her clit. The tip of his shaft grazed the sweet spot that always made her tremble, repeatedly so.

"Say you're mine," he demanded huskily, his free hand bracing her throat.

She felt her walls clench. "Rowan," she gasped in pleasure.

"Say you're mine."

Arching into his chest and granting him access to her breasts, she couldn't control the volume of her moans. He played with her pebbled nipples, giving them equal attention.

"I'm yours," she cried out at his next thrust—hard and deep. "Yours."

"You're perfect," he whispered. "I can't get enough of you."

As he laced their fingers together, she pressed a kiss on the back of his hand. Chocolate and honey collided in the reflection, and she saw *everything* in his gaze—that unyielding devotion, that pure adoration, that unconditional sentiment of being appreciated for who she was.

But before she could analyse those stars in his eyes, his perusal darkened again, and his lazy thrusts became feral and uncontrolled. He pounded into her without restraint, working his fingers in sync to bring her to the stars.

"Rowan," she choked out.

"Come for me, baby. Let me see how beautiful you look when you fall apart while my cock fills your tight cunt so nicely."

Ava unravelled with a loud moan, blending with the sound of his verbal praise and their skin slapping. She gripped the sheets tightly, trembling as he kept pounding into her as she reached her climax.

"That's it," he murmured. "Perfect."

She listened to his low grunt as he buried his face in the crook of her neck. To his loud moan when he came hard, stilling as he released deep inside her, her name dancing on the tip of his tongue.

"Oh, fuck," he rasped out, pulling out and plunging back in. "You've ruined me for everyone else."

As he pulled out fully, she winced slightly at the feel of his cum dripping down the inside of her thigh.

He made her turn around so that she would lie on her back to look at him. He kissed her softly, chuckling when he felt her legs still shaking from her recent orgasm.

"That good?" he teased.

"It was decent," she mocked back.

"Idiot." He pecked her nose, a lazy smile etched on his blood-rushed lips. "Give me a few minutes. I'm going to teach you a lesson about getting railed thoroughly."

She wondered, at that moment, if he knew how deserving of love he was. How loved he was.

"Hey, lover boy?"

"Yeah, sunflower?"

"I really like you."

He sighed softly, tenderly kissing her cheek, then her lips. "That's a good thing because I adore you. Like a lot."

He pulled her to his chest as he lay down, allowing her to listen to the rapid drum of his heartbeat. "We can be anything you want us to be until we figure everything out. I've been yours for as long as I can remember. I'm not going anywhere."

She peered up at him. "Even when you hated me?"

"Especially then. No one can spike my temper like you do, but no one has ever taken the time to get to know me and support me the way you do."

Ava could feel herself free-falling, but all she wanted to do was bring Rowan with her, because she was intent on catching him and never letting go.

CHAPTER THIRTY-ONE

MONTREAL, CANADA

"Be careful in turn eight. Watch out for track limits."

Rowan nodded at his race engineer's remark. "I've got it."

Driving at a slower pace to keep his tyres warm, Rowan drove through the circuit. Slight drizzle was falling on the entire track, though the weather forecast had predicted heavy rain by the end of the qualifying session.

"My call is to leave the intermediate compounds on."

Rowan scoffed as he flew past another car almost at a full stop on the side of the track. "I'll be fine. I won't slip if that's what you're worried about."

"I'm not," Jamie chided.

"Liar."

There were less than two minutes left before the end of Q3. From afar, Rowan saw the starting line and got ready to start his qualifying lap.

He wasn't one to boast, but Rowan liked to think he was

one of the best drivers in the rain. He knew how to control his car, its anchors, its grip. Knew how to handle the speed and anticipate the braking.

And having a wet qualifying at the Circuit Gilles-Villeneuve was exhilarating. This track was a thrilling one because it was quick, flowing, and filled with many heavy-braking chicanes.

The start of his lap went smoothly, knowing by his unbridled speed that he had just set the fastest lap-time in sector one. With that unrestrained pace, he focused on the dry line created by other cars to drive through the rest of the track. But taking turn eight, he felt his rear slip, causing him to lose time and drive off track before regaining control.

"Shit," he muttered under his breath.

He finished the lap, knowing he had set the fastest time in sector three as well despite his minor error.

"Tell me we have it," Rowan asked, decreasing his pace.

A beat passed before Jamie's voice filtered through. "You had it, but your lap time has been deleted because of the track limits in turn eight."

"Damn it." He shook his head, disappointed. "Don't tell me 'I told you so.'"

Jamie chuckled. "I wasn't going to."

"You were thinking about it, though." He had run a lap at the beginning of Q3, so he would start Sunday's race based on that first run. "What's my position then?"

"P3."

"Good."

Rowan was gutted, but he had to tell himself it was a great qualifying result, regardless.

When he parked his car and got out of it, he congratulated his teammate who had qualified second, then Miles who, obviously, was on pole.

Watching Miles go up to his father to share a tight hug, Rowan felt his heart twist until an unbreakable knot formed. He tore his helmet off, unable to shake that longing feeling away.

A firm hand clapped him on the back, and Rowan grinned at Tate who had come to congratulate him. "I'm proud of you."

Rowan understood then, that family didn't necessarily mean sharing the same bloodline. Tate was his family, and that girl smiling proudly at him from afar was his family, too.

His home.

❧

ROWAN CHECKED the time on his phone again, exhaling frustratingly when he noticed Avery hadn't responded to him.

Was she ignoring him? Was she angry at him?

"Trouble in paradise?" Thiago asked from his side as they sat in the hotel's lobby, waiting for their respective PR officers to accompany them to the track.

Thiago's PR officer was busy having a conversation with the receptionist, but Avery was nowhere in sight. She hadn't answered any of Rowan's text messages since last night. He was worried. To the point he'd felt anxiety rattle his entire body because the mere thought of her leaving was destroying him.

"Not sure what you're talking about," Rowan answered before adjusting the cap on his head.

A knowing smirk touched the corner of his teammate's lips. He lifted his shoulders in a shrug, able to see directly through Rowan's nonchalant lie. "You should give her a call."

Rowan's jaw tightened. "Wow, thank you loads for the suggestion. Why didn't I think of that? She isn't answering, genius."

Thiago frowned. "Do you want me to give it a try?"

Shaking his head, Rowan dialled Avery's number again. "I've got it."

As he pressed the device to his ear, he watched his teammate type on his own phone, a growing smile brightening his features.

Such a lovesick imbecile.

"Hi!" Avery finally answered. Rowan let out a relieved sigh at the sound of her voice, straightening himself. "I'm sorry. I wasn't ignoring you. I'm just not feeling well, but I'll be down in a minute—"

"Where are you?" he cut in, standing up.

He heard a sniffle from her side of the line, and he scurried to the lifts, his heart pounding with disquietude. "My room. But I'll be right there."

"You don't sound okay. What's your room number?"

"Rowan—"

"Room number, sunflower," he repeated firmly.

"208."

"I'm on my way."

Rowan's pulse was deafening as he knocked on her door. He observed his surroundings, finding relief when no other team member of Primavera Racing was lurking around. Most of them were already at the circuit, anyway. Still, taking the risk was worth it. It always was when it came to her.

As soon as the door opened, he surged into the room, tucking Avery into his chest.

"Are you okay?" he asked, breathless, tightening his hold around her small frame. He felt his heart churn when her small hands fisted around the back of his shirt, as though she didn't want to let go of him, either.

"I'm fine," she said hoarsely.

Rowan pulled away, slightly confused by her tone full of fatigue. When he looked at her, he raised his brows in surprise. "You look like shit."

She rolled her eyes, pushing him away playfully. "You have such a way with words. Best compliment award goes to you."

"Evidently," he replied with equal sarcasm. He gripped her chin, tilting her head backwards to observe her reddened nose, puffy eyes, and pale face. "Who did this to you? Did someone hurt you? Is it Nikki? Did she say something to you? Where is she—"

"The weather," was her blunt answer. "I caught the flu or something. But I can go to work, it's okay."

The back of his hand touched her forehead, and he frowned. "You're burning up. No work for you today."

"But it's the Grand Prix!" she argued as he directed her towards the bed. "I can't miss this day."

"You can and you will. Stop being stubborn."

She was now sitting on the edge of the mattress, hooded eyes staring back at him. She pushed her glasses back up the bridge of her nose, sighing softly when he kneeled before her.

"Who's going to replace me?"

Rowan winked before undoing her shoelaces. "You're irreplaceable. But I'll check with Thiago to see if his PR officer can work with me today, too."

Avery nodded, contemplating his words for a few heartbeats. "Okay. I'm so sorry. I wasn't feeling well yesterday after dinner, and I thought I'd feel better if I went to bed early. I hate that I'm letting you down today."

"Hey," he coaxed, rising to his full height before going into her suitcase to retrieve a pyjama set. "It's not your fault, baby. I just—I was so worried about you. You haven't been answering me, and I thought you were mad at me for something."

Avery lowered her gaze. "I didn't mean to make you feel that way."

"I know," he murmured, helping her out of her Primavera Racing polo. His heart ached when she grunted in agony. Her body must have been aching. "I don't know how to take care of others, but I promise I'll take care of you."

Her expression softened, yet it was evident she wasn't comfortable with the fact that Rowan was putting her well-being above everything else. "But you need to get to the circuit. Like, now."

"I know, and I'll leave soon. But you come before anything else in this entire world."

"Never before racing," she tried to counter.

"Always before everything," he pressed, holding her gaze.

Deep down, Rowan wasn't certain anything could ever overpower his love and dedication to Formula 1, but maybe he could make an exception for Avery. He was, at that exact moment.

"Don't be late," she whispered. "You'll get in trouble."

"I've got this."

When she had changed out of her work attire and tucked under her bed sheets, Rowan walked towards the mini kitchen and started brewing some tea.

"I can't believe I wasn't there to help you last night and this morning," he mumbled, taking a deep breath to calm his nerves.

Seeing Avery so frail and worn out was akin to being set on fire. It was torture. He hated seeing her like this. She was always such a vibrant, sparkling person.

"No worries," she said so quietly that he almost hadn't heard her. "I'm fine."

His phone chimed, and he let out a heavy breath.

TITO

Everything ok?

ROWAN

Avery caught the flu or some shit.

Taking care of her now but I'll be down in a few

TITO

I hope she feels better soon!

We just need to leave in five so be quick. I'm covering for you.

ROWAN

Thanks. What did you say?

TITO

That you're taking your morning shit

ROWAN

Dumbass

"Okay, here."

He set a steaming cup of tea with lemon and honey on her bedside table, along with a glass of water and painkillers he had found in the bathroom.

"I know you're not feeling well at all, but try to get as many fluids in as you can. There's chamomile tea here and water. Shoot me a text if anything goes wrong. Tate will have my phone and I'll figure something out to send someone to check up on you."

A small smile tugged her lips upwards. "I love this side of you."

"Which one?"

"The caring guy."

"I only care about you," he admitted gruffly. "You know that, right?"

She nodded, tremors racking her entire body.

He couldn't leave her. But his phone rang, and he declined Thiago's call.

He tucked the covers until they were secured under her chin. Rowan didn't quite know what to do—she was shivering yet burning up all at once. "You okay, baby?"

She blinked, nodding. "I'll be okay. I promise I'll watch the race from here."

"Just try to get some rest, that's all I'm asking." He brushed her sweat-dampened bangs away from her forehead, feeling an ache in his chest to see her so fatigued. "It's killing me to see you like this."

"I'll be okay," she repeated.

He let his lips tilt in a minuscule smile. "I'll bring you soup after the race."

"Sounds good."

Leaning forward, Rowan planted a lingering kiss on her

burning forehead. He left a caress on her cheekbone, smiling when she watched him in awe. His heart clenched, and it cemented something in him.

"I lo—" He stopped himself and cleared his throat, surprised by the words that had almost slipped out of their free will. "I'll be back soon. Please get some rest."

"Good luck, champ. I believe in you."

Rowan squeezed his eyes shut and took another deep breath as she turned on her side to lie in a comfortable position. He flexed his fingers and finally turned on his heel, but whilst his heart urged him to stay here and take care of her, his head was telling him to stay focused and concentrate on his career.

He left her room with a heavy chest, only to find Eliott walking out of the lifts and heading towards his direction.

"What are you doing here?" Rowan asked coldly.

Eliott jerked his chin towards the end of the corridor. "Coming to check on Ava. She was supposed to leave with us fifteen minutes ago."

Rowan grabbed the back of the photographer's neck, forcing him to walk back into the lifts. "She's sick. She's not coming today."

"Seriously?"

"Yep. She's taken care of."

Eliott shrugged. It took every ounce of willpower for Rowan not to smash his head against a wall. Not only was this guy interested in his girl, but it seemed like, lately, he was getting too close to her—prying too much into her business.

Besides, Rowan didn't want that man anywhere near Avery.

"And what were *you* doing here?" Eliott finally asked when they stepped inside the lifts.

Rowan tucked his hands in the pockets of his jeans. "Why do you care? Went to check on her since she's my PR officer and my shadow."

"You can be such a dick," the other guy mustered.

"Thank you."

Eliott only narrowed his gaze on him, and Rowan couldn't help but think this was the beginning of trouble.

❧

ROWAN WAS on Thiago's tail as they drove inside the hairpin. As his teammate reaccelerated after the turn, Rowan followed him closely by staying aligned with the car, hoping to seek a slipstream and gain extra speed as they flew down the straight line. Whilst the dirty air caused slight turbulence on his vehicle, he managed to control his speed, sensing the heat of the circuit and the sparks igniting on the asphalt mixing with the thrill oscillating through his veins.

Lap 12, he read on the sign a mechanic had brandished when he crossed the line.

Fifty-eight more to go.

He hit the brake late before taking the chicane, and when his foot pushed on the throttle to regain full speed, he felt his car lose control.

Everything was a blur to Rowan as the car dragged through the track at an unstoppable speed. When the vehicle came to a halt by crashing into a protective fence, he heard a buzzing sound in his ears, the smell of smoke enveloping him in a cloud.

One moment he'd been driving normally, the next one he lost his front end and spun, hitting the barrier and causing a wheel to detach from the vehicle.

Then, complete darkness.

CHAPTER THIRTY-TWO

MONTREAL, CANADA

THROUGH THE HAZE of turmoil fogging his mind, Rowan managed to lift a thumbs-up and grin broadly at Tate when the latter tried to snap a picture.

"Enjoy while it lasts, prick," Rowan grumbled when his friend snickered. "No, 'I hope you're okay', no 'your crash was scary as fuck', no nothing. Just you, snapping photos of me while I'm high on painkillers and wearing this stupid hospital gown."

Tate's shoulders were lifted in a lazy shrug after he took a seat on the armchair placed in the corner of the room. Rowan was waiting for the doctor's approval to leave, which shouldn't take too long now.

He had been taken to the nearest hospital after his crash. After several tests, he had been told everything was alright and that he was lucky nothing had broken with an incident including that much G-force.

"Stop being so melodramatic," Tate drawled as he opened a packet of crisps to munch on. "You're alive."

"Great observation," Rowan responded.

His head was still pounding, and the doctor had advised him to stay away from screens for the next twenty-four hours. As he tried to make himself more comfortable, he rubbed his face as a groan erupted.

Suddenly, a photograph of chocolate eyes that had already been embedded in his mind resurfaced and caused his heart to go into overdrive.

He peered at Tate who was busy scrolling through his phone. Clearing his throat, he asked, "Heard from Avery?"

Tate didn't so much as look up. "When are you going to start calling her Ava?"

"Never." He loved calling her Avery. Loved being the only person using her full name.

"Well, *Ava* is worried sick about you."

Rowan sat up. "You've been texting her?"

Tate scoffed loudly before locking his phone and putting it in the pocket of his hoodie. "Yes. You asked me to check on her all day long because she's got the flu. She woke up from her nap to watch the race, and now she can't stop asking me how you're doing."

"Can you tell her I'll call her when I get back to the hotel?"

"Already done."

"Thanks. Is she okay?"

"Marvellous," his friend deadpanned. "Tired and very weak, is what she told me. I already called room service to bring her some soup and painkillers."

"Thank you, man."

Rowan tipped his head back, allowing a frown to touch his brows when he closed his eyes.

"You really do care about her, don't you?" Tate asked quietly.

Rowan only nodded. There was no denying it. "I'm an idiot."

"Your words, not mine."

Rowan sighed heavily and finally opened his eyes, only to find his friend watching him curiously.

"You *really* like her," Tate observed.

Tate knew Rowan best. His secrets. His fears. His strengths. His weaknesses. And whilst Rowan had been able to keep everything regarding Avery a secret from the world, Tate was no fool.

"Yeah," he breathed out. "So much that it's killing me not to be able to touch her in front of everyone else. Have you seen this woman? I've never met anyone like her. She's so selfless, smart, brilliant, and fun to hang out with. She's the only one besides you who knows about my father and everything about my past. She's my best friend."

"Hey!" Tate hollered, an aggravated look taking over his features. "You're such a cunt!"

Rowan glowered. "Fine, you're *both* my best friends. But I don't know, she's just the most special person to walk this planet."

A surge of intense relief seeped through his veins as he finally admitted out loud, to someone other than himself, that he had unwavering, strong feelings for Avery. He'd never felt like this before, and he wasn't sure what it was.

But if Avery was a drug, then damn him for not wanting to find a cure. Being utterly intoxicated by everything about her was akin to flying high, to racing at full speed. He never wanted that haze of euphoria to fade away.

The corner of Tate's mouth curled upwards. "I don't know if you're high on meds or high on love. Either way, this is epic. I always knew you had a thing for her."

"Really?"

"You've been trying to get her attention ever since she arrived on the team. Always spiking her temper, firing back at her comments, always watching her not-so-discreetly."

Tate was a quiet man, but thoroughly observant.

"I almost told her I lo—" Rowan stopped himself, eyes widening. "That I care deeply for her."

Tate snickered. "Why are you saying it like it's a problem?"

"Because it is."

"I don't see how."

"I don't even know what love is. You know I wasn't surrounded by it when I was a kid. For all I know, whatever this is with Avery could be mistaken as intense lust—"

"It's not just that," Tate cut in.

"I know. I just don't think I'm good enough for her. She deserves way more than what I can offer. And I don't deserve to be loved."

"The bullshit that comes out of your mouth is truly baffling, Rowan."

Rowan scoffed. "I'm just telling the truth."

"No, you're confused. There's a nuance. So what? You think you're not good enough for her, so you're going to leave her?"

Rowan shrugged. "If it makes her happy..."

"It would tear her apart, and you know it. It would destroy you." A beat of silence passed. "Is that why you're so terrified to tell her you love her? Because you think it's not earnest enough? Because you think you're not allowed to feel it because of your childhood and what your fucker of a father made you believe? You talk about her like she's your saving grace, you protect her like you'd take a bullet for her. Is that not clear enough for you?"

Rowan reared back. "Why are you getting angry?"

"Because—" Tate rubbed his face. "You're my best mate. I just want you to be happy."

"I don't deserve her. I'm not a good man—"

The only thing he was worried about was the detriment he would be facing by prioritising Avery's happiness and destroying himself by doing so.

"Stop it, Rowan. Stop fucking with your own emotions."

Slumping against his pillows, he sighed, trying to ignore the buzzing in his ears and the weight pressing against his heart. "Sorry."

For a moment, Tate was silent, simply observing Rowan with shining eyes. Like seeing Rowan in this state was hurting him, too.

"I'm proud of you, you know," Tate said earnestly. "For accepting the intimacy she's providing you. But you need to allow yourself to be loved and to love her, too. I've watched you yearn for this kind of affection your entire life. And I don't know a single person who isn't more deserving of finding love than you, mate. So I'm not sure what you're waiting for to tell her how you feel."

He couldn't breathe. "I'm just struggling. I think she could be happier with someone else."

"Don't do this to yourself," his friend murmured. "I like this chick. She's cool, funny, snarky, and she's perfect for you. The way she's patient and holds your hand, the way she helps you be the best version of yourself without judging. She pushes you forward and encourages you. Why would you want another man to have her? You told her about your father and your past, you told her everything. Just because you think you don't deserve her doesn't mean you should stop yourself from exploring those feelings. You can't control the way you feel about her, so just accept it. And you make her happy, so fucking happy. Don't take that away from her."

Taking a shaky inhale, Rowan tried not to let tears escape. "Jesus, don't make me cry. Why are you so quiet all the time and say stuff like this out of the blue?"

"I just wish you would get your shit together and marry Ava so that I can win the bet I made with Riley and your mother."

"You made a bet—You know what? I actually think you're a complete shithead."

Tate rubbed his nose with his middle finger. "I think the right words should be 'Thanks, Tate. You're the best friend I've ever had.' But it's whatever."

CHAPTER THIRTY-THREE

LONDON, ENGLAND

AVA JUMPED UP with a start when a knock resonated loudly. She dropped her phone, a loud thud echoing when the device hit the bureau. She looked up and sheepishly smiled at Eliott.

Hopefully, he hadn't caught her texting Rowan. Or blushing at his risky messages. Or smiling like a fool at his verbal applause. Or complimenting her on the outfit she'd been wearing today. Or thanking him again for bringing her breakfast every day for the past week.

"Still not off?" Eliott asked, gesturing towards her laptop.

She calmed her racing heart, and closed her planner—hiding the nerves rattling her body. "I should be done in a few. What about you?"

"I just got done editing the recap video of the Canadian GP," Eliott said as he stepped inside. "Still a bummer you missed it."

She lifted her shoulders in a shrug. "The flu got me good."

"You feeling better now?"

A subtle smile spread across her lips. "Yes. I mean, it was over a week ago, so I'm all good."

"That's cool." Eliott tucked his hands in the pockets of his jeans and bounced on his heels. "Have you eaten yet?"

She had some plans with Rowan, but for obvious reasons, she couldn't say that to her coworker.

"Not yet," she responded. "I'm having dinner with my housemate and a few friends."

Not a complete lie since she had asked if Rowan was down for eating over at her house tonight.

"Oh. I wanted to ask if you wanted to grab a bite in town or something."

She couldn't help but smile sweetly. "I appreciate the offer."

When he rubbed the back of his neck, Ava held her breath. It had been a few weeks since he'd been invading her space more than usual—always following her everywhere, trying to check who she was messaging, hanging around when she was supposed to attend meetings with Rowan.

Obviously, Eliott was suspecting something. And she didn't know what, to be precise. So, all Ava could do was keep her answers short, cold, and create more distance between them.

As much as she appreciated him and found him to be a funny guy, Rowan's safety came above everything. She would protect her man with everything she had.

"Okay." He took a deep breath in and spat out the next words so fast that they were barely comprehensible. "Iwouldliketotakeyououtonadate."

Ah.

Of course, Ava had understood it all.

She tilted her head, ignoring Rowan's message. "Sorry, I didn't get that."

Eliott exhaled. "Sorry. Nervous. Um, I'd like to take you out, Ava."

She lowered her gaze, searching for the right words to say without hurting her friend. Her eyes landed on Rowan's message, and there was no doubt about the direction in which her heart was gravitating.

ROWAN

I'm right outside your office.

Please shout "DOUGHNUT" if Eliott tries to make a move on you

But I'm really looking forward to hearing you reject him. Cause at the end of the day, it's my cock that's filling you up.

Ava snorted, covering her mouth as she read the messages.

"Are you laughing at me?"

She found Eliott's gaze again, sighing softly to calm herself down. "No. Oh my gosh, sorry. Look, I really appreciate you, but I can't go on a date with you."

He frowned. "Why not?"

"Because..."

"Because why?" he pressed, aggressively. "It's just a date, Ava. I didn't ask if you wanted to shag right here and right now."

"Wow," she cut in, lifting her brows, surprised by his tone. "I'm seeing someone, Eliott."

"Who?"

"It's none of your business."

He narrowed his gaze. "Is there a specific reason why you won't tell me?"

"Just keeping my relationship private."

Elliott's jaw clenched as he took a step back. "You know what? I deeply regret asking you. You don't have to lie if you're not interested."

Standing up, Ava felt anger seep through her system, but she controlled her tone to stay gentle and soothing. "I'm not lying. I really am seeing someone. I didn't mean to hurt you or anything."

The man she had once referred to as her friend only shook

his head in disappointment and turned on his heel. "You're such a bitch. No one would date a girl as prudish as you, anyway."

Rounding her desk, she folded her arms across her chest, rapidly slipping her gaze to the door when Rowan's silhouette appeared. "Calling me a bitch because I told you no is very low coming from you, Eliott."

"Well, I think I have every right to—"

"Avery," Rowan cut in as he marched inside the room. "I'm having an existential crisis. I need my publicist to help me sort out this mess."

She emitted a soft sigh of relief, though she could see the fury blazing around Rowan's pupils. The wrath emanating from his demeanour. The curl of his hands.

She knew he didn't need help. He had come to save her.

"Sure," she said, keeping her gaze on Eliott.

The latter didn't say a word and exited the room, making sure to bump into Rowan's shoulder.

"Lovely seeing you!" Rowan called out, a faux smile on his lips.

He then slammed the door shut, turned the lock, and strode towards Ava with anger-filled steps.

"Are you okay?" He tucked her into his broad chest, one hand cupping the back of her head.

His torso rose and fell rapidly as she looped her arms around his waist. She was trembling with rage, shaking with sadness because the sentiment of culpability was too overpowering. But when he caressed her hair, coaxingly, she couldn't help but bask in his comfort.

"I'm fine," she murmured. "We're in trouble."

"I know." He kept the volume of his voice quiet, just in case. "We'll figure something out, okay? I won't let anything happen to you."

"And I won't let anything happen to you, either."

He kissed her temple, and she felt a smile form on his lips. "Look at us, having each other's backs."

"Always," she whispered.

When Rowan placed a delicate kiss on her forehead, she couldn't help but smile.

She watched stars shine in his gaze, causing her heart to burst open. "Keep doing that and I'll fall in love."

And so, Rowan planted another kiss on her forehead. And another one. And another one until he started pecking her cheeks and nose and jaw.

Soft giggles fled around the room. Ava pulled Rowan down, bringing her lips to his forehead. She heard him sigh, and when he looked into her eyes, that gleam swirling around the edges of his irises told her everything she needed to know.

Rowan pulled her into a long embrace, and despite that unbreakable feeling of safety in this moment, she couldn't help but feel like their world was about to crumble down.

CHAPTER THIRTY-FOUR

SILVERSTONE, ENGLAND

"OKAY, YOU'VE GOT this, mate."

"Can you stop the sweet talk when I'm driving?" Rowan grumbled. "Update me on the situation instead."

"Understood," Jamie answered. "The safety car is going in on the next lap. Nineteen laps to go afterwards."

"Awesome. Let the fun begin."

The British Grand Prix was, without a shadow of a doubt, one of Rowan's favourite races on the calendar. Not only was it Primavera Racing's home Grand Prix, but also because the circuit's layout was thrilling, being one of the fastest tracks. Besides, races were always filled with exhilarating moments.

He had started on pole, but the race was red-flagged during the first lap when an incident at the end of the grid occurred. Several cars had been involved in the collision, and one driver had been sent flying violently into a barrier.

Fights after fights with Huxley as the latter kept trying to overtake him, Rowan had to pit during lap seventeen when he had made contact with his rival, causing a puncture on his front right tyre.

Miles had been leading ever since the incident, but Rowan wouldn't let him win. This victory would be his, and no one else's.

Last week, he finished P2 in Austria. So far, he was having an amazing weekend and was intent on standing on the highest step of the podium today.

Pushing on the brake when he got too close to the Imperium Racing car, Rowan zig-zagged to keep his tyres warm. He watched sparks fly behind his rear wing as the car dragged on the asphalt, desperate to claim his win once the green flag was waved in the air to replace the yellow one.

Then, the safety car went into the pit lane, leaving the circuit to the drivers to finish the race.

Rowan accelerated at the same moment Miles did, going flat-out before braking late before the corner, attempting to overtake on the outside. Miles' car was quicker and swifter in turns, so Rowan didn't manage to take the lead back.

❧

Two laps later, Rowan started chasing Miles down the long straight. Coming wheel to wheel, he pushed his rival slightly out on the pebble, making a move on the exterior of the turn and staying ahead.

Rowan was back at the front, and he would fight to stay there.

As he raced in a corner before pushing on the throttle to escape the queue of cars lining up behind him, Rowan glanced in his rear-view mirror to watch Thiago trying to go around the outside of Miles Huxley, but he went off the track in the process.

"Come on, Tito," Rowan muttered. "Let's make this a 1-2."

❧

Slipping off the track limits, Rowan went into the grass, yet managed to stay out front when he fell back on the circuit.

"Twelve laps to go," Jamie announced on the radio.

Though Rowan had speed, great tyre management, and complete control of the strategy, he wasn't sure if he could hold Miles Huxley off for too long. Imperium Racing was too fast. Too good. But Rowan loved a good challenge.

❧

It appeared like there was a problem with the Imperium car as Huxley's pace shifted drastically. With the sun beating down on Rowan, he felt his suit clammed with sweat sticking to his body, his chest heaving as he took a tight corner.

Managing to catch a glimpse through his rear-view mirror of Miles slowing down and allowing Thiago to overtake, he felt a surge of pride wash over him.

"Get him, baby," Rowan praised, grinning under his balaclava as he took Beckett's corner. "That's what I'm talking about."

❧

There were only five laps left when another yellow flag was brandished.

"What happened?" Rowan groaned in slight annoyance as he hit a button on his steering wheel to set his pace at ninety kilometres per hour.

"A McMillan stopped on the track in sector three. He can't take corners."

"Ah."

Once again, not surprising.

"Keep delta positive."

"Yup."

It took two laps before the green flag was brandished again.

When Rowan sped up, he observed his teammate trying to put as much distance as he could between him and Miles. So, Rowan decided to help by slowing down.

"I'm going to give Tito DRS as soon as it's available."

"Good job," Jamie praised. "Great teamwork."

Rowan scoffed. "Look at me doing the strategist's work again."

"You and your massive ego will kill me one day."

Rowan only chuckled at his race engineer's remark.

Anticipation thrummed through his system as he led the race lap after lap, keeping his teammate on his tail in order to secure a double podium.

His fast car roared through the track, leaving sizzling sparks in its wake.

The high temperature coming off the circuit blended with the July heat caused his breathing to stagger, beads of perspiration falling down the bridge of his nose.

He didn't lose focus in the high-speed corners. Aimed the apex of the corner with millimetric precision. Handled the vehicle easily.

The moment Jamie announced it was the last lap, Rowan pushed at full throttle and fled through the entire circuit flat-out, causing his tyres to degrade rapidly. He didn't care though, because he had just done the fastest lap time, and had won the British Grand Prix.

ROWAN GRINNED BROADLY as he brandished the trophy high in the air, listening to the overjoyed screams and delighted cheers coming from below.

When he glanced down, all he could see was a sea of red—

mechanics, engineers, fans—praising him and Thiago, chanting their names.

And through that mass of people, he managed to find Avery. Standing there, a beautiful smile on her lips as she looked up at him as though he was a shooting star. No matter where he was, no matter what surrounded him, he could always find her like she was the missing piece that completed his puzzle.

He winked down at her, and she winked back.

❧

NOT A SINGLE CALL from his father, not even a mere text. Rowan was used to this. He felt so numb that he didn't feel a single shred of pain now.

He was done pleasing his father. Done pushing himself to his limits to be validated. Done hurting himself just to be neglected like he'd been his entire life. If even winning didn't mean a single thing to his father, then he needed to focus on the people who were there for him.

Regardless of his destructive thoughts, the message he had received from Avery's father brought a grin to his lips.

ANDREW MADDOX

Thank you so much for inviting us to this weekend. It was awesome! Massive congrats on your win.

Hit me up when you're free to grab a beer or something. If that's cool with you of course

I'm so happy my daughter found a persevering man like you.

Cheers!

Feeling a warm sensation dancing inside his chest and setting his entire body to cracking embers, he lifted his gaze to look at

Avery who was waiting for him to finish dressing up, scrolling through her phone and chuckling on rare occasions.

"You look handsome in this photo." She showed him the screen that displayed a shot of him standing on the podium, racing boot in hand, grinning a moment before drinking the champagne from his shoe.

"Hope you'll have it printed."

"To hang it above my bed?"

He hummed. "There's an idea."

She feigned disgust by scrunching her nose, and returned her attention to her phone. "I'm alright. I'd rather not see your annoying face first thing when I wake up."

"That's a shame," he chided. "I'm sure my prettiness has the same effect as a ray of sunshine."

She chuckled. "You wish."

She was so captivating. So beautiful.

And he was on the brink of making the biggest mistake of his life.

"Avery," he breathed out shakily, standing up.

They needed to head out for post-race interviews, but he just needed one more moment with her—one last moment. Away from the entire world. Away from cameras and prying eyes.

Her gaze collided with his, and he felt his knees threatening to give up on him just at the sight of her doe eyes. "Everything okay?" she asked.

"Come here, baby."

The instant he winded his arms around her body, aligning their drumming heartbeats in perfect harmony, he sighed in relief.

No matter how tightly she held him, no matter how hard she clung to him like her life depended on him, Rowan still doubted he was good enough for her.

The questions never stopped ricocheting against every corner of his mind. Never ceased being loud and driving his thoughts into a frenzy. Sometimes, he couldn't sleep. Couldn't focus—paralysed by fear.

"I'm really proud of you," she whispered in his ear. The murmur dug a hole in his chest, expanding and widening until his entire body ached.

He felt a lump make its appearance slowly, agonisingly, in the back of his throat. Closing his eyes, he tried to ignore the stinging sensation flooding his waterline.

"Thank you," he whispered. "For everything."

With her ear pressed to his chest, he wondered if Avery was able to sense his sudden dismay. "Are you okay? Your heart is beating so fast."

"I'm grand," he lied. "Still coming down from today's high."

She was silent for a moment, tightening her hold around his waist. "Okay. We need to go."

He let her go with a heavy heart, but just as she was about to open the door, he grabbed her elbow and made her turn around. Slanting his mouth on hers for a slow, passionate kiss, he swallowed her gasp and let his tongue brush hers, sealing himself to Avery by this invisible cord tying them together.

The tip of his nose grazed against hers when they pulled away. "Avery..."

"Yes?" She flicked her gaze between his. Rowan was on the cusp of breaking to pieces.

He memorised the precise brown of her irises, frowning. Who knew this particular shade had become his favourite colour? "Nothing. I just..."

"It's okay," she murmured, smiling softly. "Take your time. We can talk later."

But Rowan wasn't sure if eternity was enough time. He was confused, scared of the strong sentiments he felt for her. Part of him wanted her for every lifetime he'd be granted to experience, but that sombre part was still convinced she deserved better. Deserved someone who had the courage to shout and profess his love from rooftops, deserved someone who could easily give her the love she merited without any term or condition.

For the first time in his existence, Rowan wasn't sure whether to listen to his heart or his head. Teeter towards happiness or destroy himself by letting her go.

CHAPTER THIRTY-FIVE

LONDON, ENGLAND

SOMETHING HAD SHIFTED drastically. Something Ava couldn't fathom and hadn't anticipated. Something that was wounding her so deeply that she felt like her walls had crumbled down.

Rowan had gone from spending nights with her, stargazing and sleeping together, to not talking to her anymore.

She didn't know what she had done wrong.

She had sensed that something was happening inside his head, though. That he was combating some demons. She hadn't braced herself for this cataclysmic tempest—one that had obliterated her.

But she should've held his hand. Should've encouraged him to open up instead of giving him space to lose himself in his detrimental thoughts.

She was adamant about communicating all sorts of sentiments—whether they were negative or positive. She knew

Rowan struggled with words, with opening up, but he had shut himself off in the blink of an eye, and it was hurting her.

It had been nearly a week since she last heard from him. At first, she had given him space because that was maybe what he needed. Perhaps he was starting to feel overwhelmed by those new feelings consuming him.

Ava knew he reciprocated her sentiments. Those deep, unwavering, affectionate feelings.

So, what happened?

"You okay?" Gabe asked softly, rubbing her shin as her feet were resting in his lap.

She swallowed the thick lump inside her throat and nodded, keeping her absent stare on the television screen. "I'm fine."

She wasn't okay, let alone fine. Gabe knew it, but he didn't push her.

Perhaps Tate would be able to help her.

AVA

Is Rowan okay?

TATE

I think so? He's in the room next door. I can check on him.

We went out for drinks last night and he seemed more than fine. But you know him, he keeps to himself and smiles even when something bothers him. I did sense him being pensive, though.

The fissure she felt pierce through her vital organ left her internally bleeding. She wiped the rivulet of tears that had escaped, tapping her response rapidly. Gabe's touch was still soothing, but she couldn't manage to find the strength and embrace his comfort with her spiralling thoughts.

AVA

Was he with someone else?

TATE

Another woman?

Jeez, Ava. Of course not. He'd never do that.

Why? What's going on?

She decided to text Rowan directly. Because she was tired. Because she would fight for him just like he'd normally fight for her.

Maybe Rowan was bored of her. Maybe he wanted to stop everything and see someone else. Either way, Ava needed closure. Needed answers.

AVA

I don't understand what happened.

Can you please answer me? At least tell me you're okay.

I'm worried and I can't act like I don't care about you because you know damn well you're my entire world and beyond.

Talk to me, Rowan. Please.

His answer was immediate, but instead of sending a torrent of relief towards her, his message left her agonising with an unfathomable pain.

LOVER BOY

You should go out with another man. Anyone else.

I'm not the one you want.

CHAPTER THIRTY-SIX

LONDON, ENGLAND

AVA KNOCKED ON his door again, wrapping her cardigan around her torso as the late evening breeze brushed against her shaking body.

When the front door opened, the wound in her heart deepened, leaving fragments to fall into the pit of her stomach. Rowan stood there, bloodshot eyes staring back at her as though he was surprised to see her there. As though he was shocked that she was willing to fight for him.

"You're such a fucking cretin, Rowan," Ava choked out, letting her hands fall to her side.

"Nice seeing you, too," he deadpanned, stepping to the side to let her enter his quiet house.

"Is it?" she bit out. When her shoulder grazed his chest, she felt sparks ignite on her arm, but they diminished instantly when he didn't grab her hand, or wrist, or hip. When he only closed the door and stood before her, immobile. "Because it looks like you're avoiding me, and I don't even know why."

Rowan's mouth gaped as he ran a hand through his dishevelled hair. That was when she noticed how fatigue-stricken his face was. How he was letting the same affliction consume him.

"Actually, I know why," she said bitterly, frowning. She didn't pay attention to Praline who had come to beg for her attention. "You're pushing me away because you think I don't want you, but you don't know *anything*, Rowan. You're so used to people leaving so you're walking away, thinking I'm going to abandon you when it's not the case. So you're saving yourself the trouble of hurting by pushing me away instead. But you don't get to do that. You don't get to make that decision without talking to me first."

Rowan didn't respond. His entire expression was blank, yet his eyes were glinting with sorrow.

"I'm right, aren't I?"

His answer was a simple nod. Barely existent.

Ava didn't want to say those words out loud, but she forced herself to. After letting out a breath, she asked, "Do you want to put an end to this? To us?"

Rowan's lower lip trembled, his features hardening for a flickering heartbeat. Then, he shook his head. "No."

A cloud of turmoil had started invading her senses. "I'd rather you tell me the truth."

"I just—" His voice cracked, and he shook his head, like he didn't know what he wanted to confess.

"You what?" She glanced away, blinking to prevent tears from falling. "You thought it would be okay to tell me who I want to be with? You thought it was okay to ignore me, thinking I'd put all of our history in the bin like it didn't mean anything to me? You thought what?"

"I think I don't deserve you!" he shouted then, his chest rising and falling.

She swallowed thickly, not even rearing back at his outburst. "Why do you keep doing this to yourself? Why can't you just accept for once in your life that someone wants you? All of you.

Your demons, your scars, everything. Is it so hard to believe that I want to fight for you?"

His jaw tightened, making its muscle tick. His hazel eyes that she had fallen in love with were shining with unshed tears, and she knew he was hurting just as much. "I'm not good enough for you. I can't give you what you need."

"That's not for you to decide," she argued, feeling a tear cascade down her cheek. The sight of her detriment made his fingers twitch by his side, but he kept the immense distance between them. "You can't tell me what's good or bad for me. You've given me everything. Why are you throwing it to waste like that? You have flaws, imperfections, but that's what makes you so real! You constantly give me everything I've longed to have in a lifetime, and that's exactly why you're my favourite person."

Ava's vision was blurry, and she felt her entire body tremble with rage.

"I don't want to lose you," she whispered, her voice cracking. "I refuse to let you push me away."

He gestured to the door. "There are tons of guys out there who would treat you better than I do."

"That's bullshit!" she cut in, stepping forward. "That's bullshit, and you know it. Stop making these excuses. Stop thinking I want someone else because I don't."

"You're the one who said we needed to cut our deal if we wanted to see other people."

The world stopped spinning, her mind going into a frenzy at the realisation. "Is this what all of this is about? You've met someone, haven't you? And you're pushing me into someone else's arms to make it easier to leave."

Rowan's expression hardened. "I haven't met anybody else."

Incessant rivulets of tears stained her cheeks, and she couldn't stop the wild tremors skittering across her body. "That deal was for *you*. Because *you're* the famous F1 driver who always meets new people. Because *you're* the guy with girls chasing after you. *You're* the guy who could meet, at any moment, a woman who has everything I don't. This was all for *you*, Rowan. Don't you dare turn it around on me."

"But do you not see the way I just disrespected you?" His voice was hoarse with sadness, features woven with undeniable chagrin. "The way I left your place days ago and haven't answered any of your messages since then? How I left you thinking you weren't enough, leaving you worried. I'm not a good person, Avery, and you'll soon realise it. I just don't get why you came running to me after everything I put you through. Why you want to be with me when—"

"I love you, you idiot!"

Rowan stilled, blinking as he inhaled sharply. Shock drew upon his face as though he couldn't quite believe those words had fled past her lips.

"I love you," Ava repeated softly, taking another step forward until she finally stood before him. Close to him. She batted her tears away, a small smile spreading across her lips. "I know you want to be with me, too. I know you're terrified of those feelings, and of what's at stake when you commit to a serious relationship. But we're not your parents, okay? We're us. We're everything. We're an entire galaxy, and you know it."

"Say that again," he asked, almost inaudibly.

Ava chuckled. "I love you, Rowan. You're my best friend. I've wanted a best friend my entire life, and it just makes sense that it's you. You picked me up when no one noticed I had fallen."

A sob erupted from the back of his throat, and he finally closed the distance by cupping her cheeks, setting her whole body to life again. She grabbed his wrists—coming home to her anchor—blinking out another stream of tears, tremors rattling through her body.

"Why?"

"You have the audacity to ask me why I'm in love with you? I could write an entire novel about how incredible you are, about how amazing and appreciated you make me feel. You are fully loved, and it's hurting me that you don't realise it."

"I'm sorry," he murmured, over and over, dropping his forehead against hers. "I thought it was for the best to let you be free and see someone else."

"It was the worst thing you could have done."

"It's been killing me," he admitted, sniffling. "I've been trying to convince myself to let you go, but I don't want to. I'm just trying to protect you."

"From what?"

"From being fired," he clarified. "You're so passionate about your job, and it's beautiful to see. I know we tend to forget about reality, but I couldn't stand the thought of you being forced to leave because of our reckless decisions. Remember, it's your job or me."

Ava held his gaze. "And it's you that I choose. Wasn't I clear enough? Did you think we would've been able to work the rest of the season together and act like we were okay if we had called it quits?"

He shook his head. "I didn't think it through."

"Not your smartest move, Emerson."

He sighed heavily, brushing a tear away from her cheek. "I'm aware. I'm so sorry, baby. I didn't mean to hurt you."

"I really thought I had done something wrong," she whispered, knitting her brows together. "If you feel too overwhelmed, or if you need space, I just want you to tell me. I will understand."

He nodded. "Okay. It's just that—" He paused to take a deep, tremulous breath in. "I've never felt this way about anyone before. And all my life, I've been used to living in someone else's shadow. I've been told, repeatedly, that I'm not good enough and I've always been the second choice. It's destroying me, and I don't want to be that person to you."

When she cupped his broad neck, she could feel his steady

pulse beneath her palms. "You're my first choice. Always. Until the galaxy turns to dust. Until I draw my last breath. I promise."

Rowan accepted her words when a tear freed itself. He kissed the inside of her wrist, evoking a trail of chills to roll down her spine. "You're my whole world, too, you know. You're even more than that. You're my anchor. My everything. You keep me grounded. You make me feel like I'm enough despite all the mistakes I repeat."

A sob tried to rise in the back of Ava's throat. She cried quietly in relief because he still wanted her. Because that spark had never been extinguished—hadn't even faltered. But she also cried with raw sadness, pained by the fact he still didn't believe he was good and golden.

"Please don't cry," he murmured, kissing her cheekbone and collecting her tears one by one. "It's killing me to see you like this. I'm a complete dickhead, and I know it. I really am sorry, Avery."

"Don't do this ever again."

"I won't," he promised. "I swear I won't. When you started giving me space to reflect on my thoughts, I was starting to get suffocated without you. It's like I couldn't really breathe unless I held you. And I don't know why I tried to convince myself it was a good idea to tell you to go on a date with someone else. I punched a hole in the wall after I texted you earlier."

Frowning, Ava grabbed his hand, causing him to wince. Reddish marks had already bloomed on his scarred knuckles, tiny splits cutting the skin open.

"You need to stop punching walls," Ava murmured, pulling him towards the bathroom.

"It was either the wall or Tate's stupid face. He tried to shake me to my senses."

"What would we do without Tate's sense of humanity?" she deadpanned, hopping on the counter.

Settling between her parted legs, the corner of his mouth tipped upwards as he allowed her to take hold of his warm hand.

She dabbed disinfectant on a cotton pad before wiping his knuckles delicately. Like she was scared to hurt him even more. Like she wanted to make him comprehend, through the delicacy of the actions, that he was allowed to be treated as if he were made of porcelain.

Nothing was indestructible, but there was nothing such as being too broken. Ava had never thought of him as a hopeless man; she'd never wanted to fix him. All she wanted was for him to heal, embrace the wounds he wore akin to battle scars, and find the courage to move forward. Every step he had taken—whether with her or in his F1 career—was like a gold medal he could hang amongst his greatest achievements.

"Is Tate still here?"

"No," Rowan answered quietly. "He knew you'd show up. I hoped you would."

"I'd cross an entire ocean for you," she whispered, finding his mesmerising gaze.

"So would I. The entire world."

"I know."

He slid his other hand on her thigh, applying a certain pressure. When he kissed the tip of her nose, she felt all the affliction that had invaded her body disappear. "What you make me feel is beyond comparison. What I feel for you is strong and powerful. Freeing, but so grounding all at once. You make me feel like the happiest man alive. I'm just afraid I can't give you what you need."

"Can you please stop saying that?" She threw the cotton pad away, trailing the tips of her fingers up his forearms, watching chills arise beneath her touch. "You're a good man, Rowan. You make me feel seen, cared for, loved. You make me feel beautiful, and that's a feeling I never knew before you. You've given me more than what I ever wished to have in a partner."

A dimpled smile graced his features. "Good. You deserve an entire sky full of stars."

She poked the little divot on his right cheek, mirroring his act of happiness. "I've missed this."

"I've missed you." His hands went from her legs to her hips, pulling her towards the edge. "Do you forgive me?"

"The only thing I was angry at was you shutting yourself off and pushing me away when there was no reason to. But all your feelings are valid when you're with me, so of course I forgive you."

"Thank you, sunflower."

Toying with his silver chain, she bit the inside of her cheek. "I have a question..."

His fingers slipped beneath her blouse, setting her skin ablaze. "Anything."

"Did you go out for drinks with Tate, hoping you'd be able to move on by—"

"I'm stopping you right there because the answer is no. No, I didn't want to flirt with another woman. No, I didn't speak with another woman. No, I don't want anyone but you. I just went out to grab a beer or two to clear my head. Nothing else."

"Okay. Sorry. You know how I tend to overthink when it comes to this."

Rowan's fingers cupped her chin delicately. When he started sauntering his tender gaze over her face, she felt like combusting under the intensity of his scrutiny. "There's only you for me. There aren't enough words to describe your beauty, but you know what I love most about you? It's this,"—he tapped her temple, a smile touching his lips—"sexy brain. Your mindset, your resilience, the way you handle every situation with care. The way you see the good in everyone. The way you're just so amazing."

She lowered her stare before blinking, unable to control the torrent of emotions coming to mist over her eyes. "Thank you."

The very instant Rowan brought his lips to hers, she felt sparks igniting on every inch of her skin. Setting her on fire. She gasped, as if she'd resurfaced after nearly drowning, just as he cradled her face to deepen the kiss.

Rowan moaned as though he couldn't get enough of her. As though he felt alive and high on adrenaline, just by the simple tangle of their lips.

"Let me show you how much you mean to me," he whispered against her mouth, brushing her jawline with the pad of his thumb.

"Please."

He smirked. "So desperate."

"So cocky."

"You won't be complaining when my cock's inside you and making you scream while I fuck you into oblivion," he droned, obliging her to wrap her legs around his waist. Effortlessly, he picked her up and walked them towards his bedroom.

Her fingers worked to unbutton his linen shirt, a soft chuckle flying past her lips when he pinched her bottom. "I think we should test out this theory."

"I already know how it's going to go." Depositing Ava on the bed, he hovered above her, hands placed on either side of her head, letting his chain dangle in the air between them. "And I know I'm right."

"You have such a massive ego," she bit out, resulting in him scoffing softly.

"Oh, come on, I'm quite literally the best person you know."

She smiled, and he stilled, as if her mere presence had paralysed him. He sat back on his heels, hands delicately caressing her jeans-clad shins as his eyes softened.

"You are," Ava confirmed.

Rowan's grin was akin to a ray of sunshine—procuring her an intense sensation of serotonin. "That's what I thought," was his smug response.

Pulling him towards her by hooking her pointer finger in his chain, she noticed his smile before their lips sealed for yet another breathtaking kiss.

She didn't know how long they kissed, but all she knew was that she was lost in a complete haze of euphoria and desire.

Rowan's hands were roaming all over her physique, like he was trying to convince himself she was real. Ragged breaths were echoing inside the room, their bodies trying to eliminate every shred of distance between them.

His fingers tangled with her hair just as his lips found her jaw, leaving a trail of open-mouthed kisses down her neck. Tilting her head to grant him more access, she sighed, locking a leg around his hip and pulling him into her. Instantly, their hips started to roll in tandem, his hard erection pressing directly on her centre.

"Need you naked," he mumbled, lips grazing at her collarbones.

Ava couldn't form coherent phrases, so she only nodded. He pulled away, sitting up before grabbing the hem of her shirt to pull it over her head.

"So beautiful," he whispered as her blouse got discarded on the floor. His perusal lingered on her breasts nearly spilling out of the lacy fabric, descending his gaze to her stomach.

He watched her with a starlit delicacy, a lover's gaze so tender and filled with so much adoration, that the thought of hiding barely crossed her mind.

As he started unbuttoning her jeans, Ava watched how dark his eyes were, how his pupils had expanded with unrelenting lust.

When her pair of jeans joined her shirt on the floor, Rowan didn't waste a second to worship her body by planting soft kisses all over her skin. Her throat. The swell of her breasts and the valley between them, making sure to give equal attention to her peaked nipples. Her stomach—every single inch, every single dip and curve. Her navel. Her thighs. Her shins. Up towards the inside of her thigh, making sure to leave a few marks—claiming her.

But there was no need to leave a trace on her skin when he'd been etched into her soul ever since the first time they touched.

"You are so beautiful," he whispered, planting a kiss above her pulsing heart. "I can't believe you're mine."

And there was something so innately beautiful about the way Rowan loved Ava so fiercely. Even if he hadn't said those words out loud just yet, she could feel deep inside her bones that her sentiments were reciprocated. She wanted to believe they were.

"Rowan," she breathed out when his lips grazed the hem of her underwear, the roughness of his beard burning her skin, yet making her want more.

He settled comfortably between her parted legs, a taunting smirk dancing on the corner of his mouth. "Patience, love."

"Such a tease."

"Such a brat," he bit out, earning a scoff in response.

"Keep complaining, and I'll leave you here with a raging hard-on."

"Yeah, right." Scoffing, he tugged her panties to the side, exposing her aroused core. "You're dripping wet for me, baby. Ain't no way you're walking out of my house without getting off. Multiple times, preferably."

The very instant he latched his lips around her swollen clit, Ava fell back on the pillows, a soft moan rising from the back of her throat. Rowan grunted, his tongue flicking fiercely around her clit as he kept his gaze on her.

Through the fog of pleasure nearly blinding her vision, Ava tried to maintain his challenging gaze, threading her fingers through his locks. She tugged at the roots when his tongue went flat out from her entrance to her sensitive bud, before he went back to devouring her.

Ava writhed, moaned, arched her back, and ground against his mouth until she came hard, breathing raggedly.

Rowan only stopped when her legs ceased to tremble. He rose up, grinning before leaning in to kiss Ava softly.

The taste of herself on his lips made more arousal pool in the pit of her stomach, and her burning desire for him nearly made her combust into a wildfire. She made haste to undress him without breaking their heady kiss, a few chuckles blending with the heavy sighs evaporating into each other's mouths.

They broke apart to let Rowan shrug off the rest of his clothes.

And suddenly, time stood still. Everything around Ava shifted to a blurry semblance, her whole attention brought to his left pectoral.

She pushed herself on her elbows, trying to breathe and not let emotions consume her. "You're such an imbecile."

Rowan chuckled, his own eyes glittering. "I just went down on you, made you climax, and now you're insulting me?"

"You tried to leave me, and you got a sunflower tattooed above your heart." She sniffled, raising trembling fingers to feather-lightly trace his new tattoo. The fine lines and details were beautiful. He'd filled the blank space with a symbol that, perhaps, gave him peace and joy. "You're an idiot."

"I know," he breathed out, grabbing her hand and guiding it to flatten it against his skin. His heartbeat was powerful—erratic. "I knew I wanted this done a few weeks ago."

"Why?"

"After you showed me the stars and told me my constellation was one of the brightest. After you showed me your perfect body, showing you trust me enough to see you. After I just realised I feel everything for you... I just knew that I needed to fill the blank space."

Carefully, she ran her finger around the tattoo without touching it. "It looks recent."

His cheeks flushed. "You're going to call me stupid again... But I had it done last night."

"Last night? But—were you drunk?"

"Tipsy," he corrected wryly. "I know, I know, it's not good to get a tattoo when you have alcohol in your system, but drunken actions are sober thoughts."

Knitting her brows together, she laughed. "That's not the exact expression, but okay, lover boy." She found his tender gaze again. "Why all of this? Getting this tattoo and then pushing me away?"

"I was just so confused. I've never felt this way about anyone before, and it's scary, you know? Even now, I still think I don't deserve to be loved, but I'm willing to learn and do this with you."

"Thank you." She brushed his jaw, smiling. "What's the meaning of the sunflower, then?"

He mirrored her smile. "It's a sign of positivity. Of something colourful despite the darkness surrounding me. And it's a reminder of the girl who's stolen my heart—the most special woman to have entered my world."

Ava locked her lips to his, kissing him softly. "I love you," she whispered against his mouth, and he shivered before retreating.

"I know."

Ava wasn't upset. Wasn't disappointed because he hadn't said the words back. She didn't need him to, because she just knew he loved her beyond measure. She'd felt it weeks ago.

Their gazes locked when he wrapped his hand around the base of his erection, his free hand running from Ava's knee to her hip.

"Get naked, baby," he ordered, pumping slowly. She could see a bead of pre-cum leaking from the slit. "Now."

Ava pulled the remaining pieces of clothing off her body, leaving her completely bare before Rowan's eyes.

He'd seen her like this before, but there was something different in the way he was looking at her now. Something raw. Something real. Something unwavering and everlasting.

"Good girl," he rasped, planting a hand next to her head when she was lying down again.

Without warning, he rubbed the tip of his shaft along her

wet folds before entering brusquely, causing both of them to gasp and moan loudly.

"Yes," Ava sighed, digging her nails into his shoulders as he started pounding recklessly into her.

"I'm the only one who fucks you this good." He pulled out to the tip. Slammed back in. Wrapped a hand around her throat and forced her to look into his dark eyes. "You're mine."

Ava nodded, unable to contain her moans. "Yes."

He applied pressure around her airway, his thrusts feral and uncontrolled. "Who do you belong to?"

"You," she gasped, eyes rolling to the back of her head, her legs locking around his hips. The new angle made him whimper. "You," she said louder.

"That's my good fucking girl," he praised. "You're doing so well."

Rowan released her throat as he slowed down yet kept his thrusts deep and hard. Taking one of her legs, he raised it until her ankle rested on his shoulder.

"Fuck," he moaned at the new position. Slowly, he pulled out and rammed back in. "You feel so, so good, baby."

He started circling her clit in sync with his rapid thrusts, the bed rattling against the wall. Ava rolled her hips to meet him halfway, fingers holding the bed sheets so tightly she knew her knuckles had turned white.

Rowan's skin was shining with a thin sheen of sweat, his breaths heavy and bated. Whimpers loud, moans unrestrained.

"Say it again."

"I—" A hard thrust made her moan. "Love—" Another harsh one. "You."

His rhythm became animalistic, intent on rapidly sending her towards the pinnacle of pleasure.

"Come for me," he encouraged as he felt her walls clench around his pulsing cock. "Let me see how pretty you look when you fall apart."

When the pressure applied against her clit became nearly

unbearable yet heavenly, Ava unravelled, moaning loudly. She chanted his name, over and over, completely at his mercy.

"Stunning," he praised huskily, continuing to pump to help her ride down her euphoric high.

"Rowan," she cried out, exhausted by her orgasm.

"I'm close." He released her leg, slowing his pace down. "Can I come on your tits?"

"Wherever you want."

"That's right," he said, pulling out to straddle her torso. "You're mine. The only cum that's going to fill that tight cunt of yours or cover this perfect body is mine."

As he placed his slick cock between her breasts, he pushed them together with the help of his hands and started fucking them, slowly at first, until he found the perfect rhythm and angle.

Ava couldn't help but find this thoroughly hot, bringing her hand between her legs as she watched his expression filled with pleasure. Lips parted, he was breathing heavily, beads of sweat falling down his temple, meeting the ones rolling down his toned chest.

"Does watching me fuck your tits turn you on?"

She nodded. "Yes."

He rubbed her nipples, groaning. "You've got no idea how many times I wanted to do this."

Ava was already close. Circling her clit rapidly, she moaned softly and encouraged Rowan to attain his high, too.

"You fuck me so good," she praised sultrily. "Come for me."

By the way his shaft was twitching and his breaths were starting to stagger, she knew he was close. He threw his head back, brows pinched together, and she watched his abdomen contract.

His pace picked up, and in unison, they came together, their raptured sighs a euphonious melody of utter pleasure.

"SOMETIMES I STILL CAN'T BELIEVE YOU'RE mine," Rowan murmured, tracing featherlight circles on her bare back. "I just look at you, and I'm in complete awe and adoration of the person you are."

Ava looked up at him, watching the glow of the television illuminate his handsome face. "Really? Why?"

"Because you're you," he explained. "You're this ambitious young girl who has such a bright aura. I've always been attracted to you, but I never thought you'd like me back."

"Well, look at how the tables have turned."

"I'm glad I kissed you back that day."

Rowan kissed the tip of her nose, ecstasy etched on his face with the tops of his cheekbones rosy and the glint in his eyes sparkly.

"So, lover boy," Ava started, a mischievous smile tugging her mouth upwards. "Want to be my boyfriend?"

Rowan threw his head back, exposing the strong column of his throat as he barked out a loud laugh. "Jesus, you're so goddamn unexpected and unpredictable. I'm supposed to be asking *you* out."

"You should've been quicker," she protested.

He pushed her to lie down, pinning her wrists to the mattress and narrowing his gaze on her. "You did not just say that to an F1 driver."

"I did."

"You're so annoying," he muttered before engulfing her in a tight hug.

"Is this any way to talk to your girlfriend?"

Rowan hummed contently, and Ava felt whole. Complete. Safe. "Girlfriend. I like that."

CHAPTER THIRTY-SEVEN

LONDON, ENGLAND

"MORNING," AVA GREETED happily. Gabe and his boyfriend were already sitting in the kitchen when she entered, the strong smell of coffee lingering in the air.

"Why are you looking at me like that?" she asked warily, retrieving a mug from the cupboard and flicking her gaze between the two men who were staring back at her, expressions forlorn.

When her roommate exchanged a glance with his boyfriend, Ava immediately understood something was wrong.

She had woken up with a bizarre feeling stirring inside her gut, as if something terrible had happened. The deafening silence confirmed her doubts, and she couldn't help but frown when Gabe rubbed the back of his neck.

Ava brought her fingers to the corner of her mouth. "Do I have toothpaste on my face?"

"Worse than that," Elijah said.

"Please elaborate."

Gabe slid his phone across the central island, and when Ava caught it, she nearly felt a gust of wind swipe her off her feet in an awakening tornado.

"No, no, no," she mumbled, scrolling through the phone, feeling her hand shake in the process. "This can't be happening."

She asked, repeatedly, whether this was a joke or not.

When neither of the men answered, she knew this was real. Very, terribly real.

She was looking at a photo—well, more like hundreds of photos—of her and Rowan sharing a tender kiss when he had dropped her off at her house yesterday morning.

Their secret was out in the world, and there was no more turning back.

CHAPTER THIRTY-EIGHT

LONDON, ENGLAND

Rowan knocked softly on her door, entering reluctantly when she authorised him to access her space.

The bubble of anxiety had only expanded, but seeing Avery procured him the solace he desperately needed.

"Hey, sunflower," he whispered, the sliver of sound erupting laced with hurt. She was wrapped in thick layers of blankets despite the summer breeze outside, a book resting on her lap as she gaped at Rowan with puffy, sad eyes. "Fucking hell. It's killing me to see you like this."

"Hi," she croaked out, causing his heart to crack open at the sound of sorrow woven into her quiet voice.

Closing the door, he rushed towards her.

Rowan kneeled before the armchair she was sitting in. "How are you feeling?"

A veil of guilt misted over her eyes, and he instantly placed what he'd been holding on the floor to cup her face, brushing her bangs away from her lashes.

"I'm so sorry," she said, a lump evidently stuck in her throat. "I never meant for this to happen—"

"It's not your fault. It's not mine, either," he assured softly. "Someone beat us at our own game."

Avery leaned into his touch, closing her eyes—losing herself in a world where their secret hadn't been exposed. Pain was etched upon her angelic face, and Rowan wanted nothing but to set the world on fire. No one and nothing was allowed to touch Avery.

"I brought something that's going to make you feel better," he said before reaching for the paper bag he had set aside. "Food."

As she peered inside the bag, she smiled, but the act of delight wasn't genuine at its fullest. "Mini éclairs and a lemon meringue tart?"

Rowan hummed. "I know you love them. But there's also a pain au chocolat from your favourite bakery."

Brown eyes met with his, and she sighed. "Thank you. You know me so well."

He squeezed her knee. "Funny you should say that, because I keep expecting a ten-page essay with facts I should know about you."

Avery emitted a chuckle. *Bingo.* There was her dimple and radiant smile. "That's your thing. I can't just steal your ideas."

"True."

Setting the pastries aside for a moment, she rubbed the side of her nose and gulped. She, too, looked too nervous to be thinking of anything else. "How did it go?"

When the disaster had exploded on the internet, Rowan's phone had been blown up by both his team principal, Simon, and Thiago. After pacing around in his living room, listening to Tate trying to help (with irrational and unfazed thoughts, of course), and declining his mother's calls, he had decided to go to the headquarters to sort everything out.

Rowan grabbed her hand and kissed the interior of her wrist. "They had an emergency meeting."

Bewilderment lit her eyes up as she straightened herself. "That bad? We made such a mess. Oh my god—"

Rowan rose to his full height before tearing the duvet off her body. "Come here." They switched positions in the armchair as he pulled her into his lap. She curled into his chest, and he kissed her temple, caging her in and procuring unyielding safety. "Everyone's been trying to reach you."

"I turned my phone off after Nikki sent me an email, brief and clear that said, '*I warned you. You're done.*'"

"Ah, shit," Rowan muttered, rubbing his tense jaw. "She wasn't at the meeting, though. She's not important enough to make that decision, so don't rely on her email, okay? She just wants to scare you off."

"But what did they specifically say?"

He sighed, looping his arms around her waist. "We need to break up."

Instant tears swamped her eyes, but Rowan continued: "Let me finish. And please, don't cry." Avery only nodded. "Either you leave or I do."

"You can't leave Primavera Racing!" she exclaimed, outraged. "It's your home."

"It's yours, too," he argued, frowning.

"Being in this team isn't as significant for me as it is for you. You're their driver, and I'm just a replaceable press officer. You cannot leave. No other team is going to worship you the way Primavera does. They're your family. It's my fault that we ended up here, so I'm the one who's going to face the consequences."

"What do you mean?"

"I initiated the first kiss—"

"Yeah, because I was too much of a pussy to kiss the girl of my dreams."

Avery whacked his chest gently. "Don't take the blame for me, I'm begging you."

Tucking a rogue lock of her ebony hair behind an ear, he tipped his head back and exhaled loudly. "I want to protect you. I want to think about our future—as a couple, but also as me, the F1 driver, and you, the publicist. They told me they didn't want our relationship to impact my racing or my mindset. They fear that I'll lose my focus as I keep falling in love with you."

"You—"

He smiled gently. "Yes, sunflower. I'm falling for you. So fast and so damn hard, and I'm loving every moment of it. I think I fell a long time ago. I just don't want to lose you, so I'm not sure what the wisest decision is. They're supportive of us, though. No one saw it coming; most members of the board were surprised, but we just can't continue working together."

He had fallen a long time ago. The only difference between now and then, was that he was accepting of the free fall—before, he'd wanted to crawl upwards to save himself.

Trembling hands found his own, interlacing their fingers together. A natural fit. Two magnets meant to be. "See why it's a good team for you? They love you, Rowan. They just want what's best for you. Are you going to be fined? Lose points in the drivers' standings?"

"No. This has got nothing to do with the FIA and all. The worst that can happen is bad press."

She nodded, pensive. "While you were at the meeting earlier, I made a decision."

He felt confusion brim his senses for a beat. Avery was a woman with logic, rational thoughts, and smart outcomes. "Tell me about it."

"I'm quitting. I'm leaving Primavera." She let out a shaky sigh. He hated seeing her so sad. So powerless. So out of control of her emotions. "I've been wanting to leave the team for quite some time now."

His heart ceased to beat for a few seconds too long as shock rattled through his bones. His grip around her waist tightened, as though he refused to let her slip away.

A lump had made its appearance in his throat. "Why? Did I make your life such a misery when you worked for me?"

She glowered at his lack of seriousness. "No. I'm just choosing you. And I'm choosing myself over anything else. I need to take care of my mental health, and that's why I'm deciding to walk away."

Finally. She was taking care of herself. Though Rowan was utterly devastated to let go, he felt pride wash over him. Felt happiness overpower the chagrin, because she was finally putting herself before others. "Good. I'm proud of you, baby."

"I can't deal with Nikki anymore. She'll keep pestering me until the day I die. I don't want you to feel guilty, because none of this is your fault. You're the reason why I stayed on this team. I loved working with you, loved challenging you and riling you up, but I need to go. I know it's a tough decision, but I think it's the smartest one."

The smartest for their couple to last, he supposed. He didn't want to watch her go. She was his anchor. His favourite person. But her well-being always came above all. "Where are you going to go?"

Avery shrugged. "Another team. Whatever team. As long as I'm still in the paddock and around to cheer you on."

"Okay," he whispered. "I support your decision. I'm your number one fan. I know you'll just thrive and shine wherever you go."

"You seem mad," she murmured, tracing the divot between his eyebrows to make it disappear.

"Just very sad we won't have to be stuck to each other's ass every single day."

"Liar," she teased. "I know you're happy to get rid of me."

"So damned ecstatic!" he agreed sardonically, chuckling.

"Things are getting serious between us. I think not working together anymore might be best for our relationship."

Though it pained Rowan to be separated from the only

person who believed in him, he still nodded in understanding. "I agree."

"You do?"

"Of course." Cradling her face, he caressed her cheekbone with his thumb. "Seriously, baby, I'm your biggest supporter. And I'll stand by your side the whole time. I'm really proud of you."

"I'm proud of myself, too. You know how difficult it is for me to realise when something isn't good for me. I'm just exhausted to work for someone who's intent on ruining me instead of cheering me on, because I know my worth. I know I'm a great press officer."

"You're genuinely the best," he said in a murmur.

"Stop with the flattery," she mocked.

Despite her efforts to put a smile on his face, Rowan couldn't manage to let delight draw on his expression. "I don't know what I'm going to do without you."

"We still have each other. Differently. But I'm always here for you."

"And me for you." He pressed his forehead against hers. "We'll figure everything out. You're my best friend, Avery, and I'm not letting you down. I'll help you find the best job in a top team because you deserve this. Because you're an amazing and hard-working person who'd burn herself down before letting her entourage be touched by a single flame. And I want to be with you. Under the spotlight, in the open, for the entire world to see. So, in the end, I do think it might be the best decision for us to part ways."

"Agreed," she whispered. "Also... I don't want to let you down, but I don't think I'm ready to face Nikki yet. I've taken a couple of days off, so I won't attend the race, but you'll be in good hands and—"

"It's okay. Think of yourself for once. Please. Take the time you need to process what just happened, to write a resignation letter, and to figure things out. I'll be a call away, but you know I'll defend you with everything that's in my possession."

"Thank you," she whispered.

"Anything for you. Thank you for choosing me."

After kissing her softly, sealing unspoken promises to her soul and tethering his eternal devotion to her heart, he bent down to pick up the second item he had put down. His heart stopped beating for a few milliseconds as nervousness started to rack through his body.

"What's this?" Holding the bouquet, she focused on the unique petals, grazing them with her fingertips.

"I made it. The flowers are made from paper, so that they never die. Each petal is a sheet filled with lyrics of songs we've been listening to. Of songs that remind me of you. Some of them are pages from novels you said were your favourites."

Avery was starstruck and in awe for the longest time as she analysed every rose, every petal, until she halted on a particular flower with Rowan's handwriting splattered across the piece of paper.

Until the galaxy turns to dust, was what he had scribbled all over.

Chocolate eyes found his gaze before Avery's arms came to loop around his shoulders, pulling him into a bone-crushing hug. "This is the best thing someone has ever made for me. Thank you. You have no idea how much I love you, Rowan."

He kissed the side of her neck, inhaling her perfume. "I know. And my feelings for you are just as strong. I won't let anything happen to you. I won't let anyone tear us apart. We'll be fine."

CHAPTER THIRTY-NINE

BUDAPEST, HUNGARY

ROWAN UNZIPPED HIS racing suit, keeping his gaze ahead as he ignored the horde of photographers snapping pictures of him. Under normal circumstances, he would grin at the cameras, wink playfully, and throw roguish smirks at everyone crossing his path. But today, all he wanted was to shield himself from the world.

Despite having Donna, Thiago's PR officer, following him while the scandal sorted itself out, Rowan felt empty. Utterly empty. His other half wasn't there to attend interviews with him. Wasn't there to cheer him on and give him the reassurance he needed.

Rowan was great at ignoring everything the media said. But he couldn't exactly ignore what they had said about his girlfriend, the murmurs echoing inside the paddock, the glances people working for Primavera Racing would throw his way.

Avery had debriefed him—had asked him not to let anyone get to him, no matter how much he yearned to shut them up.

"Your little bitch isn't following you?" a voice filtered through the noises dancing around him.

Rowan halted and pivoted, tuning out all the sounds surrounding him as his blood pumped through his system. Angry. Burning. He flexed his fingers, lifting an eyebrow in defiance.

"Say that again and watch where my fist lands," Rowan warned Eliott as the latter passed by.

"You don't want to get in trouble," Eliott said, a coy expression etched on his features. "Oops, I forgot. You were already banging your PR officer."

Alex Myers, who had been walking alongside Eliott, pulled the latter away. "Why are you such a dickhead?"

"Yeah, Dalton," Rowan interfered. "Why?"

"Rowan," Donna said slowly, like a warning, handing him his phone. "Just walk away."

"I've got this," Rowan assured softly, urging the press officer to leave before turning back towards the man he wouldn't mind strangling. "Listen, Eliott sweetie. The tiny amount of respect I had for you vanished the instant you lashed out on Avery when she refused to go out with you. Your ego can't handle rejection? Fine. But calling her a bitch for absolutely no reason? Try again, and I'll run over all your precious little cameras."

Shock drew itself upon Eliott's face as he cradled his camera to his chest. "I just—"

"You what? Thought it's okay to talk trash about the nicest person on the team? About the girl who's helped you countless times with your workload? You're such a fucking hypocrite. I bet you're the one who leaked all those photos."

Eliott's face was crimson with embarrassment. "You have no proof."

"Yet," Rowan bit out. "Get out of my way before I do something I regret. And maybe you should quit, too. Avery wouldn't have left—at least not so suddenly—if you had been mature enough. This isn't a place for kids."

"She's quitting?"

"Yes, genius." Rowan brushed past Eliott, making sure to bump into his shoulder aggressively. Hands curled into balls, he tried to control his anger. "Don't even think of looking my way because I swear I'll end you. I hope the guilt keeps you awake."

Rowan's footfalls were hurried as he took a deep breath in, ignoring Alex's calls, intent on finding shelter where no one could look or judge him.

He had just gotten out of the first session of free practice, and there was so much he needed to do today—go into debriefing with his engineers, talk strategies for the race, get ready for another session of practice—so wanting to hurt a co-worker was not the solution.

When his phone vibrated in his palm, he grunted with so much frustration that incredulous stares were thrown his way.

"What?" he snapped once he'd accepted his father's call.

"What's that drama with your PR officer? Is she the reason why you're so bad at racing?"

"Jesus, why do you care, Stephen? If you're calling just to be the awful man that you are, just know that I have better things to do than listen to your bullshit."

Hanging up, Rowan didn't even care if he had been merciless. He was done with that man who pretended to be a fatherly figure to him when he'd been nothing but the cause of his pain all his life.

"Hey, Emerson!"

God, couldn't he catch a damned break?

Turning on his heel, he faced Miles Huxley trotting towards him, his Doberman puppy in tow.

"What's up?" He bent down and showed his hand to the dog, a slow smile spreading across his lips. "Can I pet it?"

"Sure," Miles answered. "This is Rosie."

Rowan scratched Rosie's head, causing her tail to waggle happily. "Hey, Rosie. You're a sweetie."

"How's Ava holding up?"

For a split second, Rowan forgot about the fact Avery and Miles used to be friends. He straightened himself, sighing. "I called her earlier this morning and she said she was fine. I know she is, but I know she isn't okay, either. She's probably seeing all the weird shit people say on the internet and it's most likely driving her insane. All she wanted was to protect me."

"I don't follow news on socials, but I genuinely think your fans would root for you two. I mean, yeah, it's a shock to everyone, but so what?"

Rowan only raised his shoulder in a half shrug.

Miles scratched the back of his head. "Heard she might get fired?"

"Wrong," he scoffed. "She's quitting before they can even tell her she's out. She's taken the weekend and the upcoming week off, but I think her team also needs space to think of something. They're losing their best publicist."

Rowan wasn't very close to Sophie McKinnon, but from the few interactions he'd had with her, he knew she was the type of person who wanted the best for her employees. Hopefully, she'd wait for Avery to explain herself before instantly firing her.

Running his fingers through his hair, Miles said, "Look, it might be weird, but I'm looking for a personal press officer. All the ones I've worked with at Imperium are useless and don't listen to my needs. I think this deal could save both Ava and I. What do you think?"

Rowan was surprised by the offer. Miles Huxley wasn't an asshole per se, but he liked to make the world think he was the unattainable World Champion who wouldn't let anyone close to him. "I'll ask her about it, but we both know her answer. She'd be happy to reconnect with you."

It was no secret that Rowan would do anything to save the love of his life. If helping her find happiness meant watching her work with his biggest rival, then he would accept the torture and wish to the stars that Avery would finally be at peace.

"Sweet." Miles held Rowan's gaze. "I'll take care of her. You know that, right?"

Rowan slipped his gaze elsewhere, hoping the burning sensation in the back of his throat would go away. "Yeah, I do. And it's what she needs. I wish I could've helped her."

"Don't beat yourself up, man." Miles extended his fist, encouraging Rowan to accept this new sort of alliance. "Focus on what awaits you tomorrow. Look on the bright side; you won't have to hide your relationship anymore."

CHAPTER FORTY

SPA-FRANCORCHAMPS, BELGIUM

"Focus, Rowan. Please," Jamie ordered.

"I am," Rowan countered, his fingers flexing around the steering wheel.

The visor of his helmet was dotted with droplets of water, nearly blinding his field of vision as they cascaded down the transparent polycarbonate. But no matter the weather's circumstances, he knew the route of this iconic circuit by heart. The track was slowly drying, but the car in front of him still sprayed minuscule beads of rain towards him. Following the dry line, Rowan tried to chase a slipstream, seeking top speed to attempt an overtake.

"You're not," Jamie said bluntly.

The unbridled speed as he flew through the Raidillon and Eau Rouge was incomparable. Known as two of the most dangerous turns in the motorsport universe, they were also Rowan's favourites. Because of the thrill. The danger. The sharpness of every twist and turn.

In all the years he'd been racing, Rowan had always been able to concentrate on his results and goals—nothing else. When he was in the car, nothing else mattered.

But today, out of all days, during one of the most important races of the season, he simply couldn't minimise his spiralling thoughts.

Whilst Avery had insisted, on multiple occasions, that she was fine and coping with the situation healthily, Rowan couldn't help but worry.

He hadn't seen her in almost two weeks. He wasn't used to the distance, to this void of emptiness. He'd been so accustomed to being with her almost every single day for the past few years. Sure, the first two seasons were spent firing insults at each other and wishing for the other's downfall, but he would still see her every day and try to grab her attention, desperately so.

He just needed to hold her and help her ride those reckless waves before the tempest would settle down.

"Heavy rain predicted in the next hour," Jamie announced, bringing him back to reality.

Rowan blinked, forcing himself to focus on the race.

"Again?" Rowan's fingers pushed the clutch to move one gear forward, his pace increasing when he passed the chicane. He waited to attain top speed in the straight line to continue his casual conversation with his race engineer. "How many laps are there left?"

"Fifteen. We might be able to avoid the downpour. Catch Huxley and take back what's yours; P1."

Rowan had started from pole.

He wanted to win.

Not for his father. Not for his team. Not for anyone, but only for himself.

Focus, the euphonious voice echoed inside his head.

Taking a deep breath in, he pushed at full throttle, passing through the corner of La Source.

Turning too wide, he slipped slightly, but regained control easily.

Focus, Rowan.

So he did.

CHAPTER FORTY-ONE

LONDON, ENGLAND

"How are you feeling?" was Kamari's question when Ava took a seat on the stool facing the bar.

Despite the fact Dawn's Café was quite busy at this time of the day, most of the customers were watching the Belgian Grand Prix with undivided attention.

Ava was glad she could steal some of Kamari's time to talk. The coffee shop's owner was wise, resilient, and empathic despite her guarded façade.

Ava lifted her shoulders in an indifferent shrug, as though she was numb to the feeling. Truth was, she was everything but. She was someone who always felt deeply, who was sensitive. She couldn't help but blame herself for putting hers and Rowan's relationship out in the open like this.

So far, she had ignored all calls and text messages from her colleagues. Had only talked to Thiago when he had asked if there was something he could do to help. She still couldn't believe

Primavera Racing had asked Rowan to leave if he wasn't ready to let her go.

Ava knew how much Formula 1 and this team meant to Rowan. She wouldn't have allowed him to walk away from the only things he loved.

"Oh, darling," Kamari whispered. She pushed a coffee and a pain au chocolat towards Ava, a small smile on her lips. "Rowan texted me saying your favourite breakfast is a crispy pain au chocolat."

It wasn't even breakfast time anymore, but she still felt disoriented. A soft chuckle escaped Ava's mouth, her chest tightening. "He's right."

"So? Tomorrow's the day?"

Tomorrow would be the day Ava was going to resign from her position as a PR officer at Primavera Racing. Sophie had reached out to her the day the secret was revealed, kindly asking her to come to the office to talk whenever she felt ready.

After spending over a week resting, reflecting on the situation, and trying to sort everything out, it was finally time to move on.

"Yes." Ava stirred her coffee, keeping her absent stare on the midnight blue cup. "Do you think it makes me a weak person? To leave without fighting?"

"No," her friend answered instantly. Truthfully. "You're one of the strongest people I know. You travel all the time. Put up with imbeciles at work. Put everyone else's happiness before your own. I think you wanted to leave Nikki's team for a while, so it's fine. Maybe you're quitting because your secret's been exposed, and it was the cherry on top, but you're mostly doing it for you and Rowan. To save your relationship. Do you know how many couples call it off when they work together? Working with your partner 24/7 can be so frustrating if you're not used to it."

"That's what I'm telling myself."

Slipping her gaze to the wide television screen, she frowned, seeing that the start of the race was still delayed because of the heavy rain.

Typical Belgian weather.

Ava was gutted not to attend that particular race. The circuit was in the top five of her favourites in the calendar.

"You'll be okay," Kamari assured softly, bringing Ava's attention back to the barista. "Do you know what you're going to do after the summer break?"

There would be a four-week break for everyone working in Formula 1 after the Grand Prix. To enjoy the summer. To rest. To disconnect and rewind. And all Ava needed was to escape to a world alone with Rowan.

Ava nodded after wiping the corner of her mouth. The pastry was delicious, and she made sure to tell Kamari so before answering the question. "You know Miles Huxley?" Kamari nodded. "He's my childhood friend. He's looking for a new PR officer and he's going to hire me on private terms. I'll still be working with Imperium Racing, though."

The stunning entrepreneur arched an eyebrow. "Going to the enemy?"

"Sorry," Ava answered with the same teasing tone. "Didn't mean to betray you all."

"Well, as long as you're happy. I'm rooting for you. And if you need someone to defend you, I'm your girl."

"DO YOU WANT ME to go in with you?"

Drifting her gaze away from the large building, Ava found Rowan's tender gaze. She placed her hand above his, which was resting on her thigh, and applied a soft pressure.

She couldn't believe this was her last Monday here. Couldn't realise just yet the fact that she was about to walk in, resign, take her belongings, and never look back.

"I'll be okay."

"I know you will. I'll still wait for you outside of Sophie's office."

She tucked a strand of hair behind an ear and took a deep breath in. Nervousness had been stirring inside her chest ever since she got inside Rowan's Porsche.

"Thank you." She kissed his cheek, earning a smile and a scarlet blush on his cheekbones. "I can't believe I'm saying goodbye to Primavera Racing."

Rowan brushed her bangs away from her forehead, delicately. "As much as it hurts to know you're leaving us, I know you're going to a much healthier environment. Huxley is a total dickhead on the track, but I know he'll treat you right. If he doesn't, I'll kill him. And if anyone dares to hurt you, I swear I'll set the entire place on fire."

"Careful," she started with a teasing tone, "I'm going to start thinking you care."

"You wish," he spat playfully. She watched Rowan's hazel eyes drift somewhere behind her shoulder and linger on the landscape. "That lake."

She shifted in her seat to look at the sunshine beaming down on the still water, a sentiment of nostalgia squeezing her lungs. "What about it?"

"I can't even tell you how many times I caught you staring at it. Just admiring it."

Ava raised her eyebrows. "You used to stalk me?"

"Not stalk." He rolled his eyes, resulting in her rolling her eyes back at him. "Just finding you. I would always find you, no matter where we were. And the car launch at the beginning of the season? The night you announced you'd be my press officer... I swear you took my breath away that night."

"With a broken shoe and a missing contact lens?"

He chuckled. "Especially because of that. You're unique in my eyes." His features softened, a soft sigh escaping his parted lips. "I'm so sorry, Avery. Sometimes I can't help but think this is all because of me. I influenced you to sneak around, break the rules. But just so you know, I don't regret a single thing. You make me feel alive, and safe, and at peace."

Before Ava could voice her gratitude, her phone chimed. The notification sent her mind into overdrive, shock rippling through her veins. With lips agape and unblinking eyelids, she read the message over and over again. At this exact moment, she couldn't help but think the universe was on her side.

Rowan leaned in. "What is it?"

Ava met Rowan's curious yet concerned gaze. "Remember how I told you Gabe's boyfriend works in IT? I'm pretty sure what he did is illegal, but he managed to trace the IP address of the person who leaked the photos."

❧

WHEN SOPHIE WELCOMED her into her office with a kind smile, Ava couldn't help but sigh in relief.

Here goes nothing.

"Tea?" Sophie asked kindly.

Ava shook her head to deny the offer.

"Coffee?"

"I'm alright. Thank you."

"A pain au chocolat?" the woman asked then, a faint hint of mischief woven into her tone. "I know a certain someone who has forced everyone on the team to always leave the last one on the tray for you."

Ava closed the door, the confession sending her mind into overdrive.

Rowan Emerson would be the reason for her undoing.

"I had no clue," she whispered. "How do you even know?"

"I observe everyone who roams through these hallways." Sophie's lips curled into a polite smile. "How were your days off?"

"Fine." Ava walked up to the desk and handed an envelope to Sophie. "I'm resigning."

Slumping back in her chaise, Sophie only watched the letter, a frown on her brows. "You are?"

Ava lowered her arm and laid the envelope down. "It was either me or Rowan who had to leave. I can't let him protect me. I caused all of this chaos, so I'm the one who has to leave."

Sophie's frown deepened. For a moment, she stared absently at the envelope, her lips pressed in a hard line. "I'm surprised, to say the least," she confessed, peering up into Ava's eyes. "I never thought you would choose love over your career."

"I'm sorry," Ava whispered. Had it not been for Rowan and for the way he'd captured her heart, she would've fought to stay. Wouldn't have put her entire career at risk.

Sophie raised a shaky hand. "Don't apologise. I saw Rowan at the emergency meeting, and that man loves you so fiercely. I've seen the way he looks at you in secret. A Formula 1 driver never leaves a team unless he's got a better deal with another one. Unless his contract is over and he needs to depart. But for a second, a tiny second, I really thought he would leave for you."

Ava's heart churned. "No. He loves Primavera too much."

"He does, as we all love him. He's very different from Thiago, but he's an equally talented driver." Sophie gestured for Ava to sit, and she obliged in silence. "You know, when I decided for you to become Rowan's new publicist, it wasn't just to spite you. I was aware of the resentment you both shared towards one another. Sure, I forced you to be a team in the hopes the hatred would go away, but I made that choice because I know you both. Your personalities, your strengths and weaknesses. I knew you'd complement each other well. I wasn't wrong, because you champion each other. You're a good duo."

Starting to rub the hem of her sleeve between her thumb and forefinger, Ava offered a gentle smile to the woman before her. "I know I didn't show much enthusiasm at the beginning of the season, but I liked working with Rowan. As much as I loved working with Thiago."

"I'm glad to know that. You've always been one of my

favourite employees, Ava." Sophie's eyes shone with something like regret, guilt. "I wish you had been brave enough to tell me you were developing feelings for Rowan."

"You'd have fired me, too."

"No," the lady whispered. "I would've moved you back into Thiago's team. Did you know you could've signed an agreement to state you and Rowan were together? The non-fraternising clause is there for a reason, but we cannot control who you fall in love with. We're aware of the amount of people who break this rule."

"I didn't know this agreement existed."

"Because Nikki kept assuring you there was no way we could find a compromise, right?"

Ava inhaled sharply, feeling tears burn the back of her eyes. She blinked, uncertain of what she was supposed to say.

"I have to ask," Sophie continued. "I have a feeling you're not leaving just because of the drama. What's the cause of your departure?"

"I've been wanting to leave for a while," Ava admitted, her words stuck in her throat. Sophie's expression shattered, leaving hurt etched on her features. "It wasn't because of you. I loved working with and for you. You taught me so much, and I truly appreciate all the opportunities you've given me. I just—have never been on good terms with Nikki. It's been very tough for me to work under her command for the past three years."

"Oh, Ava..." The woman knitted her brows together, a few beats passing before she spoke up. "Why haven't you talked about it?"

"I didn't want to cause any trouble."

"I should've listened when Thiago came to see me and said she was acting inappropriately towards you and the rest of the team. There were so many signs that I didn't catch. I'm—what did she do?"

Where to start? "Well—"

The door burst open, and the person she had been avoiding for days finally emerged back into her life.

Talk about perfect timing.

Nikki planted her hands on her hips. "Is it done? Is she fired?"

"Lovely seeing you," Ava muttered.

"I see you didn't use those days off to tone down your attitude."

Bitch, Ava wanted to scream. But she had dignity. Had the tiniest ounce of respect left. She only held her breath. Stayed silent, just like she'd always done in Nikki's company.

She only looked at Sophie, gesturing towards the other woman as if saying, *"See how she's acting with me?"*

"Nikki," Sophie cut in coldly, shaking her head. "Act like an adult. Ava's been nothing but respectful to you."

"She slept with Rowan," Nikki argued.

Sophie blinked, rearing back at the outburst. "Come sit for a second."

With slight reluctance, Nikki approached before slouching down in the other chair. This time, Ava didn't lower her gaze when Nikki glowered at her.

"So? Is she leaving the team?"

Ava's anger started to thrum against her temple. "Yes, I am. Happy?"

"Finally! I warned you, and you didn't listen. You took your job as a press officer as a literal joke. It was a shame to have you on my team."

"Sophie's team," Ava corrected bitterly. "You were an awful team manager. I've never seen anyone lack sympathy as you do. I am one of the best publicists to work in F1, and you know it. You're just jealous not to have my position. You're envious that I work so closely with the drivers. I've seen the way you look and flirt with both Rowan and Thiago. I know about the times you asked Rowan to join you in secret. But he's never wanted you."

"Shame," Nikki mustered with disdain. "I'm much better than you."

"That's not what he seemed to be saying this morning whilst he was between my legs."

"Excuse you?"

"Girls," Sophie cut in. "Let's keep it classy."

Ava sighed, turning to her recently former boss. "Sorry. I didn't mean to blurt that out. I hate to snitch, but Nikki has been sleeping with someone on the team."

"Who?" Sophie asked slowly.

"Are you seriously ratting me out?" Nikki bellowed.

"Check your inbox," Ava suggested, ignoring the fuming blonde.

The tension in the room was thick and palpable as Sophie read the email. Trembling fingers hovered above the keyboard before curling into a fist.

"Nikki," Sophie said quietly, coldly. "You've been sleeping with Eliott Dalton? Bribed him to stalk Ava and Rowan then asked him to leak the pictures?"

Nikki's silence was confirmation.

"Why did you do that?"

"Because Ava has Rowan. And I despise her. She has the man I've been running after for years, and the only one who wanted me was sweet, young Eliott. He does everything I want. He, too, wanted to ruin Ava for—"

"That's enough," Sophie interrupted. "Pack your belongings. You're fired."

❧

"I'M PROUD OF YOU," Rowan murmured in her ear as he draped an arm around her shoulders, pulling her into his side. She'd bask in his warmth all day long if she could. "You fierce girl."

"Thank you. For always standing by my side."

"Just returning the favour, sunflower."

He was holding a bag with the last items they'd retrieved from her office. Sure, it was bittersweet to pack her belongings, but Ava thought it was a freeing feeling, too. Rowan had helped her pack whilst reminiscing on their private moments in there; when they got to know each other, when they shared breakfast, when they talked about work, but also moments where professionalism wasn't in the picture.

The door to the lifts opened, and they faced another person who had ruined their lives.

Ava felt Rowan stiffen, but all he did was pull her even more into him. "Eliott," he acknowledged. "I wish I could say it's fancy seeing you here, but it's really not."

Ava elbowed her boyfriend in the ribs. She only glared at Eliott and walked past him, not wanting to deal with him unless he gave the apology he owed her.

"What are you doing here?" Eliott asked when she was nearly out of the building. "Are you not ashamed of what you did?"

Falling in love with Rowan was, without a shadow of a doubt, the best thing that had happened to her.

Ava turned around, a ball rising to block her airway. "Glad to see you, Eliott. I hope you're happy I'm leaving."

"Wow," the photographer droned, his brows rising. "You two are truly the perfect match."

"Thanks. I think so, too," Rowan quipped. "You're not invited to the wedding, though. Bummer, 'cause your photography skills are kind of decent."

"Stop," Ava told him brusquely.

Rowan only winked down at her.

Eliott swallowed thickly, keeping his gaze on Ava. "Did you get fired?"

"Not officially since I handed my resignation letter before Sophie could let me know."

When he didn't say anything, she only shook her head, deception making her chest tighten, and pivoted. That was the exact reason why Ava wouldn't let people in; being nice always meant getting betrayed in the end.

"One question." She turned back around, finding Rowan's hand to twine their fingers together. Eliott didn't miss the gesture, lowering his gaze to their connected palms. "Why? I've been nothing but nice to you. You were one of my favourite colleagues. Just... why?"

"I liked you, Ava," Eliott answered quietly. "I wanted you to be with me, not with that prick."

"Watch the tone you take when you talk about Rowan," she said with a chilling softness.

Rowan's fingers tightened around hers.

"I'm not going to apologise. I knew you were hiding something, and Nikki knew it, too. You wouldn't have been able to keep your relationship secret much longer, anyway."

And that was it. No more explanation. No further apology.

Ava scoffed. "I hope getting an older woman's pussy was worth it. What I did was nowhere as hurtful as your actions. You shouldn't have betrayed me."

"I'm being suspended," Eliott announced after swallowing. "I hope you're happy now."

"No, Eliott. No, it does not make me happy. But you deserve so much worse."

Without another glance back, Ava left the building with a heavy heart. When Rowan squeezed her fingers in reassurance, she found anchoring honey eyes, stealing her breath away. He stopped walking, cupped her face, and leaned in to kiss her. Softly. Deeply. Passionately.

She felt a weakness in her knees. A certain weight being lifted off her shoulders.

"What was that for?" Ava asked as they pulled away, smiling.

"Because I admire you. And what you just said to Eliott was really sexy. And because you're just my favourite person. And you deserve the world. I promise I'm going to give it to you."

He already had.

Walking away from the organisation that had given her a place in the motorsports industry to find another home where she hoped she could be herself, Ava couldn't help but think this was the beginning of liberty. Happiness. And the greatest love story of all time; the one she had written on her own.

CHAPTER FORTY-TWO

LONDON, ENGLAND

IT WAS A sunny Sunday morning when the realisation hit Rowan like a wild tidal wave, sending all his thoughts into a frenzy and his heart into racing mode.

They were sitting on his patio, enjoying their usual post-sex snack.

Ava had just tipped her head back to allow the sunlight to cast warmth upon her flesh, a small smile touching her lips. With her untamed curls, her rosy cheeks, and her contagious goodness, she looked like the most beautiful woman to have ever walked into his orbit. She *was* the most extraordinary woman in his life.

"I'm excited to go to Australia for a few weeks," she said happily.

"Yeah?"

Opening her eyes, she met his stare and nodded. "Yes."

There was something unequivocally enticing about the way the sun's rays turned into starlight when they shone directly upon her skin, making it seem like constellations had made their appearance on her face. Like she was made of angelic stardust. Like a sunflower turning towards light; towards positivity.

Rowan couldn't keep his smile from spreading wider, his fingers twitching when he felt the need to close the distance and touch her. Hold her.

"What?" she asked, tilting her head sideways.

"Nothing," was his answer.

Everything, actually. She was simply everything.

When she got distracted by the romance novel she'd been reading, he grabbed the notebook he was doodling in.

He wrote a note he would rip out later to put in a box he had made for her. A box containing all his favourite memories with her—photos, notes, tickets, anything.

AUGUST 5TH.

THE DAY I FINALLY REALISED THAT I'M HOPELESSLY IN LOVE WITH YOU.
I'M GOING TO MARRY YOU ONE DAY.
I LOVE YOU WITH EVERYTHING I HAVE.

"Can I tell you a secret?" Rowan asked softly—so softly he hadn't heard himself through the loud thud of his heart.

She smiled beautifully. "As long as I get to share one, too. A secret for a secret."

He jutted his chin towards her. "Ladies first."

For a few heartbeats, she seemed to sort out her thoughts. Then, came her earnest confession: "I always thought you were the most attractive driver on the grid."

Rowan tipped his head back, barking out a laugh. "Baby, that's, like, a universal fact. Everyone knows I'm the sexiest."

Avery only shook her head, allowing her grin to widen, as though she had expected this exact response.

"Your turn."

He felt perspiration clam his palms, his heart beating so wildly that it felt like it was on the brink of explosion.

Rowan roamed his gaze over every curve and line of her angelic face, sighing softly. She was his. She was his, and he'd never felt so happy before.

I love you. I love you. I love you.

Once upon a time, he'd been a boy who didn't believe in love. Who couldn't understand its meaning. Today, he was a man who was learning and who, finally, felt like he was deserving of it.

"I told my mum I was going to marry you."

Avery's eyes started to glimmer, happiness drawing upon her features. "You did?"

Rowan simply nodded.

"Good," she whispered. "Because I intend on making you my husband one day."

CHAPTER FORTY-THREE

BRISBANE, AUSTRALIA

ROWAN DIDN'T KNOW if this was a good idea. Detrimental hesitancy was burning through his vessels as he stood before the grand door, feeling the cold wind brush against his cheekbones.

"I can't do this," Rowan mumbled, his hand hovering above the doorknob. "Unless you two want me to strangle him."

"Dramatic," Tate said after exchanging an amused glance with Avery. "It'll be fine."

It was the first thing Rowan had noticed when they parked in the driveway—Stephen's car. He'd said, *"The fuck is he doing here? Turn around. We're leaving."*

Avery grabbed Rowan's hand, her soft touch bringing him back to life and making the haze of anger dissipate. "It's going to be okay. It's just dinner. You don't have to talk to your father. You can just ignore him."

Grunting with defeat, he pushed the door open and walked

into his childhood house. Rowan wasn't sure why his mother never moved out of here. Sure, the domain was big and beautiful, surrounded by acres of land and wildlife, but this was way too big for Julia.

Regardless of the reluctance blinding him, being home felt divine. As much as he loved racing, Rowan needed the time off to rewind and disconnect.

"I don't know why Mum invited him."

"Maybe she wants to see if you can all get along after everything that's happened," Avery said softly.

"I doubt it."

Tate clapped the back of Rowan's neck. "Come on, it'll be nice. We're back home, your mum made her famous lamb chops, and Nora will be there. Stephen is just part of the decor, like always."

With a heavy sigh, Rowan made his girlfriend and best friend understand the gravity of his dismay. He truly resented Stephen, but he was willing to eat in his company. For his mother. Avery only tightened her hold around his hand—a silent promise she wouldn't let go.

"We've got you," Tate promised as he closed the door behind them. "Julia! Your fave son is here."

Emerging from the kitchen, an apron secured around her hips and a bottle of wine in hand, Julia squealed in excitement when Tate strode towards her to engulf her in a tight embrace. "Tate! You look handsome."

He returned the hug, taunting Rowan with a grin. "I know."

"Ah, here's my other son," she acknowledged in a mocking tone before coming up to Rowan, wrapping an arm around his waist. "Hi, my love. I'm so happy you decided to come home for a few weeks."

"Hey, Mama." He kissed the top of Julia's head, tucking her into his chest. "It's good to see you, but why, exactly, did you invite Stephen?"

Julia rolled her eyes. "He invited himself. Heard from Riley you lot were back, and he decided to crash dinner. He promised to be on his best behaviour."

"Mum," he muttered coldly. "Kick him out."

The sad smile taking over her features made his chest ache. "Let's just have a nice evening, okay? Can you do this for me?"

Some parts of Rowan regretted his childhood and early adolescence—the way he'd acted, shut himself off from the world when his anger consumed him. He wished he'd been able to save his mother, help her heal in some way.

Julia pivoted and didn't waste a second to hug the ray of sunshine that was Avery Sharma-Maddox. The sight of the two women Rowan loved most sharing a tender moment made his heart swell. "Thank you for coming. I'm so glad Rowan came to his senses."

"What are you talking about?" Rowan asked.

"You've been head over heels for this girl ever since she started working for Primavera Racing. And don't deny it. Your mother knows it all."

When Julia looped her arm through Avery's to drag her into the kitchen, the latter peered at Rowan with raised eyebrows, a soft chuckle flying past her lips.

It appeared like his entourage had known about his foolish crush on Avery for a long time. Way before he even knew about it, and realised she'd stolen his heart by igniting his temper.

"How are you doing, honey?" his mother asked Avery before they disappeared into another room. "Does my son treat you well?"

Tate looked at Rowan, raising his left hand and pointing to his ring finger.

The bet. Right.

What a bunch of fucking idiots.

Rowan sighed, tucking his hands in the front pockets of his jeans as he walked into the living room. So far, no sign of his father. He hoped this family dinner wouldn't ruin his holiday.

He wanted to come back to see his mother, sister, and niece, but mostly to show Avery his roots and the life he'd lived before moving to England.

Rapid footsteps echoed from the staircase, and a wild toddler with curly hair jumped into Tate's arms, giggles filling the air.

Rowan watched Tate engulf Nora tightly before making her spin, a slow smile spreading across his lips. "Hey, girl. Damn, you're the size of an adult now. When did you grow up so much?"

"I missed you," the little girl said, winding her arms around Tate's neck.

Rowan feigned hurt, putting a hand on his chest. In reality, he loved the bond his best friend and niece shared. It was special and unique. "What about me? I'm your real uncle."

Nora grinned, pressing her cheek to Tate's. Strangely, her features resembled Tate's. Rowan thought he was dreaming. "Tay-Tay is my favourite."

This evening promised to be excruciatingly long.

"WELL, LOOK WHO decided to show up."

Entering the dining room, Rowan took a breath in and lowered his gaze so he wouldn't meet his father's. He caressed Avery's back as he rounded the table before taking a seat beside her, instantly putting his hand on her thigh to ground himself. Julia was sitting on his other side.

"You okay?" Avery whispered. He simply nodded, applying pressure on her skin.

"Why are you even here, Stephen?" Rowan gritted out, observing Tate pour some wine into Julia's glass. "You've avoided all sorts of family gatherings your entire life."

"Rowan," Riley warned as she adjusted Nora's t-shirt.

"Stephen," Julia sighed at the same time. "You said you would behave."

Stephen shrugged sheepishly, slurred words evaporating in the air when he defended himself. "I didn't do anything wrong. Just made a comment. Not my fault if he's a sensitive kid."

"Is he already drunk?"

Everyone answered Rowan's question with a nod.

"Awesome."

"Let's eat and enjoy dinner," Julia suggested sweetly. "It's been months since the boys have been home. Plus, Rowan brought his special lady."

Nora laughed softly, diffusing the tension with her small voice. "Special lady. You lied to me, Uncle Wawa."

"Me?" Rowan exclaimed. "I would never do that!"

"You did," Nora said with a pout. "You said you wasn't in loves with her, but I know you are."

Laughter echoed around the table. Weaving her fingers through his, Avery brought his attention towards her and winked. He only shook his head before releasing her hand to dig into his meal.

He wondered if Avery knew how much he loved her. Just because he couldn't voice those words out loud yet, didn't mean he couldn't show her. He rapidly nudged her knee, and she nudged his back.

"Ava," Riley asked, "did Rowan show you around the backyard?"

She took a small sip of water. "Not yet."

"He'll have to. You should walk around the ranch, too. You'll see the horses and the motocross circuit he built with Tate when they were twelve."

Avery smiled. "I'd love that."

Rowan nodded. "I'll show you in the morning. Sunrise is beautiful over here."

Stephen cleared his throat. "So, Ava. Did you manage to find a job after sleeping around with my son? I bet it doesn't look good on your résumé."

Rowan's shoulders stiffened, his fingers flexing around his fork. "Don't call me your son, and don't talk to her that way."

"I did." Ava's thigh pressed into Rowan's—coaxing, reassuring. Her tone was calm, her voice as feathery as usual. "I just signed with Imperium Racing and Miles Huxley on private terms. I'll be starting as soon as the second half of the season starts."

"Mmh." Stephen took a sip of his red wine, eyes narrowed on Avery. Rowan clenched his jaw, unable to shake that sensation of fury off. "It's your fault Rowan's so distracted all the damn time."

"Here we go," Tate said under his breath. "Can we not do this here? Or ever? This is ridiculous."

From the corner of his eye, Rowan saw his sister down her beverage rapidly. *Typical.*

"Pardon me?" Avery frowned at the man sitting at the end of the table.

"She has got nothing to do with my results," Rowan protested. "I can't believe I even have to explain myself."

"Well," Stephen argued, "maybe you would have won more than one race if you hadn't been busy sticking your dick in your press—"

"You can't be serious." Rowan's chair rattled as he stood up aggressively. He was ready to drag this man out of the house.

"Sit down," whispered Julia, tugging on his sleeve gently.

His fingers curled. "No, Ma. I'm exhausted, okay? I can't deal with him. Why would you even let him enter the house after everything he's done to you?"

When his mother only lowered her gaze, he felt a lump grow inside his throat.

Sounds of cutlery colliding filled his senses for a flickering heartbeat, but all Rowan could see was red. And his father's smirk.

"You don't get to show up to family dinner and disrespect my girlfriend. She's been nothing but nice to you when I invited you to races, making you feel welcomed as a guest. Races where you only pointed out my mistakes instead of cheering me on for my great results."

"You never won a championship," was Stephen's argument, and the reason for Rowan's temper to explode.

"So?" Rowan passed his fingers through his hair frustratingly, shaking his head. "Your hyper-fixation on this is driving me nuts. I started racing to make *you* proud. Because you were dying to have a son with big accomplishments under his belt, who does great things. All I wanted was to make you happy, but all you saw were my mistakes, struggles, and results. It's been like this ever since I was a kid, and instead of cheering me up when I failed, you kept dragging me down and undermining me."

Standing up, Stephen knocked out his chair to the ground. "Because it's a shame to be the father of someone who can't—"

"Stephen!" Julia hissed.

"With all due respect, sir, I think that you should stop." Avery stood up, finding Rowan's pinkie finger with her own. His hand was trembling, but even at that exact moment, the feel of her skin couldn't help him stay calm. "Rowan has the privilege of being one of twenty drivers in F1. Do you know how hard it is to get into that sport? How an opportunity like this comes only once in a lifetime? Some drivers can't even renew a contract after a season or two, yet Rowan has been with Primavera for nearly a decade now. He's making history with the team with the longest contract extension. He's a fierce driver with a millimetric accuracy that no other driver can match. He's ambitious, driven, and passionate. A World Champion title doesn't define him as a driver. It's his place in this universe that does. His popularity shows how much he's looked up to and admired from all ends of the Earth. Rowan is one of the best men I know, and it's a shame you can't see it. Yes, he makes mistakes and cannot be the best all the time, and that's okay. He's the kind of person who has a mindset made of steel. He rises after failing, embraces his vulnerability to forge it into fortitude, and doesn't linger on his regrets. Rowan is an incredible man, and I'm so sorry that you will never realise this."

Speechless, Rowan turned to Avery, a burning sensation rising in the back of his throat whilst a veil of tears rapidly blinded his vision.

He'd never had someone else other than Tate come to his defence. To his rescue.

"Pop off, Ave," Tate cheered, raising his glass in the air.

Rowan swallowed, finding his father's shocked stare. "Seriously, Stephen. How many times have I begged for your attention? For your validation? This is all so meaningless now. You don't mean anything to me, just as I know I don't mean anything to you. You come to races for your own reputation. Just so that people will give you some sort of validation. But when was the last time you came here to spend some time with us without mentioning racing? When was the last time you checked up on Riley, or Nora, or Mum?"

Stephen was barely able to stand on his feet. "Stop making me look like the bad guy here."

"You are the bad guy. You were barely a father figure to Riley and me, and you know it damn well. What kind of father lifts his hand on his son? What kind of man emotionally manipulates his own kid? You should have left us for good instead of destroying everything in your path."

"I was a great father," the drunk man slurred.

"Really? When's Riley's birthday?"

No answer.

Riley poured herself another glass of wine, and sighed loudly.

"When's mine?"

No answer either.

Rowan gestured to the door. Though his chest felt heavy and aching, he knew this was the right decision to make. To free himself. "Leave. I don't want you to contact me again. You walked out of my life the day you walked out of Mum's. I can't believe it took me nearly twenty years to tell you to go."

Stephen took a step back, aiming a finger at Rowan's chest. "You ungrateful little shit. You would never be here without my financial help."

"Yes, and thank you for helping me reach my goals. Now, I'm a fucking multi-millionaire, and I can buy my little cars on my own."

Angry, Stephen was ready to lunge at Rowan, fists ready to strike him in the nose. And this once, Rowan would strike back. Avery caught his wrist, stepping in front of him—ready to shield him.

"Don't you dare lay a finger on him," she warned so softly, so steadily.

"This is cute," Stephen chuckled dryly. "Just you wait until you realise he's a sad, broken boy who will never exceed your expectations."

"Once again, you are wrong about him."

But Tate caught Stephen's arm, pulling him back. "Okay, buddy. I'm done watching this shitshow. Apologise to Ava, Rowan, *and* Julia, and walk away."

Scoffing, Stephen wriggled out of the punishing grip, glaring at Tate. "*This* is a shitshow? Does Rowan know you slept with Riley?"

Time stopped, and all heads turned to Riley who was already on her third glass of wine. "Great. Thank you for this."

Tate stumbled back, his wide eyes finding Rowan, an apologetic gleam brightening his irises. "Rowan—it was years ago—"

Rowan raised a trembling hand—fury and deception and confusion burning every nerve in his body. He shook his head, the buzzing in his ears becoming louder.

"I need a moment," he said, tone clipped. He refused to look at anyone in the room as he turned on his heel. “Stephen, leave. Mum, let him go, and stop hurting yourself. You can’t keep doing this to yourself, and I’m begging you to never open the door for him again. You deserve so much better.”

Rowan walked outside the moment thunder clashed in the sky, the front door slamming in sync with the universe’s wrath.

CHAPTER FORTY-FOUR

BRISBANE, AUSTRALIA

THUNDER WAS RUMBLING amongst the cataclysmic clouds, the wild wind brushing Avery's strands of hair away from her face.

She brought her knees to her chest, chin tipped back as she observed the angry sky, listening to rain crashing down on the concrete and the booming roar of the heavens.

It was past midnight, and the only source of light came from the patio's lamp, casting a golden luminescence on her profile. The mugs that had once been filled with hot chocolate were empty, and all there was left was each other's unwavering company.

Rowan couldn't manage to find the strength to look away from her. She was so mystifying and electric—somehow more enthralling than the thunderbolts cracking through clouds.

Rowan buried his hands in the pockets of his fleece jumper, scoffing softly as he went back to getting lost in his thoughts.

"How's your hand?" Avery asked, peering at him.

He showed his hand, flexing his reddish fingers and bruised knuckles. "You should see the other guy."

She snorted softly, inching closer towards him to drape the blanket over them both. "Was punching him necessary?"

"No, but it's what I had to do. I don't make the rules. I'm sure the main male protagonists in the books you read act the same way."

"They do," she agreed, nodding. "Are you really mad at Tate?"

Rowan shrugged lazily. "No. To be fair, I'm not that surprised. He's always had a thing for Riley."

With a soft sigh escaping her mouth, Avery leaned her head on his shoulder, allowing her sweet fragrance to swivel around their peaceful cosmos. "I have crazy thoughts running across my mind right now."

"Tell me about them." He draped an arm across her shoulders and kissed the crown of her head. After spending an hour or so outside, Tate had come to explain himself, but Rowan had struck his right fist into Tate's nose before he had the chance to open his mouth. Tate had only sworn, clutching his nose as he muttered he had deserved it.

An hour later, as Tate went back inside, Avery had come out. To sit in silence, talk about anything and nothing, to help him ride those reckless waves of emotions. She'd whispered many times how proud she was of him, and her comfort and support were exactly what he needed.

"What if Tate is Nora's dad?"

Rowan stiffened, settling his gaze on a puddle of rain where droplets crashed into it relentlessly. He wasn't stupid enough to pry into his best friend and sister's secrets, but the thought made him angry. For Nora, who deserved to know who her father was —Tate or not.

"That's between them," Rowan said.

"But it would make sense," Avery murmured.

"It would."

Letting out a sigh, he tipped his head back. "I don't know why they hid it from me. And how the fuck Stephen somehow knew about it."

"Probably because they were scared of your reaction. And because it was just a one-night stand, right?"

He cast an incredulous glance her way, his lips tipping upwards. "You and I both know they railed each other more than once, baby. But whatever, I'm not mad. Just surprised. I'd be happy for them if they dated."

Avery hummed in understanding, passing her fingers through the hair on his nape, causing him to sigh in relief. "Feels good?" He nodded. "What's going on inside your head, lover boy?"

Rowan leaned into her touch as she cradled his jaw, her thumb brushing the faint dust of freckles on his cheek. "Today was hectic. Should I feel bad for what I said to Stephen? Because I don't. It makes me feel like I'm a terrible person."

"You're entitled to feel like this, but I promise you're the best person ever. This situation was messing with your head, and I think you really needed to say this to him. I'm truly sorry that he's never going to see you for who you are. You're one in a million, Rowan. I'm so glad the universe has brought us together."

He tucked a strand of hair behind her ear, sighing softly. "Thank you. For having my back, for being the incredible woman that you are. I don't know what I would do without you. I don't even see the rest of my life without you."

Avery held the power of disentangling all the knots that had formed in his nerves. She kissed him softly, sensing his growing despair, and he smiled against her lips, resulting in her mirroring the action earnestly.

"Make me forget about tonight?" he asked when they parted ways.

There was a gleam of mischief alighting the edges of her irises. "I have an idea, but you're going to think I'm insane."

"Doesn't change from the daily thoughts I have of you."

"Thanks, idiot." She stood up and threw the blanket at him.

"You love me," he supplied with a grin as he watched her zip her coat up to her chin.

"Doesn't make you any less stupid."

Rowan leaned back in the chair, crossing his hands behind his head. "Okay, show me what you've got."

She marched backwards until she stood under the pouring rain. Rowan straightened himself, frowning as he watched her spin around, a squeal filled with excitement escaping her mouth.

He shook his head, baffled by the sight before him. "You're insane, woman."

"I told you!"

"What are you doing? You're going to catch a cold." His heart swelled until it was on the verge of combusting. The sight of her genuine delight and her unfaltering smile set the wild birds inside his stomach free.

"So?" She lifted her shoulders in a shrug. "I know a guy who takes great care of me when I'm sick."

"Lucky lad," he droned. "Wiping snot off his girlfriend's nose."

"Can you stop?" She laughed, shaking her head. "I'm trying to be romantic and you're just being yourself."

He stood up and walked towards the edge of the patio, leaning against a pillar and watching Avery tip her head back.

Rain rolled down her face, black tendrils were sticking to her skin, yet she managed to be the most beautiful woman he had ever seen.

He loved her. He loved her. He loved her.

If he walked through a field of dead flowers, Avery would be the persistent flower that kept on blooming no matter how dark and grey the skies were. No matter what fell upon her. She was the vibrancy proving that nothing would stop her from being alive regardless of the moments during which petals lost their will to stay upraised—she'd still push through to shine.

The moment a lightning bolt struck in the dark sky, a single string of light flicked upon her—proof that she was part of the heavens' magic.

"I love thunder," she announced. "I love how angry it sounds. How loud it is when it booms. When I used to live across from Miles, he would come over when there were thunderstorms. Don't tell him you know this, but he's scared shitless of them, so he would come to my place, and we would play board games until it calmed down."

"What makes you love it so much?"

He grabbed his phone and put some music on. Not just any music, though. *Kiss Me* by Sixpence None the Richer echoed from the speaker, making Avery's smile widen. Then, he took a step forward, feeling the first droplet of rain crash on the bridge of his nose.

"I just love it," she explained, extending her hands for him to hold on to. Their palms fitted perfectly, and everything made sense now; they were made for each other, existing in the same universe where their stars were aligned. "The furious banging when it cracks overhead. The electric lightning bolts brightening the sky. The violent gusts of wind. The rain. I also love the sound—"

"I love you," Rowan breathed out, cupping her damp face shakily. He observed rivulets of water cascade down her skin, her eyes light up, her lips tug upwards. "I'm hopelessly, utterly, and unequivocally in love with you, Avery."

Time came to a halt. The world ceased spinning. His heart stopped thundering.

He'd known it for a while but hadn't realised it until recently. And saying those words felt freeing. Avery needed to know. Needed to understand that her love wasn't unrequited.

"About damn time, lover boy." She pushed his hair away from his forehead, chocolate eyes shining with adoration.

And then, the sounds surrounding him returned to buzzing in his ears, the coldness of the rain making him feel alive. He smiled broadly, grazing the pad of his thumb over her lower lip. Beneath his fingertips, her jaw was trembling—perhaps because of the cold, or perhaps because of the confession she had been waiting to hear. "I don't know why it took me so long to say it back. I know I've been in love with you since I met you. I just wasn't convinced I deserved it. Deserved you."

"You're the most deserving person. You are fully worthy of love," she promised softly. "And you are so loved. Always have been."

"I now realise it. I was seeking love in the wrong place for the longest time, but now that I found it with you, I'm never letting it slip away."

"Good."

Winding his arms around her waist, they started swaying to the rhythm of the music. The rain beating down on them didn't matter. The cold air didn't matter. Because every time he would be in Avery's presence, the entire universe would reduce to her, and solely her. She had welcomed him into her orbit with open arms, and within the immensity of it all, she had given him her heart, trusting that he would never so much as put a fissure in it.

He lifted her until her feet hovered above the grass, her arms raised towards the angry sky whilst their laughter echoed in symphony.

When she touched the ground again, he placed his forehead against hers, letting the violent downpour tug them downwards until they were drowning. But as long as he was in her company, knowing she returned equal affection towards him, going back to the surface to breathe and survive didn't feel like an impossibility now.

"You're a ray of sunshine, Avery. I see daylight when I'm with you. I see a whole world painted in colours when I've been fully certain it was all black and white. Loving you is so easy but being loved feels so effortless. Thank you for believing in me."

In the end, Rowan knew his persistence in chasing the slipstream was worth it. Winning didn't always mean he was brandishing the biggest and shiniest trophy—it meant he had achieved his goals, securing what he'd been running after his entire life: happiness, love, and security. And with Avery in his arms, her heart bound to his for eternity, he knew he could let himself fall, and fall, and fall, confident that she'd hold his hand the whole time and catch him before he could break to pieces.

CHAPTER FORTY-FIVE

MONZA, ITALY

ROWAN HAD A dream last night. A beautiful dream in which he won the 2023 Italian Grand Prix.

After last week's disaster at the Dutch Grand Prix where he had a major failure with the gearbox before the race's start, rendering him unable to drive at all, he was intent on winning today.

Especially since he was starting on the front row, right next to his teammate. Monza's circuit was one of his favourites because cars would go at full throttle for nearly eighty percent of the lap with a great combination of tight chicanes to warm up the brakes.

He was currently warming up in the paddock, rope-jumping with Tate monitoring his every move.

There was no room for tension and misunderstanding between Rowan and Tate. But ever since Tate's secret had been revealed, Rowan had been able to sense a slight shift in his mood.

He would always be lost in his thoughts, perplexed by whatever tormenting idea would flicker across his mind.

Rowan didn't know what had happened between his best friend and Riley in Brisbane. Maybe they'd talked, maybe they'd had sex again, maybe they'd simply acted as if the other didn't exist. Contrary to Tate, Riley hadn't apologised to Rowan. Hadn't even tried to explain herself. Rowan didn't care, though.

Taking a break from warming up, he recuperated his breath slowly, hands planted on his hips as he let his gaze travel towards the busy paddock. Journalists interviewing drivers. Photographers capturing memorable moments. Mechanics running around. Everyone was getting ready for the Grand Prix.

"You okay?" he asked Tate, searching for a dark-haired PR officer with a black uniform and a devastating smile.

It was weird not to work with Avery anymore. She kept him focused. She saw through him. She understood him. But her happiness came above all, and it was evident her new job had a healthier environment than the previous one.

Rowan was now stuck with an intern, Joey. He was nice. Didn't have any banter, though, which was quite boring.

God, did he miss her fiery comebacks. Her witty responses. Her sense of professionalism, her work ethic, and her vision of things.

"Yeah, fine." A pause, then, "Do you hate me?"

He looked over at his best friend, knitting his brows together in confusion. "Come on, mate. We've already been through this. Why do you ask?"

"Because I had sex with your sister."

Rowan shuddered dramatically. "Just when I thought I would get rid of this atrocious image inside my head..." Tate glowered. "I don't care, Ritchie, and you know it. Whatever you do with my sister is your business."

The physiotherapist rubbed the back of his neck. "So you wouldn't be opposed to us dating? Because I like her."

Rowan snickered. "You really think you're coming in hot

with brand new information, don't you? I know that, bastard. Just ask her out."

"It's not that easy, and you know it. It took you three years to ask Ava out."

A flutter of happiness crashed over him at the mention of his girl. "Trust me, you'll feel so much better once you tell her how you feel."

Tate nodded, then let a soft smile spread across his lips. "You've changed, you know."

"Is that a compliment?"

"Yep. I'm glad you have Ava. I'm happy you found the love you deserve."

"Damn it," Rowan grunted. "Save your speech for my wedding day."

"Wedding day, huh?" Tate pinched Rowan's cheek to taunt him before being hit in the stomach. "Look at you being all grown up and smitten."

"I'm not smitten!"

"A liar, that you are." Tate pointed behind his shoulder. "Look who's coming this way."

At first, he saw Indy hurriedly walk past him, as she kept her gaze ahead of herself, her high heels tapping on the concrete. Then, he saw Miles Huxley chase after her. He stopped in his tracks, fingers flexing by his side, then shook his head before turning on his heel and heading towards the opposite direction.

And finally, Avery appeared.

Looking confused, she tried to catch Miles' elbow, but the latter only shrugged her off before walking away. She blinked, then found Rowan's gaze from across the paddock. As if they were always pulled towards the other. As if, even in the most crowded place, they could find their way back home.

She waved excitedly, making his cheeks hurt when he smiled widely.

"Hey, guys!" she greeted as she approached them. Even dressed in his rival team's attire, she looked stunning. She tucked her phone and recorder into the pocket of her skirt, standing on her tiptoes to peck Rowan's cheek. "Ready to lose to Huxley?"

Tate snorted somewhere behind Rowan, as the driver feigned shock. "Goddamn brat. You didn't."

The tantalising disdain etched upon her features reminded him of the days when they supposedly disliked each other. "We're rivals now, lover boy. I've got to stay true and faithful to who I work for."

"Traitor," Tate sing-songed.

Rowan narrowed his gaze, amused. He would just destroy and punish her in the hotel room later. "You're so insolent."

She taunted him with an innocent smile. "Thanks."

"So, gonna tell us what that was with Huxley and Indy?"

"Ah." Avery peered behind her shoulder to look at Indy now chatting with Kamari in front of Primavera Racing's motorhome. "Well, they're head over heels for each other, but don't know how to tell the other. Their situation is a bit complicated. Huxley has a bit of a darker side and Indy's complex in her own way, too."

"They remind me of two people I know," Tate noted, draping an arm around Rowan's shoulders.

"Get lost," Rowan mumbled, pushing his friend away.

"I need to go. I have duties to fulfill." Avery grabbed Rowan's face and kissed him softly. So softly that he felt his knees weaken. So softly that he felt his heart batter ferociously in stark contrast to her delicacy. Now that they didn't have to hide their relationship anymore, he was more than delighted to show the world who he belonged to. And apparently, she liked it as well. "Good luck, lover boy. You'll do amazing."

"I knew you were secretly rooting for me," he said smugly. "I'm going to win for you."

She chuckled softly. "Yes, please. Love you."

He kissed her cheek. "I love you."

"You two are so disgusting," Tate muttered. "I miss the times you would scream and fight in the rain."

Avery had already turned around, but she gaped at the physiotherapist from her shoulder. "Love you too, Tate."

❧

It was on the twenty-first lap that Rowan was announced a yellow flag was brandished in the second sector.

He sighed heavily, pressing on the brake to decelerate and hitting a button on his steering wheel. "Seriously? What happened?"

"Beaumont lost his rear in turn six and went into the barrier. He's out of the car already."

Rowan nodded.

"Safety car is arriving," Jamie announced. "Keep delta positive."

"Gotcha." Zig-zagging behind Thiago, Rowan started to hum a melody, maintaining his warm tyres by accelerating and slowing down. Repeating. "Can we talk strategies whilst the safety car is out?"

"Strategies?"

"Do you want to chat about the weather? Sun's shining, if you're wondering."

"Yeah," Jamie deadpanned. "I see that."

"Awesome," Rowan drawled. "So, I think y'all should let me overtake Tito. I've got speed. I'm faster."

There was a long pause before Jamie's answer came through the radio. "Stay behind."

Rowan's fingers tightened around the steering wheel. "Fine."

"Box now, though. We're doing a double stack."

❧

On lap thirty-seven, Rowan found a slipstream, roaring off on the track at top speed. He was back to being P2, chasing after his teammate.

After taking the chicane, smoothly, he pressed on the throttle and flew down the straight line, tired of staying behind Thiago. Though the next turn was a slow one to take, Thiago lost slight control over his car because of its lack of responsiveness, causing it to understeer.

"Come on," Rowan pleaded. "I've got speed. I'll have DRS soon."

In fact, he was already less than a second away from Thiago.

Team orders were driving Rowan insane.

Okay, maybe this race and circuit were special and close to Thiago's heart, but Rowan also deserved to win here.

"Rowan," Jamie warned.

"Can I fight with Tito? Please? It looks like this race is boring anyway. Let me give the public a bit of action."

"Can you stop being so cocky?"

"Never," the driver scoffed.

"Just—Ah, be careful."

Rowan grinned. "Thank you. You're the best."

When Rowan braked late before passing through the corner on its interior, hoping to find a gap and slip in front of Thiago, his teammate drove off, putting some distance again between the two cars.

They fought for several laps. Thiago was an insane defender, in the best way, always ahead of Rowan and anticipating his moves. When Rowan would drive on the inside of a corner, Thiago would slip in front to prevent him from doing so. When he would try to overtake, Thiago always managed to keep his position.

Their wheels nearly came in contact more than once, though, and the thrill of taking those risks was making Rowan's bloodstream thrum with exhilaration.

Through the chicane they went, and Rowan was finally ahead of Thiago, claiming the lead with a smooth, delicate move.

"Woo!" Jamie cheered. "Come on, baby. Ten laps to go. Get that win."

❧

Rowan hugged Thiago as tightly as he could, and patted him on the back to congratulate him on the great result.

A 1-2 for Primavera Racing in Monza was an indescribable feeling. One of the greatest achievements they could've done as a team.

"Congrats," Thiago said, smiling broadly. "You deserve today's win."

"Thanks, man. I love fighting with you."

His teammate ruffled his hair, chuckling. "I know that, but next time find someone else to fight with. It's not like there's eighteen other drivers on the grid or anything."

"You're such a petty bitch," Rowan mocked, fist-bumping him before walking towards Tate.

He took off his helmet and balaclava, taking a deep breath to take everything in. Accepting the bottle of water his physio handed to him, he felt a pang hit his chest, obliging him to look towards the small crowd that had already formed below the podium.

He found Avery, standing on her own yet smiling at something one of her coworkers had said. Then, chocolate met honey, and the world came to a halt. She waved at Rowan as he lifted his bottle of water.

"Where's the water I hate?" he mouthed.

She shrugged, trying hard not to smile. "You should be grateful I'm not trying to poison you anymore."

"I kind of miss those days."

She smiled, and Rowan wondered how she had the power of rendering his entire entourage into a complete blur. He was supposed to head towards the reporter for the post-race interview, was supposed to go into the cool-down room before the podium, was supposed to stay focused, but he just couldn't move.

Her lips moved: "I'm proud of you."

Rowan winked, his heart swelling. Her beautiful smile fed his soul, gave him a purpose. At that moment, he knew everything would be all right.

❧

HE COULDN'T STOP SMILING at the crowd chanting his name when he lifted the trophy in the air. He kissed the prize, then pointed at Jamie and Tate.

There was a sea of red flooding the entire circuit; fans of Primavera Racing coming to watch the podium, dressed in vibrant rouge as confetti fell from overhead.

Again, he found Avery, who was supposedly cheering for Miles who had finished third, but he knew that she would always support him no matter where she was.

He winked, tipping the trophy towards her.

He had told Avery that he would win for her. And so he did.

❧

"STAY AWAY FROM ME! I'm not supposed to fraternise with the enemy."

Rowan wheezed out a laugh, wrapping his arms around Avery, regardless of her remark. "The enemy," he echoed, still chuckling before bringing his lips to the shell of her ear. "Should the enemy fuck you like he hates you tonight? Would you like that? I expect you to wait for me in the hotel room with your uniform on. I'm going to fuck you all night long until I make you understand who you belong to."

Her fingers curled around the fabric of his jumpsuit on his back, and he simply knew she was blushing.

"Behave," she murmured. "Cameras are on us."

"Let them be."

The smell of champagne still lingered in the air, the aftermath of the race still electric inside his bones. He kissed

Avery's forehead, uncaring that the entire world was watching him.

"I'm so proud of you," she told him, cupping his face to bring his gaze towards hers.

He could get lost in those eyes. Dark but beautiful, filled with so much sincerity and persistent, strong love.

"Thank you, sunflower." Kissing the interior of her wrist, he let his lips tip upwards as a smile grew seamlessly. "I know I don't say it enough, but you do know I'm endlessly grateful for you, right? All my life, I couldn't help but feel like I wasn't good enough for anything. I've been wearing that façade of a sunshine boy to hide all my wounds. But you saw all of them, and you never once stepped away. You helped me heal in so many ways, and I really, really don't know where or who I'd be today without you."

Like a balm to a wound, she had healed something she hadn't so much as broken. She had embraced all those scars, all those imperfections, and had helped him turn them into fortitude.

It was true that Rowan still didn't have a World Championship under his belt. It was true that he wouldn't be as good as his teammate or the other drivers on the grid. But he didn't care, because he finally knew that he was enough. Worthy of love. Worthy of respect.

He'd been on a quest for happiness and love for so long, certain he would never find it, until Avery Sharma-Maddox walked into his life and tilted the entire world onto its axis. Until she appeared like a warm ray of sunshine piercing through thick clouds. Until she showed him that every dead flower could come back to life and find its vibrant colours if taken care of with persistence, delicacy, and patience.

He had the bare minimum, but there wasn't a shadow of a doubt that he felt satisfied with everything he had in the palms of his hands.

His passion for racing.

His career as a Formula 1 driver.

And the only love of his life. His sunflower. His whole world. His home.

When Rowan laced their fingers together, he held on tightly to hers, intent on never letting go.

"You coming home with me?"

"Sure thing, lover boy. Lead the way."

FIN.

EPILOGUE

LONDON, ENGLAND

Three years later

IT WAS THE front door slamming that brought him back to reality, allowing the nerves that had been rattling his senses to finally vanish.

Rowan inhaled deep serenity, wiping his clammy palms against the back of his jeans before picking Praline up. The cat meowed at the disturbance, her nap being interrupted by the tattooed man, before settling further into the warmth of his chest.

"Sorry, P," he whispered. "But your mama's home. Let's go say hi."

He could feel his heart thumping so wildly that he wondered if he had ever felt this nervous before.

"Rowan?"

Avery's voice resonated in the foyer, a wave of solace dancing towards him. He rushed down the staircase, grinning at the sight before him. She was busy taking her shoes off, her luggage already placed against the wall with her tote bag resting atop it.

As much as he had loved his small town house in Knightsbridge where memories remained eternal—parties, a first date with Avery involving uncooked pasta that had led to opening up, and amazing, breathtaking sex—this new place was *home*. He and Avery had purchased this country house a few months ago, and he loved this slow, quiet life—a stark contrast to his everyday routine that consisted of racing at full speed.

"Bonjour," he said excitedly, wrapping his free arm around her shoulders. He placed a lingering kiss on her forehead, her perfume already rendering him powerless and on the cusp of bringing him to his knees. "How's my girl doing?"

Avery chuckled and pecked him on the lips before kissing the top of Praline's head. "Still the same as earlier."

After the Belgian Grand Prix where she had jumped into his arms after his win, they had to separate to fulfil their respective duties. He had left the circuit before her and caught a flight with his team back to London. He had arrived home three hours ago, giving him enough time to prepare the surprise.

"Tired?" he asked in a murmur, brushing a rogue strand of hair away from her cheek.

"Exhausted." Yet a smile broke free on her lips. Yet her eyes shone with happiness. He cocked his head at the brightness emanating from her, like golden threads dancing around them. She was glowing, was absolutely exquisite.

Rowan didn't know a single person who worked harder than Avery. She always tended to give her all in her job to make Miles happy, to be appreciated by the people surrounding her. And he knew her efforts never went unnoticed.

When he grinned, her gaze dropped to his dimple. "I ran a bath for you."

Slight surprise flashed in her eyes. "You did?"

Rowan hummed and let their cat down. He watched Praline stretch out before strutting towards the living room. "How about you go relax? I'll bring you a glass of wine. We can order some food tonight and watch your favourite movie."

She watched him suspiciously, her gaze narrowed as it sauntered from his face down his body. He'd already showered and eaten a snack after coming back from the airport. Usually, he would celebrate the Grand Prix—no matter his result—until dawn, but he couldn't bother to party today because he had a surprise to prepare. One of the biggest importance.

"You want something from me." Not a question, but rather a straightforward statement that made him chuckle wryly.

"I do?"

"Yes. What is it? Did you break something? Did you *burn* something? Do you need money?"

Rowan snorted before placing his hand on the small of her back, urging her towards the stairs. "Baby, I'm a multi-millionaire. I can give you the damn fucking moon. And no, I didn't do anything."

She only hummed in contemplation and marched upstairs, allowing him to marvel at the generous curves of her backside.

"What?" he asked. "Can't I do nice things for my girlfriend?"

She only peered at him over her shoulder and lifted a brow. He pinched her bottom and slapped it, but when they attained the top of the staircase, the amusement filling his senses diminished.

"I'm in the mood for Indian food." She hadn't noticed the sudden nervousness taking over him as she aimed for their bedroom.

But all Rowan could hear was the loud and rapid thud of his heartbeat.

"Whatever makes you happy, sunflower."

He rubbed the back of his neck, took a deep breath in, and followed Avery into the bedroom.

A soft gasp rose from her throat, and she stopped walking.

Rowan felt time stop. Felt the world cease spinning. Felt his heart flip upside down.

He peered at her expression, his lungs tightening at the sight of utter awe and admiration etched on her features. The blinds were down, the whole room swamped in darkness save for the bright constellations illuminating the ceiling that put in evidence the rose petals scattered across the floor and the bed.

One of their favourite songs resonated in the background, but not loud enough to conceal the deafening thrum of his pulse.

Avery brought a trembling hand to her lips as she peered heavenwards, mumbling, "Oh my god."

Marry me was written with stars in the stellar sky.

Discreetly, Rowan reached towards the console to his left, and grabbed the velvet box he had hidden behind a photo frame. He dropped to one knee just as she pivoted to face him.

A small sob rose from the back of her throat as she gaped at the diamond ring displayed before her.

"Rowan..."

He couldn't control the tears misting over his eyes, and he smiled broadly, tremors racking through his body. His voice, though, didn't waver as he said, "If there's one thing I'm certain about, it's that we're meant to be together. Meant to spend this lifetime and all the next ones together. If there's one thing I'm positive about, it's that I'm yours and you're mine. Avery, I love you. I love you so much that sometimes I can't breathe. I want to spend the rest of my life loving you, travelling the world with you, and watching you shine so bright and thrive in everything you do. I want to spend each day waking up next to you and listening to your voice, to the joyful chuckles of yours that are like the soundtrack to my life. Marry me, Avery."

Rowan watched a tear stream down her face, a smile full of adoration spreading across her lips.

He swore he'd seen the subtle nod of her head, but all she

said was, "Oh my god, Rowan." Then scrambled off to the en-suite dressing room.

He was still kneeling, downright confused by her response. He'd been expecting tears, smiles, giggles, and the cliché "a million times, yes" but not... that. Not her running away.

He cleared his throat and frowned, glancing at the ring. The beautiful diamond that Zoya, Avery's mother, had helped him choose.

"Avery," he droned. "You're supposed to say yes."

He'd been positive she'd agree. Unless she wasn't ready, which he doubted.

"I'm looking for something in my lingerie drawer."

He blushed, unsure of how to act. How to feel. Had she rejected him? Had she not wanted this? They had talked about it, more than once—about marriage, eventual children. Rowan couldn't understand her reaction.

"I'm flattered, but I just asked you to be my wife and—"

She came back hurriedly and kneeled before him, then popped open a squared box where lay a silver band.

"Marry me, Rowan."

He choked on air, his eyes widening at her demand. She was so unpredictable and unexpected.

"I was going to propose to you," she murmured when he couldn't find a sliver of strength to form a single coherent thought. "During our vacation in Australia."

He felt a tear escape his eye as he looked into her star-filled gaze, glinting with so many emotions. "Are you serious?"

She nodded, her beautiful smile never faltering. "I knew I loved you the moment I couldn't get you out of my head. I loved you the moment you *saw* me and never walked away. No one gets me like you do, no one renders life as exciting as you can. I want to marry you, and I know our life will be filled with so much joy and nurtured by the power of our love."

Rowan swallowed the lump in his throat a moment before

releasing a long, shaky exhale. “God fucking damn it, Avery. You’re absolutely insane.”

She chuckled and plucked the silver band out of the box. “I take that as a yes.”

Her small hand grabbed his left, trembling one. The ring hovered above the tip of his finger, but she looked at him, gentle and loving, waiting for a clear response. He was absolutely starstruck, not believing she’d beat him at his own game.

“Yes,” he breathed. “Of course I’ll marry the hell out of you.”

Avery chuckled, the melody feeding his soul. “That’s what I thought.”

Slipping the ring on his finger, Rowan shook his head in disbelief before taking the one meant for her, setting the box down.

“Your turn,” he murmured, kissing the back of her hand.

The way she looked at him made him weak. He felt an invisible force squeeze his heart before releasing it to allow it to ricochet inside his chest.

She spoke with such softness. “I’ll marry you in this life and the one after. Every lifetime we get to live together.”

Rowan’s cheeks hurt because of how much, how wide he was smiling. He put the ring on her finger, planting another kiss on her knuckles.

“It’s beautiful.” She raised her hand to eye level and gaped at the engagement ring. Gratitude shone in her dark eyes, and Rowan nearly sobbed at the sight. “I’m going to be your wife.”

Reaching out to her, he cupped her face and brushed a tear away from her cheekbone. “I told you,” he said. “Three years ago. Told you I’d marry you.”

He’d already known then that he wanted an eternity with Avery. Because she was the missing piece he’d searched for his entire life. The completeness to his soul and the salvation to his once broken heart.

Her kiss was gentle, sweet—a kiss in which she poured all her unwavering feelings for him through the entwine of their breaths and the tangle of their tongues.

"I love you," Rowan whispered against her lips.

"I know." She kissed him fiercely. "It's an honour to be loved by you."

It had become their thing—they didn't need to say it back to let the other know how much they were adored.

With an effortless movement, Rowan hoisted Avery up and laid her on the bed, their lips still locking and their tongues still battling for dominance.

Cupping her jaw, his other hand came to grip the outside of her thigh, locking her leg around his hip whilst her fingers fisted the front of his shirt.

When he backed away, she surged forward to chase another kiss, but he only stared down at her, his breath catching.

"You are so beautiful," he whispered. The constellations reflected a silvery glow upon her face, drawing minuscule stars on her skin. And just like that, she was the only thing that mattered most to him. An ethereal divine being. A shooting star in his chaotic orbit. "My fiancée. That has a pretty nice ring to it."

"Sure does, lover boy."

Rowan peppered light and tender kisses on her throat, the side of her neck, and below her ear, pushing his already hard cock into her centre, making her writhe and exhale a breathy moan.

Rowan made haste to undress her, his world coming to a stop when he looked at the red set of lingerie clinging to her body. "Bloody hell. This is so sexy."

She only kissed him, and he took care of peeling off the last layers of so-called clothing until she was bare before him, but she didn't allow him to touch her until he, too, was naked.

His hands found her waist, her silken skin a song of delicacy and pure heaven beneath his callouses. They roamed over her skin as he and Avery kissed without catching a breath, his hands finding her full and heavy breasts. He grunted at the feeling, grazing her peaked nipples with his thumbs before palming them —remembering the feeling as though he hadn't already memorised it. Rowan tried not to linger on the fact her breasts felt more firm than usual because she wrapped her hand around his cock, a gentle stroke to weaken him.

He whimpered into Avery's mouth, bucking into her hand as she stroked him hard and fast, just like he liked it.

"Fuck," he said huskily. "Let me wreck that soaked cunt of yours."

She arched off the bed when his teeth grazed the spot between her neck and shoulder. "Say please."

"Avery," he warned. He didn't want to play games today. No, he needed to make love to her. Over and over again. Sometimes sweet and slow, sometimes rough, and hard, and brutal. He'd fuck her until they were spent.

A gasp fled past her lips when his fingers dipped to her core, collecting her arousal before pressing on her clit, drawing slow, torturous circles.

"Always so drenched for me."

"Rowan," she breathed out. "More."

He smirked. "Say please."

She scoffed. When her nails brushed the underside of his erection, he groaned in pleasure and unleashed himself to fuck her hand. Avery used the momentum of distraction to flip them over and straddled him.

The corner of his lips didn't move down. "I like where this is going. Go ahead, use me."

"It seems like you don't really know what you want," she prompted.

Rowan narrowed his gaze, two fingers sliding through her wetness to plunge inside her. Her lips parted, her gaze heady with desire.

"Oh, trust me," he said, "I do. I want to watch you ride your future husband."

"You love your new title so much."

He winked, noting the tinge of crimson colouring her tanned cheeks. "How could I not?"

She started riding his hand, her breaths staggering, but he withdrew his fingers before pleasure could overtake her senses.

Rowan brought his fingers up to her mouth, and she sucked them clean without needing instructions.

"That's my good fucking girl. Come on, let me see how my cock fills you up."

He braced both hands behind his head, and she scoffed softly at his indolent behaviour as he observed her stunning body. Those thighs he loved so much. That curvy waist. Those generous tits nearly making him drool with lust.

Using a hand to lubricate the tip of his shaft against her centre, she rolled her hips to tease him, then slowly, slowly, sank until he was buried to the hilt.

"Fuck. Me." She was tight, wet, perfectly made for him.

"Patience, darling." Avery's hands found his pectorals, her fingertip grazing his sunflower tattoo.

She started undulating her hips, keeping her gaze locked to his. A moan escaped the back of Rowan's throat when she lifted herself before sinking back down in a swift motion. Repeat. Up and down, until they were panting hard.

"You ride me so well," he praised, watching her breasts bounce.

Taking them into his hands, he played with her nipples until her moans became louder and her movements more frantic. A bead of sweat dripped between the valley of her breasts, her beautiful skin coated with a thin sheen of perspiration.

"Come here," he ordered, pulling her towards him.

Their lips met in a messy kiss as he pushed on his heels to buck into her drenched core.

"Harder," she asked, breathless.

Rowan grabbed her hips, pounding into her from below, a moan escaping. One of his hands descended to her generous bottom to slap it, hard. "You like that? You don't want me to make sweet love to you, huh? You want to be fucked like the brat you are?"

Avery whimpered, nails digging into his flesh. He brought his mouth to her nipple, sucking and biting lightly, then repeated the action on the other one.

"Answer me." Another slap on her bottom. The tips of his fingers pressed into her flesh as he pounded recklessly into her, guttural moans echoing and blending with the sound of skin slapping.

"Yes," she said, panting.

Rowan withdrew and pushed her off him. "On all fours."

She obliged in a heartbeat, and Rowan couldn't help but grunt at the wetness gleaming before him. The mixture of both their pleasure dripping down the inside of her thigh.

Wrapping a hand around the base of his cock, he pumped a few times, admiring the view before latching his mouth to her clit. Avery fell forward, parting her legs further apart to allow him to plunge his tongue into her entrance.

He spat on her cunt. "You get me so hard all the fucking time."

He devoured her with abandon, switching between lapping fiercely at her clit and dragging his tongue flat-out against her folds all the while stroking his aching cock.

When he felt his balls tighten and his length twitch, he stopped abruptly before hovering above Avery's back, nudging the tip of his erection to her entrance. He needed to come inside her.

Not giving her a moment of rest, he slid right into home, thrusting restlessly as he gripped her hips tightly enough to leave bruises. It had happened before, but every time he'd apologised by kissing the marks softly. She'd chuckled and called him adorable, thanking him.

"You feel so fucking good."

She only moaned at the praise and fisted the bed sheets so tightly that her knuckles whitened.

He continued to plunge in and out, reaching over to fist her dark hair into a makeshift ponytail. She couldn't contain her moans as she arched her back, crying out his name.

His name dribbling like sin on the tip of her tongue was nearly his undoing.

"Don't stop. I'm close."

Rowan could feel her walls tighten around his throbbing shaft. He leaned forward, his chest coming in contact with her sweat-damped back and reached around to play with her clit. His fingers applied the perfect amount of pressure to make her writhe beneath his touch.

"Just like that," she panted.

Rowan kissed the back of her neck, her shoulder, her spine, and continued to hit the exact spot that made her tremble in pleasure until she came with a loud moan, her entire body shaking. The pulsing and clenching of her walls around his cock sent him over the edge, his physique spasming as he released deeply into her before stilling, ragged breaths and soft moans echoing inside the room.

❧

Rowan was spent.

He had fucked Avery not once, not twice, but three times already. The second time was sweet and slow, initiated by him after he'd kissed her entire body which was still recovering from the previous orgasm. The third one had been quick, yet rough in the shower.

As she sat with her legs crisscrossed, her wet hair falling down her back, and wearing his shirt, Rowan found her to be the sexiest and most beautiful woman. But as the tip of his fingers drew shapes on her bare legs, he was thinking of burying his tongue between them. Of having her sit down on his face whilst she'd suck his—

God, he needed to get a grip.

He smiled at the sight of her engagement ring. Looked down at the band adorning his finger.

Avery was his.

He was hers. Utterly so.

She pushed her glasses up the bridge of her nose whilst scrolling through her phone, probably looking for something to eat.

"Why are you looking at me like that?" She put the phone aside and placed a kiss on his forehead.

"Because I'm trying to realise you're mine."

All these years, he'd watched her from afar and found himself completely enthralled by the person she was. All these years, he pretended to hate her because it was easier than admitting he was attracted to someone so out of his league. All these years, he loved her because she had always been able to see something in him that no one else had dared to glimpse at.

She lifted her left hand. "Does this help?"

He lifted a shoulder in a tantalising shrug. "Even when you'll become Mrs. Emerson, I'll have a hard time realising it."

"Why?"

Rowan ducked his head, smiling timidly. A blush bloomed on his cheeks. "I always thought you were out of my league. Too perfect and good for me."

Avery lifted her brows in stupefaction. "And to think I thought *you* would never see me this way... Look at us now."

He propped himself on an elbow and grabbed her hand to kiss her inner wrist.

"I have one more surprise for you," she murmured.

Rowan sat up and watched her disappear once again into the closet.

She came back with a small bag that she gently gave him, as

she stayed standing next to the bed, hands folded before her, fidgeting nervously with the bracelet adorning her wrist.

"Two gifts in a day?" he teased, raising a brow. "You must be needing something from me."

She laughed and rolled her eyes. No amusement was decipherable through her tone, though, only slight nervousness. "Look inside the bag."

A red fabric lay at the bottom of it. Rowan took it out and unfolded it, his heart refusing to function when he understood what it was.

"Avery..."

He had barely been able to hear his trembling voice. He didn't even know if he had managed to speak.

He was holding a racing suit—a baby's. With Primavera Racing's logo, his name, and number on the back. Releasing a quivering breath, he looked up at Avery through a blurry vision, an enormous lump building inside his throat.

She was smiling behind the hand shielding her mouth, her engagement ring glittering. Her eyes shone with tears and joy and excitement. "I'm pregnant."

Rowan lunged at her, tiny racing suit left forgotten on the bed, and wrapped his arms around her waist as he spun them around. He emitted a strange sound, a mix between a scream of joy, a howl, and a sob all at once.

"We're having a baby?" He put her down on her feet before cradling her to his chest, one hand holding the back of her head as he brought her ear to his pectoral where his heartbeat battered erratically.

Tremors rattled through Rowan's body, setting his vessels on fire. He fell to his knees, unable to hold back his tears, and wrapped his arms around the back of her thighs, peppering small kisses upon her clothed stomach.

"There's a baby in you. My baby," he murmured. "We're really going to be parents?"

"We are," she said softly, emotions stuck in her throat.

Gently, Avery cradled his face and forced him to look up. He obliged, through teary eyes, and chuckled.

Though he struggled to stand on his wobbling knees, he managed to rise and embrace Avery tightly. "This is the best day of my life."

They stayed in this position for a while, holding each other and trying to grasp this new reality. Rowan kissed the crown of her head, continuously so, murmuring how thankful he was for her, for their future together.

They moved to the bed after a while of crying, laughing, accepting their new life. Avery lied down, and Rowan bunched her shirt up to the lower swell of her breasts. He placed a kiss on her stomach, another one on her navel, another one on the side of her belly.

"Hey, you," he murmured. "It's me, your dad."

Peering up at Avery, he watched stars shine in her eyes.

"We're having a baby," he told her again as though he couldn't believe it. She only nodded, smiling. "What size is it now?"

She passed her fingers through his damp hair. "According to my app, it's only the size of a raspberry."

Rowan's eyes widened. "It's tiny."

"So, so small. I'm entering my eighth week."

His throat tightened. His chest swelled. He felt a powerful wave of protectiveness surge through him, needing to keep his girl and their child safe. This feeling of ecstasy, of unwavering joy... He never wanted it to fade away as he imagined their future. Though he was terrified of becoming a father, he wouldn't let the fear take away his only source of happiness.

Rowan came to lie down by her side, propping himself on an elbow and using his free hand to caress her stomach. "Eight weeks? When did you—"

"Just last week," she cut in. "I needed an appointment at the doctor's for confirmation. And then I needed a suit to be made to tell you."

"Wow," was all he could muster. Rowan felt like he was floating in a fever dream.

"You're happy, right?"

The sound of her brittle voice made his chest ache. He cupped her chin, bringing her gaze to him before he leaned in to kiss her lips softly. "I've never been happier."

"This is so scary, though."

Of course, it was. She was still young—only twenty-six—and travelled the world for a living. He, too, was still racing and thriving, but he didn't let the disquietude obliterate his happiness. They hadn't planned on having a child for a while. Still, Rowan had never experienced such joy. "I know, but it's okay. We're going to be great parents. I just hope our kid isn't as infuriating as you."

Avery whacked his chest playfully before glancing down at her belly. Rowan shifted to kiss her stomach again, smiling against her skin when she chuckled.

He laid his head on her bare stomach, listening to the even thump of her pulse. He closed his eyes, imagining what life would look like in five years. Either a mini-Avery or a mini-Rowan running around, wanting to follow his path and become a racer.

A frown settled on his brows when a shattering thought washed over him.

What if—

"What's wrong?" Avery asked in a whisper, fingers tangling through his locks.

He opened his eyes and swallowed. "What if I'm a terrible father? What if—"

"You'll be the best," she assured fiercely, her hand moving to cup his cheek. He leaned into her electric touch. "You are not your father—never have been. You're an extraordinary man who will bring so much light and joy to our child's life. You bask in shimmering golden light. You have a mindset made of steel that keeps you from falling back into darkness. You are good, and brave, and everything a woman dreams of having as both a husband and the father of her children. Don't you start thinking you won't be good enough, because you know you are. And I know that you will not allow your kid to have the same life as you did. You're going to give him, or her, the best life ever. Filled with love, travelling, and so much racing."

Rowan loosened a breath and only nodded, letting her words imprint themselves into his mind.

"You're going to be the best Mama ever," he said. "I hope this kid is as feisty as you."

She lifted her brows. "You won't be able to handle both of our attitudes."

"Watch me." He drew circles around her belly button, content. "I bet it's a boy."

Avery smacked his shoulder gently. "No bets. I've had enough with Tate's."

"He already knows?"

Rowan smiled at the thought—of his best friend with his kid. Yeah, that child was in good hands.

"He was there when I took the first test. I was having bad morning sickness, so he suggested I take a test."

Rowan frowned. "Where was I?"

"Doing PR stuff with Tito."

Rowan scoffed. "I can't believe he knew before me."

"He cried. Then scooped me up. Kissed my cheek. And I vomited again."

He barked out a laugh, grinning so wide his cheeks were hurting again.

Before he could say anything, a phone vibrated. "Speaking of the devil," she said before taking the call.

"Hey, Uncle Tate," she chimed, putting the call on speaker. Rowan gaped at her, utterly in love and never wanting a life where she wasn't in it.

"So?" Tate's deep voice resonated excitedly. "Did he say yes? I need to win the bet with Julia and Riley. I said you two would get engaged within three years."

Avery chuckled. "You knew he was going to propose too, though, didn't you?"

The only response was Tate howling.

At that moment, Rowan knew everything was going to be all right.

ACKNOWLEDGMENTS

I hold Ava and Rowan very close to my heart; they are so special. If you were able to relate to either of them at any moment throughout the book, I am sending you lots of love. Remember that you are loved and enough. If you enjoyed Chasing the Slip-stream, please leave a review on Amazon to help a little Indie author out! It would mean a lot to me.

Ivy—Rowan is and will always be yours. You met him before anyone else did, and claimed him the moment you read about him. Thank you for being such an amazing friend, and for making the beautiful covers for this series. Always so grateful for you!

Nyla—Honestly, this book would still be a draft without your support and encouragement. Your friendship means the world, and I'm so happy to have you on this journey with me. Thank you for always being the first person to read my books, for cheering me on, and for giving me your unwavering support. I really wouldn't be here without you. I adore you!

Hannah—Thank you for everything. This book wouldn't be as great without your help.

E—You're my biggest cheerleader, and I love you for that. Your friendship means everything to me. Thank you for always listening to me, crying and laughing through our endless voice notes, and always pushing me to do better.

Célia and Sarah—This book is for you.

To my other beta readers—Jessica Rita Rampersad, Bee, Phoebe, Casey, Austeja, Fernanda, Deidre, Sheila, and Simone;

thank you all for helping me perfect this book in any way you could.

To all my readers—I hope you fell in love with the wonderful story of Ava and Rowan. I wouldn't be here without any of your support, and I am immensely grateful and thankful to be able to share my love for writing with you all.

And to Jeremy—If there's one person who constantly reminds me of how strong I am, how amazing I am doing, and how worthy I am of beautiful things, it's you. You'll always be the Rowan to my Ava. I love you.

ABOUT THE AUTHOR

Kanitha P. is a twenty-something sports romance author. She's a passionate writer who likes to write relatable characters, an avid reader with a soft spot for romance, and a Formula 1 enthusiast.

When she isn't writing or busying herself with her big girl job, you'll find her reading, baking, shopping, or running.

Her mind is in constant overdrive, causing ideas for new books to spring up every other day. She's currently working on book three of the Full Throttle series, which is Indy and Miles' story, and has other exciting projects in store.

Follow Kanitha (also known as Kay) on her social media to keep up with updates.

instagram.com/kanitha.author
tiktok.com/@kanitha.author
goodreads.com/KanithaP

Printed in Great Britain
by Amazon